Their World Was Crumbling Around Them . . .

Captain Marshall Wales—A proud, bitter, defeated man, he was alone since his wife deserted him . . . and now his troops were prepared to do far worse.

Alice Cameron—A stubborn matriarch and staunch Confederate, she had sent her husband to war to support the cause . . . but was unwilling to see his beloved Red Oaks destroyed by anyone, not even his own countrymen.

Duane Cameron Hollander—The green-eyed, auburn-haired beauty had her mother's spirit . . . and more. With her husband in Richmond, she was free to make Captain Wales forget his sense of duty.

Vance Channing—He had lost all sense of duty to his commander, Captain Wales. Now he wanted Duane enough to fight for her, cheat for her . . . perhaps enough to kill for her!

Books by Ben Haas

The Chandler Heritage
Daisy Canfield
The Foragers

Published by POCKET BOOKS

THE FORAGERS

BEN HAAS

A KANGAROO BOOK
PUBLISHED BY POCKET BOOKS NEW YORK

Distributed in Canada by PaperJacks Ltd., a Licensee
of the trademarks of Simon & Schuster, a division of
Gulf+Western Corporation.

POCKET BOOKS, a Simon & Schuster division of
GULF & WESTERN CORPORATION
1230 Avenue of the Americas, New York, N.Y. 10020
In Canada distributed by PaperJacks Ltd.,
330 Steelcase Road, Markham, Ontario.

ISBN: 0-671-81700-0

First Pocket Books printing September, 1965

2nd printing

Printed in Canada

For my wife

Note

This is completely a work of fiction; none of the people in it ever lived, nor did any of the specific events ever, to my knowledge, occur, except for the mentioned battles, including Fort Pillow. But this is not to say that it is without basis. One Southern lady is quoted in a readily available reference book to the effect that she would prefer invasion by the Yankees to having the Confederate cavalry stop over with her for a second visit. To anyone who knows anything at all about armies, there is nothing surprising in this.

THE
FORAGERS

1 _____

It was only eight o'clock in the morning on this day in August 1864, but the heat was already merciless. The sun had barely cleared the tops of the brown, drought-baked pines that stood about the land in scraggly clumps, but it was already an enemy and a scourge, a malevolent, silent white dazzle that consumed all coolness, all moisture, leaving the air hot and dry and unsatisfying, sucking all nourishment from it, so that the men breathed in gasps through the bandannas they had tied around their faces to shield them from the red dust stirred up by the feet of their horses. The dust had already powdered their gray or brown or varicolored rigs that passed for uniforms to an even crinkly red; and it had coated their mounts, too, so that they looked like a sorrel-horse troop—or the remnant of it—as they plodded along this narrow little back-country Virginia road.

Captain Marshall Wales, C.S.A., riding at the head of the column, reined in. This damn blouse, he thought, feeling the miserable little trickles of sweat oozing from beneath his arms and coursing down his ribs. I can't stand this. His lips worked soundlessly as his fingers fumbled with the buttons, and when the heavy uniform jacket was off and rolled up and wedged between his crotch and the fork of the saddle, he said aloud, "Thank God." He raised his arms to let the air get to his sweaty flanks; presently he swung the horse around to look sourly at the detail strung out behind him.

The ten men were in no marching order: they were scattered in a ragged formation involuntary and dic-

1

tated by the relative fatigue of their mounts. Wales saw that not a man or a horse had his head up; the riders sat slumped with weariness, and the horses, tender-footed, had their heads down to watch where they stepped.

Marshall Wales shook his head grimly. They might as well be on foot, he thought, his first concern the instinctive one of the cavalry officer for the mounts of his troop. Good God, he thought. You can't ride the heart out of a horse and expect a night's graze on broomstraw and blackberry briars to—what is it, Job? —to clothe his neck with thunder. If we don't get some horses soon, we'll become infantry. . . .

And the men, he thought. Hell, the horses are in fine shape compared to the men. The poor, used-up bastards, he thought. I hope we find a cow today. We've got to find a cow. Or some chickens, or something. . . .

"All right," he called, not loudly, for this was strange country. He made a signal with his arm. "All right. Let's close it up."

Grudgingly, and in their own good time, the men lifted reins and kneed their horses, slowly closing the gaps. Wales sat quietly, watching them. A scraggly lot, he thought. But I'm no better. He looked down at the dust-smeared remains of what had once been a white broadcloth shirt. God knows I'm as scraggly as anybody can get. Thirty-two and I look forty and feel sixty. I can remember when I weighed almost two hundred. Didn't think I had an ounce of fat on me. Now look at me. Nothing now but ropy muscle and loose skin sagging in folds where the fat I used to brag I didn't have used to be. And smell . . .? Christ on the mountain, I'd sell my soul for a real bath. If I weren't used to it, the smell of my own body here in this hot sun would be enough to make me puke.

Heat waves shimmered between himself and the men coming toward him; the detail seemed to ripple, to be vaporous, unreal. Maybe they are, Wales thought crazily. Maybe I am too. Maybe we all are—like ghosts, like Flying Dutchmen, doomed to ride ceaselessly back and forth across Virginia on nags too weary to trot,

never eating, never resting, starved and shot at . . .
He brushed impatiently at some sort of hot weather
insect droning stickily about his ears. Watch that,
Wales, he told himself. No abstract thinking. You
promised yourself—no thinking at all on this detail.

. . . But I can't help it. Lightheaded. This heat. Or
hunger. Or maybe Vivian again. Or maybe all three.
Whatever it is, I feel queer. My head feels as if somebody had scooped out my brain and stuffed a dry rag inside there instead. God, what a desolate country.
Nothing but scrub pine and weed fields. Of all the places
to send me to look for food. . . .

He felt saliva pouring frantically into his mouth at
that final word; his yearning belly knotted suddenly
and painfully. We've got to find something today. He
balled his fist and brought the knuckles of it hard
against the pommel of his saddle. I don't know where,
but we've got to! We're finished if we don't. . . .

One of the detail, the first man of the ten, with a
sergeant's chevrons on his dust-and-grease-smeared
blouse, kneed his horse into a sort of a trot and pulled
ahead of the rest. Dully Wales watched him come,
thinking: and only four years ago he must have been
a fresh-faced, clean-cut youth. But the face of the
sergeant now would have frightened a plat-eye, one of
the evil spirits of Wales's native South Carolina. The
sergeant—his name was Lacey MacLeod—had a
weathered, seamed and dust-caked beardy mass for a
face, featureless as a mud pie because of the filth, except for the long white scar which no dust ever seemed
to obliterate and which lifted the right corner of his
mouth in a perpetual snarl that looked inexpressibly
evil. The sergeant reined in alongside Wales, licked the
dust off his lips, and hawked and spat. "Any sign of
Lieutenant Channin', Capn?"

Wales shook his head. "He'll be back after a while,
I reckon. Keep the men closed up, Mac. No telling
what we're liable to run up with in this Godforsaken
country. I don't want half of them off picking black-
berries if we bump into trouble."

"That's the truth. But if a Yank was to stick his

3

haid outn the bushes right now, he wouldn't last any longer'n it'd take to barbecue 'im."

Wales grinned. It hurt to stretch his dry, sun-baked lips. "Only we're supposed to be looking for food, not Yanks. Me, I'd prefer a sirloin steak, given a choice."

"Hell, if I was to see a steak, I wouldn't know whether to eat it or wear it. Anyhow, I'll keep 'em closed up." MacLeod sleeved sweat off his face, leaving a paler track through the red dust on his forehead; then he rose in his stirrups and swung his arm in a half-circle, his voice a croak of indignation and disgust. "Ain't this the wust country you ever see? I swear, it's meaner'n gar broth seasoned with tadpoles. I thought I'd done fought all *over* Virginia, but I reckon I never did git to the butthole of it afore now!"

Wales nodded. "The further we get into the uplands the worse it is. But maybe that's just because of the war. Maybe all these fields of weeds were full of cotton and oats and corn once, sergeant, well plowed and well cultivated, like the fields back home, like the fields—"

He broke off, biting his lower lip. *Like the fields back home on Ashbrook, you were going to say.* Stop it! his mind shrieked. You promised. You weren't going to think about Ashbrook any more. You weren't going to think about Ashbrook and you weren't going to think about Vivian. . . .

He shook himself all over, the way a dog does to shake off water, aware that the sergeant was watching him curiously. Damn it, I can't help it.

Because Ashbrook is like this now, too, he thought—just weeds and pine trees looking brown and dried in this ferocious sunlight; fallen-down rail fences that would howl the charge of shiftlessness and poverty in normal times—and this—this air of utter desolation, of desertion, as if every living thing in this country were hiding, cowering, holding its breath, waiting . . . He ran his hand through sweat-drenched hair. As if all life were suspended, he thought, until the engine of war has passed, until the last dying thunder of its ironshod wheels . . .

Ashbrook is like this, he thought. Maybe all of South

Carolina—I don't know. All I know is that you can't blame Ashbrook on the war. You can't blame Ashbrook on anything or anybody but her. She's the one who deserted it—abandoned it . . . Something else, he thought, just one more thing I owe her, God damn her, God damn her soul—

"Capn?" The sergeant's voice was worried, inquiring.

Wales moved in the saddle, trying to still the awful, strangling hate that was rising inside him again. "The thing about it is, Mac," he heard himself saying, "it's so damned quiet and empty." He saw that the rest of the men were coming up now. "Keep 'em all together, Mac. Keep your eyes open. And don't let that wagon straggle. Come on now. Let's see if we can't meet up with Channing." He swung the horse around, having to knee the tired animal hard to get it into motion. I hope we find a bridle somewhere, he thought. I don't know how much longer this one will last. Every time I lift the reins I expect them to come loose in my hands.

The detail moved on, the only sound in the flat stillness of the morning the muffled, reluctant plop of hoofs in soft dust, the squeak and jingle of horsemen's gear. A phrase from some poem came to Wales's mind: *And no birds sing*. He tried hard to remember the name of the poem, remember who'd written it, but none of that would come to him. It was another one of those smothered memories of the time before he had become a soldier—a time remote and dreamlike now, fantastic in its remembered lushness, pathetic in its naïveté—a time, a past, long since drowned in the one harsh reality after another of a present that had no future. *"La Belle* something," Wales said aloud and gave it up then, aware that his uncertain concentration should be on the terrain anyway.

Old, rain-bleached post-and-rider fences lined each side of the road, their gray rails displaced by weather and decay, their upthrust poles stark and awry. All along their lengths they were clotted with the green vines of honeysuckle, choked with masses of blackberry bush, sassafras sprouts, and joepye weed. Good

5

cover for infantry, Wales thought nervously. A company of infantry could set up an ambush . . .

Good Lord, he thought bitterly. I'm like an old woman alone in a house at night. Seeing danger everywhere, starting at every noise . . . never able to relax. Always taut, always with this damn knot of fear in my belly, afraid of something nameless even when there's nothing real to fear . . . habit. I've got the habit of fear, the habit of dread . . . maybe I've become a coward. Maybe this is how it feels when you're losing your guts—or your mind . . .

The sweat ran down his ribby flanks in slippery trickles. He could feel it slipping past his belt, oozing down the inside of his thighs, moistening and chafing them where the constant friction occurred against his saddle. The sergeant, having closed up the detail to his satisfaction, came trotting alongside again.

"You don't reckon Channin's run into anything, do you, Capn?"

"Eh?" The sergeant's voice jolted Wales out of his preoccupation.

"I said, you don't reckon Lieutenant Channin's run into any trouble, do you?"

Wales shook his head. "Channing? I don't think so. You can say what you want to about Channing, but he knows how to make a scout in strange country."

"Uh-huh," the sergeant said tonelessly.

Wales looked at him sharply.

"Don't think much of Channing, do you, Mac?"

The sergeant squinted at Wales appraisingly. Wales could almost read the man's mind as the sergeant gauged just how frankly he could voice an opinion of one officer to another. But Channing was a newcomer to the troop, whereas the sergeant and Wales had been together for three years.

"I reckon the lieutenant's a good enough fightin man," the sergeant said finally.

"He's damn good. You know that, Mac."

The sergeant spat. "Guts is one thing," he said slowly. "Brains is another. Besides, he likes that trigger on his

6

gun too much." The sergeant paused, searching for the words he wanted. "He enjoys this damn war too much."

"Well, if somebody can enjoy it, more power to him."

The sergeant shook his head.

"He enjoys the killin part of it too much."

"I don't know," Wales said. He frowned. "Maybe," he said slowly, "that's what makes a really good soldier."

"Maybe. If it does, though, I ain't a good one."

"No," said Wales seriously, "I guess you aren't. I guess I'm not either."

But Channing's lucky, Wales thought. He doesn't seem to feel the things that we do, to see or hear the same things that we see. The look on a man's face—that blank, this-can't-be-happening-to-*me* look, full of outrage and hurt and despair all at the same time, the way a body swells and turns black and stinks in the hot sun, that pitiful, mindless screaming of the wounded —none of that ever gets through to Channing. God, Wales thought. God, but he's lucky. He doesn't even notice it. But I—Christ! If I lie awake one more night, seeing all those things over again, hearing them—

Oh, they give you words to justify it, he thought. Words to square it with your conscience, and it sounds good when they say it. It sounds right and noble. Words—I've heard them so many times from so many courthouse steps. But now I look at a dead man, and all the juice seems to have gone out of the words. They don't make sense; they've got no relation to a dead man at all. Nothing makes sense any more. I joined the army because I wanted to protect Ashbrook and Vivian, and now they're gone—both gone. But I've still got to kill Federals. If I could just even hate them, damn their blue-clad souls. But I can't even do that. All the hate I have available is used. All the hate I have is concentrated, focused, like the sun through a burning glass. Because she didn't have to—

"A body ain't supposed to like it," the sergeant was saying. "The more you do of it, the more you don't like it, lessn somethin's wrong with you. But Channin'— I seen a hen house once that a mink had done gone

7

through. Slit the throats of thirty-five chickens an' didn't eat a one—jest killin an' killin for the hell of it."

"So Channing's a mink, eh?"

"I ain't sayin he is an' I ain't sayin he ain't. But I know this: if his teeth was any sharper, I sho wouldn't want him in no hen house of mine!"

"All right," Wales heard himself saying. "But I reckon a mink doesn't have any trouble sleeping at night."

The sergeant jerked his head around; Wales could feel the sergeant's narrowed eyes on him speculatively. This kind of fear, Wales thought, it communicates itself easily, like a disease. That was a mistake, saying that.

He did not look at the sergeant. After a while the sergeant asked softly, "Something ridin you, Capn?"

"No," Wales's voice was short, a rebuff. I've got to watch that, he thought, reproaching himself. It's not fair to the men. To them, their confidence in me is the only thing in this insane war they can depend on. If they lose that, they might crumble as I can feel myself crumbling. No. Just because I have no confidence in myself, no confidence in anything, it wouldn't be—

He did not complete the thought. Instead, he jerked erect in the saddle, and his hand streaked back to unsling his carbine; his thumb jerked back the hammer. There were hoofbeats drumming around the bend ahead.

As if his gun coming up were a signal, the detail exploded, men scattering like a startled covey of quail. Horses plunged into the brush; raised gun barrels gleamed in the sunlight. There was the sound of only one horse. It should be Channing, Wales thought tensely, reining behind a screen of wild plum trees. But it could be a Federal outrider too. . . .

Then, except for those drumming hoofs, the morning was silent, with a silence that hung taut and crystal-clear over the hot, red-powdered road and the sprawling, exhausted weed-choked fields and the close, airless groves of pines. Wales was aware of blood thumping in his ears, of his throat squeaking infinitesimally when he

8

swallowed, of the twitching knot of nerves bunched in his lower belly. He was aware that he needed to make water. It was always this way before a fight; always he ceased to be a man and became a tense, tight-wound mechanism which the sound of gunfire would release from all fear and murky thought and send into furious, instinctive action. But it was different this time, he suddenly realized. There was not only the physical tightening process of fear this time; there was mental dread, too, cold and logical, a premonition, a certainty that his time had run out, and if this was a Federal coming, if this was portent of a fight—

Then Channing came around the bend, running his horse hard.

Wales stayed tense, staring past Channing for any sign of pursuit. Satisfied that there was none, he let out a long, hoarse breath, the tension unwinding, reaction spreading weakness throughout him. Then he reined his horse toward the center of the road. The knothead, he thought, slow anger staining the relief within him. He'd better have a good reason for running that horse like that. Wales pulled himself erect, ramrod straight in the saddle, sitting consciously like an officer, while he waited for Channing to come up.

The lieutenant pulled up his horse so close to Wales that lather from it splattered Wales's shirt, and Wales saw that the animal was badly blown. His eyes swung up to Channing's face.

It was a face that had always puzzled Wales. An affinity for violence and bloodshed like Channing's should have been accompanied by a hardness in the face, sharp-planed lines and grim mouth and cold eyes, probably blue. But Channing's face, even leaned by hunger and powdered with dust, had the soft, handsome, soulful look of a yearning child. His mouth was as gentle-looking and full as a woman's, even a weak mouth for a man. Only the eyes, in any measure, bore out what Wales knew of Channing's propensities, and even they were not blue but brown. There was something shallow about them, Wales had always thought. You could not look through them into Channing's

9

thoughts; they stopped somewhere this side of his brain. But Wales had seen Channing after skirmishes in which Channing had used his saber and then, when most soldiers were sick and trembling with reaction, Channing had been elated and there had seemed to be a glow burning somewhere back behind the brown of his eyes, giving them luminosity.

Something of that glow was burning in them now, but Wales could not tell what it was from: it seemed to be triumph; and Channing's face was broken in a smile of pride, his white teeth stark against the red dust. All of that self-pleased triumph suddenly irritated Wales profoundly.

"All right," he said harshly. "What's all the hurry?" He looked at the lathered, spread-nostriled horse.

Channing waited a moment before answering, sitting there looking at Wales with those glowing brown eyes. Wales wondered if that were insolence he saw in them. He thought: Like an animal, all right. He can smell the fear and indecision in me. He waited, watching Channing's grin broaden just slightly. Then Channing said:

"How would you like a cow?"

Cow.

The one plain word did an indescribable thing to Marshall Wales. It made something leap inside him; it set up a fluttering of disbelieving joy. He could feel the weariness and fatigue and hopelessness crack and slough away from him. Suddenly his mouth was drenched with saliva, he was drooling like a wolf; the dull hunger in his belly flared to unbearable sharpness. He leaned toward Channing, jabbing with a finger he could not keep from trembling.

"By heaven," he snarled, "if you're joking—"

"I was." Channing waited just long enough for Wales's mouth to open and close speechlessly one time. "What I really meant," he went on, grinning, "was maybe a dozen cows."

Wales stared at him blankly, uncomprehendingly.

Channing rocked back in his saddle with exaggerated negligence.

"You see, Marsh," he said quietly, "I found a plantation." He unlatched his canteen from the saddle and yanked the leather plug from the neck of it.

"They're virginal, Marsh," he said, looking at Wales across the mouth of the canteen. "They're ripe for the picking. I tell you, Marsh, the war ain't come near 'em. Cows, chickens, and—brace yourself, Marsh—*a pen full of pigs!*" He tilted the canteen back and drank thirstily, while Wales leaned forward, hands gripping the saddle in an agony of impatience. When Channing was through drinking, he lowered the canteen and wiped his mouth with deliberate slowness. "Ahhh," he said. "I was thirsty."

"God damn it!" Wales roared, shaking all over. "Will you quit horsing around and make your report?"

The grin faded off Channing's face. Something wild flickered in his eyes and then was masked. He sat erect in the saddle. "Yes, sir," he said in a flat voice. "Captain." He started to raise his hand in a salute.

"Oh, don't be an ass," Wales snapped. "Where are the animals?"

By this time the men had crowded close around, their faces strained forward, their eyes full of eager, feral brightness. "Oh, Lawdy," one of them whispered desperately, almost in Wales's ear. "Oh, God, I hope hit's true!"

"All right," Channing said. "I tell you, I've done found more meat than we'll know what to do with. First of all, about a mile up the road, I saw some smoke over in a clearing in some woods. There was a wagon trace running up that way, and I followed it and I come up on a po-white shack. Figured there might be something there worth picking up, and sure enough, there was a calf stobbed out in the yard. Yearling bull, looked weaned, and no sign of the cow. But you could count his ribs, and I thought to myself, Old Captain Wales, he'll have my hide if I don't do better'n this."

"We'll want that calf too," Wales said flatly. "Get on with it."

"So I sneaked back out of there before anybody saw me and I went on up the road. 'Bout four miles further along I come to a driveway all lined with oaks leading off from the road. 'Aha,' says I. 'This looks interesting.' But I had more sense than to ride up the driveway. I circled and found me a ridge and used my telescope." He sucked in a deep breath and looked around at the men. "I tell you men," he said, "you ain't seen anything like it since '61! Cows out in pasture, chickens running all around, pigs in the pens—why, even geese on the lawns!" He shook his head. "There's enough meat there to feed the whole damn brigade!"

"You're sure?" Wales's voice pressed him hard.

"Hell, Marsh." Channing sounded hurt. "I tell you, I saw it with my own eyes."

"All right. Any sign of the enemy?"

"None. You don't reckon all that would still have been there if there was Bluebellies around, do you?"

"I don't know. I'll think a little straighter, maybe, when I've got some fresh meat under my belt." Wales let out a long breath and his voice softened. "You've done a good job, Vance." He turned to the sergeant. "Now, Mac. Get that wagon and the men under cover in those pines yonder. Then report to me and Lieutenant Channing. I want to work this exactly right so we don't lose anything . . ."

"Right?" Channing's voice was startled. "Hell, there ain't anything to it. All we got to do is—"

Wales shook his head impatiently. Without answering, he put his horse over the tumbled-down rails of the fence and struck through a field of stirrup-high weeds that rustled dryly against his boots. He climbed a slope into the dim closeness of a thick grove of pines and there, stiffly, dismounted, pulling his pants away from his sweaty thighs, savoring the circulation of air against the saddle-rubbed flesh.

Channing was right behind him, and in a moment MacLeod came up and swung down too. The three men squatted in a circle, sweat streaming down their faces, for it was even hotter here in the pines than in the direct sun. The tethered horses nibbled briefly at the pine straw on the ground and then raised disappointed and disinterested heads.

Wales pulled off his hat and dragged his arm across his streaming forehead. Now, he thought. I have got to make my mind work. Can't afford to botch this. Not if it's what Channing says . . .

"I didn't think you'd be interested in the calf, Marsh." Channing sprawled out on the ground, back propped comfortably against a tree. "Not after hearing about the plantation."

"It's meat," Wales said briefly. "And we've got a regiment to feed." He looked at Channing. "You're sure nobody saw you either place? Not at the white-trash shack and not at the plantation?"

"Positive."

"Good. Well, we want it all. We've got to have it all, the calf, the stock at the plantation, everything. So we'll split up and move fast. Mac, you and I'll take the wagon and collect the calf. Vance, you'll take the rest of them and high-tail it to the plantation. You'll move in quick, before they have a chance to hide anything. And listen to me now. I want my instructions followed and I want them followed to the letter."

He arose stiffly and went to his horse. He dug into the saddlebag and then came back to them. He handed Channing a packet of folded foolscap. "That's for the requisition receipt," he said. "You fill in the name of the owner up at the top and you list very carefully the property you're requisitioning and the price you set on it. Then you pay the owner and get him to sign the requisition as a receipt."

Channing took the paper and stared at it blankly.

Wales raised his hands and dropped them in a helpless gesture.

"Well, damn it," he said, "nobody else will feed us. We haven't had any food from the Commissary Department in two weeks. They impress food back home and it never gets here. God knows what happens to it, I don't. So we've got no alternative but to feed ourselves. Either that or starve, and I don't know about you, but I'm sick of starving." He shook his head, and then his voice became more businesslike. "Being from the West, you're new in the Army of Northern Virginia,

13

Vance. But I reckon you've been here long enough to know that the only way we can take anything from a civilian is to pay him for it. Under the impressment act there's supposed to be a fixed schedule of prices, but I don't know what they are. Anyhow, we've got no authority to impress anything; we can't even give an order on the treasury. We can't steal and we can't impress, so all we can do is bargain, make the best trade we can, and pay for it."

Channing's mouth dropped open. "Bargain?" he asked, flabbergasted. His hand dropped to his holstered pistol. "Bargain, hell."

Wales's mouth drew tight. "We're not irregulars and we're not bandits, Vance. My orders are strict." He opened his hand to reveal a huge roll of bills. "I don't know where the colonel got this," he said, "and I didn't ask him." He split the sheaf of money in two and handed the bulk of it to Channing. "If that won't cover it, just tell them that I'll be along in a little while. But make the best deal you can. Get everything. And I mean . . . everything."

Channing took the block of bills and riffled it absently with his fingers. His face split in a sardonic grin. "Why don't I just pick some daisies and pay for it with those?"

Wales looked at him coldly.

"We draw our pay in that money. If it's good enough for us, it's good enough for anybody else."

The sardonic grin faded. "Yes, Captain," said Channing meekly. He stood up. "I'm sure the people will be glad to accept it. All true patriots are glad to accept it. It sure as hell beats wiping with corncobs."

Wales throttled a beginning surge of anger. I'll not let him bait me any more, he thought. But, by heaven, there is one thing . . . He pointed a finger warningly at Channing.

"I want the civilians treated with the utmost courtesy."

"Yes, sir," said Channing. "I'll be very careful how I treat the civilians, Captain." Wales noticed again that suppressed excitement in Channing's eyes, in the tense-

14

ness of his manner. He wondered at it briefly, dismissed it, and went on.

"Nothing's to be killed. None of the animals. You can kill enough chickens to give the men some breakfast—that's all. The rest of it goes back alive. It'll take us at least two days to get back to the regiment, and the only way to keep meat from spoiling is to take it back on the hoof. No killing. Is that clear?"

Channing nodded. "Yes, sir. Very clear." He grinned unexpectedly at Wales. "And we'd better get going. People got a way of smelling it when there's an army around, and while we may not be an army, damn if we don't smell bad enough for one."

"All right," Wales said, aware of hunger in him now sharp as a saber blade. He arose and strode to his horse almost briskly. "Mack, get the men formed up for Lieutenant Channing and tell the wagon to come with us. And tell them no straggling. Not if they want meat for breakfast."

He led them back down the slope and out to the road, and all the while two words were reverberating over and over in his head. Meat . . . A plantation . . . He could not tell which of them stirred the deepest, the most fundamental hunger within him.

2

The thread of smoke drifted straight up, a thin columnar wisp barely visible against the scalding blue of the unclouded sky. Channing pointed toward the grove of trees from behind which it came. "There," he said. "The shanty's up yonder."

Wales looked at the smoke. He was aware that the sweating of his palms made his bridle reins slick, that the dust had turned to mud on the inside of his hands. He had been on this sort of mission before, though not for a long time, and he did not look forward to what he had to do. He rubbed his hands on his pants, and that did not help either.

"One calf, you said," he grunted.

"Not much of one." Channing chuckled. "A damn rack of bones."

"Hit'll make soup, anyway," the sergeant said.

"Well, yonder's the turnoff. I guess we'll be leaving you."

Wales reined his horse around so that he could face Channing. "You remember what I said. Move in quick—but handle it easy."

"Yes, Captain," Channing said. He flashed a quick, too-cheerful grin at Wales and reined around, spurred heels cocked for a thrust.

"Channing," Wales snapped.

The grin faded off Channing's face. "Huh?"

"You've run that horse enough this morning. A trot will do."

Channing opened his mouth, then closed it without a sound.

Wales swung his own mount around again. "Come on, Sergeant."

The wagon trace was nothing but a pair of narrow, deep-cut ruts leading up through a weed field. The sore-footed animals picked their way along carefully, sometimes grunting when a hoof slipped against a dried clod in such a way as to put pressure on the quick. We shouldn't be riding them when they're in this condition, Wales thought. And yet there's no alternative. Men, horses, no one is spared. . . .

That's all I can do too, he thought. That's my only recourse: to grunt when it hurts and keep on going. There must be some reason for it . . . Soldiering. That's all it boils down to. And some men make a career of it. . .

Thirty-two years, he thought wryly. My mother en-

16

dured the wounding pain of delivery and devoted two decades to careful nurture. My father protected and inculcated. The Academy and Mr. Dardine's three years of private tutoring taught me Greek and Latin and sums, and the Grand Tour taught me women and drinking. Then Vivian . . . Vivian taught me—What did she teach me? Love? Love and how to survive it . . . So much care, so much attention, so much education. And for what? Why, to steal a calf.

I've managed a plantation and fourscore slaves. I've led cavalry through war in more nightmare fields and exploding forests than I want to remember. Now to my roster of achievements is to be added larceny by requisition.

The phrase had a clever sound to it. Larceny by requisition. He repeated it in his mind, and this time it sickened him all through. He shook his head and grunted a single profane word under his breath. Riding beside him, MacLeod looked up curiously. "Cap'n?"

"Nothing, Mac." Marsh Wales shoved back his hat and mopped sweat from his forehead. "I was just thinking out loud. About the war."

"Oh," the sergeant said. He hawked and spat. "Hell, I done quit thinkin about that."

"I reckon I'm dreading this chore we've got to do. You know how confounded messy these things can get."

"Yeah," the sergeant said.

"I've done this before," Wales said. "Sometimes I think it's the worst part of the whole damn business."

"Sometimes," the sergeant said. They rode on in silence for a while. After a few moments the sergeant said, "But to my mind the lonesomeness is the wust part of it."

"Huh?"

The sergeant looked out across the weed-clogged fields, not at Wales. "I said the lonesomeness."

"Oh," said Wales.

"I didn't know," the sergeant said. His words came quickly, as if he were forcing them out before they dried up. "I didn't know a man could get so Goddamned lonesome until I got in this war." His words trailed off in thoughtful silence. Presently: "I been on my own a long time. I never felt like I needed nobody until now. But I seen so many die. It sets a man to figgerin. And that's what I'm scairt of most—dyin the way they do sometimes, yellin and hollerin out there in the middle, with nobody payin 'em no mind. All alone . . . It must be hell to lay out there dyin and not even have anybody to call out for . . . not even have anybody who would give a damn if you was dead." He looked away from Wales. "I ain't got anybody," he said. "No wife, no family, nobody—except mebbe the men in this outfit. It . . . it scares me sometimes that I ain't got nobody but them."

He laughed self-consciously. "Guess I'm gittin old. 'Spect what I need is a good roll in the hay with some old whore."

"It might help," Wales said absently.

"If this thing jest *ever* gits settled . . . I'll swear, we whup them up one side and down the other, and hit jest seems to git wusser every time we whup 'em. Look how we butchered 'em at Cold Harbor. Look how we piled 'em up at Spotsylvania. And still they come on. I useta be pretty sure we was goin to win, but now I ain't so sure who's goan whup who. But I do know this—soon's somebody gits whupped, I'm goin home. I'm goin home an' I'm goan git married up an' screw for six months solid." He broke off to curse his horse when it stumbled. Then: "You're a married man, Capn. Tell me sumpin."

Marsh Wales's hand clenched so abruptly on the bridle that the pressure jerked his mount's head back. The horse snorted. Wales whirled around to look at the sergeant, thinking savagely, Goodamn him, if he's trying to be smart—

But there was no guile, no hidden layer of expression, on the sergeant's face. The sergeant was not even looking at him. Wales relaxed slightly, feeling his face burning foolishly. Of course not, he thought. I haven't told anybody, not even the other officers in the regiment. There's no way he could know.

"All right," he said heavily. "I'll try to."

18

"Well . . ." The sergeant looked away from Wales again. "I was just thinking—being married *does* help that lonesomeness some, don't hit? It does make a difference, don't hit, when you *know* there's somebody waitin for you to come back?"

"Yes," said Wales. "Yes, it makes a difference."

Stop it! something inside him was shrieking. Stop it, damn you! How did we get to talking about this anyway? His hands trembled on the reins. And they might be together right now. Locked . . . Embraced . . . Goddamn you, stop it!

"You're wife's named Vivian, ain't she, Capn?"

"WHAT?" His voice was a roar as he swung, face livid, toward the sergeant. *"How did you know that?"*

The sergeant instinctively jerked his horse sideways as Wales leaned toward him, face working.

"Why—why you talk in yo sleep sometimes. An' our bedrolls ain't usually far apart. You—you holler out for her in yo sleep sometimes."

"I do?" Wales half raised a clenched fist. "And what else do I do, Sergeant? *What else do I say?"*

The sergeant stared at him blankly for a heartbeat, then blinked his eyes. "Why, I don't rightly know. Hell, Capn, I don't listen to you. I don't know of anything, 'cept that last night, for instance, you kept callin for 'er. Not loud. Jest over an' over."

"I see." The savagery left Wales's face; now he could feel a sick dread seeping into his entrails. He sighed and slumped back in the saddle. "I see, Sergeant."

"I didn' go for to git you all riled. I'll move my bed tonight if you want me to. But, say, Capn, are—you all right? This sun's enough to knock out a damn brass monkey, an' you ain't been looking so good lately nohow."

"I'm all right, Sergeant. I'm fine." Wales mouthed the lie abstractedly. He was aware that he was trembling: wrists, hands, thighs, all shaking with a sudden, involuntary vibration. Stop it, he told himself. The sergeant will see it. Stop it, damn it all.

But, oh, Christ, he thought. So that's it. Calling for her in my sleep. Even after all these months. In the midst of hate for her so strong it makes me sick to my guts. Calling for her in my sleep like a Goddamned baby.

"When we gits to this place we're headed for," the sergeant said, "I aim to soak my hat in water. Good for the head, ridin in this sun. Might be a good idea you do it, too, Capn."

"Yes," said Wales. "Yes. I reckon that will be a good idea." The trembling was stopping now. He made himself concentrate on the reality of the morning: these fields, these woods. Here the trace turned into the trees; there would be a clearing beyond, where Channing had said the calf was. I hoped I had beaten it, Wales thought, and then, to avoid despair, he made himself give orders. "Tell Houston to pull up here with the wagon and wait. Then let's move in quiet. We want that calf before they can hide it out."

"Lands," the woman said, "but ye sure did give me a turn." Her voice was a flat, high, nasal whine. "I made sure ye was Yankees acomin up the lane." Standing there in front of the ramshackle cabin, she looked up at them with a smile of relief. Wales saw that her teeth were intermittent, like the pickets in a worn-out fence, and yellow and snuff-mottled. "I tole Carson—thet's my youngest chap—I told Carson to run hide under the house." She turned and screeched, "Carson! You, Carson! You kin come out now. These gentlemens ain goan hurt us!" In the quiet, dead heat of the morning her voice reminded Wales of the shriek of a rusty well pulley or a dry wheel hub.

Wales looked down at her from the saddle, feeling a stab of pity not unmixed with distaste. He had never seen this worman before, but he had seen her kind many times. He knew the rigor of her life—chopping cotton in the brutal sun; scrubbing clothes with raw homemade lye soap in water she'd first hauled from some spring, then heated in a black iron pot in the back yard; bearing children with a regularity a plantation owner would not have imposed on a brood mare; a vassal to her husband, moving through a life just as

20

hard and more precarious than a slave's, with no more hope or future than a mule hitched to a sorghum mill and laboriously traversing endless circles within the radius of the halter rope. Called poor white and meriting that; called trash, too, and sometimes meriting that also. Her world was bounded by the fields and the cabin; she had accepted poverty and shiftlessness and hopelessness as wedding gifts; female, but with no chance to be feminine in a world full of work that would kill a man. He had seen many of them and had always pitied them for their hopelessness, but he could not help the distaste because of what their lives made of them, old, wornout and sometimes hideous, at thirty. . . .

Like this one here. The face turned up to him was a rabbity mask of sallow skin stretched tight across flesh-less bones. The watery eyes were the pale bleached blue of fabric soaked too long in her own harsh soap; their expression was at once trusting, friendly, and hopeful, but not optimistic, as if she had had no real experience with trust and hope ever having turned out to have been warranted. The missing teeth gave the mouth a puckering aspect and made the face look chinless, as if it dwindled out rather than finished; her hair, drawn close back to her head in a bun, was pale and sunbleached, like dirty straw, and frowsy with un-combed, escaping strands. Her hands, twisting and knotting the slack of her shapeless dirty dress, were chapped and calloused into thick-nailed talons. Her body was thin and breastless, her chest almost concave. As she stood there in the characteristic poor-white slouch, spine and shoulders question marked, neck ewe-twisted forward, she reminded Wales of a warped slat.

The one-room cabin behind her was as weary and ill-used as she. The square, hand-hewn logs had been put in green and had long since dried and warped; the mud chinking had fallen out so that Wales could see daylight through holes in the wall. The ridge of the roof slumped like the abused spine of a sway-backed horse. The field-stone piers that supported the four corners of the house were crumbling and awry and in

21

danger of slipping out. As Wales watched, a towheaded, dirty-faced child of about five, a crust of mucus scabbed along his upper lip, scrambled from beneath the cabin and ran to the woman, hugging her tightly about her skinny legs. The little boy was dressed in a ragged shirt made from an old sack with the corners cut out for sleeve holes and nothing else.

"Have any Yanks been along?" Wales asked. The child looked up at him with wide, fearful eyes from behind its mother's slaunched hips. Wales tried not to look back at the child, but for some reason he couldn't keep his eyes from it. Finally he smiled in what he hoped was a friendly and reassuring manner. The child did not answer the smile but continued to look at Wales with that grave fearfulness, one finger jammed in its mouth.

"Ain't seed none yit, but we been lookin for 'em most any time. We doan ever know when they goin to come up."

"I see," said Wales. His palms were sweaty; he rubbed them back and forth along the dusty saddle skirts and then swabbed them on his trouser legs. "Well."

He swung down. "Ma'am, is your husband home?"

"Laws, no. Wisht he was. He done gone off to fight. Nobody here but the least un an' Smithfield, my oldest. He's out ahind the hill, plowin."

"Smithfield—how old is Smithfield?"

"Smithfield be twelve this November. I declare, I do wisht both you gentlemen would light an' git comfortable. I'm so glad to see you I doan know what to do. Lafe—thet's my man—he says to me afore he went off, he says, If ever you have any trouble whilst I'm gone, you go to the Confedrat soldiers an' they'll holpn you."

Wales licked his dry lips.

"Yes, ma'am. We try to look after our people. But it's mighty hard to do with no more rations and supplies than we've got. That's why I'm here, ma'am. If the army's going to look out after anybody, it's got to have something to eat." He took a deep breath to go on, but she interrupted:

22

"There's some cold hoecake an' I'd be glad for you gentlemen to finish hit off. There ain't much, but hit's all—"

"No, ma'am, thank you, ma'am." O hell, thought Wales. Hoecake . . . He was not hungry any longer; his stomach roiled with queasiness. He swung his gaze to where the yearling bull, scrawny and slat-sided, nibbled at the sun-dried grass not far from the dooryard.

"The truth is," Wales blurted, "we came to see if you'd like to sell your calf yonder."

For a moment confusion fogged her bleached eyes, then her weathered face broke into a grin at the joke. "Lands, Colonel, I sho wish I could holp ye, but I sure cain't do that. Why, thet calf's our winter's meat. Hit's all we got. We done et hits mother when she went dry, an' all the hawgs went an' died with the cholery. I sho wish we could holp ye, but times is moughty hard round these parts."

"Yes, ma'am," Wales said. I will not look at the child, he told himself, but he could not keep his eyes away from it. Still it cowered behind its mother, that washed-out-blue, fearful gaze fastened on him like a juvenile and timorous basilisk. "Times are mighty hard everywhere," Wales heard himself saying. His stomach churned at the unctuousness of his own voice. He shook his head. "We sure need that calf. I'm afraid we're going to have to insist that you sell it to us."

She stared at him uncomprehendingly for a moment, then all the welcome and trust went out of her eyes. "No, sir," she said, moving back a step. "I wish ye well, but I cain't sell the calf. Ye're welcome to the hoecake, but I sure cain't spare nothin else. Why, mister, you don't know how hit's been around here. You don't know what a time I done had since Lafe went off to fight. Hit ain't easy for a lone woman with two little chaps to make out. Smithfield does the best he can, but he's still jest a chile an' hit all falls on me. I told you whut pigs the cholery didn't git we done et, an' our ole cow too. Why, we been livin off hoecake an' poke sallit an' savin the calf for winter, an' if Lafe don't come home atter the calf's gone, I don't know how we're goan make out at all. I jest don't know. So please don't think me not wantin to do all I can to holpn our army, Colonel, but I purely cain't let you have the calf."

"Ma'am, military necessity—" Wales began, but again his own voice sickened him. He choked off the phrase, watching her lower lip tremble, watching the claw hand pluck nervously at the shirt of the child who hugged her legs. Damn it, he thought. Now how can I do this?

Why does it have to be me? he thought bitterly, standing there in the bare, clean-swept little dooryard before the poverty-stricken cabin, feeling the merciless hammer of the high sun on his back. He swallowed hard; it seemed to him that the figure of the woman danced and rippled slightly before his eyes; his throat was rancid with nausea. I've got to get out of this sun, he thought. But why does it have to be me?

"Captain." The sergeant's voice came from behind and above him. "Capn, don't you think there'll be enough at that other place withoutn—"

Wales moved over into the shade of a dogwood tree. His body was drenched with sweat. It would be so easy now, so simple, to thank the woman anyway and mount up and ride on. But he knew that it simply could not be done. He remembered the gaunt face, the burning eyes of the colonel, as the colonel had given him his orders. *Everything you can find,* the colonel had said, handing him the money. *Everything, regardless of your personal feelings, regardless of what temporary hardship it works on the civilian populace.* Those were his orders, and he knew the desperation behind them. He had seen the sick, starved men drag themselves forth to battle and die as much from their own weakness as from enemy fire. If I just had time to think about it, Wales told himself. But I don't have time. I don't even want to think. I don't dare think. I have orders and—

"Ma'am," he heard himself saying, "I'm just as sorry as I can be. I wouldn't for the world want to see harm or hardship either come to you and your children. But you must realize—this is war. Soldiers need meat. Your

24

husband—he's a soldier. You wouldn't begrudge him the calf?"

Her face screwed up; her lips trembled; tears began to course down the yellow, leathery cheeks. "L-Lafe wouldn't see us starve. He'd come home afore he'd see us starve. I'd git 'im to come home, but I don't know where at he is. He—he said you soldiers was good people. He said them Yanks was devils, but you'd holpn us iffn we needed hit." Her voice was a thin whimper; hearing it, the child suddenly began to bawl loudly and incoherently. "You ain't goin to take our last bit of somethin to eat, mister? *We're on your side . . ."*

Wales cursed silently to himself. It was not working. He had tried a trick that all soldiers knew, he had tried retreating to a cool, dark hiding place within himself, detaching all the thinking and feeling part of himself from reality so that it could not be hurt and scarred by reality. When you did that, what was left of you, outwardly still Marshall Wales, would function independently, but what it did would never really touch you.

Only it was not working. It was not working at all.

"Ma'am," Wales said softly, "I have no choice. We're prepared to pay you well for the calf. I'm prepared to offer you three hundred dollars for the calf." He took the roll of bills from his pocket.

She stared at the money as if it were something slimy. "Confedrat money! Lafe said I wasn't to have nothin to do with hit! You know hit ain't worth anything! Lafe said did I have to sell somethin, not to take nothin but gold! Mister, don't you know how hit is around here? I cain't buy anything with thet stuff!"

"I'm sorry," Wales said again. He balled up his fist and struck it against the hard leather of his saddle, and his horse, startled, jumped sideways. It was not working. It was not working at all, he thought, panic-stricken. He was still exposed, rawly, to everything that happened, and there was no way he could disengage himself. He was aware that he was gritting his teeth so hard that the tendons in his temples ached. He was also aware that, senselessly, he was beginning to hate the woman —to hate her with a deep, sick, weary hate. To hate her for being so helpless and owning the calf; to hate her for having children and owning the calf; to hate her for existing in this one place and at this one moment of time when she had no business existing and owning a calf . . . as if she had plotted to put him here in her dooryard before the commentless gaze of the sergeant and make him strip from himself the last vestige of manhood. As if she were a contributor to his own degradation instead of being the victim of it. Damn her! he thought savagely. Why can't she be gullible enough to take the money? She knows we're going to have the calf anyway!

He said loudly, harshly: "Sergeant, get that calf." He pulled a piece of paper and a pencil stub from his pocket. "Ma'am, I'll have your name, please, so I can put it on the receipt." He turned his back on her and put the paper against his saddle leather, starting to write, the pencil almost indecipherable on the pulpy softness of the paper, sweat-dampened from its sojourn in his pocket.

He did not even look up to see if MacLeod were going after the calf, but he could hear the shuffle of the hoofs of the sergeant's horse. He heard the woman let out a formless shriek; he turned to see the child sitting where it had been flung aside in the dust, head thrown back, mouth gaping, an amorphous bellowing wail slowly gathering volume. He stepped around the horse and saw the woman running past the mounted sergeant to where the calf still grazed serenely. The calf looked up with sudden fear as the woman approached; it backed off as she flung herself at it. She caught it, arms locking about its neck. "No, no, no, no," she sobbed. "No, you ain't gonna take hit! No, no, no, no! *Smithfield! Smithfield!*" As if in her desperation her last hope was that the masculine presence of a twelve-year-old boy, his simple masculinity, could prevail where her femaleness was helpless. "*Smithfieeeeeyulld!*"

Oh, shit, thought Wales sickly. But the sergeant was taking over now. The sergeant swung down with more alacrity than Wales had seen him use recently. He stood thoughtfully for a moment, hands on hips. The calf swung its head wildly, almost shaking the woman loose. She clung desperately. The sergeant looked at the woman and the calf as an axman would look at a tree he proposed to fell. Then the sergeant stepped forward. He bent over, grabbed the calf's tether rope and, digging in his heels, inexorably reeled both the calf and the woman toward him like fish on a line. The woman dug in her feet; the sergeant's shoulder muscles bulged against his shirt. Wales saw the veins standing out on the sergeant's forehead. When the sergeant had the calf and the woman within his reach, he let go of the rope and seized the woman's arm. At his touch she broke away from the calf, exploding into savagery. Her shriek was like that of a panther as she hurtled at the sergeant, clawing and kicking. Hastily the sergeant threw up a hand to shield himself. She grabbed his upflung arm and kicked out with her splayed, leathery feet. The sergeant raised his arm and lifted her from the ground. For that one moment her body was in the air, her entire weight supported by the sergeant's arm. While she was thus off balance the sergeant shifted quickly; he pushed away her claws, grabbed her in a hug, and dragged her across the grass, kicking and screaming, back to the dooryard. Suddenly he let go, dropping her on her rump in the dust and stepping back hastily. But she made no further attack. Instead, she bent forward, weeping, a hand reaching out in an instinctive gesture to the screaming child. She pulled the child to her flat breast and they both sat there in the dust crying, filling the air about the dooryard with high-pitched, shrieking sobs of utter hopelessness.

MacLeod went back to the calf and yanked up the stake that held its tether and dragged the fearful animal toward his horse. The calf balked, planting its legs. The rope strangled it, forcing out its tongue, popping its huge white-rimmed eyes. The calf hoisted its tail. Leaving behind it installments of fear-inspired splatter, it yielded, let itself be pulled. Holding onto the rope, MacLeod swung into the saddle.

Wales had finished writing now. But he knew the

27

woman would not sign the receipt. So he signed it for her, not knowing her name, but putting down the only name he knew, Smithfield, with an *X* under it, and writing "his mark" under the *X* and going to the woman then and gently dropping the three hundred dollars in her lap.

Still sobbing, she looked down at the money, and it was as if it were only then that final realization of the catastrophe sank home. She scrambled to her feet, the money falling unheeded from her lap into the dust. She thrust out a bony arm at Wales as he hurried back to his horse and mounted. There was a figure coming over the hill; that would be Smithfield, and Wales did not want to go through all this again with a twelve-year-old boy. The woman shook her gnarled, soap-chapped fist. "I shoulda knowed hit!" she screamed. "You planter! You God-damned so-high-and-mighty *planter!*" The hate she put in that word made the back hairs rise on Marshall Wales's neck. "Ye wouldn't have the guts to do this if my man was jest home! Ye're all alike, damn ye! Ye jest wait! Ye—jest—wait!" And then, in hopelessness and exhaustion, sinking to the ground again beside the crying child.

Wales and the sergeant went down the lane at a trot, the bull calf hurrying along, half running, half dragged at the end of the rope. Behind them they could hear the woman's sobs, diminishing now, dying away into long, racking, throat-scraping gasps. At last, by the time they reached the end of the lane, all they could hear was the crying of the child.

3

Houston, the wagoner, fumbled in his pocket for one of his few remaining sulphur matches and grunted a curse. He looked over at the sergeant who, riding alongside, matched the gait of his mount to that of the wagon.

"Well," Houston grunted, " 'pears like times is gittin better." He jerked his head toward the back of the wagon, where the calf did its best to keep up, almost obliterated in the billowing red dust from the wheels.

"Yeah," the sergeant said. There was no enthusiasm in his voice.

Houston swung his slope-browed head curiously toward the sergeant. Houston was a gray and grizzled badger of a man, broad, truculent, a wonder with mules. He took the match he had fished from his pocket and held it down to ignite against the iron shoe of the wagon wheel. When it fired, he touched it to the corncob pipe clamped between his teeth.

"What's the matter?" he asked. "You sound like hit doan't make a hell of a lot of difference to you one way er another." He took the pipe out of his mouth and spat.

"I'm hongry as you are," the sergeant said tersely.

Just then the calf let out a sudden, high-pitched blat. Both men twisted around, and Houston hauled the mules to a stop. "He ain't chokin, is he?" Houston tried anxiously to see over the tail gate. The sergeant dropped back, then spurred forward. "No, he's all right. Jest homesick, that's all."

Houston chortled. "Holler all you want to, you little

booger," he shouted back at the calf. "Hollerin won't keep you outn the stewpot!"

"Aw, shut up," the sergeant said.

"Whut in time's ridin *you?*" Houston sounded indignant. He jerked his thumb in the direction of the cabin, now a mile behind. "Whut happened back there, anyhow?"

"Huh? Back where? Back there? Nothin. Why?"

"Nothin. I jest wondered." He leaned far over and lowered his voice, jerking his thumb again, this time toward Wales, riding a few lengths ahead of the wagon.

"Him. What happened to him back there? When y'all come outa that lane draggin that calf, the capn had a kinda sick, greenish look to his face, sorta like he'd jest swallowed a hoptoad. I figgered somethin musta happened."

"Naw," the sergeant said quietly. "Nothin happened."

"Um. Well. Anyway, leastways we got some meat. Great God Almighty, my backbone's durn near stuck to my belly button. I tell you one thing, brother, I done had my bait of that damn roasted corn." He sucked on the pipe with a bubbling sound. "Roasted corn for breakfast, roasted corn for dinner, roasted corn for supper. I-God, hit's a wonder we doan't all sprout."

The sergeant didn't answer. After a while he said, "You seed hit too, huh?"

"Seed whut too?" Houston looked at him blankly.

The sergeant made a gesture. "The capn. Seed the way he looks nowadays."

"Yeah." There was a pause, during which Houston cursed the mules for a brief, pungent interval. Then he said, "You doan't look so damn purty your ownself."

The sergeant shook his head irritably, not even listening. After a while he said, "You mind Flem Porter?"

Houston thought for a moment. "Oh. Him. Yeah, I mind him. That boy kinda broke up when we was rear guard comin back from Gettysburg. Stood up there in the rain an' waved his saber at that troop of Yanks an' yelled at 'em he was a rooster an' then started to flap

30

his wings an' crow. Yeah, I mind 'im. He got his God-damned head shot off. I mind 'im all right. Why?"

"I seed hit comin," the sergeant said. "I seed hit comin in Flem Porter a week, two weeks, afore hit happened."

"Yeah?"

"Yeah." The sergeant considered, letting his words out carefully, adjusting the phrases as they came so that he was saying exactly what he wanted to say.

"I seed hit in his eyes. The first thing was, he quit lookin at you when he talked to you. His eyes got secret-like. You know how it seems to hurt a dawg when you look 'im straight-on an' he turns away? Hit seemed to hurt Flem Porter too."

"Yeah," Houston agreed. "I seen 'em like that." His face went grave and serious and he chewed on the stem of the pipe thoughtfully. "*He* beginning to do like that?"

"I doan know. I cain't tell for sure. There's somethin wrong, though. There's somethin ridin 'im. I doan know if hit's one thing in particular or jest everything in general. But hit's in *his* eyes too. He'll still look at you, but you can see him forcin hisself to do it. Like he was somewhere else all the time. Like he was a thousand miles away, even when he's talkin right at you."

"I-God." Houston scratched at his beard. "I doan't like to hear you say that. I doan't like to hear that at all. When a man gits thataway, he can git you killed."

The sergeant said nothing.

"What ought we to do?" Houston asked anxiously. "You reckon he's fit to keep on soldierin?"

"I doan't know," the sergeant said tersely.

"I doan't mind takin orders," Houston said. "But, I-God, when there's lead flyin around every which way, I want the man what's givin 'em to have his wits about 'im."

The sergeant did not answer this, and they rode on in silence for a while.

Presently Houston asked, "What about Channin'?"

The sergeant said an obscene word and spat.

"I doan't know," Houston said earnestly. "He seems like he's got plenty of piss an' vinegar."

"He ain't dry behind the ears yet," the sergeant said. "He doan't know a Goddamned thing but how to pull a trigger."

"Well, I ain't no officer lover," Houston grunted softly. "But I will say that Wales plays it right straight an' doan't hand out no more crap than he's got to. And he's right smart mean in a fight hisself. But, by damn, if he's fixin to go off the deep end, that's a hawse of another color."

"I didn't say he was fixin to," the sergeant snapped. "I jest said I was a little worried about 'im."

"Well, damn it, now you got me a little worried too. What you aim to do about it?"

"I aim to keep an eye on 'im," the sergeant said. Some of the irritation went out of the set of his shoulders and his voice was softer. "I ain't goin to let nothin happen to this outfit that I can help," he said. "I'll watch 'im. We'll see how he makes out. An' if it looks like he's dangerous to have around, I'll think of somethin. Jest calm down an gimme a little time . . ."

Houston took the pipe out of his mouth and spat. "Time," he grunted sourly. "There ain't no time in this war but from one minute to the next. That's all the time there is."

Planter, she had called him. *Planter*. He could still hear the hate in her voice, the sheer cold, naked hate that had made her use the worst insult she could think of. *Planter* . . . What does she know about planters? Wales thought, kicking his horse so that it moved another pace or two ahead of the wagon. What does she know about planters? What is a planter to her anyway? A man on a big horse that comes around and takes half the crop for rent for allowing them the privilege to squat on land he didn't have slaves enough to cultivate anyhow. A man who buys more slaves and rides up next year and says, "You'll have to move. I aim to put all of this in tobacco." That's what a planter is to her.

32

That's all she's ever seen of a planter. What does she know about it? What in hell does she know about it?

They're movers, he thought. He blinked his eyes, rubbed at them with the back of his hand. You're movers! he wanted to yell at the faces that were haunting him. When he raised his head, he could still see them, shimmeringly superimposed on the rolling, gully-cut, pine-clad country that stretched dry and brown ahead of him. The face of the woman, the blurred, rabbity face collapsing in stricken hopelessness; the unceasing blue-eyed stare of the dirty child, still enough baby to suck its thumb . . . He felt smeared, plastered, so befouled with what he had done to them that there was no way he could imagine of ever getting clean. The more he stared ahead, searching the vacant, baking terrain for any sign of danger, the more the two faces got in the way of his looking and sickened him to his bowels.

But you're movers! he yelled silently at them. You don't know. You don't know, he thought defensively, but more calmly. You've never owned land. You don't know what it is to be obsessed by it.

To grow up on it, he thought, and know that your father and his father grew up on it, and to plan for your children to grow up on it. To feel your roots going down so deep into it that there's no way they can be pulled loose. To plan over it and sweat over it and dream for it and grieve over every ounce of it that's washed away. To own it and have it own you. Like Ashbrook, he thought helplessly. Christ! He squinted at the vaporous faces. Your roots don't break, he yelled at them silently. They don't cut. They just pull up. But mine—

Cut, he thought.

She cut them.

Something twisted inside of him. He grabbed at the pommel of the saddle, clenched it with a convulsive grip. He was racked with the sensation of being sucked unwillingly, helplessly, into a vortex, because now memory was surging back on him and there was no way he could fight it off, the memory of spring in 1863 and the furlough, the last furlough before the roots were severed, before the top withered and died, before the world caved in. . . .

South Carolina had looked good after Virginia—it had looked calm and prosperous and remote from the war. A thin, gentle spring rain had been falling as the train entered the low country, and it seemed to give the landscape a sheen, a sort of luster, shining it up the way rain makes a horse's coat shine. Wales could remember the tightness in his throat, the stirring deep in his bowels as the train rattled and clacked past the remote tangled darkness of cypress swamps, chugged past immeasurable reaches of low, flat fields, fresh-plowed and fresh-planted and peaceful, so different from the roiled and blasted terrain of Virginia from which he'd come. He could remember the way fatigue and tension had flowed out of him, replaced by the good, wonderful anticipatory excitement of being almost home.

Ashbrook, he had thought eagerly, Ashbrook and Vivian. The two names echoed over and over inside his head, fueling almost unendurable fires of impatience.

Then, at last, all the other stations had been passed. All the other crossings had been blown for. Now there was only the end of the line; now there was only home, and the train was slowing, the whistle blasting hollowly. Suddenly every soldier in the car was shoving and pushing for possession of the windows, fighting for the first look at home, fighting for the first sight of a face among that knot of people standing tensely, expectantly, on the platform in the rain. Wales remembered how excitedly he had scanned the crowd as the train rocked into the station, trying desperately to pick Vivian out of the throng, searching for the unmistakable gleaming yellow emblem of her hair. But there were too many open umbrellas, like wet black mushrooms.

What he couldn't remember was how he had fought his way through the sea of gray-clad humanity in the coach, each man scrambling to extricate his possibles and be the first one out. He could not remember that, but he could remember landing on the cinders beside

34

the car, what meager gear he had in his hand. He could remember searching that swirling clot of rain-wet, re-united humanity all about him with a sort of foolish panic. Where was she? Why hadn't she come?

Then all those bobbing shiny black umbrellas had parted and she was there, standing at the edge of the platform.

For a moment he had not moved. He had only stood there and looked at her, a little stunned for the moment with the knowledge that she was real, not a memory seen in campfire smoke, his mind not fully able to grasp the fact that he was home.

Then she had said his name, and he was going to her.

Her hair had smelled like lilacs.

She had not changed; she had not changed at all. Her hair was worn in exactly the same way, a long yellow fall, shimmering, molten-looking even in the gray rain. Her face was the same round child's face, her eyes the same great blue child's eyes, wide-spaced, a little up-turned at the corners, her body still trim, small, com-pact, her whole aspect almost doll-like, a creature out of one of the paintings of Fragonard he'd seen years ago on the Grand Tour. Physically she was the same. If the year of separation had done anything to her, it was not visible. But when he released her and she took a step backward and looked up at him, he was aware of some-thing that had not been there before; he could find no name for it; it was—an intensity, he thought. Then he forgot it as Uncle Clint pulled at his arm, turning him around. The old Negro, family carriage driver for as long as Wales could remember, was trembling with emotion, and Wales had had to put his arm around him, give him an embrace, before he could turn back to Vivian.

He put his hands on her shoulders and held her away from him, looking at her, his lips moving sound-lessly. He could not think of anything to say that he could say here on the crowded platform. At last he heard his own voice, banally, "How's Ashbrook?"

35

"It's all right," she had said, "I think. You're so thin."

"Pining for you," he had said. "The place is all right?"

"Yes," she had said. "Yes. Ashbrook's fine."

"You look fine too."

"Thank you."

He recognized a yearning in her eyes that matched his own. He handed his bag to Uncle Clint.

"That's all the gear there is," he said. "Come on. Let's get started. I want to get home."

It was as if he had never been away. She lay so closely against him in the darkness that every contour of her body was fitted against him; her head was in exactly the same spot on his arm that it had occupied every night of their marriage that had been spent together. She had never been able to go to sleep unless her head were cradled on his arm.

Wales let out a long breath of satiety.

Her hand moved slowly, caressingly, down his chest. "Is there any wifely duty I can perform for you?"

He laughed shortly.

"Not without rendering me unfit to return to my regiment."

She burrowed her face down tight against him.

"Oh, I'm so glad you're home."

He lay thoughtfully silent for a while, his fingers stroking her back.

"I'm an extremely lucky man," he said at last.

"Umm?" Her voice was drowsy.

"I said that I am an extremely lucky man." He paused. "I never really knew how much I loved you," he said. "Not until I was away from you. Then, it was . . . Well, I couldn't get used to it. I never did get used to it. I haven't felt right for a year. Until now."

"I know," she said sleepily against his chest. "Incomplete."

"That's it," he said. "That's it exactly. Incomplete."

They lay quietly for a few moments.

"I worried about you so much," he went on. "About leaving you here on Ashbrook. It's a big job, running

36

a place like this. I was a little afraid. You haven't had too much trouble, though, have you? Everything's been all right, hasn't it?"

For an instant he thought her body stiffened against his. Then she murmured, "Yes, everything's been all right." Then her breathing became regular and he knew that she was asleep.

The next morning they had ridden over the plantation—he and Vivian and old Uncle Clint trailing behind on a sorrel mule. They had ridden every part of it, and Wales had drunk in the sight of it avidly, absorbing the look of it, the feel of it, into himself as a drunkard absorbs alcohol. There were the fields, already turned and planted and now baking flat and black under a sun fierce enough, though not yet even a semblance of what it would be later. There were the pastures, lush with spring grass, spotted with the lazy, drowsing shapes of cattle. There were even the swampy necks of woods, where water stood between the cypress boles in flat dark ponds and white herons, disturbed at their fishing, rose slowly with majestically striving wings. The three of them—Wales and Vivian and Uncle Clint—stayed out all day, not even riding back to the house for dinner, eating a luncheon from a hamper Uncle Clint carried on the mule; and at sunset they had just completed their circuit and were pulled up on the crest of the hill that overlooked the main house, its windows now aglow with candlelight.

The horses blew softly through their nostrils and jingled their gear as they rubbed their heads against their legs to mop the sweat off. The night air was cool and moist and clean, pungent with the last sun-distilled odors of grasses and weeds, flavored with the dank, stirring odor of the distant swamps. Night birds flew overhead to roost: doves made whirring, whistling sounds; a big owl flapped past noiselessly; swifts and bullbats darted and circled in crazy patterns. From beyond the plantation house a slave's voice lifted in a high, clear call to the cattle to come up for milking, and in the night hush Wales could clearly hear the squeaking of a well pulley as someone drew water.

He let out a long breath, relaxing in the saddle. He was tired and sweat-soaked and he felt wonderful. There was no discontent anywhere within him. He was completely at peace, swathed in satisfaction, and Virginia and the war were only dimly remembered fantasies of a dream from which he'd at last awakened, incredible and insane aberrations that had no relation to this, the only world that existed and was real.

Beside him Vivian said, "Uncle Clint, please ride down and tell Mama Louise that we'll be in for supper in about half an hour."

"Yas'm," the old man said and lifted rein, kicking his weary mule down the hill.

Wales and Vivian sat for a moment longer without speaking. Then Vivian said, "Well?" It was a small, strained, and uncertain sound.

"Well, what?"

"Well—I . . . I hope everything is all right."

Wales turned in the saddle to look at her, unstirruping one foot and bringing his leg around the pommel. She was not looking at him; she was looking down the hill at the big white house below, serene in its groves of bamboo and myrtle, as if the light from the windows of it had somehow hypnotized her.

Wales fished in his pocket and found a cigar. He bit the end off of it, spat, and then struck a match on the sole of his boot and lit the cigar. He blew smoke.

"If you don't move the cattle down to the lowground pasture," he said, "you're going to get the hill overgrazed and it'll go to bitterweed."

"Oh?" she said.

"And you've got to watch the way King lays out his plowing. Straight up and down a hill makes the ground wash."

"I see," she said. "I didn't know that."

Her body was very tense and rigid on the sidesaddle; suddenly Wales thought of a little girl awaiting punishment from a parent. Instantly he was touched and regretted his impulse to tease her. He sidled his horse up close to hers.

"You've done a wonderful job," he told her softly, reaching out to hook a finger under her chin and turn her face toward his.

He heard the breath go out of her in an audible sigh of relief; her face flooded with gratification, almost literally lighting up; her eyes beamed.

"Whew," she said.

"What's the matter?"

"I—nothing. Only . . . well, I didn't know. I don't know anything about running a plantation. I just did the best I could. For all I knew, I might have been ruining it. And I know how finicky you are about it. I know how much Ashbrook means to you, and I was—well, I was just scared I wasn't doing things the way you wanted them."

"You've done fine," he said.

"Oh," she said, "you don't know how relieved I am to hear that." She laughed. It was carefree but a little shaky. "I was afraid that I might have bollixed it up so bad that you'd run me off when you got home."

"No," Wales said, "I'll try to put up with you awhile longer."

"Well," she said lightly. "I just knew how much you love Ashbrook—"

"Yes." He turned away from her to look down at the beckoning windows of the house. "Even more now than when I left it." He made an inarticulate gesture with his hand. "You and Ashbrook. No matter how bad things got, I had you two to hang on for. When I was so scared or so tired or so baffled that the whole world seemed crazy and nothing made sense, I could think about you and Ashbrook, remember how you look, remember how this place looks, and then everything would make sense again. There would be a reason for doing what I was doing, for killing people I'd never even seen before—" He broke off. "You two, you and this place, when everything got all mixed up, remembering you straightened it out again."

She was silent for a moment. Then she said, lightly

—but not so lightly either—"I think I'm a little bit jealous of Ashbrook."

He blinked at her. "Huh?"

She laughed. "I'd just hate for you ever to have to choose between me and this plantation."

Wales looked at her in the twilight. He was conscious of a twinge of irritation. "You ought to know better than to say a thing like that," he snapped. Suddenly he reached over and seized her, pulling her to him. "You know who I love," he said fiercely.

Her face was very pale in the dusk, her eyes very large. She stared at him long and with a strange appraisal, her gaze serious. "Say it," she whispered.

"Say what?"

"Say who you love."

"I love you."

"Not Ashbrook?"

"You."

He felt the curious tenseness go out of her. He felt her relax within his grasp.

"I had to hear you say it," she whispered.

After that the days had blurred together. They had fallen into a rhythm of living not too dissimilar from what they had known before the war. It was almost as if they were trying to use the magic of ignoring it to make the war go away. But it hadn't. As the halfway mark of the furlough slipped by and the remaining time began to dwindle, Wales began to feel haunted. He found himself cherishing time and hating it simultaneously; he found everything he said and everything he did shadowed by awareness of the future. He was a hostage to time, and everything he did was a little bit spoiled by his awareness of it and a little bit sweeter because of his awareness of it.

He had not realized that Vivian felt the same, until that night near the end when, as they lay welded together in the bed, exhausted after one of those oddly desperate, tender clashes in the dark, she had begun to cry. Not loudly, not violently; at first Wales had not even realized what was happening. Then he felt the wetness of tears on his chest.

"Here now," he said. "What's the trouble?" A woman's crying had always profoundly upset him.

Her voice came muffled from against his shoulder.

"Oh, Marsh, it's almost time for you to go back. And I can't bear for you to go back. I can't. Marsh, please. Please don't go back . . ."

"*What?* Honey, I have to go back. You know that."

"Have to?" She pulled herself away from him and flung the question almost savagely. "Have to? *Why* do you have to?"

"Why, I—" His mind moved futilely for an instant. "Why, I just have to. That's all."

"No," she said. "No, you could resign your commission. The conscription couldn't touch you. We own more than twenty slaves. You'd be exempt from conscription . . ."

Wales sat up in the bed. His voice was almost angry.

"I'm not going to hide behind my slaves."

"No." Vivian's hand moved soothingly over his arm. "No, I didn't mean that, Marsh. But I need you. Ashbrook needs you. Please, you could stay home—"

"No, I can't, either." He shook his head. "No. You don't understand."

His words came slowly, carefully, trying to make her see exactly what he meant.

"Ashbrook needs me more up there," he said. "This war has got to be won without ever letting it get to South Carolina. It's got to be won without ever letting it get to Ashbrook. I've got to do what I can to help keep it in Virginia."

He spread his hands in a gesture she probably couldn't even see in the dark.

"You don't know," he said. "You don't know what ruin there is. In war. Nothing seems to mean anything in war. Nothing is worth too much to be destroyed. Why, the plantations up there," he said. "I've seen houses that would make two of ours here leveled to the ground and nobody give it a second thought. Livestock dead and rotting in the fields. Crops ground into the dirt by armies moving across them. Death and desolation everywhere, as if God had just taken His hand and rubbed it, palm down, across that country. Why . . ." He searched for words to make her see. "I remember one time in the Valley there was an apple orchard. That orchard must have been a hundred years old. It was last spring and the trees were all in full blossom . . . it was a fine orchard. Only," he said harshly, "there was a brigade of Federals dug in in the orchard. We brought up the horse artillery and cut loose on them. The artillery just dug up the orchard. It knocked the trees over and broke them off and leveled the orchard and churned the ground so that it looked like a fresh-plowed field. A hundred years old, that orchard, and in three hours there wasn't a tree left standing. You can't imagine it," he said. "But I've seen it. Do you think I want the war to get to South Carolina? Do you think I want something like that to happen to Ashbrook?" He clenched his fists. "I don't give a damn about political reasons," he snapped. "I don't even give a damn about abolition. When this thing's over I'm going to free these niggers anyhow and get the whole thing off my conscience. But I don't give a damn about any of that now. What I've got to do is *to try and keep the war away from my plantation.*"

There was a long silence in the darkness.

"You understand, don't you?" he asked finally.

She pulled away slightly, rolled over in the darkness. She did not answer for a moment, and Wales became aware that he was holding his breath. "Yes," she said at last, "I understand. I'm sorry. I know you don't have any choice. I know you're right. But I hate so much to see you go. I'm so afraid . . ."

"Afraid of what?" he asked tenderly, as though to a child whose fears he had to dispel.

"Afraid for you." Her voice a tiny pathetic wail in the night. "Afraid for myself . . ."

He wanted to gather her up in his arms, to pet and comfort her. But first he had to reason with her.

"Look," he said. "First of all, don't worry about me.

I'm not fool enough to get myself killed when I've got a wife like you waiting for me to come home."

"Just thinking about it scares me—"

"Please," he said. "Please don't be afraid." He was puzzled by the faint trace of irritation that marred his pity. "There's nothing here to be afraid of. The niggers are loyal . . . loyal as rocks. I've known them all my life, and there's not a one I wouldn't trust as far as I'd trust myself. King, LeRoy, Cuffo, Uncle Clint—you just give the boss niggers their heads and they'll practically run the place for you." He licked his lips. "Besides, if you should have any trouble, it's only a ten-minute ride to John Everett's place on a fast horse. I'll have Uncle Clint keep a fast horse saddled all the time and always be ready to ride. That way, if you ever need help, just send word and John Everett will be right here. He may be too old to soldier, but he swore to me that he would give you all the help he could while I was gone."

"All right." She said it hesitantly. "I know Mr. Everett will help me. He already has—a lot. But the . . . the emergencies aren't what I'm afraid of, Marsh."

"Then what in heaven's name is it?" He hadn't meant to let the irritation boil through into his voice like that. But there was no help for it; he could quiet logical fears, but how could he cope with illogical ones? "What else could you possibly be afraid of?"

There was a brief silence; when she spoke her voice was small and unsteady. She said, "It's . . . just day-to-day that I'm afraid of, Marsh."

"Huh?"

"I mean—I'm afraid I can't keep on running Ashbrook the way you want it. I'm not a planter, Marsh. I'm just a woman. I never had to be a planter before. There are so many problems, so many decisions, so many things always coming up—and nobody to handle them but me. It just scares me, Marsh."

"Nonsense." Wales sat up abruptly in the bed.

"Look," he said, "if I thought it was going to be for much longer, I wouldn't even ask you to do it. But it can't be for long. Why, we've whipped the britches off

43

of every general the Federal Government's got. Mc-Clellan, Pope, Burnside, Hooker, the whole bunch . . . It can't last much longer. The North won't stand for it lasting much longer—you'll see. In the meantime"—he made a violent gesture with his hands—"the most important thing we've got is at stake. Ashbrook's our home. It's all we have—if anything happens to it, we've nothing left. We've both got to do everything we possibly can to protect it. I'm not asking you to be a planter or run a model plantation, sugar. All I'm asking is that you just hold Ashbrook together while I'm gone. You can do that. I know you can. There are women doing it everywhere now, and I know that you're braver and smarter than any of *them*."

She was quiet for a while. Then she moved over next to him and some of the tenseness was gone out of her body, and he lay back down.

"I'm sorry," she said. "You're right. I'm being an awful coward. Gracious knows, what I've got to do is nothing next to you having to go back to Virginia and let those Yankees shoot at you." Her voice went cold and hard. "Oh," she said, "how I hate those God-damned Yankees for trying to kill you." Wales blinked. He had never heard her use a profane word before. She was suddenly tight against him. "Oh, Marsh, oh, Marsh, I love you so much. I'd die if anything happened to you. I love you so much. I hate those Yankees. I hate this crazy, senseless war!" She was up against him so closely he could feel every throb and stir of her body, the jerking of her diaphragm as she tried not to cry.

"I'll do the best I can, Marsh," she whispered.

"I know you will," he said, stroking her hair. "And, please, please don't cry any more, honey . . ."

And she hadn't. Not even when she saw him on the train going back to Virginia.

Not even when she kissed him there on the platform, kissed him so hard and clung to him so fiercely that he'd had to reach up and take her arms and pull them away when the conductor cried urgently and finally, "*'Board!*" Her eyes had been big and shining, but no tears were in them. Her mouth had worked, words coming from it at last:

"I love you—oh, please be careful and hurry home!"

But there had been no time to answer. The press of gray-clad men had swirled by Wales and picked him up and shoved him on the car. The train had started, jerked to a stop, then started again. Wales had looked out the window. She was standing on the platform, waving frantically, standing on tiptoes the way women do when they wave goodbye to trains. She looked very small, even on tiptoes.

The whistle blasted. The train picked up speed. Wales had pressed against the window, his heart sinking as he watched her flow away from him, watched her recede, diminish, until all he could see was a doll-sized figure still standing there on the platform waving.

Then the train had gone around a bend and he hadn't been able to see his wife any more.

The spasm of memory had emptied Marshall Wales. Now he slumped, spent, against the cantle of the saddle. His head drooped in the hot sun. A sort of bile worked raw and bitterly in his throat. His lips moved slightly, mouthing soundless words at the unanswering fields of Northern Virginia.

God, he said fiercely. God, how I hate her.

4

"Why, damn 'em," the sergeant was saying, panic in the words. "They'll done have everything et up afore we kin even git there!"

The sound of his voice pulled Marshall Wales back to reality. The outraged spasm griping his empty belly tod him the sergeant had spoken of food. He raised his head, and all at once he was aware of a peculiar sound in the flat, dead morning air. It took a moment for his brain to register what it was—the frenzied, indignant, pathetic squawking of chickens in mortal fear for their lives.

"Over yonder." The sergeant pointed. He was fidgeting in the saddle with an impatience like that of a man needing to make water badly. "That's where hit is."

Squinting through the bright, dancing glare that hung over the road, Wales saw and recognized at once the plantation driveway—a double line of oaks, still a half mile distant. Like twin files of soldiers, the giant old shaggy-headed trees seemed to march from behind the shoulder of a ridge to their intersection with the road, and it was from behind the ridge, where the driveway must have ended, that the shrill, desperate sound of the chickens came.

"Them hongry bastards'll have everthing devoured!" the sergeant half wailed, as the screaming mounted to a crescendo.

In that moment Wales's mind clicked fully back into the present. Suddenly his mouth began to water; a quick, greedy fear that matched the sergeant's rose within him. "By God, they'd better not!" he snapped. He could feel his heart pounding. "Damn them, if they eat up everything, I'll flay 'em alive!" He snapped the order: "Tell Houston to get those mules on the bit and let's go!" His spurs jabbed the horse viciously. It broke into a lurching, reluctant trot. Behind him Wales could hear the wagon jolt and clatter, the calf bawl piteously as it tried vainly to keep up.

But it seemed to take forever before they reached the oaks, before they swung into the broad, sand-clay drive between the trees. Then they were out of the sun and entering coolness, the checkered shade a benison, the horses' hoofs muffled on soft, moist sand shadowed by the interlocking foliage. The oaks stretched away before them, a giant cathedral-like aisle with a vaulted

46

ceiling of rippling leaves. A quarter of a mile ahead of them Wales could see where the oaks merged with more greenery. There the driveway seemed to end, and all at once he caught the gleam of sun on window glass. He blinked, coming out of the lustful delirium in which he had been certain he'd be cheated of breakfast; he reined in the horse so quickly that it snorted, and put out a hand to check the sergeant. The sergeant looked at him in surprise.

"God damn it," Wales said. "This is no way to come up. Slobbering like a couple of starving mongrels. There's a house up there. We don't want to go charging into the yard like a couple of Yahoos."

The sergeant batted his eyes. "Yes, sir," he said.

One last chicken raised a final despairing cry. The desperate squawk was cut off abruptly at its highest pitch, but some vibration from it seemed to throb on in the air. The sergeant shifted nervously in the saddle.

"Don't worry," said Wales. "Channing swore there was plenty of livestock." He tapped his hand against his thigh. "Sergeant."

"Yes, sir, damn it, Capn."

"I want an iron hand kept on the men. There's a procedure for this business. We'll have no looting. We're still soldiers in the Army of Northern Virginia, and these are our own people, not Yankees. This is not going to be any Roman holiday. I want you to see to that."

"Yes, sir," the sergeant said. He made a jerky forward motion with his whole body. "Capn, all them chickens will be gone—"

"All right," said Wales. "Come on." He lifted rein and they moved slowly and deliberately up the driveway.

Wales's stomach was still plunging and twisting like an unbroken animal fighting a tether. He could hear it growling. He looked up at the arch of leaves overhead. This shade feels good, he thought. Channing said— But, no. He must have been exaggerating. He had to be exaggerating. It will be like all the others—a shell, picked clean, with nothing but some leavings for us to

47

take if I've got the guts to go through that business all over again with somebody else. But . . . everything *does* look good this far.

They were nearing the end of the driveway now. They could see that the driveway faded into a long, high wall of tangled hedge and wild rose riotous with blossom, a green screen blocking off all view of what was behind it. There was so much foliage, but Wales squinted hard, and in a moment he was certain that beyond the hedge he had seen the heights of a roof, lavish with chimneys.

He felt a curious tingle of anticipation that had nothing to do with hunger. He was suddenly possessed with an eagerness to see what was behind that hedge. He wanted to whip up the horse, but instead he deliberately slowed it to an even more leisurely gait. He saw now that the driveway continued on through a notch in the hedge, and he and the sergeant approached that opening warily and almost respectfully. Then they were through it, and as the wall of hedge fell away behind them and they entered the main yard of the plantation, Wales reined in, his jaw dropping and his throat suddenly blocked with an upsurge of quick emotions: amazement—envy—but most of all a strange, wrenching, eerie sensation that somehow he had just come home.

"How did they do it?" he heard himself whisper. "How did they manage to do it?"

It was a big house and an old one. Probably a very old one, likely built before the Revolution by an owner who had been his own architect, a man who had known nothing of buttresses, arches, frills, or falsework, but who had only wanted a big frame box to live in, a two-story rectangle to which, later, as an afterthought, he had added a gallery with columns.

He had built well. The lines of the house soared up straight and clean and unadorned into the shifting, shadow-patterned heads of the tall red oaks whose foliage brushed its roof. White weatherboarding gleamed; spacious windows amiably winked shafts of sunlight out toward Wales. A rambling gallery on the front looked shady and inviting. Vast green lawns

48

sloped away on every side, like the skirts of a seated, stately dowager, accented with a jewelry of flagstone walks and marble benches. Wales rubbed his hand slowly across his stubbled cheek. Beside him he heard the sergeant's voice, full of exultant greed. "By God," the sergeant was whispering over and over. "By God, if we ain't done struck it rich!"

But how did they do it? Wales wondered blankly.

Because it was not the dimensions of the place. He had seen bigger plantation houses and more ornate ones than this. It was the look of adequacy and care. Ruin was what his eyes were used to: not only the quick, jagged ruin of battle destruction, but the slow, rotting, slumping ruin of neglect and disrepair—Virginia was porous with that now. But there was no ruin here of any kind; this place was prosperous and in order. The house shone with fresh paint—in a time when scabby, peeling surfaces were ugly attestation to patriotism. The shrubbery was trimmed and thinned, the lawns neat and free of weed growth. Ashbrook, Wales thought . . . It looked like this before she— But they saved theirs, he thought, envy clawing at him. Somehow . . . Whoever they are, they have saved theirs.

Then his eyes moved to the eight gaunt horses, scabby and dust-caked, hitched on the emerald lawn. He felt an odd sense of outrage: here was a dream profaned with dirty reality. He made a quick jerking motion with his hand.

"I want those horses moved around behind," he said thickly to the sergeant.

"Yes, sir," the sergeant said. His voice was quiet and full of awe, as if he were in an empty church. Then it took on its normal harshness. "I doan hear any more chickens."

"No." Wales, too, was aware of the silence. "But don't worry . . ." He left the sentence dangling, hushing to listen.

Because there was a new sound now, strident in the placid, shaded air. It cleaved through the silence and shattered it, coming high and shrill from far to the rear of the house. Wales felt the short hair rising on his neck. That quick babble of whoops and yells and hollering—a high-pitched, choppy sound like the gobble of hounds pulling down game. But it was not dogs. Wales recognized immediately the ugly hunting cry of man after man.

There was an interval while he and the sergeant sat frozen and stared blankly at one another.

The sergeant was the first into action. "By God!" he grunted ."They done hit trouble!" He rammed spurs to his horse, and the action jolted Wales from his halted indecision. The hoofs of the animals gouged great hunks from the turf as the two men galloped their mounts across the lawn and fumbled for their guns.

There was a vast back yard, too, as carefully landscaped as the front, jeweled with flower beds, shaded by more of the big oaks, crisscrossed with flagstone walks, encircled by a low trimmed hedge of boxwoods. Beyond the hedge Wales saw a wagon drive running toward a distant complex of slave quarters, barns, and outbuildings.

Four men were coming up the footpath. Wales heard the shoes of his mount clatter and slide on the flagstones as he reined in abruptly, staring at that procession.

Two soldiers led the way, and between them, half shoved, half carried, was one of the biggest Negroes Wales had ever seen. Another soldier shambled behind the Negro, and he was rhythmically punching the black man in the rump with short, vicious jabs of a carbine barrel. The group struggled toward Wales and the sergeant without seeing them; the soldiers had their hands full with the slave.

Because he could have obviously wrenched loose in an instant if he had chosen; just as obviously he did not dare use the full potential of his giant muscles. The most he dared to do was dig his heels in the ground: Wales saw the white undersoles of his huge bare feet flash as he planted his heels and braced his legs and then was borne along by the men holding his arms and the impetus of the gun barrel at his butt; his chocolate skin shone with sweat; his eyes were white and rolling. But all at once his eyes fastened on Wales and immediately and inexplicably he quit fighting; suddenly he started to move forward willingly.

At his quick and unexpected co-operation the two soldiers who held him looked up. Abruptly their drumfire yammer of imprecations slid into quick, uneasy silence. In the noiseless morning the voice of the soldier with the gun whanged out loud, clear, unaware, and ugly:

"Awright, you black bastad. Move along er I'll skin ye with this gunsight. I know yo kind, nigga. I done sold a million like you. I know how to make you step around. You know whut the lieutenant's goan do with you? I'll tell you. The lieutenant's goan take you an' cut off yo—"

He saw Wales then too.

". . . balls . . ." he said sickly.

All the men stopped then. They looked at Wales in an embarrassed silence.

"Sergeant," Wales said quietly.

MacLeod nodded. He lifted rein and moved his horse across the lawn over to the men. He said something to them in a tone inaudible to Wales. The men did not look at the sergeant. They looked down at their feet.

The sergeant said something else. The men nodded soberly. Still holding on to the Negro, they moved toward the captain, not looking at him either. The Negro came forward willingly, not digging in his feet at all now. The whole crew of them stopped at Wales's stirrup, and he looked down at them bleakly from his saddle, consciously exercising the godhead that the man on horseback has over the man on foot.

"All right," Wales said quietly. "What are you doing with him?"

The two of them holding the Negro, the stocky, redheaded one called Boomer and a corporal named Dalton, spoke up both at once. "Sirhewassirwecaughtim—"

"One at a time—Dalton?"

The corporal licked his lips. Wales recognized a cer-

51

tain hangdog shame on the corporal's face, but there was an edge of defiance, or self-justification, in his voice. "Sir . . . Capn . . . Jeff Davis caught thisaheah nigger tryin to lead a cow into the brush. We done told these people not to try to hide nothin, but he was tryin to hide a cow. We wasn't aimin to hurt 'im, Capn, but we sho-God aimed to teach 'im a lesson."

Wales nodded, letting himself show no expression.

"Davis?"

The soldier with the carbine stepped around from behind the black wall of the Negro's body. Wales looked down at him without letting his distaste show, but he had always hated underbred, scrub stock of any kind. The soldier looked up at Wales with a weasel's eyes in a weasel's face. Forehead and chin both sloped away from the sly, pointed nose; the eyes glittered with the mindless cunning and the senseless impartial hate that Wales could remember seeing in the eyes of small predators. The narrow face and sun-wrinkled web of the neck had a crust of dirt on them—not just the dirt of soldiering, but a dirt that seemed permanent, that seemed to have accumulated over unwashed years. The soldier sniffled wetly. Before he spoke he clamped two fingers to his nose, overhand, and blew it. The sheet of mucus whirled, gleaming, from his nostrils; Wales drew back his foot and it missed the stirrup. The soldier dragged his sleeve across his face and sniffed again, then he began talking in a high-pitched voice that seemed to come from the upper reaches of his nasal passages:

"That black bastad had aholt of a cow, Capn. I seed 'im tryin to sneak 'er outn the back of the barn real quiet. I says, 'Nigger, where at you takin that air cow?' He doan even answer me, jes goes on walkin down the lane to'rd the woods. I says, 'Nigger, bring that air cow back heah for I blow yo black ass off,' an' I run up an' grab her halter. By God, I ain takin no crap off no big black buck. I done bought an' sole too many them black sonofabitches not to know how to handle 'em. I says, 'Nigger, goddam yo time, bring that air cow back heah or I'll beat yo head off with this yere gun.' Still he doan pay no nevermind. I tried to shoot 'im then an' my gun misfars an I starts to beat his haid in an somehow the gun got knocked outn my hand. By God! So I grabs 'im an he pulls loose an' Boomer an' Dalton seed 'im an' grabs 'im. When he sees he's whupped, he quiets down. By God, Capn, if I had the handlin of 'im, I'd sho as hell teach 'im to mind when a white man talks. I'd pure burn his black-assed hide offn him, that's what I'd—"

"All right, Davis," Wales said, not sternly, just with an absolute firmness that shut off the tirade the way a sluice gate closes off water. Then he looked at Boomer and Dalton.

"Let him go."

The two soldiers released their holds and stepped back. The Negro straightened up, crossing his arms, massaging his biceps where the fingers had dug. He raised his face slowly toward Wales, and the captain found himself looking down into a countenance as broad and black and blank as a tarred shovel blade. There was no fear and no arrogance, neither stupidity nor intelligence—only an impassive waiting.

"You," Wales said sharply, "what's your name?"

"Name Yance, Cuhnel." The voice was deep, steady, respectful.

Wales focused an angry, an intimidating glare at the slave's eyes. The black pupils against the yellow cornea refused to accept it; they were opaque, impenetrable. Wales felt a throb of frustrated irritation.

"All right. What have you got to say for yourself?"

"Why, Cuhnel, dat cow belong to Miz Cammun. I din want no Yankees stealin Miz Cammun's cow. I din know dese sojermens on our side—I tought dey Yankees."

"Weren't you told not to bother any of the livestock?"

"I say din want no Yankees having Miz Cammun's cow. Doan want Yankees havin nuthin. Got no use for Yankees round dis yere place."

Wales rubbed his chin thoughtfully. He knew that he was enmeshed in a game now, an ancient game with rules unwritten but explicit and formalized, one he was thoroughly familiar with. Somehow, with the invisible antennae of a race dependent on noblesse oblige for survival, this man had recognized the one person present who could not in good conscience condemn him for his attempt to save his owner's cow. Not only could not condemn him, but who, under other circumstances, would have perhaps rewarded him. Wales could see all the structure of the game now; he was aware of what would happen. And he knew that there was no way he could help losing.

He tried to make his gaze more threatening.

"All right," he said. "But you knew these men were Confederates, not Yankees. Don't tell me that you didn't."

"Naw, suh," the Negro said. His countenance lost none of its wooden impassiveness. "I couldn't tell. Dey kept deir hats on. How was I to see dat dey didn't have no horns?"

The sergeant let out a whoop. "I-God!" he yelled, pounding his saddle. "No horns! I-God, that's a good one!"

Even the corporal grinned; even the redheaded soldier, Boomer, chuckled. The soldier named Davis looked disgusted; Wales shifted in his saddle and tried hard not to let his own expression become any less grim.

"Now you listen to me," he said harshly. "I reckon you're one of the boss hands around here. You've got sense enough to do as you're told. Now, I'm telling you and you tell your people. I don't want anything touched. I don't want anything moved or hidden. You understand? I want your people to go on about their work and leave the livestock alone. The next slave I find messing around a cow or a horse is going to get the hide taken off his back."

"Yassuh," the Negro said immediately. The opaque eyes lightened a bit with what could have been respect. Wales knew that the slave realized the game was over; Wales was telling him that he accepted defeat but would not lose another round. "Yassuh, I tells 'em."

"All right," Wales snapped. "Now go along."

"Yassuh. Thankee, Cuhnel." The Negro bobbed his

head soberly and respectfully a single time. Then he turned and stepped wide around the three soldiers and moved with a measured, almost dignified gait down the path toward the slave quarters. Wales watched him go, feeling partly that he had handled the situation well, partly that he had let himself be made a fool of. He raised his hands and dropped them in a baffled gesture, thinking: It's a good thing we don't allow them to play poker with us.

He took a deep breath.

"Corporal, find Lieutenant Channing and tell him to report to me immediately. Keep your eyes open and don't let anybody else get away with anything. Davis, it was good work catching him with that cow, but no more roughing anybody up like that, not even one of the niggers, understand? Sergeant, keep an eye on them and get us some breakfast and I'll pay my respects . . . Cameron, eh?" He swung his horse around toward the back door of the house.

The old woman, who was standing on the steps and who must have been standing there all along, said gravely, "My thanks, Captain, for the way you persuaded your men to release my slave. I was about to take action myself."

Wales stared at her, openmouthed.

Her hair was snow-white, her face the face of a proud old hawk. Wales was reminded of engravings he had seen of George Washington's face, with the high hooked nose and the cold blue eyes, the dry, harsh little lines at the mouth corners. This was such a face, feminized. She wore a severe dress of black with a little lace at the throat. Her figure was small, frail, delicate. In her hands she held coiled a great black drover's whip.

"I can use this thing a little," she said, unsmiling, seeing his eyes drop to it.

Wales remembered then to jerk off his hat; he swung to the ground and introduced himself.

The woman waited for a few seconds, and Wales felt oddly awkward and silly under those icy eyes staring from their vantage above him. Then he saw her subtly relax, a trace of a smile easing the lines at her mouth corners.

"I am Alice Cameron, Captain," she said, holding out her hand. "Unfortunately my husband, Doctor Ward Cameron, is with the Fifty-third Virginia, somewhere near Richmond. But I hope you will allow me to welcome you to Red Oaks in his name."

"Thank you," Wales said.

"You spoke of a Lietenant Channing, I believe," she went on. "I presume he's the young officer who accompanied these men—I didn't quite catch his name earlier. However, if that's he, the lieutenant is at present refreshing himself upstairs."

"Refreshing himself?"

"Bathing."

There was a moment of outraged silence, while Wales gawked at her blankly. "Bathing?" he managed at last, trying hard to keep the strangled anger out of his voice. "Taking a bath? *Now?*"

"Why, yes. He was very dusty." Her eyes went up and down his long, travel-soiled figure. "Like yourself. Won't you allow me to have one prepared for you too?"

Wales swallowed hard and looked at the corporal.

"Dismissed," he snapped. "Mrs. Cameron, that's most hospitable of you. But I must see Lieutenant Channing immediately and—"

"Captain, Captain . . ." Her voice was gently remonstrative. "Surely you'll allow the young man time to finish his ablutions." She smiled ruefully. "I'm afraid our hospitality's more in the word than the deed nowadays. But we still have some ham and the chickens have fortunately continued to lay. And there's yet a little coffee. I trust you'll breakfast with us?"

Ham? Eggs? Coffee? Wales blinked. His mind flailed, trying to make sense out of her words. Nobody in Virginia had any coffee. And certainly no one in his right mind would admit to possession of any to a foraging party. Didn't Channing tell her? he wondered. Doesn't she know why we're here? Why, she must know, he thought; no one could be that naïve. Unless . . . He felt hope stirring in him. Patriotism, that's it. Maybe because her husband's in the army she's willing to give freely. He felt vastly relieved. At least, he thought, I won't have to go through anything else like that business back yonder.

"I wouldn't want to put you to any trouble, ma'am . . ." But in the middle of the words he raised his head, sniffed, nostrils widening, yearning vibrating through his nerves. Faintly, drifting from a nearby window of the separate kitchen wing of the house, came the taut, rich, delicate fragrance of brewing coffee. Wales swallowed. ". . . but I'd be delighted," he finished. "If it wouldn't be any inconvenience. But first I've got to see to my men. With your permission, I'll be along directly."

"By all means, Captain. See to your men. I've given them permission to kill as many chickens as they need for breakfast." She drew the coil of the stock whip tighter in blue-veined, waxy-skinned hands. "Asking them to limit their slaughter to roosters, of course. How do you like your eggs, Captain?"

"Ma'am?" he said blankly. "Oh, fried, please. Not too hard."

"Very well, Captain," she said. "I'll see to it. There's hay in the barn for your horse." With that she turned and entered the latticed door of the back porch. Wales looked for a long time at the door after it had closed. He rubbed his hand through his sweat-plastered hair and put his hat back on. Then he turned and gathered up the reins of the horse. "Come on," he said to the animal and pulled it around.

Leading the horse, he walked slowly down the path toward the barn. His movements were groping, almost blind, like those of a sleepwalker as, stunned, his eyes swept over his surroundings, feasting on them visually, hungrily—the thriftiness and good husbandry everywhere; the perfectly kept barns and slave quarters and outbuildings; the fields . . . especially the fields. The path ran along the spine of a gentle ridge, and from this height he could look out over the plantation for a fair distance on either side. The fields lay peacefully under

57

the merciless sun, clean of grass and lush with corn, peas, yams, even some cotton. Wales looked at the fields and thought of all the ruined countryside he had ridden through until now and shook his head in bewilderment. He had the eerie sensation of being caught up in a dream that he could not break free of. He knew this was reality—the bright, harsh sun, the gravid earth, all this fructifying growth—but he could not believe it. This was quiet, orderliness, serenity, and growth. But there was no quiet or serenity, no growth or orderliness in Virginia any more. Every rational impulse told him this must be an illusion.

But it was not, and he could not fit himself into it.

Because, he thought, maybe I'm the illusion. Maybe the war is the illusion. Maybe this *is* reality and all the rest of it's a dream and—

His hand gripped the reins so tightly that the horse's head was jerked forward and the animal snorted.

"No," Wales said aloud. No, he thought, his throat going dry, feeling the trembling beginning in himself again, all at once terrified because he knew he was about to start remembering and would not be able to bear it. "No," he said hoarsely. His hand made a futile gesture in the air. But this was not reality. Reality was Ashbrook, the five chimneys of Ashbrook the last time he had seen them, stark against the sky on a winter afternoon. Right after I got the letter, he thought helplessly. Unable any more to help remembering—

As he had ridden up there had not been a sound around the place where the house had been. The iron-bound cold of December had gripped everything; the rutted, weed-grown earth was frozen hard beneath the feet of the shambling old livery-stable nag. There had been nothing in the afternoon but silence and a hard, still cold.

But he had not even felt the cold. Because somehow, amid all the grief and hate and rage, it had never occurred to him that anything had happened to the house. He had been born in it and grown up in it and so had his father before him, and despite everything else that had happened to him, despite every other cataclysm, the house of Ashbrook had been fixed in his mind as one of the unyielding verities of life, as enduring as a pyramid of Cheops. He had thought about it all the way out from town, the interminable distance on the slow old livery-stable horse; his heart had pounded and he had worked himself up into a lather of unendurable impatience to see it again. He had pictured it standing in its grove of cane and myrtle, knowing that at least that much would have endured.

And now he saw that there was nothing left of it but five gaunt chimneys, tall and soot-blackened against the lead-colored sky. Five chimneys and a formless mound of charred rubble. . . .

His breath was coming hoarsely; he was panting as he dismounted and walked stiffly toward the debris. That was when the trembling had started: then was the first time. He was already trembling when he ground his toe against a blackened board and watched almost curiously the way the board disintegrated into charcoal.

After a long time spent circling the house's remains, an aimless, distraught time in which he went no further into the rubble and recognized no item among the cinders, he found himself moving toward the slave quarters. He had had to fight his way through a season's brush that had grown up, untended, between the house and the quarters, and when he had reached the long double row of empty cabins in which the slaves had lived, he had halted at the head of the alley between them and watched the open doors swing gently and untended in the winter wind. Later he moved down between the cabins, looking idly in each one.

He was startled when he found life.

In almost the last cabin. A skeletal, attenuated black figure swathed in rags, crouching over a smoking fire it was trying to get started on the hearth. Wales had stared, unseen. "Uncle Clint!" In the hush the crackle of his own words startled even himself.

The figure came slowly erect, turning with horror and fear on its face, and then the fear had changed to a grotesque radiance of excited joy. The old carriage driver came stumbling across the cabin, his mouth working soundlessly, and fell on Wales. His embrace was redolent of smoke.

After a while they sat on a bench in the lee of the cabin, out of the cold wind that was rising, and Wales looked up toward where the phallic chimneys stood out lonesomely against the metallic afternoon. It was then he asked the question he had come all this way to get answered: "Uncle Clint . . . how did it happen?"

Uncle Clint shook his head. "Seem like she mighty upset atter dat time you come home an' go back," he said. "Seem lak when you go back it tear her up purty bad. She say to me one time, 'Clint, I go crazy I stay in dis empty house. I nebber knew a house could be dis empty.' She say, 'Clint, I scream if King ax me one mo time when he mus' chop cotton. Whut I know 'bout choppin cotton, Clint? I jes a woman—I no plantuh . . .'

"Atter while she has me drive her to Sumter t'ketch de kyars to Columbia to stay wif a quaintance dere. She say, 'Clint, you come git me in a week.' I say, 'Miz Vivian, whut about de place?' She say, 'Let de place look atter itself. You an' King look atter de place. I sick o' de place.' So I take her, Missa Mahsh, an' den it git to be a regular thing. Ebry udder week she say, 'Clint, carry me in to ketch de kyars again.' Ebry udder week, reglar. Den, one weekend, she come back an' dat man come back wid her. She say, 'Clint, dis Missah Ahmstrong. He cotton buyer. He fum England, Clint, come all de way cross de ocean buy cotton an' carry hit home tru de blockade.' "

Wales's hands had had to do something. He was surprised to find his pistol in them. His hands kept spinning the cylinder of the pistol. It had made a dry, whirring sound as Clint paused, and everything inside of Wales had felt frozen and stiff and very far away.

"What did he look like, Clint?"

"He mighty hansome man, Missah Mahsh. He big, tall, slim man; wide shoulders, little hips, dress very fancy. He quiet talkin, very polite, got gray hair over he ears an' little brown mustash. He says, 'Very please

60

meet you, Uncle Clint,' an' he gib me silber dollar. Miz Vivian, she say, 'Uncle Clint, Missah Ahmstrong stay heah few days whiles we talks business.' "

Wales had not felt frozen and stiff inside then. He stared down at his knuckles, watching them getting white around the grip of the pistol . . .

"Didn' think nuthin ob dat . . . Miz Vivian, she say she so lonesome she cain sleep in dat big house by herself no mo. She hab Dorene, dat gingerbread house gal she trainin, sleep in her room ebry night since you done go back. Atter Missah Ahmstrong come, Dorene she keep right on sleeping dere."

"Yes?" Wales had said in a stranger's voice.

"Yassuh." Clint nodded. He looked down at the ground.

"Den one evenin atter sundown when he been heah mebbe three days I meets Dorene down heah at de quarters. I say, 'Gal, how come you down heah? You blong up dere at de big house wif Miz Vivian.'

"She says, 'Miz Vivian, she tole me spend de night in de quarters tonight.' "

The leathery old face turned up to Wales then was twisted in pathetic misery.

"What I gwine do, Missah Mahsh? What I gwine do? I ain nobody. I ain nuthin but old nigger carriage driver. How kin I go up dere and say, 'Miz Vivian, you stop now. Doan you do nothin like dis . . .' "

When he finally went on, his voice was so low and dry that at first Wales thought it was the wind in the live oaks.

"De man he go back to Columbia next day. Miz Vivian, she quit goin for a while atter dat. Den one day a coupla months later de man come back."

His throat worked hard.

"Dorene come back an' sleep in de quarters agin.'

"Yes?" Wales said again, the cylinder of the Colt's spinning round and round, the brass-capped nipples winking in the dull light.

"I stay wake all dat night, Missah Mahsh, de night when he come back. Dat de longest night I ebber spent. Fust cock crow, when de sky gittin gray, I heah sumpin.

I heah wheels on de driveway. I heah a carriage goan out. Soon hit light, I make me 'scuse go up to de big house.

"Dey wasn nobody dere, Missah Mahsh. He gone. She gone. De baroosh gone outn de carriage house 'long wif de chestnut team. An' dat de last I done seed ob her. I went ober to Missah Jawn Everett's, but he done had a stroke an' he very sick. He die two days later, an' atter dey buries him, Miz Everett move back to Charleston. Dey ain nowheah to go. Dey ain nobody to go to. Dey ain nothin to do. 'Cept wait," he finished, standing up. " 'Cept wait twel you come back."

"Yes," said Wales, finality in his voice, standing up too.

"De niggahs doan know whut to do," Uncle Clint said. "King, he say he boun you dead—Miz Vivian not go off if you wasn't. He stay heah fo a while an' den he say you dead an' she gone—he think he go see kin he find freedom. He go. Cuffo go. All de boss niggers go. Nobody lef heah but de trash." Uncle Clint's voice became sodden with contempt. "Trash!" he spat. "Dey tear de big house apaht for kindlin wood. Dey go through de drawers. Dey go through de trunks. Dey joke an carry on. Dey say, 'Looka me, look. I plantation boss. I fancy, same like white bukra . . .' Dey do deir mess on de flo. Dey tear up *eberyting!* Den one night we wakes up an' finds de big house on fiah. Two ob dem cavortin round in de bedroom knock ober a candle. Big house burn up fo we kin put hit out. Den dey all scared. Dey all run off. Now ain nobody heah but me."

"All right," Wales had said, looking again at the chimneys, then turning to survey once more the weed-choked fields in the distance, where unharvested cotton, beaten from its bolls by rain and weather, lay in dirty gray hanks in the blackberry bushes and broomstraw clumps. "All right . . . Well, I'm going away again, Clint."

"Where you gwine, Missah Mahsh?"

"I don't know." Wales put the gun back in its scabbard. "I'm going back to the war, I reckon. I don't know of any place else to go."

Uncle Clint's anxious hand shot out and gripped his arm. "Den take me wid you, Missah Mahsh. I cain stay heah by myself no longer."

"I'm not going to leave you, Clint. Any horses?"

"Dey all gone."

"All right. We'll take turns on my nag back to town. I'll find somebody there to look after you until I can come back."

"You comin back, ain't you, Missah Mahsh? You comin back, ain't you?" Clint's voice trembled with anxiety.

Wales turned and looked toward the soaring, forlorn chimneys.

"I always thought I was," he said.

Then he had walked on back to the house and straight past the fire-blackened piles of masonry without even halting. He had gone to where his horse was tethered and he had swung up and held out his arm for Clint to swing up behind him. "Hyah," he had said to the horse, and the animal had swung around and shambled off up the driveway. Wales's nostrils were full of the stench of burnt, rain-wet wood, and he did not look back at the chimneys. . . .

And now Marsh Wales stared out across the neat fields shimmering in the Virginia sun.

And there's your reality, he thought. Not this. But that.

5

In a broad lane which sloped down from behind the largest barn of the plantation toward the woods the men had built a cooking fire of scrap fence rails. Now they sprawled at ease around it, watching the smoke drift upward, thinly blue and pungent, tired, strained muscles relaxing on the resilient grass, trying hard to control the ravening pangs that went through them as the fat, dripping from broiling chickens skewered on sabers propped over the flames, hissed and sizzled in the embers and thickened the air with its hot, rich fragrance.

The sergeant, leaning against the rail fence of the lane, said, "Yo're lucky he didn't boot yo tail plumb up between yo ears." The sergeant was talking to the soldier everyone called Jeff Davis.

"Like hell," Davis said in his nasal whine. He spat between his teeth into the fire. The sergeant said, "You spit on them chickens an' I'll do hit myself."

"Like hell," Davis said again. "Better not nobody mess with me about roughin up no damn nigger. Not this army they better not." He sniffled and dragged his sleeve across his nose.

"Doan hit hurt you to smile?" the sergeant asked. "With that crust on yo upper lip?"

"Screw you," Davis said. "Screw the bunch of you. I done tole you, that air nigger was tryina make off with a cow. I ketched 'im, didn't I, Boomer? Didn't I, Dalton?"

"All right," the sergeant said. "You caught 'im. You want somebody to give you a leather medal?"

"Ahhh . . ." Davis turned a saber with two chickens growing brown on it. "The trouble with you, MacLeod, is that you doan know nothin about niggers."

"I won't argue that," the sergeant said. "Ain't many of 'em back in east Tennessee."

"Now," said Davis, sitting back on the grass and dragging his sleeve across his nose again, "now I knows niggers inside an' out. I done bought an' sold a many of 'em in my time. Big uns, little uns, an' in-between uns. A many, many of 'em."

"So I hear," the sergeant grunted.

"Awright." Davis looked up at him defensively. "So I was a slave trader. There ain't nothin wrong with that, is there?"

The sergeant didn't answer.

"You damn right I was a slave trader," Davis went on. "An' I'll tell you one thing more—I ain't a damn bit ashamed of hit neither. I ain't—"

"All right, Davis," the sergeant said without impatience. "All right. All right."

"Well, damn it all, I jest git tired of everybody lookin down their nose at me 'cause I was dealin in niggers. I git tired of bein low-rated all a time. Hell, what's wrong with dealin in niggers? What's any different 'bout me buyin an' sellin 'em an' some big planter buyin an' sellin 'em? I tell you, these damn muckity-muck planters got no call to look down their nose at me. I done sold a many a one of 'em a nice young nigger wench to lay up with. I done bought many a wore-out gal they was all through with too. I done seen some of the things they done to 'em. I doan see how come everybody makes so much difference 'tween me and them."

"All right, Davis," the sergeant said, with less patience this time.

"Like that damn capn," Davis went on, the sergeant's interjection not even slowing him up. "Me and th' other boys grabs that big buck nigger red-handed, an' you an' the capn makes us turn 'im loose. Why, I tell you, down home in Alabama—"

God damn him, the sergeant thought irritably. Like a confounded horsefly buzzin an' buzzin. "Well, you

65

ain't in Alabama now, Davis. You're in Nawthun Virginia. You been with the outfit only three weeks an' we ain't had a real fight yet. So maybe, if you don't mind, we'll set tight 'n see how well you make out in a skirmish before we ast the capn to turn over command of the company to you. If that's all right with you, Mr. Jefferson Davis."

Davis looked up at him, red rising under the dirt on his neck. "Well, damn your snotty time. If you didn't have them stripes on—"

The sergeant's grin broadened. "Sho, now. I wouldn't let a little thing like that stop me." I got no business tormentin him, the sergeant was thinking. But, blast it, he's so eternal noisy and hard to like. . . .

Davis snuffled, spat into the fire. "Hell," he grunted. "I wouldn' fight no nigger-lover . . ."

All the faces around the fire went white with shock. The sergeant straightened up, his eyes like two steel balls. "Now I'd sho hate to hafta kick you teeth in, Davis. But I'm goan do it if you doan't apologize. I was jest teasin you, but I doan't take that kinda talk from nobody." His voice was deadly soft.

"Well, you an' the capn jes now—Damn it, what else you goan call it? I—" Davis saw the shocked faces all around him then. He swallowed, comprehension and terror coming into his face. His hand moved out to one of the sabers propped over the fire and clutched the wire-bound haft.

The sergeant took a step forward, lightly, on the balls of his feet. "You'd better turn loose of that, Davis," he whispered.

Instead, Davis suddenly bounded erect. He shook the saber at the sergeant wildly, two crisping chickens still on the blade. "I-God," he shrilled. "I-God, doan't you come pickin on me now. I mean hit! Doan't you come pickin on me!"

The sergeant rocked back and forth on the balls of his feet. "I said, put that thing down, soldier."

"Doan't you come at me! I'll cut yo gizzard out! I-God, MacLeod, you been pickin at me ever since I come into this outfit! You all have! Jes because I was in the home guard until the last draft. Jest because I useta be a slave trader—"

"Ain't nobody been pickin on you, Davis," the sergeant whispered. "You gotta learn to take joshin. But what you called me ain't joshin. Now apologize, or I'll take that saber away from you an' ram hit up yo tail!"

"Pickin on me," Davis yelled, unhearing. "The whole bunch of yuh! Coddlin big black buck niggers! God knows, hit'd serve you right! Goddammit, the Yankees *oughta* come down heah an' free the niggers, an *then* you could coddle 'em! You could coddle them air niggers dressed up in bluebelly uniforms over to Petersburg! You could have them niggers put up alongside you an' made jest as good as you are. Then you could watch great big black free niggers chase Southern white women around . . . Hit'd serve you right! Doan't you come at me, MacLeod. I'm awarnin you! Doan't you come at me—" He waved the saber violently, chickens and all. "I'm tired of yo pickin!"

The sergeant tensed to spring across the fire; suddenly he let out a long breath and straightened up, relaxing. "All right, Jeff. Simmer down. Maybe we have been ridin you too hard. I apologize if we have. Now, if you'll apologize, we won't have no trouble . . ."

"I doan't want no trouble." Davis's voice trembled and broke on a note shrill as a woman's. "I didn't go for to call you a nigger-lover, but doan't you come at me, or I'll stick you sure! I'll do it—"

"Stop it," said Wales, coming up, taking in the tableau, not knowing what caused it and not really caring, but having to ask. "What's all this about?"

The sergeant rubbed his cheek thoughtfully and turned to face the captain, shoving his cap back on his head. "Me an' Davis merely had a little misunderstandin, Capn. We already done apologized to each other, didn' we, Jeff? You kin put the sword down now, Jeff. I'm satisfied." He grinned. "Didn't amount to a hill o'beans, Capn," he said.

"All right." Wales watched until slowly, carefully, Davis had put the saber back in the forked stick which had been supporting it over the fire. He turned again to the sergeant.

"Where are the pickets located?"

"Which pickets, sir?"

"Didn't Channing put out pickets?"

The sergeant shook his head. "Not as I been able to find out." His grin broadened. "But you kin ease off, Capn. I sent Vardaman an' Coltrane an' Brazos out. Brazos has got the road, Vardaman's out ahind them haystacks yonder, an' Coltrane's over acrosst that field in that line of woods."

Wales slapped his hand against his thigh disgustedly. So eager for a bath and breakfast he couldn't even take time to see to security, eh? All right, he thought. I'll just add that to my little list of things to discuss with Lieutenant Channing. He said, "All the men got breakfast?"

The sergeant nodded. "Yessuh. Plenty chickens to go around an' some eggs too. We'll make out fine. Could use some hoecake though."

"I'll have some sent down," Wales said. He started to add, "And coffee," but he did not. Ashamedly, he thought: I'd better see how much there is first. It's been two months since I've had a cup of real coffee and . . . He said, "Carry on, Sergeant. And you, Davis, save your saber waving for the Yankees, or we'll be having a little talk." He turned abruptly and left them then.

Halfway back to the house he stopped, looking out over the fields again. A faint breeze was beginning to stir, and the coolness felt good against the sweat-plastered shirt. He shoved back his hat, letting the wind cool his damp hair. He felt his lower back muscles, long taut with strain, beginning to relax with an easing of tension that amounted almost to an ache. Looking at the peaceful and familiar-seeming expanses of green that stretched away to the distant woods, he felt a strange reassurance. There was, for a moment, the sense of having waked from a nightmare.

Because you forget, he thought. Your thinking gets warped in an army. You no longer see things as they are for sane, normal, everyday people. You see them only in their miliary aspect, which bears no relation to reality, to sanity . . . When you look at things through the eyes of a soldier for long enough, the yardstick you use to measure things by becomes a fantastic one. . . .

Like this place, he thought. Now I'm not supposed to see it as a plantation. I'm not supposed to see all the dozens of years that went into cleaning these fields and building them up and planting and growing and creating. I'm just supposed to see this as a supply depot . . . something to be plundered and left, just another plantation, not at all important to the war, except for what I can steal from it.

But I can't think like that, he told himself. I can't help seeing— Damn it, if I were a lawyer or a politician or a preacher . . . But I'm not. I'm a planter, and the only way I can look at all this is in a planter's way: the life, the growing, keeps pushing its way through the military aspect.

In the midst of life we are in death, he thought. He watched a cloud shadow, thrown by a towering, fluffy mass of cumulus, slip over the woods, encroach a little on the sun-flooded fields. But it works two ways, too, he thought, and maybe some day all of us soldiers will learn it. Because nothing is as insistent as a seed. You can't even keep a seed from growing by dropping a body on it. Seeds like to have bodies dropped on them.

The dark flatness of the cloud shadow edged on across the fields, engulfing row after row of corn. The breeze stirred a little more authoritatively.

Maybe it will rain, he thought. I hope to Christ it will—not enough to ruin the roads, but enough to cool things off.

The cloud shadow came on, swallowing up the crops. He watched it approach. He could feel it, curiously, devouring his own moment of serenity as it devoured the field.

Of course, he thought, despair seeping back into him.

69

Of course, it wouldn't last anyway. The cows have to be taken and eaten; the horses have to be stolen and ridden into the cannon fire. Of course it wouldn't last. It's all got to be laid waste.

With me, he thought, the despair deepening into sickness, with me the one who has to do it.

He clenched his fist and raised his face to look at the towering mass of the cloud, almost directly overhead now. God damn it, he yelled helplessly, silently, at the cloud. God damn it, let somebody else do it. Somebody who's not a planter—I've already got Ashbrook on my conscience. . . .

The shadow quartered across the fields and passed on by. Wales lowered his face and looked down at the ground. He put out his boot toe and kicked a pebble over and watched a round fat bug run from beneath it in panic.

But of course, he thought, I would be the one. He saw for a vivid instant the wailing, hopeless face of the woman from whom he'd taken the calf. Why, he thought, if I can do that, I can do anything. Because I've quit being a planter. I've become a destroyer now; it's my trade. I have a talent for it. Destruction follows me like a dog at heel. Vivian, Ashbrook, the woman, this plantation . . . I am a pestilence, he thought.

He could feel the trembling beginning again then, that involuntary twitch of muscles. Stop it, he commanded the muscles. He was suddenly angry at himself. Stop it, I say! If not me, the Federals anyhow. It hasn't a chance to survive. It might as well be me as them who does it. . . .

But the trembling would not stop. Wales began to walk toward the house, moving stiffly and carefully because of the trembling. He looked up at the sky again, brazen, unholy blue once more now that the cloud had passed. He squinted into the merciless sun.

But this is the last time, he yelled soundlessly at the hard bright glare. This is the last time. A man can only do so much—he can only take so much. This is the last time—d'you hear? It's not fair. It's just not fair. . . .

He lowered his face then and dragged his hand across his eyes to wipe the sun brightness out of them. This is the last time, he said again, more quietly, to himself, and went on walking toward the house.

Mrs. Cameron herself answered his knock at the front door, and her smile was cordial. "Come in, Captain Wales. May I take your hat?"

She put it on a rack next to Channing's slouch hat, which had the brim pinned back rakishly. Mine looks tired alongside his, Wales thought wryly, following Mrs. Cameron down a hall, past a drawing room which he saw only fleetingly, and into a dining room.

Everything in the dining room was solid and honest and clean and polished. Fine, heavy woods massively hewn and precisely fitted shone in the morning sunlight; the delicate hunters and huntresses on the English wallpaper pursued a multitude of stags untiringly above the wainscot; silver gleamed richly from the great sideboard; so did the place settings on the white linen cloth of the big oval table. From somewhere there was coming the pungent, incomparable odor of frying ham, and Wales felt his mouth pour full of saliva.

"If you'd like to wash up, Captain Wales . . ." The woman indicated a direction and a door, and he went down a hall and into a small room fitted with a mounted basin served by a hand pump. There was real soap in a dish and soft, clean towels on a rack. He looked at them unbelievingly.

That was the moment when he realized that he had been deceiving himself. He realized then that what he faced was something infinitely more delicate and incomparably more messy than the affair with the poor-white woman who had owned the calf. He could see now the texture of a web being spun about him—a web of obligation. Why, naturally, he thought. I was a fool to think there'd be anything easy about this. She knows what she's doing. We've taken her unawares and she's helpless. Caught flat-footed. The only thing she can think of to do is to make sure we're as kindly disposed

71

toward her as possible. After all, you catch more flies with honey. . . .

He looked at his face in the mirror above the basin. It was the first clear view of it he'd had in several weeks and it was startling. There was no recognition in the deep-socketed gray eyes that stared at him from the glass, the high-boned, sunken cheeks, the thin, cruel mouth; the face was neither his face as he remembered it nor thought of it. A beard-stubbled long blade of a face, he thought, without humor or pity or kindness anywhere in it. My God, that's not me. Surely that's not me. . . .

Well. He touched the stubble. It's a good face for scaring old ladies into compliance with the foraging practices of the Confederate Army. It's a good face for that.

What this face would do in a case like this, he thought, would be to accept all her hospitality and then, casually, loot her, unswayed by pity, respect, or remorse. And since the face is mine, he thought, that is exactly what I shall do. Because the face belongs to me.

Still a little shocked and awed by the matter-of-fact savagery of the face, he stripped off the dirty shirt and pumped a basin full of water. The cool cleanliness of it, the thick, rich lather were indescribable luxuries. She said I could have a bath later, he reminded himself. Like Channing. I wonder, he thought. I wonder if I could scare hell out of Channing with this face. God knows, he's got it coming to him.

With each scooping cascade of water he threw against himself he felt a little younger, a little less exhausted, a little less like the face in the mirror. But when he was as clean as he could get himself and had distastefully shrugged back into the dirty, sweat-soaked shirt, the face had not moderated its cold, passionless capacity for anything by one jot.

Well, he thought, first to breakfast, then to business. He realized that his palms were sweating. God, he thought. Face or no face, I would give anything not to have to do this. He rubbed his palms against his pants; his hands felt dirty, and he washed them again. Then

72

he went out into the hall and back to the dining room, and when he reached the doorway he stopped.

First of all, before he even saw her, there was the old, familiar, faint, rainy smell of lilacs.

He walked into it unwittingly. First there had been the vaguely musty air of the dark hall; then as he reached the entrance to the dining room there was the known perfume. It was not that it struck him; it was that it triggered something within him before he was even consciously aware of it: something jerked and wrenched upward from deep within him without his knowing why, and his fingers dug convulsively into the casing of the doorjamb as he halted, and only then did he recognize the fragrance, while another part of his mind was already wondering crazily how she had come to be in the room before him.

Then he saw her, standing in the dining room beside the table, a silhouette against the blinding aura of the sun raying in through a high window. He took a step forward in unreasoning quick excitement, his lips forming her name. Then she turned and he saw the trick of the light and his own instinctive reaction to the lilacs, and the swollen eagerness within him collapsed like a pricked balloon; reason and sanity came back to him, but his legs still trembled with a helpless weakness. He blinked his eyes against the glare and halted, feeling a naked, awkward foolishness and an involuntary grief. Her hair was not yellow—it was red—and she was much taller; it was hard to see how he could have been so— I've got to sit down, though, he thought. I've got to sit down.

Mrs. Cameron came from the kitchen then and noticed him. The girl, still considering the silverware on the table, as she had been doing when he had walked in, had not yet seen him. Mrs. Cameron crossed between the girl and Wales. "Oh, Captain Wales," she said, and Wales did not miss the brief, warning tap of her fingers on the girl's elbow. The girl started, looked up, and saw Wales for the first time. A polite smile leaped to her face. "Captain." Wales was aware of a

73

faint, tense shrillness under the polite modulation of Mrs. Cameron's tone. "May I present my daugther, Mrs. Hollander?"

The girl came toward him, her hand out, graciously. Lilacs, Wales thought. The Goddamned lilacs . . . He felt his face burning with the rise of blood. Channing should have warned me, he thought. Damn him, he knew. That was why he was smirking like that. He should have warned me.

"It is a pleasure, Captain Wales."

Her voice was soft and rather deep for a woman's; the contrast to her mother's was pleasing. Wales became unpleasantly conscious of the rankness of his sweaty shirt, of the two-day stubble still on his face, the dust and horse sweat and grease on his uniform trousers.

"Your servant, Mrs. Hollander," he said as gracefully as he could.

The girl had a triangular face, very wide at the cheekbones, tapering to a small, prominent chin. Her skin was the sheltered clear alabaster of unfreckled redheads; her eyes, deep sea-green and long-lashed, looked enormous against the paleness. Her lips were long and full and red, without either sensuality or puffiness. Her gaze at Wales was direct and apparently completely friendly. She hasn't realized yet, Wales thought. Maybe her mother has, but she hasn't. She would be beautiful if her mouth were smaller, he thought. Vivian's was . . . He released her hand.

"Mother was just telling me," the girl said, "that we're to be honored with your presence at breakfast." The long lips smiled more widely; her teeth were white and seemingly perfect. "First a lieutenant and now a captain. Our lonely plantation certainly has become a crossroads all at once." She moved back around the table, a hand gathering the fullness of the sea-green skirt that matched her eyes, her face, seen in profile, pale and clean-lined as a cameo.

"But I'm afraid my lieutenant must have drowned in his bath," Wales heard himself saying, vaguely surprised at hearing anything but harshness coming from

74

his mouth. "Has there been any word from him recently?"

"Oh, I'm sure he'll be down shortly. Captain, I do hope you've got some news from Richmond. My husband's there and the mail is so——"

"I'm afraid I haven't been to Richmond lately. We've been operating mostly up and down the Weldon Railroad since early in July."

"Oh." A shadow of disappointment disarranged the cameo for a moment; Wales saw her throat work as she swallowed. "Mother and I were hoping . . . My father is somewhere around Richmond, too, and we never hear anything any more. Well." Her face cleared. "We're delighted to have you, Captain. Those men of yours—the ones camped down by the quarters—I suppose they'd like some bread and salt and coffee, and I thought I'd send some down to them. How many do you have, Captain Wales?"

"Eleven." Wales blinked incredulously. It's impossible, he thought. Where would they get coffee for that many men?

"Very well. I'll see to having it sent immediately. If you'll pardon me . . ." With a graceful motion of excusing herself she left the room.

"In these troubled times it's good to have a stout staff like Duane to lean on," Mrs. Cameron said when her daughter had gone. "I'm very proud of her. But of course you mustn't praise your children in their hearing. Won't you sit down, Captain? I've already eaten, but I do hope you won't mind if I drink a cup of coffee with you. We so rarely have visitors."

"I'd be honored," said Wales, moving quickly to hold her chair for her. Then he retreated around the table and seated himself. A door opened somewhere and he was assailed by the rank, wonderful odor of fried ham. Everything else was forgotten as a thin, ancient colored woman moved like a polite wraith to the table and put a heaped-up platter before him. He had served himself and was eating before she could even return with the coffee.

The rich scent of the coffee distracted him from the

ham, and he remembered his manners then. "Please forgive me, Mrs. Cameron. It's been so long since I've sat down to a meal like this that I'm afraid I let myself—"

The old woman smiled. "By all means, Captain, eat. Eat, eat. Our men have been away for a long time. We've sorely missed the satisfaction of watching a man address himself to good food."

Wales lifted the coffee cup with genuine reverence; he teased himself with it before he allowed himself to drink from it He let the moist, revivifying steam filter up his nostrils, let the aroma throb along every nerve. Then he took a great swallow and set the cup down almost empty. At once the old colored woman was there to refill it. Mrs. Cameron poured cream from a pitcher into her coffee and spooned it with a faint, tinkling sound of silver against china. After a moment she laid down the spoon and raised the cup and took a ladylike sip. She set the cup back in the saucer and said:

"We're starved for news here, Captain. We're so isolated we get hardly any word at all. I do hope you'll bring us up to date. How are things going now with Mr. Lee and his army?"

Wales looked at her over the brim of his cup, holding it poised like a mask. Her face was set with the alert, birdlike politeness of any woman entertaining a strange visitor; it was innocent of any guile that he could perceive. Wales took a mouthful of coffee and held it for a moment, rolling it on his tongue with sensual appreciation. Then he put down his cup.

The coffee seemed to leave an aftertaste in his mouth, somehow at once bitter and cloying. And perhaps it was only that his deprived stomach was no longer capable of coping with a full meal, but the food seemed hard and undissolving inside of him.

"Miserably," he said.

"Oh." She had not, evidently, expected an answer so frank, and she arched her brows.

"Things are going miserably." Wales looked at the backs of his hands laid flat before him on the tablecloth. The skin seemed ineradicably dirty against the whiteness of the linen; corded tendons stood out in them; the long fingers moved idly, involuntarily, like restless serpents. "They couldn't be worse. We might as well be in a bottle."

"How so?"

"I—oh, I guess the government knows what it's doing. But we're tied to Richmond. We're locked in. Grant keeps up pressure against us all the time. I had to bring my men through Union lines on this detail. We'll have to recross them when we go back. I'm not even sure we'll be able to do it. But—well, I don't want to upset you, Mrs. Cameron. But I can't overemphasize the gravity of the situation."

She looked puzzled. "But there've been battles. Unless I've been misinformed, haven't we killed a vast amount of Union soldiers since Grant took over? I seem to have heard—"

"You've heard correctly." Wales wished the Negress would bring him some more coffee. His mouth was dry; his throat felt harsh and choked, and the words came only with effort.

"We fought in the same woods we whipped Hooker in," Wales said. "Around Chancellorsville. Why, we killed thousands of 'em there. We fought them at Spotsylvania, and the dead bodies were piled up there four deep. We fought them at Cold Harbor, and I swear to you, we killed them like flies." He shook his head in baffled horror. "But still they come," he said, his own incomprehension in his voice. "Why, Grant—that man's a criminal butcher!"

"Well, then," she said, "obviously the North will not tolerate those kind of casualties for long."

"I don't know," Wales said. "You hear talk like that, of course. But we might as well face it. Grant has got us on the defensive now. For the first time. That's more than any other Yankee has been able to accomplish." He picked up his spoon and toyed with it and laid it down again. It made a small tinkling sound on the edge of his saucer. "If Atlanta falls . . ." he said.

"You make things sound very desperate, Captain."

77

"Things are very desperate, Mrs. Cameron." Wales raised his head and looked at her levelly. "Things are about as desperate as they can be."

"But . . . but surely we'll triumph in the end. After all, what does Grant amount to when we have General Lee? Why, haven't we been outnumbered all through the war? And haven't we been consistently successful?" She took a sip of her coffee and put down her cup. "Surely, Captain, right and justice must count for something. Our men are fighting for something they believe in, not for bounties. Certainly we must ultimately prevail."

"We might," said Wales. "But not without food. Not without ammunition. Not without clothes and shoes to see us through the winter, and not without horses for our cavalry and artillery. Right and justice are mighty, all right—but they aren't much help when you're weak with hunger and you've run out of bullets in the middle of a Federal charge." He shook his head. "We've never had much," he went on. "And with Sherman cutting us off from the Southwest, now we have nothing except what we can scrape up ourselves. While the enemy has everything. And guards it well. We used to be able to take a great deal of what we needed from generals like Pope and Burnside and Hooker, but Grant's a different case. You don't steal a wagon train from Grant."

"Nevertheless," she said, "I'm certainly surprised to hear an officer in the army preach such despair. Why, it—it's almost shocking."

Wales took a deep breath.

"I'm not preaching despair, Mrs. Cameron. I'm merely trying to answer your question truthfully. You asked me how things were going, and I've told you." He bit his lip. "I don't mean to say we're whipped. The Yankee elections are coming up. We've hurt them hard, as you said. And we may hurt them still harder yet. If we can just hurt them so hard that they'll repudiate Mr. Lincoln, elect a government willing to negotiate for peace, why, we can still maybe come out ahead of the game. But we can't keep up that kind of pressure without something to do it with. We can't do it on thin air. It's . . . discouraging."

"I'm sure it must be." Mrs. Cameron's voice had turned sympathetic now. "Duane's husband is in the Quartermaster Department and he says in his letters that it's indeed heartbreaking. He says it's a constant struggle to obtain the barest necessities. But I had no idea it was truly so bad. However"—she picked up her spoon and began to stir her coffee again—"I understand that our army hasn't had to sink to the brutal level of the enemy in supplying its needs so far. I understand that General Lee absolutely will not countenance any looting of the civilian population." She looked at Wales directly over the rim of her cup. "I understand that he forbids pillaging."

"That is correct," Wales said quietly. Then he added gently, "We pay for everything we get."

The old woman went on as though she had not heard him. "Nevertheless, Captain." She set down the cup. "Nevertheless, we feel it's our patriotic duty to do what we can. We want to share. We have a few hams left in the smokehouse. I hope you'll allow us to make you a present of some of them. And I want you and your men to feel free to dine without stint while you rest here. We are all keenly aware of the great sacrifices you soldiers are making, and we are all quite willing to assume part of the burden ourselves."

Wales knew that his mouth was opening and closing like a stranded fish's. He stared at her with astounded blankness, his body rigid with incredulity. She was looking down at her coffee cup; the sunlight struck blue glints from her sleek white hair.

"Mrs. Cameron," Wales heard himself manage at last, softly, "the lieutenant didn't tell you why we're here?"

With an almost imperceptible motion she made known to the old Negress that she wanted her cup refilled. "No, Captain." She looked at him squarely. "Nobody has told me anything, except that almost a dozen soldiers would require breakfast this morning." She paused. "Why? Is there something else?"

79

"There is, ma'am." Now, Wales thought. Now how do you do this? How do you sit across a white-clothed table on a sunlit morning, while outside you can hear the quiet, comfortable, busy sounds of a well-ordered plantation, and tell a defensless, white-haired old woman that you are here to destroy it, to strip it clean and bare as a branch in winter? How do you do that? he wondered. In Christ's name, how does any halfway sane and honorable man go about doing that?

He was surprised to hear his own voice proceeding in a calm monotone, unagitated, without qualms, divorced from the part of him that was causing his hands to sweat and the muscles in his back to pull taut with strain.

"You are quite right about the army's attitude toward foraging, Mrs. Cameron. We don't, as you put it, loot or pillage. But we have got to have supplies, and we're prepared to pay for what we need."

"Pshaw, Captain! I wouldn't think of accepting money for a few hams."

But he noticed that her white, brown-flecked old hand was clutching the dull-gleaming silver spoon very tightly.

"I'm sure that's very gracious of you, Mrs. Cameron. But we would insist on paying." He was amazed at the gentle reasonableness of whoever it was speaking, this other person divorced from him, finding the right words, the patient words, the courteous and diplomatic words. He wanted to scream. Goddamn it! he wanted to scream. I can't go through any more of this today! But the implacable and collected voice went on without a break.

"I am, as a matter of fact, empowered by the Confederate Army not only to pay you for the hams, but to pay you whatever sum you may ask, within remotest reason, for *any* livestock or food or other supplies which you are able to sell to us. I am to assure you that such items will be turned over directly to the army for the sole purpose of maintaining troops and enabling them better to defend your state and country." He leaned forward across the table, the disembodied and involuntary voice unctuous and regretful. "I beg your deepest indulgence for any inconvenience we may have or will cause you, but I also beg you to put before any consideration of self or person the welfare of the army which stands between you and the enemy. I am certain, of course, that we will need have no cause to doubt either your patriotism or your generosity."

When the voice had ceased, the room was silent for a moment. Wales was acutely aware of the solid, imperturbable ticking of an old china clock on the sideboard. Now, he thought with panic, knowing that he had no more resources within himself to call on if she began to cry, now it'll break loose.

But she merely said quietly, without looking at him, "A very pretty speech, Captain. What, precisely, do you need?"

Wales made a gesture with his hands.

"Everything," he said.

He watched her thin bosom rise and fall beneath the black of her dress. For a moment her face lost its hawklike imperiousness and confidence, which had been there all along, directly beneath the hospitality. For one almost imperceptible instant Wales saw the face of a tired old woman.

She looked away from him; he could barely hear her sigh. He watched the fingers of her thin, blue-veined hand, with its brown-flecked, waxy-looking, almost transparent skin, toying with a wrinkle in the fine linen cloth of the table. She squeezed the wrinkle tightly between thumb and forefinger, plucked it, let it drop, and sighed once more. When she looked at Wales, her face again wore its hawklike mask.

"I was afraid of something like this when your men rode up. Now, Captain, I hope you will listen to me very closely."

"I am listening, Mrs. Cameron."

"Very well . . . Captain, I'm certain that you'll find us as co-operative and patriotic as you could wish. But, please—let me ask you now not to let external appearances deceive you. It's true that here at Red Oaks we may have a little more than we immediately need. But only a little."

She looked at him intently across the table.

"My husband is a man of intelligence and foresight, Captain. Any child could have seen this war coming—Doctor Cameron foresaw what would happen far in advance. He foresaw the blockade too. He had the initiative to lay in a considerable supply of items which we could not raise here on our own place. Paint for our buildings, coffee for our table, even shoes for the mules—small luxuries and necessities such as those.

"But, Captain, that was back in 1860. That was four years ago. For the last two years we have been unable to replenish our supplies at any price. Perhaps the presence of these small luxuries"—she gestured at the table—"this coffee, this salt—maybe these have caused you to misjudge our resources. We aren't wallowing in abundance here, Captain. We've got only the minimum. Just enough so that with careful management we can last through a few more months of war. No more than that."

She brushed at her hair with a gesture at once feminine and distracted.

"We're awfully remote here, Captain," she said. "So remote, it's true, that you're the first band of soldiers we've seen. But our remoteness, our isolation, isn't necessarily an advantage."

She looked toward the window.

"There are over sixty slaves out there," she said quietly. "And as far as I know, not a full-grown white man within twenty miles. You've heard of Nat Turner's rebellion, Captain. You know what they are capable of if once the idea of freedom, of vengeance, ever gets into their heads."

She paused, seemingly trying to gather her thoughts. After a moment she went on.

"They have stayed loyal so far," she said. "They've stayed loyal because nothing has arisen to even give them an idea that there's any alternative. So far we've maintained control by issuing the same rations, keeping up the same routine, even, as best we can, applying the same discipline as my husband did when he was home. There have been no changes to set them to wondering . . ."

Her voice hushed as the old Negress padded in and poured more coffee. When they were alone again, she went on.

"Now suppose all at once we can no longer feed them. Of course, then there will be immediate discontent. Tell me, Captain, what will happen then? If you upset this—this delicate balance we've contrived, what will they do?"

When Wales did not answer, she said harshly, "What you are proposing, Captain, is the ruin of Red Oaks. If we lose control of the slaves, my daughter and I will have to refugee to some city for our own protection. Have you ever seen a plantation left to the mercy of the Negroes, Captain, with no overseer, no control? What will it be like?"

Those words seemed to hang in the air for a long time after her mouth had closed in a dry, tight line. Wales blinked. He thought he could smell again the soggy pungence of rain-soaked burnt wood, hear dry leaves rustling in the iron-bound cold of a December afternoon. She had made the one claim on his pity that could not fail, and yet he somehow had to resist it. There was a gigantic effort of will, a conscious one, then, as he did the only thing he could do. He coldly forced all that part of him capable of feeling pity, compassion, or even capable of reasoning logically, into some limbo deep within him, so that it would not get in his way. He knew that the effort it took was one he would pay dearly for later. But what remained was all soldier, functioning methodically and mechanically, invulnerable for as long as his will held out, with no soft places to be touched.

"I repeat," he became aware of her saying, "that there is no abundance. But what we have we will be delighted to share."

Wales looked at her directly. "Ma'am," he said slowly and with absolutely no expression in his voice, "the

83

Confederacy must ask that you not withhold anything which, in my discretion, would be of value to the army."

She looked back at him unwaveringly. Motes danced in the sunbeams streaming through the high windows of the room; in the yard a chicken, unscathed and forgetful, clucked and churred as it snuggled down in its morning dust bath; far away somewhere a cow bawled faintly and lonesomely.

"In your discretion. And in your discretion what would that consist of?"

"In my discretion, ma'am, the army's first need is fresh meat—livestock on the hoof. But it needs horses too. It needs harness and leather, flour and meal, gunpowder, and anything else it can get."

"I see." She nodded. "But the quantities?"

"All we can lay our hands on," he told her then.

"In short, you propose to plunder us completely. Strip us bare."

Wales pushed back his chair and stood up.

"I have a choice of feeding sixty slaves or sixty soldiers." He bit his lip, trying hard to think of some solution for her, some answer. But what he said was lame and he knew it.

"You have garden truck, ma'am. We'll not disturb that. You have your corn crop—it'll make meal. And your slaves should be able to hunt and trap some game. We'll leave a cow so that any children on the place will have milk. More than that I can't promise you, but I don't think you'll starve. Believe me, the Confederacy requires that you sacrifice so that in the long run you will not lose everything . . ."

"But I've told you!" For the first time her voice rose; now this was an impatient cry. "I've told you! We will! We will lose everything!"

Wales realized that his fists were clenching. "As well lose it now as when the Federals come through," he told her harshly. "At least we'll pay you for it."

"In Confederate money," she said scornfully.

"Legal tender," he said "Of our own government."

"Fit only for wallpaper," she said acidly. "Valueless as the promise of a drunkard!"

"Redeemable in silver after ending of hostilities," he said.

"But I've made my contribution." Her voice was determined, outraged. "My husband's an elderly man. He has no business sleeping on the ground or charging into a battle. But he's a doctor and he knew doctors would be needed, and he would go. I could have stopped him if I had tried hard enough. But I didn't. I let him go because he thought he had to.

"And my son-in-law," she went on. "He is a young man—younger than yourself, Captain. My daughter loves him and her life is bound up with his. To lose him would be to lose her. Yet he has gone to take his risks, as I'm sure you have taken yours. I don't plead for special indulgence, but surely you must see that—"

"I am sorry, Mrs. Cameron," Wales said flatly. "I believe you said your son-in-law is in the Quartermaster Department. If so, you need have no fear that he is in danger of his life. And as for your husband—he's bound to have written you about conditions in the field. He's bound to have told you how desperately needed such supplies as you have are."

"I have his last letter here," she said unexpectedly, reaching into a pocket of her dress. "I carry it about with me. Will you allow me to read from it?" She unfolded a worn sheet of paper.

"He says: 'Thank Heaven that I have left you well provided for. I have one less worry in that respect than most of the poor fellows here. But what you have would do no good here, for it would be only a drop in a bucket that has no bottom . . .' So you see, Captain—"

"Mrs. Cameron," Wales said, "I simply have no alternative."

Her face was expressionless for an interminable moment. Wales heard the distant cow bellow again. Suddenly Mrs. Cameron stood up. Her voice quavered.

"Captain Wales, I refuse to believe that you have thought about this carefully. I can't see how further consideration could fail to convince you that you would be doing us an injustice that couldn't possibly be outweighed by its benefit to the army. Please—let's both take a little time to think about this. I'll—I'll have to talk it over with Duane. In the meantime, I promised you the opportunity to refresh yourself with a bath. If you'll excuse me, I'll see to that, and then later on we can —can resume our discussion. But I must have a little while." Before he could answer, she went out of the room very rapidly, through the door to the connecting corridor, the dogtrot, as it was called, that led to the kitchen. Wales sat down heavily, staring at the remnant of ham, the last hard bite of egg, on his plate. He was no longer hungry.

"Ahhh . . ." said the voice of Lieutenant Vance Channing behind him, then—almost shining in his cleanliness—Channing strode around the table. "See you got here all right, Marsh. Man! What a difference a bath can make in the way a fellow feels." Channing reached out, took a biscuit from the plate before Wales, and, with Wales's knife, began to butter it. Then he sat down in the chair Mrs. Cameron had vacated. "They serve right good breakfasts here, eh, Marsh? Beats parched corn, don't it?"

He leaned across the table, his face bright with exultancy, his voice dropping. "What d'you think of it, Marsh?" he whispered. "What d'you think of this little shebang? It's all I said it was, ain't it? Did you see that girl?"

Wales looked at him with eyes he wished were capable of drilling holes. "As soon as you've swallowed that biscuit," he said crisply, "I want an inventory made. In writing. Of every head of livestock on this place. Every bag of meal. Every pound of coffee, every bit of harness, every pair of shoes or boots. Of anything else you find that we can use. Do you understand?"

The light went slowly, doubtfully, out of Channing's eyes. "Why, good God, Marsh—you ain't done gone and told her what we're here for? Why, why, great heavens, man, we can live a wonderful life here for a couple of days—we could've if you hadn't told 'em! Why, theyda waited on us hand and foot. That's why I didn't tell 'em. As soon as I saw up close what this place was like, I figured sure you'd want to lay over a couple of days, and then, just before we were ready to leave, we could have told 'em and the hell with 'em! I figured—"

"You figured wrong. I want the inventory and I want it right away. As soon as we can round up things and settle with Mrs. Cameron, we're heading back to the regiment. And I don't want any dragging of feet or—or lollygagging. Is that clear?"

Channing's eyes were cold now, his grin vanished, his mouth sullen. "Yes, sir," he said slowly and with exquisite correctness. "Yes, sir, Captain, that's very clear."

"All right." Wales arose. "Remember. I want *everything*. Now. If you'll excuse me, Vance, I'm going to take advantage of Mrs. Cameron's offer of the opportunity of a bath. I shall expect substantial progress within the next hour."

Channing's mouth twisted angrily. "Damn it, Marsh, you had to go and spoil it. But if you'd just act human, we could—"

"I'm sorry," Wales said. But now he was seeing again the blindly bawling, mucus-smeared face of the child pulling at its shrieking mother as the two of them sprawled in the dust. "I'm sorry," he said again, and his voice was tired. "I reckon I've used up all my humanity for today. The inventories in an hour, please." The two of them, the woman and the child—he could still hear them, the soundless, accusing crying ringing in his head as he left the room.

6

"I carried you some breakfast," the sergeant said. He squatted down and opened the hamper and took out a whole roasted chicken and a pone of bread. "Think that'll hold you?"

"Fo' Gawd," the soldier named Vardaman said. His eyes were greedy flames in the beard-and-dust-obliterated mask of his face. He seized the chicken and began to rip and tear at it with his teeth.

The sergeant stood up, turning his body in a slow arc, his eyes squinting across the fields and the far line of woods. "There's some coffee in there too," he said. "You got water in your canteen?"

"I got some," Vardaman said.

"You kin build yosef a fahr," the sergeant said. "I'll send somebody over to relieve you directly."

"Rumpf," Vardaman said, his mouth full of chicken.

"Ain't seen no sign of trouble?" the sergeant asked.

Vardaman shook his head.

"All right," the sergeant said. He picked up the hamper and said, "Gotta tote some over to Coltrane. Now doan't you git so full you cain't keep yo eyes open." He strode off across the field toward the woods, leaving the guard still squatting there against the haystack, ripping away at the chicken like a starved animal.

The sun was hot on the sergeant's back as he made his way across the stubbled field. The smell of the cut hay that had recently been scythed here was clean and fragrant in his nostrils. The sergeant's legs felt heavy and stiff; it was an effort to pick up the big cavalry boots.

But, he thought, taking this food to the pickets was something that had to be done. You couldn't leave a man on outpost without seeing to it that he got fed as soon as possible. Coltrane, Vardaman, Brazos—somebody had to look after them. Of course, he could have sent one of the others with the hamper, he told himself. But they were tired, too—just as tired as he was. And God knows, after what they'd been through, they'd earned a chance for as much rest as they could get.

There were so few of them left, the sergeant thought. There'd been so many to begin with, and now there was nothing left but a handful. Himself, Wales, Dalton, Boomer, Vardaman, Coltrane, Brazos, Houston—you couldn't count Channing and Davis. They were newcomers. They hadn't gone the full furrow like he and the others had. There wasn't that—that—his mind searched for the word he wanted. He couldn't find it. But he knew what he meant. He knew that after you had been through what he had been through with those men, each one of them somehow became a part of yourself. An organ, a limb. They were a part of you and you were a part of them. That Godawful loneliness— when it came over you, there was no remedy at all for it—he had meant it when he had told the captain that he had never been so lonely. But at least when it got hold of you, sooner or later somebody would crack a joke, pull a prank, and then it would begin to lift. The sergeant scratched his beardy jaw. Christ, he thought. I doan't know what I'd do if somethin was to happen to the rest of 'em. . . .

Which brought him back to the pocket of disturbing thoughts about the captain which he had been trying hard to think around, to avoid.

Because he's dangerous, the sergeant thought sickly. He's jest as likely as not to git us every one killed.

Not because he's scairt, the sergeant thought. I don't believe it's that at all. It's because—it's because he jest ain't interested no more. He's got his mind on somethin else. I doan't know what it is, but it's drained all the juice outa him. He's used up—he's had all he can take. Well, not yet, maybe, because he's still tryin to hide it.

The time when he will really be finished will be when he ain't even tryin to hide it no more. Until then maybe we can make out. But he's dangerous. Because there's no tellin when he's liable to break. And if he breaks at the wrong time, he'll git us every one killed. Me, Coltrane, Brazos, Vardaman, Dalton, Houston, Boomer. . . .

God damn it, the sergeant thought. I ain't used to havin to think about somethin like that. But it worries me. I doan't want to see nothin happen to Wales. I wisht I could help 'im. But I sure cain't let nothin happen to the rest of the boys neither. Somebody's got to look out for 'em. God damn it, whut kin I do?

He was at the woods now. He halted at the rind of underbrush that edged the trees and mopped sweat from his face.

Well, he thought, about the main thing, I reckon, is jest to do what I can to ease the strain on him. I doan't know of anything else. Jest do what I kin . . . He shifted the hamper from one hand to the other and went on into the pines.

The heat in here was worse than out in the field. The sergeant cursed softly under his breath. He tried to pierce the summer-thick underbrush with his eyes. "H'yo, Coltrane," he called softly.

From up a slight ridge a voice called back, "H'yo." The sergeant climbed the ridge and found Coltrane lying on his belly on the pine needles. "Everything all right?" the sergeant asked.

Coltrane nodded. " 'Cept I'm plumb starved."

The sergeant handed him the hamper. "That'll fix yo. I'll send out your relief in a little while. Bring that basket in with you when you come. I'm sick of carryin the damn thing." He went on down the ridge and walked along through the woods for a ways. He was hot and thirsty. He saw a place where the ground fell away in a long slope, and his practiced eye told him that there would be a spring down there in the hollow. He went down the slope quietly and found the spring in a brush-rimmed depression at the bottom. He lay down and drank from the cool, clear bowl, unmindful of the crawfish he could see moving around in the water-soaked leaves on the bottom. Then he stood up, wiping his mouth and looking about him.

Across the hollow a path led off into the woods. It was no more than a narrow gap in the tangle of underbrush. Moving idly, but with an habitual alertness, the sergeant sauntered over to it. He tried to guess from what he could see of the terrain ahead of him where it might lead and for what purpose it was here, but there was nothing to indicate any especial reason for it. The sergeant squatted down and looked at the path. Then he frowned. There was something lying on the ground across the path a little ways up there in that tunnel of undergrowth. He edged into the bushes and moved along the path quietly until he came to what it was that he had seen, and then he picked up a small sheaf of cut grass: hay, not yet fully cured.

The sergeant stroked the little bundle of hay and sucked at his lower lip. He looked as far as he could down the path and then he nodded to himself. He walked back out of the bushes and then he climbed out of the little hollow and struck off through the woods, moving roughly in the same direction as the path but in the arc of a circle, which would bring him back to intersection with it perhaps a half mile from its beginning. He moved through the woods very silently; no Indian could have done it better.

It was three quarters of an hour later when he got back to the plantation house, and the men were still lolling about in the lane. Even before he reached them, he heard the voices, shrill and angry as quarreling sparrows; and as he came up he could see Boomer, the red-headed soldier, and Jeff Davis confronting each other, arguing loudly, Boomer's voice sullen and Davis's a high, drawling whine.

"Ahhh—go screw yosef." That was Davis.

"Well, blame it all, if you didn' take hit, who did?"

"Well, I didn' take hit. You musta laid hit down somewhur. I didn'—"

"Awright, awright." The sergeant's voice split the contention apart. "Awright, what's all this yammerin?"

"I hadda twist of tobacco," Boomer explained sullenly, his florid face like an upset moon. "I tooka chaw offn hit an' laid hit down whilest we was cookin chickens, an' I jest remembered hit an' now hit's gone. Davis was right there aside me an' I asked him did he see hit an' he thought I was claimin he took hit—an', by God, now I think he did!"

"Oh hell," the sergeant said wearily. "Like a coupla younguns. Davis, pull out yo pockets."

Davis began a nasal protest. "I said pull 'em out!' the sergeant grunted fiercely.

Still muttering, Davis emptied his pockets. A few crumpled bills, a filthy rag, a hawk-billed knife, some matches, a rabbit's foot: this was the meager inventory of his personal possessions. The sergeant felt a faint, involuntary pity, a passing sadness. Why, he's like me, the sergeant thought, and for only an instant Davis had reality for him. If he was to vanish, he doan't even own nothin big enough an' heavy enough to leave behind for people to look at an' say: That belongs to Davis. Whutever become of him? If he was to vanish, he'd vanish clean, with his whole thirty years right there in his pockets with him.

His voice was gentler when he said, "Awright, Davis. Fix yosef back up. Boomer, if you cain't keep track of yo own tobacco, you ain't old enough to chaw nohow. Now, you two go find Corp'rul Dalton an' tell him I want to see 'im."

He watched them saunter off up the lane, still arguing, and he shook his head. That damn little Davis, he thought, even when you feel sorry for 'im, you cain't hep despisin the bastad. It's like the little bastad was born with somethin about him that sets people's teeth on aidge . . .

His thoughts were interrupted by the sound of a door slamming up at the big house. In a moment the sergeant saw Lieutenant Vance Channing striding down the path toward him. The sergeant sighed.

He's got a burr under his tail, the sergeant thought,

noting the white face, the flared nostrils, the set mouth
I reckon Davis ain't the only one been catchin hell this
mawnin.

He stood slackly as the lieutenant came up.

"Sergeant!" Channing's voice was sharp and ugly.
"Git the Goddamned men up off their tails an' put 'em
to work. I want an inventory of every damn thing on
this place an' I want it in an hour. You understand?"

The sergeant nodded. "Yes, sir," he said easily. "You
mean everything?"

"Everything," the lieutenant snapped. "Turn the place
inside out—slave cabins and all. Anything that's fit to
eat or we can use . . . Now, dammit, don't stand there
looking at me—get busy!"

"Yes, sir," the sergeant said without alacrity. "We'll
need some keys, Lieutenant. The smokehouse is locked
—reckon some of the other buildins too."

"I'll get you your keys," Channing said hoarsely.
"Now get to it!"

The sergeant nodded and turned without any further
speech. "All right, boys," he said to the men still lounging around the fire. "Hit looks like our holiday is
over. . . ."

After the sergeant and the men had moved off, Channing stood there in the lane tautly, his hands clenching
and unclenching in frustrated anger.

The bastard, he thought, the damned overbearing
bastard. He's gone and spoiled everything. All I wanted
was one day without them knowing why we were here.
Without them being upset and mad. I could have done
it in one day—I swear I could. Because I knew I could
soon as I saw her. Now he's gone and ruined it all. But
the time will come . . .

Still fuming, he strode back toward the house. It's not
like she was a prancing little virgin, he thought. She's
broken in. She knows what it is. Husband away for
months . . . Christ, it would have been like falling off
a log! I— He sucked in his breath as the back door
opened and the sea-green dress glimmered in the sunlight. Damn him, he thought with utmost bitterness. Oh,

93

damn him to hell. He went to meet her as she came down the steps.

She's mad already, he thought. I can tell from the way she's walking—those short, choppy steps. Well, it don't make much difference now. Still and all—it won't hurt to be nice. Might get a kiss before I go. Then I'll know I was right, anyhow. He swept off his hat.

"Mrs. Hollander. Should you be out in this heat?"

The girl turned the pale, triangular face up to him; the great green eyes were stormy, the large mouth set. He swallowed hard, noticing the thrust and fall of the tight bodice in cadence with her angry breathing; the lilac smell of her perfume was maddening in his nostrils.

"It appears I have no other alternative, Lieutenant. I just found out from my mother that you're fixing to make an inventory of all our belongings and property so that you can loot us. I certainly have no intention of letting your men turn our place upside down without being out here to keep an eye on them. Tell me, Lieutenant, where are you going to start—what are you going to steal first?"

Vance Channing shook his head regretfully. "Mrs. Hollander, Mrs. Hollander, please. I don't want you to think that any of this is *my* idea."

"Oh, I'm sure it's not, Lieutenant. I'm sure it's not." He couldn't be certain how much sarcasm she intended. "Of course you're not the kind of officer who would deliberately rob—"

"Please, Mrs. Hollander. Don't say that word . . ."

Christ, Channing thought. She's even better when she's mad. Look at those eyes! And that underlip poked out. Lord, I'd love to—

"It's exactly that, Lieutenant. What else do you call it when you swarm down on somebody with soldiers and make off with all their belongings, even the very food from their mouths?"

Channing tried to smile placatingly. "In the army," he said, "it's called foraging."

"Yes. Foraging. But the army has a different name for everything, doesn't it?" Her voice was full of scorn. "I know all about it—my husband and my father have

94

told me. In the army you don't retreat; you withdraw in good order. You don't get whipped; you just get your flanks turned in. And you don't steal, either, do you? You just forage."

"All right. I stand corrected, ma'am. And I wish there was something I could say." His face sobered as he saw that his grin was merely increasing the storminess in her eyes. He made a careful effort to sound earnest and sincere. "Mrs. Hollander," he said pleadingly, "believe me, I *am* sorry. If this were my command, I'd leave your plantation unharmed. But that's a decision not in my power to make. That decision rested, unfortunately, with Captain Wales, and I am merely his subordinate. He directed me to make an inventory and I have no choice. Please, ma'am . . ." He directed a look at her that he knew was sad and upset and that begged for understanding, a look just a little like the expression of a small boy in trouble. He always knew what sort of look he was directing at a woman; he never looked at a woman without arranging his face first. He had the looks catalogued, down to the finest gradations. He had learned that a man could control a woman with his eyes, if he were clever and patient enough, just as a horse could be controlled with reins. He had learned that if he did it just right he could look a woman right into bed with him.

Now he was gratified to see the swirling anger in her eyes subside a bit.

"Perhaps," he suggested diffidently, "you would feel better if I gave my word that everything will be done in a correct and orderly fashion. Believe me, Mrs. Hollander, you have no idea how distasteful to me my orders are."

She took a deep breath, and at the magnificent motion of her bosom beneath the tight silk, Channing could feel the palms of his hands go sweaty; he could hear the blood pounding in his ears. I could have even had two days, he thought. They're not looking for us back at Regiment until Friday. Damn that Wales!

Then the girl let out that breath and dropped her head. She looked down at the ground for a moment,

95

while Channing waited. When she finally raised her eyes, he knew that the look—the look and the carefully modulated tone—these had worked.

"I'm sorry, Lieutenant," she said tonelessly. "I understand that it's not your fault." She twisted the fingers of one hand nervously with the other. "I—please forgive me, won't you? I wasn't accusing you. It's only—well, it's just that Mother and I feel so desperate, I guess. If you take everything Captain Wales said you were going to, why—I just don't know what we'll do. It's not easy for two women to manage a place like this alone, even under the best of circumstances. And . . . and with the food gone and our people hungry—oh, I just don't know. I just don't know how we'll cope with it."

Looking directly at him now, she smiled—a brave, shaky little smile, not very mirthful. "Well, I suppose there's no use crying over spilt milk, is there? I suppose —I suppose you must take an absolutely complete inventory to the captain, mustn't you? He . . . he would probably check you, wouldn't he, and if you didn't, you might get in trouble, isn't that right? So I suppose . . ." She dropped her eyes again. "I suppose you will have to be very careful to get everything."

Channing's forehead was sweating; it was cold perspiration, having nothing to do with the hard, bright sunlight in which they stood. Oh, Christ, he thought. So that's it. She's beginning to find out which side her bread is buttered on now. Oh, Christ, look at her. Oh, if I was only in charge of this detail. Because she's fixing to start bargaining now. She's going to try it another way now. Oh, if I was only in charge, what a trade I could make. A plantation against a woman—wouldn't that be some trade? Yes, he thought. Now you're going to begin playing your cards—the only ones left. And if I had the command of this outfit, I'd call you for every pot. In fact, if it wasn't for that damned sergeant running to Wales with everything, I'd—No. No, damn it, that's too risky. It wouldn't work.

He shook his head. "I've got my duty, ma'am. Besides, Captain Wales is very strict. I'm afraid I have to be careful to miss nothing. As a matter of fact, my men are already checking the slave quarters now, and I was just on my way up to the big house to see about getting the keys to all the outbuildings."

"Oh." There was a tinge of disappointment in her voice which she could not conceal. But the smile was still on her face, and after only a second she managed to light up her eyes to match it. "You certainly do work fast, don't you?"

"Have to," he said. "Unfortunately. I'm in no hurry myself, but—who would have the keys, Mrs. Hollander?"

"I would," she said, and she looked up at him with a taunt, a challenge in those undocile eyes of hers. "But suppose I don't choose to give them to you. What would you do then?" Her tongue moistened her lower lip. "Would you take them from me by force, Lieutenant?"

His own voice sounded very far away to him. "No. We would be forced to break down the doors."

"Oh," she said. "Then withholding the keys would avail me nothing, would it?" Her eyes locked with his for the barest fraction of a second, then she lowered hers demurely. "Very well," she said, and she sighed again. Her hand dipped into a pocket of her dress, and she brought out a ring with a single key on it.

"A master key," she said, looking at him directly again. "It will fit all locks."

"That's very convenient," he heard himself say.

"Yes. It will fit all locks on the outbuildings."

"Oh," he heard himself grunt crassly.

All at once her manner changed. She was nearly as crisp, as hostile as she had been at first.

"I still intend to accompany you on your depredations," she said. "I'm going to do everything I can do to protect our interests in this matter."

"Why, of course," he said. "I only regret—"

"I'm sure you do," she said. "I'm sure you have many regrets, Lieutenant. There is an old saying that regrets butter no parsnips."

97

He bit his lip. "Please, Mrs. Hollander," he said, trying to sound hurt.

Her manner softened. "I'm sorry," she whispered. "I suppose you have your duty. It's only that—" She broke off and shook her head, bitterly, he thought; the motion set red hair to dancing in the sunlight briefly. "Well, I suppose you don't want to delay any longer, Lieutenant Channing. Shall we begin?"

She seemed very thoughtful as they walked together down the path that led toward the slave quarters, and there was silence between them for a while.

"What did you do before you became a soldier, Lieutenant?" she asked suddenly.

"Eh? Oh. My father was a cotton merchant in Memphis. I assisted him. Not a large enterprise, you understand," he added modestly. "We had a good factoring business, but we weren't tycoons."

"Of course. And you have been in the army how long?"

"Since early 1862. I joined a company formed in Memphis, and most of my duty's been in the West. Lately with General Forrest. But my outfit's casualties were heavy and it was finally pretty well wiped out, and I found myself transferred to Virginia with a draft of men in like circumstances."

"You've seen much fighting, then?"

"A great deal," he said bleakly. He was carefully silent then, with a silence that he hoped was significant with unvoiced sorrow. After a while he added, "War is a dreadful, senseless thing."

"Yes," she said. "No one knows that better than I, what with my father and my husband both away, with our home at the mercy of—" She lifted her head, set her mouth. "Well, we'll not talk of that now. This— Captain Wales, isn't it? Has he been a soldier for a long time too?"

"I suppose so," he nodded, thinking: the hell with Marsh Wales. Why should Marsh Wales even cross your mind, you lovely, sweet-smelling, teasing red-headed goddess? I'd like to take Marsh Wales and . . .

Oh, damn you, you smell good. You smell like lilacs. I want—

"He seems a very unprepossessing sort of person," she said. "Is he supposed to be a good soldier?"

"It depends on what you mean by a good soldier." You fine filly, he was thinking. Oh, I've seen your kind before. I've had your kind before. Cotton merchant, he thought with an inner grin of wry amusement. If you could have seen me in the saloon of the *Maid of Natchez,* trimming the gillies with the pasteboards, you'd have hiked your skirt and stepped aside as if I was something nasty, just like all the other planter women used to do. Yes. A gambler. Nasty. But still, I'd get you—as I got the others that I really wanted. Oh, I know how to get you. If I just had time . . .

"You'll find Marsh Wales something of a martinet, I'm afraid," he told her, careful to keep any rancor out of his voice. "He's a fanatic for duty. He has no sense of humor, no human kindness. Personally I think he carries it to foolish extremes. Sometimes I'm afraid Marsh is a little, well, deranged. It's unnatural for a man to be as—as unfeeling as he is."

"I see," she murmured expressionlessly. Suddenly she halted, left his side to go to a late-blooming rosebush as high as a man's head leaning against a trellis. She touched crimson blossom after crimson blossom, only to have each shatter as her fingers closed on it. Channing looked at the woman, the red hair, the green skirt, the ivory-white skin, the drifting shower of crimson rose petals. The picture sent an excruciating thrust of desire through him.

She finally touched a blossom that was firm, took it, and then gave a little cry. "Oh!" She brought her hand to her mouth.

In one step he was to her. "Did you hurt yourself?"

She looked up at him with eyes blurred with tears of pain. "My hand. I seem to have punctured it on a thorn."

Channing bit his lip.

"Allow me," he murmured. He took her hand and spread it, palm up. It was warm and firm and smooth, and it was the first contact with woman flesh he'd had in months. The desire was like surf mounting and breaking within him, pounding in rising waves.

"Is there blood?" she asked in a small voice.

One red drop was welling up from a puncture on her forefinger. "A little," he said.

"Blood makes me feel faint," she whispered, and indeed her face was very pale. She made a deft motion toward her bosom and somehow produced a tiny square of white linen and handed it to Channing. Channing took it, smelling lilacs on it and another, moister, more sensual smell, a trace of musk perhaps, or the smell of the perspiration of her breasts: it was a faint undertone of aphrodisia beneath the clean, chaste raininess of the lilacs. He pressed the handkerchief to the wounded finger and doubled her hand back and said, "There," and then, still holding her doubled hand, looked straight into her eyes.

Even if he had wanted to, he knew that there would have been no way of hiding what was in his gaze.

And her eyes did not waver for an instant; then they widened slightly, but with an unreadable expression. Something had stirred in her; he was certain of that. He could not tell what it had been, but it was something. Suddenly he was aware that she was withdrawing the hand, and then she turned.

"I never did get my rose," she murmured. "Will you, Lieutenant?"

7

The pillow was soft and its slip had a satiny texture that was like the feel of a woman's body in a nightgown.

Wales lay on the bed with his face buried deep in the pillow, pushed down in it as if it were a bosom. He murmured something into the depths of the pillow, and one arm went out and groped at the emptiness of the bed. His hand moved searchingly up and down the vacant counterpane, confused, questioning, and then he stirred and said one word, "Vivian?"

The bedroom was hushed and silent, unanswering. A rising mist of consciousness began to seep back to his brain. "Vivian," he said again, and then he opened his eyes.

As reality bore in on him, the disappointment and loneliness chilled him to his marrow, and he sat up, naked and shivering. He knuckled at his eyes, fighting in his half-wakefulness to make his mind adjust to the realization that the dream had been only a dream, that she was gone, Ashbrook was gone, everything was gone; the past was gone and along with it the future was gone, too, and there wasn't any way for any of it to come back: woman, house, past, or future. There was only the desolate now; and for a moment, on the edge of sleep, it seemed to him that there was no way for him to bear that any longer.

Then, as always, the hate came to rescue him. The hot, dry, bitter hate that stirred deep in his entrails, that climbed up his throat, burning, filling his brain, making his temples pound, his hands sweat. A hate as great as the desolation, but bearable because it had a focus. A hate that bore with it a still-stunned incomprehension, a *why?* as impossible to answer as to account for the fate of a squashed bug, but which could still center on something, on *her,* rather than leaving him abandoned to the loneliness and emptiness. It always racked him, agonized him, drained him. But it was the only thing that made remembrance bearable. He dreaded remembrance; even when he was fully awake, he lived in fear of the onset of it, as a man might live in fear of a tooth he knows is going to abscess. Now, with his mind still drugged by sleep, he had no defense against remembrance at all, and he knew he would need the hate. ...

It was October, he remembered, and a thin, drizzling rain was falling, a cold rain that made the soldiers curse and shiver and that turned the streets of the camp into a red mire that could suck the boots right off a man. But it was a chance to rest and lick the wounds of Gettysburg that were still not healed; and it would have been welcome, except that he had not heard from her, had not had a letter from her or anyone else, in over ninety days.

So, he remembered, he had hated the camp and he had hated the inactivity. Because there was too much time to think, to imagine. He had imagined all sorts of things, he remembered, only he had never imagined anything as monstrous as the truth.

But he had thought about all the other things that could have happened—sickness, injury, disaster of a thousand kinds—and he had worried until his stomach was never rid of a cold leaden knot within it. *Was I right?* he thought hauntedly as he lay on the pine-bough bed in the narrow log hut that was not the size of a decent stall for a horse and that let in more cold and dampness than it kept out. *Was I right to leave her there alone?* If anything's happened to her, he thought, I'll never forgive myself. Never.

And the rain kept up and the mud grew deeper, and still there was no mail. Every Thursday the courier from Richmond rode into camp with bulging saddlebags;

there were supply wagons and sutlers' wagons, and they all brought mail, but none for him. He could feel the tension growing in him, the fear strangling him as a parasite vine strangles its host. By the time the Thursday came when he got the letter, he had already promised himself: If there's nothing today, I'm going to get a furlough. Somehow. Regardless. I'm going to get a furlough and go home and see about her.

But then it was that Thursday, and still the rain came down; the men huddled in their log huts and endured the smoke of wet-wood fires and cursed the dampness and blessed the inactivity. It was Thursday and Wales squatted in front of his hut at two o'clock, with his eyes fixed, hawklike, on the corner which the courier would have to turn, on the street which he would have to come down. He was beyond noticing the rain or the chill; he was beyond anything except the suspension of life that came with single-minded waiting.

After a while he saw the courier. The man rode hunched up in his saddle like a wet chicken, his coat collar turned up against the drizzle, and his horse picked its way through the mire almost daintily. Wales saw the saddlebags behind the cantle: they looked full and heavy. He could feel his heartbeat quicken; he heard the breath rasp swiftly through his nostrils as he watched the courier pull up in front of the hut that was Regiment and swing down and unfasten the saddlebags.

Still he did not rise. There would be a crowd, a swarm of men down there in a moment. He did not want to mix with it. He had waited this long. He would wait just a little longer. He did not want all those men jostling around him when he got his mail. Part of him shrieked at him to hurry, to fight his way through the throng, but something else within him would not let him move.

Then, at last, the street in front of Regiment was empty again. Only then did Wales arise. He got up heavily, stiff after his long vigil. He walked down the street, not hurrying, letting each boot sink deep in the gluelike mud and then pulling it out again. He was still aware of the hoarse, rasping sound his breath made in his nostrils.

The interior of headquarters hut was dim and rank with wood smoke. The mail courier was trying to warm his hands over a charcoal fire in a bucket with holes punched in the sides. The adjutant's orderly was sitting propped back in the adjutant's chair, reading a letter and smiling to himself. On the table before him lay a dozen unclaimed letters, and Wales had walked over to the table with feigned casualness.

But before he had even reached the table he had seen it—the familiar blue envelope peeping out from under the pile.

Wales withdrew the envelope, and then the tension went out of him in a great rush. He pushed through the rest of the envelopes, but there was nothing else for him.

"This all the mail, Travis?"

The adjutant's orderly had nodded. "No more'n till next Thursday, Capn, less the wagons bring some in later on." He went back to his reading. "Sorry."

"It's all right," Wales said. "It's all right." Then he left the hut and went out into the street where it was lighter. He ripped open the envelope and shielded the letter with his hand so that the rain would not make the ink run.

He could not remember afterward how long he had stood there in the mud with the rain falling on him. He knew that he must have stood there for a long time.

Because, the first two times he read the letter, it simply hadn't registered; it had no meaning for him at all.

Then he thought that somebody had played an inexplicable, obscene practical joke. He stared at the handwriting.

It was hers all right.

Near him the courier's horse stamped in the mud with a sucking, squelching noise, and its bit chains jingled. Wales read the letter again.

After that he didn't know what to do.

I have got to go somewhere, he thought. *I have got*

104

to go somewhere away from people and read this once more. This is a bad place to read, here. I must have read it wrong. He folded the letter and stuck it inside his coat and began to walk.

He turned at right angles to the street and walked past the side of Regiment's hut. Inside he could hear the orderly reading aloud from his letter to the courier; a fragment of the lines stuck in Wales's mind and would never come out. The orderly was saying, " '. . . And Old Man Howard almost cried.' " I wonder what made him almost cry? Wales wondered.

He crossed the other street and walked between two huts on its far side. He slogged through the manure-stained mud of the horse lines, where the huddled animals stamped and shivered in the cold rain. He passed on by the horses and through the bivouac of the flying artillery and then he was beyond the encampment and in an open broom-sedge field.

He crossed the field. The tall sedge drenched his greatcoat so that it was a binding weight dragging from his shoulders. His boots were great traveling gobbets of mud. When he got to the edge of the field, it was all he could do to lift his feet.

At the field's edge there was a grove of pines. There had been a skirmish in the pines one time, and the small second growth still showed the scars and blazes of artillery fire. It was quiet and private in here. There was no sound but the quiet ticking drip of water falling from the pine needles. Every time Wales bumped against a pine sapling it drenched him with a small, concentrated shower. Once he slipped on an old canteen that had no top on it. He kicked it out of the way. He found a big rotting log with honeysuckle climbing on it and sat down on a place that the honeysuckle had not covered. He opened the letter again and read it over and over. The water dripped from the pines and fell on it and made the ink run, but he knew what it said.

It said:

My dearest Marsh (and that was the only part of it that he could even imagine her writing). My dearest Marsh, I have put this letter off as long as I can, because I did not know how to write it. I still don't know how to write it, but somehow you must be told and it must be written and perhaps the best way is quickly.

I am going to have a child. All I will tell you about the father is that he is an Englishman. When you read this, I will already be en route to England with him.

I know this is not enough. But it has taken me a long time for me to get the courage to write this much and I don't have the courage to write any more.

I can't ask you to forgive me. I will ask you not to grieve over me. I will not soil you with explanations. There are no explanations that I could make to anyone. Believe me, I did not mean to hurt you. If only you were here, or if only I had the courage to write more.

VIVIAN

Wales read it through and then he raised his head. The rain fell coldly into his face and ran down his cheeks. Wales stared at the wet pines. "I don't understand," he kept whispering over and over at the pines. "I don't understand. Why?"

He sat there on the log and read the letter over and over all that long rainy afternoon. But no matter how often he read it, the letter yielded no answer; it never said anything more than it had at first. All he knew was that she was gone. . . .

Now, huddled naked on the edge of the bed, he ran his hand through his hair. It's got to the point, he thought bitterly, where there is no peace even in sleep.

Sleep?

He was up from the massive four-poster in a bound, his heart thudding with apprehension. By reflex he was across the room in a long stride, cursing himself groggily even as he swung the pistol harness off the chair and dropped it on the bed so that the ivory butts of the two long-barreled Colts were within easy reach. Should know better! he thought fiercely. Sleeping . . . strange country, strange house . . . His ears strained above the reflexive pounding of his heart for any tatter of ominous sound.

But there was none. The room must have belonged to the girl, and it was as gentle and silent as any woman's bedroom in the midmorning. The sounds drifting in from outside were the familiar, pleasant, and reassuring forenoon sounds of a plantation at work: the chiming ring of iron against iron as a smith labored; the honk of geese; the distant bray of a mule.

Wales shivered as he emerged from the last of the sleep. Only then did he realize that he was naked.

He stood there in the middle of the room, feeling absurd. He knuckled at his eyes and ran his hand through his hair and looked about the room. In the alcove in one corner was the big iron tub, still full of bath water. Across the room there was a dressing table with an assortment of female things on it—a box of rice powder, a forgotten sachet bag, a comb with a few coppery strands still gleaming in it. It had been a rare breach of modesty for a woman like Mrs. Hollander to allow him to use her bedroom, but apparently hers and her mother's were the only two rooms in the house with tubs. Wales walked over to the dressing table and looked down at it, the sight of all these feminine things, the imprint of a woman's personality, curious and unpleasantly stirring to him. Standing there, he had an eerie half-recollection, half-awareness of the murmur of crinoline, the muted, sensuous, intimate, familiar rustling sound of a woman undressing.

He turned away quickly before any of the memories could start again. He walked back to the bed, a four-poster of gleaming walnut, canopied with silk and with a satin coverlet gleaming in the stray light leaking in through the drawn curtains. The two big ivory-butted pistols looked blasphemous, lying there in the middle of the bed.

It was the bed which had seduced him. After the bath and the brisk, strenuous rubdown with the towel he had been wondrously relaxed. He had been drawn by the bed then. He had crossed the room and, tentatively, put out a hand and punched at it gently. It had been so long since he had lain on a real bed. The mattress had yielded under his touch with a surrender like that of flesh.

No, he'd thought, I can't; there's too much to do. But his relaxed muscles had seemed to drag him down. He had sat on the bed, thinking: It won't hurt it. And I won't sleep. Just a moment's rest, that's all. . . .

And then, in the dream, Vivian had been tight and warm up against him, snuggled in the crook of his arm, and he had been happy with the inexpressible relief of knowing that it had all been a hallucination, that she had never left him, that nothing had been wrong at all.

Well, you see what happens, he thought. You yielded to it because it was soft and comfortable and familiar, and all it did was start things up again. This place is bad for you. It evokes too many memories. You can't stand many more memories. What you'd better do is this: you'd better get dressed, finish what needs to be done, and get the hell out of here as quick as you can.

He dressed quickly. While he had been bathing, one of the house servants had brought clean clothes. "Miz Cammun say mebbe some Mr. Hollanduh's unduhclose an' linen fits you, Cuhnel." Another bribe, Wales thought, as he put his arms into the shirt sleeves. But, God! Is there any sensation like having clean, crisp linen next to your skin? He must have been exactly my size . . . even the shirt . . . I wonder if he won't miss the shirt when he gets back, her husband . . .

Husband . . .

His fingers froze on the buttons of the shirt. His eyes flickered to the bed. He was assailed by a sudden, un-bidden, embarrassingly vivid mental picture of a face-less man and the girl—the white-skinned, redheaded, green-eyed girl—on that bed together.

You're getting as bad as Channing, he thought savagely. Damn it to hell, you have got to stop that. He shook himself again and finished dressing rapidly, not really feeling dressed until, ultimately, the two heavy guns were buckled around his waist. He went to the dressing table and smoothed back his hair with one of the girl's brushes. It looks more like me, he thought, staring at his reflection. Not so taut, not so savage. They must have already softened me up some.

I don't know, he thought. Maybe I am being too rigid. Maybe I should leave at least—

The calf's blat was flat and frightened and came from the middle distance, and for a moment Wales thought he had imagined it. Then he remembered that the calf had been turned into the pen at the barn. The harsh, pitiable sound lingered incongruously in the lilac-scented room.

Christ, Wales thought.

All at once the quiet, ordered opulence hemming him in seemed peculiarly obscene, almost gluttonous. And they said *they* were desperate, thought Wales bitterly. And *they* offered to share their hams . . .

His eyes looked back at him sickly from the mirror and then, abruptly, went hard and cold. Decisively he turned then, hitching at the gun belt, and went out of the room.

He found Mrs. Cameron in the kitchen, in deep conference with the cook. Her back was to Wales, but when she heard him enter she turned. Her eyes went over him slowly, and her face broke into a polite, extremely charming smile.

"Well, Captain, I must say you're a more prepossessing representative of the army than you were an hour ago. Did you find everything satisfactory?"

"Extremely, ma'am. I am indebted."

"Not at all." She said over her shoulder to the cook, "And don't forget the spoon bread, Aunt Esther. Now, Captain. Now that you are refreshed, I hope we can continue our little talk and perhaps arrive at some friendly compromise. Certainly we want to be—"

"I'm sorry, Mrs. Cameron," Wales said. "I am afraid that I have no recourse other than to carry out my orders—which were to requisition and bring back everything I could find of any use to my regiment."

The old woman opened her mouth and then she closed it without saying anything. For a moment, Wales saw the same frost in her eyes that had been there when she had stood poised on the back steps with the drover's whip. Then the frost was dissolved in an expression of patient reasonableness.

"Let's step into the dining room a moment, shall we, Captain?" Her voice was bland and unaroused.

"Mrs. Cameron, no purpose would be served . . ."

"Please, Captain." There was sharpness in her voice now.

Wales sighed. "Very well, Mrs. Cameron."

In the dining room she turned to face him, and her expression had changed now. The patient reasonableness was gone; there was no charming smile. Her face was bleak and defiant as that of a captured hawk.

"Suppose, Captain, that I refuse your demands. What will happen then?"

"Mrs. Cameron, I sincerely hope you'll not find it advisable to do that. I beg you to co-operate."

"Fiddlesticks! Suppose I refuse to sell to you. We are citizens of the Confederacy, we are Virginians, and you are soldiers of our own army. I'd expect such treatment from Federals but not from you. I protest it—and suppose I will not sign your requisition?"

All right, Wales thought. Since you have asked the question. But I will try to tell you in a nice, a courteous, a genteel way.

"Ma'am," he said heavily, "you're aware that all over the South civilians have been called on to sacrifice their worldly belongings to support the war effort. And for the most part they have done so willingly. I can't believe that an obviously patriotic lady like yourself would do otherwise. But"—he found a perverse pleasure in the subtle, deliberate hardening of his voice—"but, should you see fit to do so, you would leave me no other recourse than to proceed exactly as though you were a supporter of the Federal cause."

Her face went blank with shock. "Why . . . why, of all the insolence!"

"You'd leave me no choice. Don't you understand, Mrs. Cameron? Nobody has any choice any more. This is a crucial time. The hour's past for lip service unbacked by action. If you don't support the Confederacy to the utmost, then it *must* be presumed—"

Had he still been talking to the woman with the calf, he would have hated the unctuous piety of his voice; but now, somehow, its very smoothness pleased him.

"And I with a husband and son-in-law in your army! You dare to say—"

"All the more reason, Mrs. Cameron. Look. Listen to me now." The oil had gone out of his voice and it was harshly serious. "I think we might as well understand each other. I detest having to do this. But as long as I'm a soldier I'll fulfill my obligation as a soldier the best I know how. I've got fighting men who need to be fed, and their welfare has to come first, or none of us will survive, and that includes you. I'm going to feed them with whatever I can find to feed them with—and neither pleas, tears, nor bribery can divert me from doing that." He spread his hands. "I'm sorry, but that's the way it is and I have nothing more to say."

She stood rigidly for a long moment, looking at him fixedly, her eyes unreadable. At last she seemed to relax.

"Very well, Captain." But there was no resignation in her voice. Her hands pulled at each other with the only betrayal of nervousness she showed. "Very well. I'll try to resign myself, since you leave me no alternative. I . . . trust you will be staying for dinner?"

"I hope we'll be away before that. But if we aren't, I'll certainly not put you to any additional trouble. The lieutenant and I will eat with our men."

"No, Captain Wales, I cannot allow that." She raised her head and pointed her chin at him, and Wales thought of the muzzle of an artillery piece coming up into line, defiant and dangerous. "Duane and I shall expect you and Lieutenant Channing if you are here."

111

"Mrs. Cameron, I'm sure our presence would be distasteful—"

"That," she said fiercely, "has nothing to do with it. No wayfarer has ever stopped at Red Oaks without receiving all the hospitality within our power to bestow. As long as you're here—as long as any gentleman is in my house—he is my guest and I intend to treat him as such and expect that he will conduct himself as such, within whatever limits are possible. If you are here, Captain, we shall expect you. As the victim of your foraging expedition, it may be necessary for me to excuse certain abridgements in the gentleman's code of behavior, but rejection of the hospitality of Red Oaks is not one I can overlook."

Like one of those ironclads, Wales thought helplessly. Like an ironclad warship, impossible to sink and not at all afraid of ramming head-on. Won't she ever give up? How long will it take for her to give up? Why can't they ever believe it when it happens to them? But, he thought, who can believe disaster, comprehend it? I have lived with it for almost a year, and I still don't believe it, don't comprehend it.

"Very well. If we are here at dinnertime, we'll be deeply honored."

Her eyes turned to the clock on the sideboard. "It is now eleven. We propose to have dinner at one sharp. Fried chicken, string beans, sweet potatoes, peas, spoon bread, and blackberry pie. I hope that will be adequate? Assuming, of course, that we have your permission to use two of your chickens . . ."

"I am sure," Wales said, deliberately not hearing her last sentence, "that it will be a sumptuous meal. Now I must go find Lieutenant Channing. If you will excuse me, Mrs. Cameron . . ." He turned and strode from the room, leaving her still standing there rigidly; and as he went out he could feel, was aware of, tangible and cold as the prodding point of a bayonet, her eyes boring into the ramrod straightness of his back.

Once out from under the canopied foliage of the oaks at the rear of the house, the glare dazzled his eyes and the heat was like a hammer stroke. Before he was three paces from the edge of the shade Wales could feel the sweat running down his flanks. He halted, squinting into the brightness, his eyes sweeping the villagelike complex of barns and sheds and slave quarters, seeking Channing.

The lieutenant was not to be seen. Smart, Wales thought. It was very clever of her to send the girl with him. Channing could walk right past a mountain made out of butter and not even notice it, with a good-looking woman hanging on to him.

He walked on down the path that led to the slave quarters. The double row of little brick buildings, each with its two tiny windows and heavy wooden door, was quiet and devoid of life, except for the crying of a child in the house nearest Wales. As Wales passed the window, he heard a dark, soft voice: "Hush. You hush now. Hush . . . or de sojer mens gits you . . ." Wales paused in mid-stride, then moved on. Right, he thought. We get everything.

A door opened in one of the slave huts and the sergeant entered, half a flitch of side meat under one arm. He grinned at Wales. "They been livin high off the hawg," he called, pointing at the bacon, and ambled slowly up to Wales. The captain waited for him.

"Finding much?"

The sergeant nodded, his brows lifting. "Right much. Don't believe these people even knowed they was a war goin on. Tell me, Capn"—he shoved back his hat—"how in time did they manage to make out so long?"

Wales shrugged.

"They're in back country, and they laid low and kept quiet. Stocked up before the war even started. Good planning, Sergeant."

"Yeah. But it does look like they'd of given some of this to help out afore now."

Wales looked at the sergeant. "Would you have?"

The sergeant stared back at him, and after a moment the sergeant nodded. "Yeah," he said slowly. "Yeah, I would of. I ain't the type to wrap hisself up in the flag, but I reckon I would of had to give some of it to shut

113

my conscience up. Well, I reckon they're gittin their chance to contribute to the Cause now."

"Yes," said Wales. "They aren't happy about it."

"No," the sergeant said. "I allow they're goan to be a mite unhappier, too, afore all's said an' done." His eyes narrowed and the grin left his face. "I was pokin around in the woods some this mornin when I took grub out to the pickets," he said.

"Oh?"

"Yessuh," the sergeant said. "There's a little path out yonder leads down to a hollow. I found a bundle of fresh hay lyin acrosst hit, and that kinda aroused my curiosity. So I did a little scoutin."

"Oh?" said Wales again.

"I found what I figgered on findin," the sergeant said.

Wales stood there for a moment without answering, rubbing his chin. After a while he said, bitterly, "Well, damn them."

The sergeant nodded without comment.

"Was there much?" Wales asked after a moment.

"Right smart," the sergeant said. "Didn't count 'em all. There was two-three niggers foolin around and I didn't want to git spotted."

"No," said Wales. He licked his lips. "Well, God damn them," he said.

"Lieutenant Channin's got everybody searchin the place up here right now," the sergeant said.

"Yes." Wales rubbed his chin again, his brow wrinkled in thought. "Well," he said, "we'll let this go up here. Get some men and go bring them on in."

"Yes, sir," the sergeant said. He turned to go.

"We should have thought of that earlier," Wales said.

"I reckon we was too hongry to do much thinkin, Capn."

"Well, I should have known. I should have thought of it." Wales pulled his hat off and ran his hand through his sweat-drenched hair. "I don't know," he said, and he shook his head wearily. "I don't know what in the hell's the matter with my thinking lately." He put his hat back on. "Seen Channing?"

The sergeant reached up and scratched his beard-stubbled cheek, and his face broke into a slow-growing grin. "Yeah," he said at last. "Yeah, I seed him. He went past here a little spell ago. Brought me the smoke-house keys and then said he was goin to—to recon-noiter." The grin broadened and the sergeant shook his head in reluctant admiration. "I'll say one thing. Damn if he can't really drum up the help when it comes to—doin whatever it was he said."

"I take it," said Wales, "that someone was with him."

"Yes, sir," the sergeant said. "A mighty fine-lookin lady was with him."

"Which way did they go?"

The sergeant jerked his thumb toward the same lane in which the men had cooked their chickens. "Yonder-ways," he said. His grin disappeared. "I doan't reckon they give you any trouble, did they, Capn? Not after the vittles they served up? Sholy not from the way that lady was lookin at Channin when they went by. You have any trouble?"

Wales shook his head. "Not yet, Mac. Not yet."

"Well," the sergeant said, "if they do an' you need me, jest holler."

The lane led gently downhill, falling away to a swale a half mile distant, where Wales could see the swine pens of the plantation. It was another token of the thrift and good management of the place that the hogs were penned, Wales thought; mostly people ear-marked their swine twice a year and let them run wild to forage for themselves. But you lost a lot of them that way: wild animals got them, and besides, they damaged the crops. A place that kept its hogs penned and corn-fed was a well-run place.

Then Wales saw the lieutenant and Mrs. Hollander. They were standing in a curve of the lane beside a grove of plum trees, leaning against one of the fences, talking.

That is, Channing was talking, his face idiotically bright and animated. The girl was looking up at him with silent, rapt attention. She was standing very close to Channing, the points of her bosom almost touching him, her lips slightly parted, her eyes wide.

Wales stopped.

Something about the scene struck a wild and jangling chord within him. He could feel sudden, inchoate anger ballooning inside his skull. He felt his throat tighten with it, his soul go sick with it. The girl laughed, a soft, pleasant sound in the bright, drowsy air. Wales saw her put out a hand, resting it on Channing's wrist for the briefest moment to emphasize her amusement.

Wales was suddenly aware of a pungent, meaty rankness, a harsh stench assailing him in the clean morning air. He looked down curiously and found that he had torn a stalk of Jimson weed from the brush along the fence line and was grinding the pulpy, rancid stem in his right hand. He opened his hand and let the stinking pulp drop to the ground. The anger boiled up and out.

"LIEUtenant CHANNing!"

Channing actually jumped.

But as Wales strode toward him, he seemed instantly to regain cool possession of himself. Something in those shallow brown eyes was bright and mocking as the captain stopped before him.

"Why, howdy, Marsh." Channing's drawl was unruffled. "You look mighty clean. Marsh, have you met Mrs. Hollander?"

"We've met," said Wales tersely.

"I figured I'd better look around a little," Channing went on easily. "Get familiar with the terrain, in case there was any trouble."

"Yes," said Wales. "Perhaps even find out where the pickets you didn't put out are located. Yes," he said, "that's a good idea." He stared at Channing with a loathing he knew he should not show and could not conceal. He must have been like you, he thought . . . a dog that runs snuffling after every bitch that passes. Yes, Lieutenant, he must have been a great deal like you, with the fact of a marriage meaning nothing—less than nothing—to him or to you either.

He turned his glare to the girl. And you, he thought.

116

He struggled to keep the contempt he felt out of his face. Using as a weapon what you should have consecrated . . . wearing a price as certainly and obviously as a woman patrolling the water front at twilight. He let out a long breath. "All right," he said. "Your orders, Lieutenant, are to inspect the guard. There's a man over by those haystacks, another in the pines yonder, and one out across the road. I want 'em all checked, Lieutenant. I want them all checked personally by you. In the meantime"—he waited to savor the disappointment and anger in Channing's eyes—"perhaps Mrs. Hollander would accompany me on a tour of the plantation. You see, Lieutenant, I need to . . . familiarize myself with the terrain also. Mrs. Hollander, would you care . . . ?"

"Why," she said pleasantly, as if completely unaware of any tension in the air, "I'd be delighted, Captain." She inclined her head toward Channing, who stood there rigid, still smiling, but with his eyes quite icy now, no longer mocking. "Perhaps you'll finish your story later, Lieutenant? I'll be breathless until I hear the end of it."

"Yes." Channing's voice was toneless. "Yes, I'll finish it later, Mrs. Hollander. You may be assured. Now, if you'll excuse me, I'll go . . . carry out the orders of my commanding officer." He whirled and strode up the lane.

As soon as he was out of hearing, the woman laughed. The merest suggestion of a laugh, a small, lilting sound. "Really, Captain, your appearance was fortuitous. I'm not entirely sure the story the lieutenant had begun was going to be in the best of taste."

Wales looked down at her. Above the rankness of the Jimson weed that still clung about him he sensed a breath of her perfume, a faint, lovely echo of the pillow in the bedroom.

His voice was terse. "Lieutenant Channing's taste frequently runs to matters which I'm sure a lady would find distasteful."

"Many things are distasteful nowadays, Captain." He saw that she was not unaware of the rebuke, and she

117

raised her chin sharply. "The looting of a plantation is distasteful."

Wales began to walk downhill toward the swine pens. She swung in alongside him. The sun struck glimmering flashes from the waves of her red hair. "I trust," she went on, "you're aware of all the implications of what you're doing to us, Captain Wales."

"I'm completely aware, Mrs. Hollander."

"Ah. And—you feel no compunction?"

"Compunction's too dear a luxury for a soldier, Mrs. Hollander. A thing is at hand to do and it must be done. It's as simple as that."

"Yes. So simple." Her voice had gone bitter. "War makes everything so simple, doesn't it?" She halted. "Need we go any closer to the swine pens, Captain?" They were close enough now so that the odor of pigs was rank and cloying, like something nauseous and solid tamped up the nostrils. The girl took a handkerchief from her bosom and held it daintily to her nose. Thus, when Wales turned, he could not see her expression.

"Very well," he said. "Let's turn around." His eyes swept out over the landscape instinctively. He looked off beyond the pens to the distant fields where corn rows shimmered in the blinding light. A sudden, weird impulse bloomed in his brain. To make a good job of it, he thought savagely, we should ride through that corn. Ride through it and break it down. Destroy it. He had a quick, vivid mental image of hoofs trampling stalks, crushing and grinding . . . then an involuntary shiver washed over him; his head cleared; he was full of shock and amazement at the monstrousness of his own impulse.

Why, I meant that! he thought eerily. What's the matter with me? I'm just here to find food—these people haven't done anything to me that I must revenge myself for. Why? Why did I . . . ?

"Yes," he said heavily. "Let's turn around." More and more, he thought, frightened, I am losing control. I have got to watch that. I mustn't allow—

When the girl removed the handkerchief, he saw that the animation had gone out of her face too. Wales

118

wondered if somehow she had just realized the uselessness of all her devices.

Then he saw that she had not. While he watched, she forced the vivacity back into her face. She took his arm with a too-ready gesture, and the pressure of her fingers on his biceps was too tight. "Please," she said. "Come, Captain. Do you always have to be so grim and businesslike? You interrupted my walk with your lieutenant. The least you can do is to let me complete it with you as my escort." Her voice seemed to have risen a pitch; there was a desperate edge to it; its coquetry sounded shrill and tinny.

"All right," Wales said tonelessly, and they began to walk up the lane together.

"Why, Captain, I believe you're quite human after all. I was beginning to wonder."

"That's not strange," Wales said tiredly. "I often wonder myself."

"You certainly frightened me when I first saw you—all dirty and bearded and gun-hung."

"I'm sorry. But until your hospitality I hadn't exactly had a great deal of time for prettifying myself."

He was not even listening to her. He was weighing what he had left within himself, wondering how much longer and what pressures the determination and purpose within him would survive. He was aware that something here kept draining him of resolution and stiffness. Not the women: he felt a certain amount of pity for the old one and little but contempt for the young one. It was, he decided, the place, the plantation itself. It was something he did not know how to fortify himself against. Just being here had opened up old scar tissue that he had healed at great cost; wounds were bleeding again, draining, and he was not sure he had anything left to close them with. He felt a sort of panic rising in him. Whatever it was he had been standing so close to the edge of for so long he was about to fall into. The ground was crumbling beneath him. The woman's quick, desperate, inane chatter hardly registered in his brain.

119

"Well, really, Captain, beneath it all you proved to be a most interesting man. Not handsome. I won't insult your intelligence by calling you a handsome man. Interesting is much better. Not that you're bad looking. On the contrary . . . But, really, good looks don't mean much in themselves, do they, Captain?"

"I'm afraid not," Wales said absently.

Something in his voice stemmed the flow of chatter. They walked in silence for a moment. Wales was aware that the girl could not fathom his mood and was disturbed by it. They climbed up the lane through the dry, hot sunlight, following the rutted wagon tracks that made a path through the riotous growth of summer grasses and weeds. Wales could feel the sweat pouring down his sides beneath the shirt; he could feel the girl's fingers digging into his arm. There was something fierce and anxious about the way the sharp-tipped nails pressed into his flesh. He was intensely aware of that pressure, but it stirred no lechery in him—only weary disgust.

If you were to ask your husband, Mrs. Hollander, he thought bitterly, looking at her from the corner of his eye, I doubt that he would agree that it was worth it.

Then there was a little sting of remorse. Maybe I'm unjust, he thought. Maybe I'm not thinking normally any more. Maybe I've become a sour, ranting, holier-than-thou creature. Maybe she's only being friendly and my warped mind is putting a warped interpretation—

Her voice interrupted his thoughts.

"Tell me about yourself."

He recognized it as the woman's last desperate gambit to break his mood, to capture his interest. He shrugged. "I'm just a soldier."

"Yes." Her voice was dry. "That's very obvious. But you weren't always a soldier. Or are you a professional?"

"No. I'm a farmer—a planter—by profession."

"You own a plantation?" Wales could sense the heightened interest, and inwardly he nodded, following her maneuvers with a detached portion of his mind. She believes she's found what may be the touchstone, he thought.

"Yes. In Clarendon County, South Carolina. At least"—his voice sounded wonderfully calm to himself —"at least it used to be a plantation. It's just a wilderness now. A—" The calm broke fractionally; his voice faltered slightly. "A ruin," he said.

"A ruin? Why, what happened to it?"

"I was in the army . . . and I had no overseer."

"But surely . . ." She frowned up at him questioningly. "Surely you just didn't ride off and leave the place to go to rack by itself?"

"No."

She halted him by pressure on his arm. "I don't understand, Captain Wales. Perhaps it's none of my business. But didn't you have relatives, parents or someone?"

"Yes," he said, feeling a turgidity rising through him, feeling too many emotions boiling up from all the places inside him he'd hoped were dead, aware of an outward pressure at his temples as if his head might explode from its burden of hate and grief and regret and anger and shame. "Yes, there was someone left with it. My wife."

"Oh," she said, the one word toneless, not signifying any understanding yet.

No trembling, Wales told himself. None of that. Not with her hand on my arm. He withdrew the arm. She had lowered her eyes as if uncertain of the propriety of looking at him so inquiringly.

After a moment she said tentatively, "It's a very difficult thing for a woman to manage a plantation."

"Yes," said Wales. He heard himself add, without meaning to and in a voice ugly with savagery, "Especially when she is in England."

"England?" She raised her face again, her eyes very wide.

I didn't mean to get into this, he thought, feeling the pressure on his temples increase. How did I get into this?

"England?"

"Yes," he said fiercely. "England." Suddenly, perversely, he was seized with the necessity of telling her. So she would know. So she would understand exactly what effect her tinny coquetry had on him, why he would be impervious to it, why nothing she could do could possibly move him. All right, he thought. All right.

He knew that his face was stony as he looked down at her; his voice was hard and stripped of all emotion.

"My wife, Mrs. Hollander," he said carefully, "became with child by another man several months after my last furlough home. He was an Englishman. She has gone to England with him. I have not heard from her. I don't know where she is or what has become of her. She left my plantation at the mercy of the slaves. The house has burned to the ground and the fields are ruined. Now, are your questions fully answered?"

"Oh," she said, the sound more an indrawn breath than a word. "Oh." Her face went white, then began to redden. She put her hand to her mouth. "Oh, Captain, I'm so sorry."

"There's nothing to be sorry about," he said harshly. "It's the fortune of war. Like losing an arm or a leg or one's eyes . . . or some hams and chickens . . ." His gaze bore into hers coldly.

Under his eyes she dropped her head and turned and walked to the fence. Clasping the top rail, she looked out over the sun-dazzled fields.

Wales stood there looking at her back. She's not as large a woman as I thought she was, he thought. She looks smaller, not much bigger than— Plotting a new course now, he thought. Figuring out what to do next.

After a while she turned.

"I see now, Captain," she said. Her face was very white in the sun glare. "I understand why you seem so—so bitter and vindictive. You have a right to, I suppose. But why us, Captain Wales? We're not the ones who—"

"My bitterness, as you term it, has nothing to do with the way I discharge my duty." His voice was thick with anger.

122

"Yes. I am sure you tell yourself that. But are you certain?" Her voice was low and intense. "Are you certain? Or is that not why you've been so merciless toward Mother and myself?" She pointed a finger at him. "I believe you hate women, Captain. You do. I can see it in your face and in your eyes and hear it in your voice. You hate us. Very well." Her bosom heaved under the tight dress, rising and thrusting. "Very well. Hate us all you please. Revenge yourself on us for what your wife has done. But, as a planter, do you have to revenge yourself on our plantation too? Must you destroy *it* to even some score for your own house and your own fields?"

Before he could answer, she swept an arm outward in a gesture that encompassed the land around them.

"Our men went off and left us," she said tautly. "They didn't even ask us if we wanted to be left. They didn't even ask us if we could do what we had to do. They just went. Father, my husband, our overseer. They never had a doubt—and they never even asked us if we had any . . ."

Her voice trembled.

"This place has been in our family since 1721," she said. "Do you think our men are fighting for the Confederacy? They're fighting for Red Oaks, for this plantation. And can my mother and I do any less? We've had to endure a lot, Captain, more than you can realize, and the only thing that's made it possible was the determination that Red Oaks would still be here, still be intact, when Father and Webb came home."

She shook her head; the red hair danced and glimmered.

"Why, we've been walking on eggs," she said. "It's been a nightmare. Keeping the slaves working, keeping them in order, never knowing when they're going to rise up and— The food is the only thing," she said. "Don't you see? It's only the food they can't get anywhere else that's done it for this long . . ."

She made a helpless gesture with her hands.

"We're not taking anything that belongs to someone else," she said pleadingly. "We're not depriving any-

123

body of anything rightfully theirs. All we're doing is using what belongs to us. All we want to do is to save something, to keep what our men went to war for in the first place. Let everyone else destroy—we only want to maintain. This place is everything to us. It means too much to sacrifice to a war that would gobble it up and never even know it." Her voice dropped; it was low and husky, throbbing now. "Then you come here and try to make us feel selfish, unpatriotic, ashamed, because we value our home place above all else. If that's not bitterness, what is it? Since when has it become moral to destroy and immoral to preserve?"

Damn her, Wales was thinking. Damn her for all her arguments that nobody can refute. That sure as hell I can't refute. What can I say? What answer can I make?

But even while his mind flailed about uselessly he heard his voice answering anyway, in that cold, oily tone he hated the sound of. "In wartime, ma'am," he heard himself saying, "the laws of morality are upside down. War itself is essentially immoral. But, given the fact of war, morals have to be adjusted to fit."

Her face was white, looking up at him, sea-green eyes blazing.

"Yes," she said hoarsely. "That's what your wife must have thought too."

The anger was instant, total, quite insane. Her face shimmered before him; for that incandescent second he was sure her hair was golden, not red, her eyes doll-blue, not blazing green. His hands whipped up, moved with the rage-born impulse to throttle. Then, with equal abruptness, the fiery blindness receded and he dropped his hands, drained and empty as if he had experienced orgasm.

He stood there panting, exhausted, confused.

But there was already contrition in her face. She was looking at him, appalled. "Forgive me, Captain. I had no right to say that. It was a terrible thing to say."

"No," he said weakly. Why can't I meet her eyes? he wondered. Why can't I meet anyone's eyes? "No. It's only the truth. It's all part of a—"

124

Then he became aware of the yelling and he broke off.

The yelling had been coming over and over from the slave quarters for the last ten seconds, but it only then impinged on his mind. He tensed, listening.

It came once more, shrill and urgent. "Captain! CAP-TUN!"

Wales whirled, forgetting the woman.

"Cap-TUNN!"

"Christ!" he said thickly. Fumbling for his gun, his heart thudding wildly, he began to run as fast as he could up the lane.

8

Thin, dirty, tattered—a scarecrow of a man—the soldier they called Jeff Davis walked reluctantly and sullenly toward the smokehouse.

They're all agin me anyway, he was thinking. Everybody's agin me. Mockin me. Tormentin me. Tryin to git me riled. Well, the hell with 'em. Frig 'em. Frig 'em all. But mostly, frig that damn sergeant.

He spat disgustedly. Cain't even call me by my right name, he thought. He had been born Samuel Alexander Davis, and everybody had always called him Sam until he'd come into this company. But the sergeant had thought it funny to dub him Jeff, and the nickname had stuck. There were lots of things that sergeant thought were funny, Jeff Davis meditated, which weren't funny at all—not by a damn sight.

Like this now, he thought. Go git them hams outn the smokehouse, Davis, he says. Sure. Go git them

125

hams, Davis. It had to be Davis. 'Cause they're up high an' they're heavy. Couldn't send one a them big uns like Boomer. Naw. Let *Davis* break *his* damn back carryin them big ole smoked hams while the rest of 'em prisses around in them air nigger cabins. Sure. Always. Send Davis.

He halted in front of the square, windowless brick building that was the smokehouse. The thin-featured weasel face turned in a slow semicircle, eyes squinting to see if anyone were watching. Then, satisfied, Davis reached up under his hat and took out Boomer's twist of tobacco, bit a chunk off of it, and stuck it back under the hat. He chewed for a moment and then spat.

There was the defiant slowness of a sulking child in the way he fiddled with the latch. The sergeant had given him a key to the padlock, but he was in no hurry to get the padlock open.

I got no business bein here, he thought. I got no business havin to leave Alabama. They tole me when I joined the home guard I wouldn't never have to leave Alabama. The lyin bastards. Then they haul off an' conscrip me outn the home guard an' send me off to the friggin cavalry in a draft. How come it had to be me? How come it wasn't one of them rich old bastards in the fancy unifoams that was drillin with us stidda me? How come everybody always picks on me?

The key finally clicked in the lock, and Davis lifted the lock free. Of its own weight the heavy wooden door of the smokehouse slowly groaned inward. The blackness inside was not inviting. Davis raised his foot and gave the door a push with his boot. He lifted the carbine: you never could tell what might be inside a place like that.

They said the home guard was safe, he thought, entering the smokehouse warily. They said we wouldn't hafta fight lessn the Yanks come right inta Montgomery. Then they haul off an' send me to Vuhginia. I-God, a man cain't put no dependence in nothin.

He looked around the dim interior of the smokehouse. The air was stiflingly pungent with the smell of salt and hickory. Hams and bacon sides, festooned from the joists, dangled mournfully like corpses after a mass hanging. But Davis relaxed. Enough daylight came through the open door to convince him that there was nothing harmful in here.

Jest throwed my money down the drain, he went on thinking. That damn colonel, he told me a hundred dollars in silver an' I wouldn't hafta go. Why, that lyin bastard. Chargin me to git me in the home guard like that and then after only a year sendin me off to Vuh-ginia. That lyin sonofabitch.

He leaned the gun in a corner. That sergeant, he thought. Doan't he reckons anybody ever gits tired? Well, blame it all, I done enough today anyhow. I'm goan rest a little bit afore I start luggin them hams. He sat down on a pile of hickory wood.

I doan know, he thought moodily, staring into the murk. I jest cain't figger out why everybody's agin me so. Unless it's cause I was dealin in slaves ...

Sure, he thought. Everybody looks down on a man who deals in slaves. But I cain't figger out why. I kin understand them damn high-tone planters—they looks down on everybody. But I cain't see why other people thinks a slave dealer's sumpin to despise. Somebody's gotta handle the niggers, ain't they?

Anyway, he thought, I bet before the war I was makin more money than that damn fancy-bred colonel that took my money an' sold me out. By God, he thought with a stir of honest pride, if I doan know nothin else, I knows niggers. I reckon there ain't anybody knows how to take a broken-down nigger an' scare the life back into 'em like I can. By God, I know how to scare a nigger bettern anybody else I ever seed. Take one that cain't hardly drag hisself an' git him so afraid he'll do anything, work like a damn horse, paw the ground like a big ole stud, to git hisself sold away from me. Pick 'em up for a song an' sell 'em for a damn good price. Doan ever let nobody tell you there ain't money in niggers for a man that knows the ropes. Coraman-tees, Foulahs, Mandingoes, Gaboons, I done handled 'em all. A man that didn't know what he was doin, he'd lose his butt. But, I-God, *I* know how to handle

127

'em! But that's it, he thought bitterly. That's how come everybody thinks he kin pick on me an' git away with hit.

It ain't fair, he thought, and he shivered, feeling unloved and lonely, all his innards full of righteous indignation. Then, after a while, he thought: I better git a ham outa here, I reckon. That damn sergeant'll come alookin . . . He started to get up and the wood pile rolled under him.

He flailed wildly for balance, finally regained it, and stood up. Well, Goddamn, he thought, looking aggrievedly at the scattered wood, as if it had deliberately betrayed him. A hell of a way to stack . . . to stack . . .

Well, I'll be a sonofabitch, he thought.

The neck of a gallon clay demijohn was peeping up through a crack between two hickory logs. Davis stared at it unbelievingly for a long moment, then his narrow, stubbled face split in a pleased, incredulous grin.

"Well, I'll be a sonofabitch," he said out loud. He swung a quick glance all around him, then he was down on his knees, clawing the rest of the wood away. In a moment he straightened triumphantly, hugging the demijohn to him, his hand yanking fiercely at the corncob stopper.

His whole thin body was shaking with excitement; his sharp nose twitched as the rank, oily fumes of white corn whisky rose from the jug and assaulted him with delicious waves.

The nigger that hid this, he thought delightedly, he got a surprise comin to *him!* Tends the smokehouse an' keeps his jug ahind the wood. Well, I-God, that's goan be one more chopfallen nigger, this time!

He started to drink and then halted. He hunched protectively over the jug, looking furtively about him. He moved to the open door and pushed it shut. Then he lifted the jug once more and remembered just in time that a nigger had been drinking from it. Carefully he wiped the mouth of it with one dirty hand. Trembling more violently now, he lifted the jug, drinking deep, almost falling over backward as he held it tilted

128

up to his mouth, the clear corn whisky running down his throat, scalding and powerful and satisfying. . . .

But he knew that time was his enemy. The sergeant had a brain like a railroad watch. It was only a matter of minutes until he would be along, prodding and hollering. Got to drink hit fast, Davis thought. Doan want nobody else gittin holt of hit.

Draught after draught spilled down his throat in a cascade of molten fire, gagging him and filling his belly with hot pleasantness all at once. Goan be drunk as a coot, drinkin this fast, he thought. Doan care, though . . . Some of the whisky dribbled off his chin onto his coat. Goan smell like a still, too, he thought. Doan care anyway. . . .

But after a while he knew that he had had enough. Any more and he would be sick. Not used to this now, he thought. Been a long time since I done had any good corn like this. But I gotta let hit settle . . . Better hide it now. Better put hit back under that wood.

But, by God, I got the laugh on 'em now! he thought. Sergeant'd mess his britches, did he knew what a favor he done me when he sent me to the smokehouse. By God, most wisht I could tell 'im, jest to see his face! Davis cackled soundlessly as he rolled the wood back in place. His little eyes were glittering. Already the whisky had bitten deep; he could feel waves of carefree drunkenness roiling up through his blood stream. Christ on the mountain! he thought exuberantly. If I ain't a lucky bastard!

He lurched over to the door and pushed it open and leaned there against the jamb for a moment. What I ought to do, he thought happily, is go breathe in his face. He'd go crazy as a hoot owl, trying to figger out where I come by it. Man, that'd be a joke, I mean! He picked up his rifle. I will, he thought gaily. I-God, I will.

He blinked as he emerged into the bright sunlight. Now, whur's that sergeant? he wondered. His eyes swept the street of the slave quarters; the little brick buildings rippled and shimmered deliciously. There was nobody on the street.

'L find 'im, Davis thought confidently. An' then I'll breathe in his dirty face an' tell 'im to go frig hisself! He moved carefully across the yard to the slave quarters, raising and lowering his feet gingerly because the ground always seemed closer to him than he expected when his heel came down.

He halted in front of the closed door of the first slave cabin in the row. He stood there for a moment, listening, rocking back and forth gently on his feet. There was no sound of life whatsoever in the cabin. Then Davis heard one faint rustling whisper. A slow, happy grin of inspiration spread the whiskers on his face. By the old Nick, he thought. You know hit's been a damn long time since I thowed a scare intuh airy nigger!

He looked down at the carbine in his hand, and his grin widened. "Ha!" he said joyously. He turned to face the wooden door of the house. He thrust the carbine forward. Then, with a mighty kick, he slammed open the door and stalked into the cabin with the carbine cocked and menacing.

"All right, niggers!" his voice blared out. "Yo time has come!"

There was a crash as a chair fell over.

Jeff Davis blinked in the darkness of the little building. Then his vision cleared. He saw the one occupant, cowering against the back wall. She was a young girl, chocolate brown, perhaps fourteen years old. She was squeezing herself against the wall in absolute terror, her eyes wide and whiteshining, her breath wheezing loudly through broad, flat nostrils.

Jeff Davis stood there grinning.

It smells good in here, he thought. It smells like niggers. He savored the smell, as any journeyman would savor the smell of his trade, as a baker would respond to the hot freshness of new-made bread, as a printer would respond to the tang of ink. It was the smell of his livelihood, the smell of money to be made. Some people don't like to smell 'em, he thought; and he took a deep breath of the musky odor compounded of wood smoke and perspiration and grease—a dark odor, a heavy, thick, rich odor, and he thought: This is like ole times.

The girl stayed huddled against the wall. She was wearing a shapeless garment made of calico roughly sewn into a tube, with holes cut out for the arms. Beneath it young breasts, small and pointed, rose and fell in terror.

Their motion caught Jeff Davis' eyes. There was immediately a quick stirring in him, deeper, more significant, than the drunken impulse to prank. Immediately the burning of the whisky was transmuted into desire.

For perhaps half a minute they remained frozen thus in grotesque tableau—the skinny, fox-faced soldier with the thrust-forward gun, and the lean, long-legged young brown girl. For perhaps half a minute. Then Jeff Davis pushed backward with one foot and the door squeaked protestingly as it swung shut. Its closing made the room even darker. Jeff Davis let his thumb ease down the hammer on the carbine. He took a single step forward, pushing the gun ahead of him so that its muzzle made a dent in the soft flesh of her belly, just above the navel.

"Awright, brown gal," he said. "Take off that air dress."

She did not move. Her eyes grew wider, their whites enormous in the dimness; her brown face shone with sweat.

Jeff Davis leaned slightly on the gun. He licked his lips. He could feel his legs trembling with desire and drunkenness and eagerness. Slowly he increased the pressure of the gun against her, rotating the barrel, boring into her flesh with the hard steel. "I said take off that Goddamn dress."

She made no move to comply.

"By God," said Jeff Davis, "if you doan take hit off, I'll shorn hell take hit off fer you!" His hand flashed out, seized the neck of the shapeless dress, pulled.

The calico was too strong; it would not rip.

Jeff Davis cursed. He threw the gun down and it slid, clattering, into a corner. Then he rammed his body against her, pinning her to the wall. His frantic hand found the hem of her skirt and jerked it upward.

At that she broke from her paralysis and began to fight him. She was strong as a young animal, supple, lean, sweaty, slippery. She did not scream; she said no word. He could hear her breath rasping through her flat nostrils: no other sound. But she exploded. In one instant she became a whirling brown pinwheel of elbows and hard-soled feet and knees and flashing teeth.

"Hell," Davis grunted. He seized her by the wrists, but his grip slipped. "Hell, nigger, I'll teach you—" He let go her wrists; one hand caught her hair, pulling her head around viciously. The other grabbed a breast, squeezing savagely.

For the first time she made a sound; she whimpered with pain, a high, thin quaver. Davis yanked her hair mercilessly. He let go her breast and used that hand to slap her face. There was a bed across the room against one wall—a rumpled heap of formless rags atop a mouse-chewed shuck mattress. Davis hit her again, and then, pulling at her hair, shoving at her face, he fought her inch by inch over to the bed. She was still making no sound but that high, thin whimper. He saw that her eyes were full of tears. He twisted the handful of hair and forced her down, and the shucks rustled dryly as the two bodies landed heavily. He put his arm across her throat and held her pinned for an instant, and then he got her dress up around her belly. But she wriggled frantically. Her kneek flashed up; all at once pain exploded throughout his groin in a sickening burst. He let out a groan, his arm pressed down; his other hand seized her hair and wrenched viciously, and at last she screamed.

Then Davis let go of her and bent over, blind with the pain in his crotch, unaware that she had quit wriggling.

It was a long time before the pain faded and he suddenly realized that she was still. He looked at her at last, and his heart stopped for a moment and his guts leaped as he saw the tilted angle of her head, dangling crazily over the edge of the bed. "Well, damn it—" he mumbled and lurched to his feet.

At that moment daylight fell across him, and Davis turned in panic toward the open door.

The sergeant's face was aghast and white as he stared back and forth from Jeff Davis to the dead Negress with the broken neck.

9

"She had a knife," Jeff Davis said.

A low, sobbing, unearthly wail rose from the distant slave quarters. It started like a pulsing moan, throbbed to a crescendo, ended in a shriek, and then began again. It could be heard clearly even here in the big dining room of the plantation house. It was, Marshall Wales thought, like the anguished cry of an animal being tortured. I wish it would stop, he thought. But it went on and on.

"Yes," Wales said, leaning his elbows on the table and looking at the soldier standing before him. Scared now. Rank with stale corn whisky and nigger smell, and scared; and yet blustery, almost defiant. After all, it was only a nigger . . . The watery blue eyes, shifting frantically, like those of an animal pushed into a corner, then coming back to focus with summoned defiance. "Yes," said Wales again. "So you maintain. Sergeant MacLeod, did you see a knife?"

"There wasn't no knife." The sergeant was standing on one side of Jeff Davis, towering over him, looking down on Davis as if the man were a cockroach the sergeant was awaiting permission to squash. On the other

133

side of Davis was Boomer, the redhead, his freckled moon of a face impassive. "There wasn't no knife," the sergeant said again, positively.

"Of course there wasn't any knife." Mrs. Cameron's voice was like the breaking of sheet ice; her thin lips were blades that sheared off the words. "The girl was a victim of unwarranted assault. This is exactly what I've been afraid of all along, Captain Wales—the natural result of turning loose an undisciplined group of rabble to loot and plunder. You must bear full responsibility."

Wales nodded. His head hurt, a dull, mean, persistent ache over his left eye. He felt almost sick with the hurt—and even sicker with the frustration of not being able just to stand up and put his hands around Jeff Davis' neck and choke him. Because, damn you, he thought, looking at the man through the pain-water that veiled his eye, because you've undermined all the position I have built up. I've been able to justify everything we've done up until now. I've been in the right— or at least nobody could prove I was in the wrong. But you and your drunken lust— Oh, she's got me where she wants me now, and she's going to make the most of it.

"Of course, Mrs. Cameron. Certainly I take full responsibility."

"I expect to be paid for the slave," she said brittlely.

"Certainly." He let out a long breath.

"And I demand that this man be punished to the fullest extent."

It would be nice to be able to throttle you too, he thought wearily. He nooded again. "I intend to see that he is." Yes, by heaven, he thought, I'll damn well see that the balance is restored immediately. He looked at Jeff Davis. "You know," he said thoughtfully, "I ought to have you shot."

The sergeant looked hopeful, but Boomer's impassivity broke in a look of shock. Shoot a man for killing a nigger? Make him pay for the nigger, sure—but hell, he didn't go to kill her—and anyway, a nigger's jest a nigger. . . .

134

Wales saw the look and read it; he also saw the confidence on Jeff Davis' face that he would not be shot. Sim Burkett, Wales thought, remembering another soldier. Why, Davis don't expect anything worse than Burkett got that time. Burkett's gun had gone off accidentally and killed an artillery horse; Wales had made Burkett dig a hole and bury the horse to teach him to be more careful with his weapon.

And of course, Wales thought, his head feeling as if someone were trying to wrench it open with a wedge, you wouldn't have to dig near as big a hole as you would if she'd been an artillery horse, would you, Davis?

He drummed on the table with his fingers.

"But of course I can't have you shot," he said. "Not without a court-martial."

Davis nodded. "I didn't go for to kill the nigger, Capn." He was trying to be ingratiating now; there was the subtle implication in his whining voice that all here were joined in a fellowship of reasonable men.

"Naw," the sergeant said. "That wasn't what you was aimin to do. We know that."

"Sure," said Davis. "Y'all know that. I wasn't aimin to hurt 'er."

"Naw," the sergeant said. "Jest rape her. Excuse me, Miz Cameron." His face turned red.

"I think everybody is aware of what his intentions were," said Wales flatly. During that interchange he had made his decision. He turned to Mrs. Cameron.

"Somewhere about here you've got a blacksnake stock whip. You had it this morning when I first came up. May I borrow it?"

There was silence in the room. Only the loud whack-whack-whack of the clock on the sideboard, only the continual mourning wail from outside. Jeff Davis' face went sickly pale; simultaneously Boomer's moon turned red. He opened his mouth, trembling with indignation. "Capn!" he blurted.

The captain looked at him. "Yes, Boomer?"

"Capn—*you ain' goan whup a white man for killin a nigger?*"

135

Wales's lips tightened. The sergeant said, gently, "I reckon the Cap'n will ask fo yo advice when he wants it, Boomer."

"Yeah, but—" Boomer was shaking all over with anger. "I never hearda nothin like that. Why—why, that's *Yankee* doings!"

Mrs. Cameron looked from Davis to the sergeant and then she looked at Boomer and then at Wales. Her eyes were frosty-blue and appraising.

Wales returned her gaze steadily.

"If I may," he said quietly.

She nodded. The trace of a smile on her mouth was quietly, insufferably triumphant. "I'll get it," she said.

"Sergeant," Wales said, "tie the prisoner's hands."

"Goddammit!" Jeff Davis burst out in a high, strangled voice that broke, "you cain't *do* this! I'm a white man! I'll—"

Mrs. Cameron had gone out of the room. Wales leaned across the table, and his eyes bore into Jeff Davis' eyes; his face was pale and taut with fury. His voice was low and savage and distinct.

"You'll keep your Goddamned mouth shut and take your medicine like a man. You get this, Davis—and you, too, Boomer. This is a clear-cut case of attempted rape, a wanton destruction of civilian property, plus being drunk on duty. That last alone is enough to have you in front of a firing squad if you stand court-martial, Davis, only this woman hasn't thought of it. Now you shut up, or by God, I'll bring charges myself. I've got a bellyful of you, Davis—" his voice trembled, rose slightly—"a flat-out bellyful of you. You have messed things up here to a fare-thee-well! I've got enough on my conscience now, having to rob our own people, leave them stranded and helpless. Don't you think I've got enough on my conscience without rape and murder too? That little nigger girl wasn't fighting any war—she wasn't doing anything but trying to keep you from hurting her . . . Christ, if the people who started this war had only known they were turning loose creatures like you—Christ! Damn you, Davis, if I had my way, I'd—"

The sergeant's hand was light but firm on his shoulder. Marsh Wales straightened up, grateful for that gentle, monitory touch. He let out a long, shuddering breath. "Consider yourself lucky, Davis."

The sergeant looked gratified as Wales turned away. Then he looked down at Davis and grasped him by the shirt collar. "Come along, knothead," he grunted, dragging Davis out by the scruff of his neck. At the door to the kitchen corridor he paused. "Where you want him, Capn?"

"Under the oak tree in back." Wales's head was splitting. His mouth was dry as cotton. After the sergeant had hauled Davis out, Wales crossed the dogtrot to the kitchen. The old Negress in the kitchen was big-eyed and as expressionless otherwise as if she had been carved from cypress. Wales looked at her. "May I have a drink of water, Auntie?"

Without speaking, she got him a dipper of cold well water from a clay crock. He tilted it up, let it course its way down his throat. *I never whipped a man before,* he was thinking. *Not even a slave. But this time it ought to be a pleasure.* His hand was trembling as he passed her the dipper. *I had everything under control here,* he thought. *I was just about to finish proving to them and to me, too, that everything we were doing was justified. Then this happens—and it's all my fault too. Rape. Murder. I was working from a moral position. I was using moral leverage—and now it's all gone. The only thing to do is to get accounts squared as quickly as possible. Now. So that they can see them squared. Otherwise all the ground is cut from under me; otherwise I'm left stripped naked, revealed as a robber and a thief.* He knuckled at his streaming left eye. *Why,* he thought, *the bastard just didn't leave me any alternative.*

"Thank you, Auntie," he said.

Mrs. Cameron entered the kitchen. The braided blacksnake whip was coiled in her hands. "A drover's whip," she said. "Do you know how to use it, Captain?"

"I have handled stock, Mrs. Cameron," he said and took the whip. He went to the door and she followed

137

him. He stopped and turned. "Don't you think it would be best for you to stay inside?"

Her face was like an iron mask. "I intend," she clipped, "to see that justice is done."

And appraise my technique, perhaps, he thought bitterly. I'll bet you've had many a poor bastard whipped in your time. Wales nodded courteously. "As you will."

"I expect you to lay on your best, Captain."

He felt his nostrils flare with restrained anger. "I trust you will find my efforts satisfactory, Mrs. Cameron."

Outside, under the oak tree, all the soldiers not on picket duty had gathered to watch, but the sergeant was alone as he tied Jeff Davis' arms around the tree. He had taken off Davis' shirt, and Wales thought, surprised: I didn't realize he hadn't any more meat on him than that. The man's a bone rack. This is really going to hurt him. . . .

His hand ran over the harsh braided leather of the coiled lash. Davis without his shirt was a fragile-looking, white, vulnerable thing, like something from moist darkness suddenly exposed to light. He was sagging against the rope that held him as if his knees had collapsed; the face turned over his shoulder was a begging mask with tears streaming from its squinted eyes; the whimpering hurt-dog noises of terror that came from his throat were barely discernible as phrases: "Please, Capn, please. Goddammit, I'm a white man—you ain't goan whup a white man? . . . Please, Capn, I'm one yo own soljers. It ain't *human,* Capn. It's goan hurt me an' I cain't stand bein hurt . . . I'm sorry, Capn, please, I'll never do hit again. Please, Capn, for God's sake, *please . . ."*

Wales just stood there, sick with revulsion at the sight of that white, twisting, skinny torso, feeling the skewering pain intensify over his left eye. All at once he realized, almost with panic, that the driving force of the rage had drained away from him; there was nothing left within him but a flat, weary disgust, nothing to spark him to do what had to be done. But I have

138

got to, he thought. It's gone too far now. I can't back down now.

The sergeant came over. "Capn," he said softly and put out a hand.

"No." Wales shook his head. "I'll do it, Sergeant. There might be trouble. Because this is highly irregular, you know, Sergeant, and I don't know how that new brigade commander that took over a couple of months ago is going to look on this. There should be a court-martial and all that—"

"All right, sir." The sergeant faded back. Wales continued to stand there, looking at the white, whimpering thing, devoid now of all self-respect and all courage in its incoherent pleadings, twisting and squirming around the tree trunk like an anguished caterpillar. I have got to get started, he thought desperately. I have got to get started some way.

"It is our custom to lay on forty for the most serious offenses," the voice of Mrs. Cameron said at his shoulder.

"Forty." Wales's mouth opened and closed. He felt his neck throb with the resurgence of anger. "Why, forty would kill this man. He . . . he's not as well-fed as your niggers, Mrs. Cameron." His hands clenched about the whip. "Sergeant!" he called.

"Yes, sir."

"Count twenty for me."

A scream of anguish went up from Jeff Davis. "Oh, Gawd! Twenty strokes!"

"Yes, sir," the sergeant said.

"Twenty strokes!" Davis squealed heavenward again.

"Well," Mrs. Cameron's voice snapped, "are you going to stand there all day?"

Wales blinked his eyes. He moved forward dazedly. He was aware that the girl, Duane Hollander, and Lieutenant Channing had just come up the path from the slave quarters. He sucked in a deep breath and let the coil of the whip snap itself out to extend full length on the dust. His hand gripped the stock so tightly that his fingers hurt.

"All right, Davis," he said grimly. "Brace yourself."

The whip flew back over his shoulder its entire length; it made a whistling noise as it came forward past his ear; there was a sodden smack as it curled around Jeff Davis. The man screamed and jumped, and when the whip pulled back there was a broad red welt across his shoulders. Lord, Wales thought dimly, you don't suppose even twenty will kill him, do you? He's in no better shape than I am. The whip came forward again.

Vance Channing's voice: "Miss Duane, this is no sight for you. Let me take you inside—"

"No, Lieutenant. This is something I must see." As he brought his arm back, Wales saw her standing there, wide-eyed, pale-faced, her green eyes fixed on him strangely.

Wales brought the whip forward again, more savagely this time, and again and again, and each time it bit home, Davis screamed piercingly. The wailing, too, was still ululating from the quarters, primitive, bereft, despairing. The two sounds mingled oddly in the still, hot Virginia air.

Scream, Davis, Wales thought suddenly and exultantly, bringing the whip forward again. Scream! All at once he felt good. There was no hesitation, no indecision now. Magically the accumulated tensions, the frustrations, were flowing out of him; the weight of the whip swinging back over his shoulder was satisfying with the first really deep satisfaction he had known in months. When, with just the right wrist motion, he brought it forward again, its lash wrapping home, there was something in the impact of it that he could feel pleasantly all through his body. He felt oddly grateful to Davis for this opportunity as he brought the whip forward once more and then again . . .

"Captain," the sergeant said.

The word cut through the rhythm and satisfaction of the whipping like a knife of ice. Wales twisted his wrist, and in mid-arc the lash halted and dropped, trailing into the dust.

"Yes."

"That's twenty strokes, Capn."

"Yes. Thank you for counting, Sergeant. Cut him down, if you please."

When the sergeant had cut the rope that bound the man's wrists, Davis slumped, whimpering softly, to the ground. His back was a striped and bloody crisscross. Wales blinked his eyes. For the first time in minutes objects around him stood out in clear definition; his eyes were free of the mist of savagery that had fogged them. He opened and closed his mouth like a fish gasping for air. He had the weird certainty that he was absolutely hollow inside, that he would crumble at any moment. He fought down a panicky urge to turn and run and hide somewhere.

"I'm sorry, Davis," he heard himself say tonelessly. "But you brought it on yourself. Pick him up, Sergeant."

"You did an excellent job, Captain." Mrs. Cameron's voice at his elbow startled him; he turned.

For a moment his face merely twitched as he looked at her. Then he let out a long breath. "Yes. I did a very fine job, didn't I?"

He coiled up the whip, feeling every muscle in his body trembling, that ache back in his head, the pain like a lance above his eye. "I did a real professional job," he said. "It's my army training . . ." He handed her the whip. "An excellent whip, Mrs. Cameron." He was consciously battling to keep the hysteria out of his voice. "Really fine. I believe it would completely skin a man if you used it right. A marvelous whip. Be careful of the blood on it," he said. "And the little pieces of skin." Then he spat into the dust.

"If you will excuse me," he said, and he began to walk toward the back door of the kitchen. He did not want to be sick in front of all those people; he could not let himself be sick in front of the men. Perhaps a glass of water would help . . .

Behind him the sergeant and Boomer were helping the moaning Davis to his feet. "Come on, Davis, come on," the sergeant was saying in a voice almost motherly. "You'll live a long time yet. Come on . . ."

Wales started up the back steps, but at that moment the back door opened. The old colored woman was

141

standing in the doorway. She looked at the limp white man being lifted to his feet and then she looked at Wales and at Mrs. Cameron behind him.

"Dinner will be ready in jest a little bit," she said.

She raised her eyes to where the sergeant was still tugging at Jeff Davis. There was a jar in her hand. She held it out to Wales.

"Heah's some goose grease for his back," she said.

10

Wales walked blindly through the house.

Christ, he thought.

He could feel hot bile sloshing against the back of his clenched teeth. He swallowed hard, and it seared his throat with its raw green acids. I've got to find some place, he thought . . . I am done in.

An open door yawned at one side of the hall, darkness beckoning within. Wales lurched inside.

The room proved to be a library. It was full of the characteristic smell of books; Wales sensed great shelves of them towering over him. Immediately he had a sense of sanctuary. He could feel a lessening of the churning in his stomach. He leaned on a big walnut desk for a moment, his head down, and then, when he felt better, he groped his way toward an old massive leather sofa. It creaked and groaned under his weight as he slumped down on it. Wales let out a long, shuddering breath.

He sat there in the dark with his legs stretched out and his head down on his chest and his eyes closed, waiting for some of the trembling to go out of him. He was acutely aware of his body: it was all stirred up—

he could hear the beat of his heart, blood pounding in his ears; every tense muscle vibrated just before it relaxed; the big ganglion of nerves in his solar plexus twitched; the pain over his left eyes was excruciating.

He ran his hand over his eyes. Behind the darkness of the closed lids he kept seeing that pale, skinny, vulnerable back shivering with the agony of the lash. It was as if the bright sunlight out there had printed it, fixed it, on the lenses of his eyes. Damn it, he thought, knuckling at his eyes. Damn it.

He was full of panic because he knew that he was at the end of his recuperative powers. Somehow he would have to find strength to heal his mind of that picture, as he had healed it of all the other things that were beyond the capacity of the mind to dwell on without losing its orderly function. A dead man lying on the grass with his hands twined in his own blown-out entrails, blue-green flies crawling on the shattered paunch . . . A wounded man, on fire from head to toe, pulling himself along with his elbows through the burning woods at Chancellorsville on a Sunday morning in May . . . Watching your own saber go into a man's eye, feeling it grate against bone and pulling it free with brains and blood and a ghastly ichor on it . . . His mind had had to take a hundred recollections like that and transmute them from vivid, sickening horrors into dimly remembered commonplaces. And it had had to cope with the business about Vivian too. Whether it had the strength, the energy left for any more efforts to preserve his sanity he did not know. But he doubted it. The assaults against it had been too fierce and too constant; even the strongest fort must yield at last. . . .

He dropped his face into his hands. Oh hell, he thought, trying to shut out all thought and remembrance with the savage word. Hell, hell, hell . . .

"S'matter, Marsh? Got the dreadfuls?"

Wales looked up, suddenly glad to see Channing, glad to see anybody or anything demanding his attention, distracting his brain from its orgy of morbid remembrance. "Oh," he said. "You, Vance. What's the trouble?"

"No trouble." Channing hooked his thumbs in his

belt and sauntered across the room, looking up at the high shelves of books, a little awed, a little contemptuous.

"Old bastard must not have done anything but read," he said. He moved over to the desk in the center of the room, hooked one lean thigh over the corner of it, and sat down, humming softly and drumming one foot on the floor.

"Something on your mind, Vance?" Wales's pleasure had changed to irritation; he put the question sharply.

Channing shrugged. "Nothing much. Just wanted to know how it feels to whip a man, Marsh."

Wales got slowly to his feet. "Get out," he said tonelessly.

Channing raised his knee up and hooked his arms around it and looked at Wales with exaggerated judiciousness. "I don't believe it agrees with you, Marsh," he said cheerfully. "I really don't. I wouldn't make a habit out of it, if I was you. It makes you look sorta—well, sorta peaked and white around the gills."

"I said get out." Wales spoke the words slowly and distinctly. His fists began to clench and unclench.

Channing frowned aggrievedly. "No need to get touchy with me. I ain't done anything."

Wales's words were slow and biting and whittled to sharp, barbed points. "You sure as hell haven't. Where were you when they were checking those cabins? Off trying to diddle one of the cows?"

Channing went white beneath the weather burn, but his perfect teeth still showed in his good-humored grin.

"A man can't be everywhere at once, Marsh. After all, you sent me off to check the guard."

"Yes," said Wales, "I did, didn't I? All right, I'm sorry, Vance. Perhaps I've done you an injustice. Now will you do me a favor and get the hell out if you've got no business with me."

"Ahh," said Channing. He released his knee and set his foot down on the floor. "Ahh, but that's just it, Marsh. I *do* have business with you." Wales sensed a new tone to his voice: silky, utterly confident, not quite gloating. Then all at once Channing's voice went hard and ugly and he stood up, his handsome young man's face distorted and rigid with hate.

"Oh, I know. You've despised me ever since I joined this company, Wales. Hell, don't deny it. I know you have. You've looked down your nose at me and low-rated me ever since I come from Tennessee. You damn planters are all alike, especially you damn South Carolinians and the snoot-nosed Virginians. You think everybody's dirt but you. I don't know how you found out I was a gambler before the war, but I ought to have knowed that I couldn't expect any decent treatment from a high-and-mighty planter bastard like you once you learned it."

Wales blinked. "Gambler?"

Deliberately Channing drew back his lips in a smile of mocking exultation. "Oh," he whispered, "I've waited for this minute for such a damn long time."

He had pulled his gloves from his hip pocket; now he emphasized every word with a slap of the gauntlets against one palm.

"Listen to me. Listen to me, Marsh Wales, and listen good! Because I'm saying that I've eaten the last bit of dirt from you I intend to eat. The last bit. Do you hear? From now on, Marsh Wales, it's going to be different. From now on you're gonna sing low and walk soft. Because there's a general commandin this brigade now that if he ever hears you whipped a white Confederate soldier for killin a nigger wench, hell itself won't be hot enough to hold you!"

Wales looked at him blankly for a few long seconds. His left eye kept watering, and after a moment he knuckled the water away. "Oh," he said at last, softly. "Oh, I see."

"You see!" Channing mocked savagely, leaning forward, his face twisted in a happy, vindictive snarl. "You see! You're blame well told you'll see!"

He straightened up and took a step backward and rammed the gloves in his hip pockets. "Whippin a white man for killin a nigger slave! Why, my Christ, Wales, which damn army did you think you was in? Where did you think you were—in Vermont or Con-

145

nectieut or one of those places? Good Lord, man, how did you figure to git away with it?"

He didn't want for an answer.

"Lemme tell you somethin," he whispered savagely. "I know you Goddamned South Carolina and Virginia bastards look down at us men that used to be with Bedford Forrest. I know that General Hampton's a South Carolinian, too, an you're probably lookin to him to back you up. But there's one thing you forgot, Wales. You forgot that the general runnin the brigade now ain't no South Carolinian. He's from the West, like I am. And he was at Fort Pillow, like I was."

His eyes gleamed ferally, and his teeth shone in the dim light, and he began to pace back and forth behind the desk. Suddenly he turned. "Let me tell you about Fort Pillow"—he grinned—"an' maybe you'll understand."

"I've heard about Fort Pillow," Wales said quietly.

"No, you ain't," Channing said quickly. "No, you ain't heard *nothin* about Fort Pillow. Let me tell you. Now. So you'll understand."

Wales didn't answer. Channing put his palms down flat on the desk and leaned forward, his voice low and intense.

"That was in April," he said fiercely. "Just a month before they sent me over here. Me and the man that's runnin this brigade now.

"You see, Wales, Fort Pillow was full of nigger troops. The Federals had garrisoned the Goddamned place with niggers. They had gunboats in the river, too, but we had the fort surrounded. There was one point they kept us from, but ole Forrest was smart as hell. While we were dickering around with 'em under a flag of truce, demanding their surrender, we moved men up there and when they wouldn't surrender, by God, we poured it to 'em!"

He brought his clenched fist down on the table.

"We stormed that fort, Wales. We went up over the side and down into it, right into the middle of them nigger soldiers. We went into 'em like hail through a tobacco field. Some of 'em threw down their guns and tried to run—we shot 'em! Some of 'em got down on their knees and begged for mercy—we shot them too! It was a sight, Wales. It was somethin to see. There was big niggers an' little ones, kids and women. But the word was out—raise the black flag—no quarter for none of 'em!" He sucked in a deep rasping breath. "Anything black that moved, Wales," he said harshly, "we killed it. No matter how big it was or whether it was male or female. And I got my share. And there was a colonel there, Wales, and he got his share too. Believe me, he did! After the fighting was over, I saw one of our lieutenants come riding up past the colonel with a little nigger boy sitting behind his saddle. The colonel hollered at the lieutenant. He said, 'Take that Goddamned nigger down an' shoot 'im, or I'll have you shot myself!' And by God, he meant it, and it didn't take long for that lieutenant to put a bullet in that little nigger! And I'll tell you something else they did, too, Wales. They nailed some of them nigger soldiers to the floor in their barracks and set fire to the barracks! I'm telling you, Wales, we had ourselves a time at Fort Pillow. Fort Pillow was something!"

"You were right," Wales said tautly, bile stinging his throat again. "I hadn't heard about Fort Pillow."

"I got mentioned in dispatches," Channing said. "So did that colonel. He got made a brigadier general. He's commanding a brigade now, Wales. This one. Ours." He rocked back on his heels, rubbing his hands together. "I thought you ought to know that, Wales. I thought you'd be interested in knowing that."

"Yes," said Wales, and that was all.

Channing waited, seeming to feel that Wales must say something more. Wales just stood there looking at him.

Something flickered for the briefest instant deep in Channing's eyes, something that disturbed the gloating exultancy. Then it was gone, and his eyes gleamed spitefully.

"Maybe it don't sink in, Marsh. Maybe you can't understand it. What I'm trying to tell you is that you've overstepped yourself this time for sure. All that needs to happen is for the general to find out he's got a nigger-lovin captain in his brigade. That's all. A nigger-lovin captain that would whip a white Confederate soldier for doing something that we got mentioned in dispatches for at Fort Pillow!"

Wales said calmly, "What would he do, Vance?"

Channing stared at him. "Why," he said. "Why, he'd have you shot if he could. And if he couldn't, he'd break you and sure as hell see you in prison."

"I see," Wales said. "In other words, you could stir up a lot of trouble for me."

"A lot." Channing's voice was happy. "The general will listen to me. If I went to him with charges against you—or if Davis made a complaint an' I backed it up . . . Well, Marsh, you might find out that General Slater ain't the only one that don't like nigger lovers. After all, the Yankees used nigger troops over at Petersburg when they blew off that big mine a few weeks ago, and I didn't hear about anybody loving them up over there." His voice rose. "You see now, Marsh? You see what I mean? You see why things are going to be different now?"

Wales nodded. "You've thought about it. I've got to give you credit, Vance. I wronged you. I didn't give you credit for near as much imagination as you've got. You can be right clever when you've a mind to."

"Crap!" said Channing. "It's too late for that stuff, Wales. You're up the creek now. Flattery ain't going to help." He turned his back, strode across the room, then whirled to face Wales again. His whole body was trembling visibly with the nervous excitement of his triumph. "We're not leaving here this afternoon," he said flatly.

"Oh? Why not?" Wales still did not raise his voice.

"Because I don't want to! Because I like it here! Because—because there's something here I want and because it's the first decent shakedown we've had in six months and I aim to enjoy it!"

"Yes," Wales said heavily. "It's been a very pleasant

148

shake-down, hasn't it, Vance? Just a murder and a whipping, that's all, with a little looting thrown in for good measure. Do you really think these people want us around a minute longer than they can help?"

"Who gives a damn what they want? They got no choice! And neither have you! We're staying overnight and maybe longer if I say so!" He thrust an outstretched finger at Wales. "And if you got any objections, you better keep 'em to yourself! You'd been better off if you'd shot 'im, Wales. There's lots of explanations for something like that. But you always was too chickenhearted for your own good!"

Well, Wales thought, looking at Channing without answering. Well, well, well. He was aware that he no longer even had the headache; the fluttering in his stomach, the trembling in his muscles, the crammed confusion and indecision in his mind—these were all gone. He felt good, alert, tight, and integrated. Why, thank you, Lieutenant, he thought. Thank you very much, you arrogant little pip-squeak . . . I must really have looked bad for you to think I was *that* far gone. Slowly, deliberately, he smiled, and he watched with enjoyment the tinge of puzzled apprehension that began to spread across Channing's face at the sight of the smile.

"All right, Vance." Wales's voice was still unruffled, conversational. "You've had your say, and now, with your permission, I think I'll have mine."

He took a step toward Channing. Channing took a step backward. Wales sat down on the same corner of the desk that Channing had just vacated.

"When I whipped Davis," Wales said quietly, "I knew that it was irregular as hell. I am aware that it might cause me some trouble, maybe a lot—although I doubt that just because you and General Slater were together in an engagement once he'd run his brigade to suit your personal prejudices. But granted that he might—it was still something that had to be done, and I did it and I am prepared to take the consequences for it. So much for that.

149

"However," he went on, "I will have to go along with you on one thing. Due to the way everything's been messed up, it's going to be impossible to get away this afternoon. Likely it *will* be necessary for us to impose on Mrs. Cameron and ask permission to stay the night."

Channing looked at Wales with an odd mixture of fading triumph and rising bewilderment, his eyes blinking rapidly. Why, you still don't know that you've lost your little gambit, do you? Wales thought. Well, we'll clear that up now. He erased the smile from his face; his mouth thinned; his brows lowered; his eyes were hard and cold as he could make them.

"And if I hear any more threats out of you," he roared suddenly, "I'll arrest you, bind you hand and foot, and let you spend the night in the smokehouse!" He stood up quickly, and Channing twitched. "Is that clear, Lieutenant?"

Wales thought of a stranded catfish as he watched Channing's mouth open and close uselessly and repeatedly.

Wales took a step forward.

"I'm a captain," he said harshly, "and I'm in command here. I intend to remain in command. Remember that, Lieutenant. When I want advice from a subordinate, I'll ask for it. When we get back to Regiment, you're at liberty to do anything you damn please and tell anybody you damn please about anything you damn please—so long as you tell the truth. If you lie, I'll call you out and do my best to put a bullet in you . . . I don't give a damn if you were a gambler before the war, or a manure shoveler in a livery stable, or General Slater's personal orderly! As long as you're an officer in my company, all I want from you is for you to behave like a soldier instead of like a gloryhound who ought to be at stud instead of fighting a war. You'll either comport yourself accordingly from here on out or, by heaven, I'll have your butt and the rest of your hide with it, and no cheap-Jack threat of blackmail will keep me from it! Do I make myself clear, Lieutenant Channing?"

"Well, by God . . ." After seconds Channing finally

managed sound, his words oddly strangled. "You'll regret this, God damn you . . . I'll tell you now—"

"On the contrary," said Wales. "This is probably the only thing I've done since 1862 that I'll look backward to with satisfaction. Now, unless you have further business, Lieutenant Channing, that will be all. You are dismissed."

Channing stared at him without moving. Their eyes locked.

This is the hardest part, Wales thought. This is the hardest, because I'm not used to looking people in the eyes any more. Mustn't falter, he thought. Must have control. He made his gaze cold and hard as iron, impersonal, contemptuous, and authoritarian. He looked at Channing like a father utterly disgusted with a not very bright child.

Silence stretched between them with a taut, loaded intensity. Out in the hall the grandfather clock went: Chock. Chock. Chock. Chock.

Then Channing yielded. His eyes rolled aside. He licked his lips. "All right, Marsh," he whispered. "You got nobody to blame but yourself." Suddenly, almost desperately, he wheeled around.

"Channing," the captain said to his back.

The lieutenant stiffened, then turned.

"There's one more thing." Wales's voice was even and definite. "If I find you attempting to make love to that girl in her husband's absence, I'll take it upon myself to shoot you. That's a promise."

"Why, you—"

"It's a promise," Wales repeated softly, almost wearily.

Channing's jaw worked, but he said nothing. He spun again and stalked from the library, slamming the door behind him with a crash that echoed through the caverns of the quiet house like thunder.

In the vibrating silence afterward the clock in the hall chimed once.

Wales stared at the door for a while, a slow, wry grin spreading across his face. By God, I enjoyed that, he thought. Right and wrong, everything clear-cut. For

151

once, an issue a man doesn't have to puzzle over . . .
Then he sobered. He was aware of the trouble Channing could cause—perhaps better aware of it than the lieutenant himself was. Not only the brigade commander . . . there were plenty of men in the army, powerful men, who would react the same way. No measuring of right and wrong, who had done what; no examination—only the fact of two colors. Yes, Wales told himself. Channing had a lever with which he could raise plenty of hell.

But right now, Wales thought, reluctant to worry away his feeling of renewal, of refreshment, I'm not going to bother about that.

He looked over the books on the shelf and at last took down a copy of Carstairs' *Manual of Animal Husbandry*. He had read it before; it was a sound volume. He went back to the sofa and looked at the book for a moment and then raised his head, his eyes glinting. I really enjoyed that, he thought happily. Much refreshed, he leaned back and began to read.

11

The dinner was both lavish and perfect. The fried chicken was a rich, tender, crusty golden brown. The gravy was thick and tangy, the biscuits light, flaky, and too hot to hold, dripping with sweet-sour white butter fresh from the spring-house. The translucent, delicately patterned china, the heavy silver, the crisp, gleaming linen: these fostered in Wales a peculiar feeling of unreality amounting almost to eeriness—a nagging, uneasy sensation of having been here before. It was a feeling that was emphasized by the table talk flowing murmurously about him. Immutable tradition prohibited any controversial subject at mealtime—no war, no politics, no accusations or recriminations, nothing but polite trivia. Already the women had woven a familiar pattern of discussion—acquaintances and family histories and relationships—a pattern Wales could remember from countless meals like this at countless tables like this in an era that now seemed like the pleasant dream that often presages a nightmare. But that was in another country, he thought with a shiver. And besides, the wench is, for all practical purposes, dead.

"Yes," Mrs. Cameron was saying. "Yes, my mother's first cousin was a Rayburn. She married a Compton. George Compton of Richmond. Perhaps you know him, Lieutenant?"

Wales watched Vance Channing shake his head, politely. "No, ma'am. Although I know some Comptons in Memphis. Would they be related?"

"Oh, my, yes! George Compton's younger brother, Archibald, went to Tennessee in '38. He married a girl from Richmond, Mary Anne Dawson. They had two *delightful* children, both girls. I was so *very* fond of them. Of course, I haven't seen them since they went West; they're both married now and have children. It seems so very hard to believe, for, of course, I remember them as little girls in pigtails. Perhaps those are the Comptons?"

Channing nodded, smiling. The women, Wales thought. The world dissolving about them. Ruin confronting them. And still time, still inclination for excavating forgotten cousins. Why, when the graves open on Resurrection Day and the dead stalk forth, the last sound in the universe will probably be the voice of one female cadaver exclaiming to another, Why, you must be my cousin Betsy from Nashville!

". . . And I'm very well acquainted with Mr. Arch Compton. He and my father have been associated in several business enterprises . . ." Wales listened to Channing's suave voice almost admiringly. Cotton factor's son, Wales thought wryly. But he knows I wouldn't expose him. Let him have his lie; that part of it's no business of mine at all. Anway, I have lost my small talk. It's fortunate he has enough for both of us. He went on eating, blanking his mind to the shuttling, enveloping web of trivia, wondering what the sergeant would find hidden in the woods, now that the confusion had died down enough for the detail to get away and investigate.

"Captain Wales?"

The girl's voice brought his head up and around.

"Ma'am?"

"Won't you have some more chicken, Captain Wales? There's plenty of it."

"Yes," her mother said. "By all means, Captain. Since you will be riding soon, you will need proper nourishment."

Wales looked at them for a moment. He looked from the girl, seated at the head of the table, to the old woman opposite himself and then back at the girl. "Thank you," he said quietly. "But I'm afraid that necessity has forced me to change my plans. With your permission, Mrs. Cameron, I should like to keep my detail here overnight."

At once he could feel an air of silent tension blanketing the table.

"By all means," Mrs. Cameron said after a while. "If it is really necessary, Captain."

"I'm afraid it is. The—unpleasantness this morning got us all disorganized and delayed things considerably. And besides—"

"Besides," Mrs. Cameron cut in, "you would like to look around some more to make sure that you haven't missed anything, eh, Captain Wales?" A faint edge to her voice was the only betrayal of rancor. "Well, I can assure you that you haven't. When you leave here, we shall be destitute and the Confederacy will be richer by everything we possess. I can only hope it will hasten the end of the war."

"I can assure you that it will play its part," Wales said. He looked at her steadily. Butter wouldn't melt in your mouth, would it? he thought. No. All right, then.

"But, yes," he said, "I did want to be certain that we . . . hadn't overlooked anything."

The old woman fixed him with a cold blue stare designed to shrink him. "Do you accuse me of withholding any information, Captain?" I? her tone challenged, full of barely controlled outrage. I? Alice Cameron, lady by birth, heritage, and instinct? You dare imply that *I* could be untruthful?

"Why, no, Mrs. Cameron." Wales's voice was carefully bland and innocent. "I am sure you've been entirely open and straightforward with us."

"Well, then," the old lady said. She dropped her eyes to her plate and, with an ineffable daintiness, forked up a tiny portion of rice and consumed it with such delicacy that *eating* would have seemed a gross, crass term to apply to the action.

Wales looked sidelong at the girl. Her eyes were on her plate and she did not look up. But as he watched, her fork trembled slightly, a sliver of chicken came unimpaled and dropped on the tablecloth. The fork clinked as she made a quick, futile gesture with it. Swiftly, and still without looking up, she returned the chicken to the edge of her plate in a smooth, unobtrusive motion. Wales saw the confused red mounting beneath the pale skin of her throat. He smiled slightly and without any humor at all.

"It would be impossible for me to believe," he said, "that you would withhold anything from the Cause."

Perhaps it was the very lack of sarcasm in his voice that caused the old lady to raise her head and look at him keenly from across the table. Gently, as if it were crystal, she laid down the fork. Now, Wales thought . . . And I'll bet her expression won't even change.

"As a matter of fact," he said, "I haven't any idea that the livestock my sergeant found hidden in the woods beyond the hayfield belongs to you. But I'd appreciate it if you could tell me who does own it, because I've instructed my men to go get whatever animals are there and bring them in."

155

High in the oak foliage outside the window a cicada was making a dry, hot buzzing sound. It went on interminably, rising and falling, filling the room with its harsh, sawing rasp. Wales had been right; her expression didn't even change. He looked at her with no triumph on his face, and she looked back for a long moment with no discernible defeat; and then, without yielding, Wales lowered his eyes and, with innocent preoccupation, took a bite of chicken.

From in front of him he could feel the old woman's eyes and from his left the eyes of the girl.

The cicada buzzing drew out unceasingly with its nerve-scraping monotony.

Wales raised his head finally and looked at the stony face of the old woman directly and frankly.

"The sergeant found a path into the woods down by the spring. There was a bundle of fresh-cut hay lying in the path. Our surmise was that the hay was dropped by a slave carrying fodder to hidden livestock. If I am wrong, I shall have to beg your apology."

"I'll see that the nigra is soundly whipped for his carelessness." Mrs. Cameron's voice was like the dry sound of a dead stick breaking.

"Yes," said Wales, "I imagine you will."

"Captain Wales—" the girl began. But Vance Channing's voice interrupted.

"Great heavens, Marsh! Haven't you got the decency to take a lady's word? You—"

Wales lifted his head and looked at Channing with a slow contempt that dried up the outburst.

"Shut up," he said.

"Why—" Channing's eyes blazed. The table jumped up and banged down again with a tinkle of silver and china as he sprang to his feet, one hand dropping toward his pistol. "Why, you— Nobody tells me—"

"I did. I meant it." Wales didn't move. His voice was cool and remote and unconcerned as the tinkling of ice slivers. "Sit down, Lieutenant."

Channing's mouth opened and shut like a stranded fish's; his left hand clawed the air in a rage-filled, impotent gesture. Wales actually turned toward him for the first time. "I said SIT DOWN!" he roared.

Mrs. Cameron's voice was unruffled and gentle. "Sit down, Lieutenant Channing, if you please. He's not worth your notice. No gentleman would embarrass a lady at her own table like that."

Channing stood hesitant, hands clenching and unclenching, face a mottled red. Wales knew that Channing had no physical fear of him, but Channing knew that Wales could expose his genteel tissue of lies about his upbringing with the one despised word, *gambler*. Almost with amusement Wales observed the transparent workings of Channing's mind and finally saw him come to a decision. At last the lieutenant seated himself slowly, lips working soundlessly. Then words broke from him. "I promise you ladies," he said in a thick, strangled voice, "that Captain Wales will pay for his high-handed actions today. I promise that—"

"Oh, hush," said Wales. He turned back to Mrs. Cameron. "Actually you were very wise to disperse your animals like that, ma'am. It would certainly be a necessary precaution against a Yankee raid."

She didn't answer. Instead, with that same incredible, detached delicacy, she picked up her fork and began to eat.

Unbelievable, thought Wales admiringly. Simply unbelievable. If I had her iron control—

Presently she sighed, as if she had reached a decision. Once again she rested the fork, patting her mouth daintily with her napkin.

"Very well, Captain." Her voice was weary and full of resignation. "If that's what you want. If you want me to plead with you, to beg you to leave us something, I shall. That's what you've been after all along, isn't it? Not just to strip us, but to humble us?"

"Why should I want to humble you?"

"Because," she said, "we had the temerity to withhold part of our substance from the glorious Confederacy. Because we did not choose to throw everything away in an orgy of patriotism and join our fellow Virginians in utter ruin for the great Cause. Because we haven't seen fit to offer up Red Oaks as a burnt sacrifice to a struggle that is unmatched in the history of the world for sheer needless, stupid futility."

Wales stared at her blankly for an instant, surprised more than shocked by her frank voicing of this heresy. It was rare to hear anything like that. No matter what you think, he told himself, it's bad luck to say things like that aloud. Especially when hope and luck are all we have left—and not much of either at that . . . He said:

"You're not, I take it, a sympathizer with the Cause, then, after all."

Her shoulders lifted in a faint shrug.

"Abstractly, yes. Concretely, when it means that you rob me blind, no. In that, I think, you will find me not too different from most other loyal Confederates."

"The women who donated their wedding rings—" Wales had no desire to bait her, but he was troubled with a perverse curiosity as to how she would answer.

"A meaningless display. You can't eat a wedding ring. I will give you mine if I can get it off. Here." She raised her hand, tugged at the gold band. "This silver service on the table—you can have that, too, if that is a measure of patriotism. But to take the very food from our mouths—"

Then, quite abruptly, Wales had had enough of it. All morning long he had listened to reasoned arguments, sarcastic semantics, from himself as well as them. But he had still not made clear to them why he was here. He had not even made it clear to himself. Now he had to face the necessity of doing so. Disgust and anger at all this nit-picking flared in him, and he pushed back his chair.

"All right," he said harshly, getting to his feet, feeling his head beginning to ache again. He walked across the dining room to stare out a high window at the lush fields lying helplessly under the merciless white rape of the sun.

"All right," he said again. "Let's forget about patriotism." A Negro, plowing, moved across his vision. A dark, slow, torpid pair of blots in the sun glare, man and mule. Pushing against the earth, Wales thought,

158

spending sweat and strength to peel out behind them a six-inch deep gash in its crust. You will not even be able to see it next year, he thought. You will not even be able to tell they passed.

"Needless," he said. "Stupid. Futile. All of that. Agreed." His own voice sounded a long way off. He whirled and faced the big snowy-linened table. He could sense hate coming from the table; he sensed it and disregarded it. He was not talking for them now; he was talking for himself, explaining to himself.

"Patriotism," he said sarcastically. "The Cause. You're not any more sick of those words than I am. They're buzzard words. Sure, they sound good when you say them at a barbecue or read them in the newspapers. But when they start circling around, you can be sure somebody is going to get hurt or die. Buzzard words . . ."

He rubbed his palms up and down his trouser legs.

"I agree that the correct words are the ones you used," he said to the table. "Needless. Stupid. Futile. But it's too late now. The time to have used those words was four years ago. There was a time when they could have been used to good effect, when they would have borne some weight, when, if all of us had used them, we wouldn't be in this mess. But we didn't. And the time is past now and I'm no longer concerned with the needlessness of it, the stupidity and the futility. It's gone too far for that. All I'm concerned with," he said, "is the men who're out there fighting it. It's gone so far," he said, "that there is no way out for any of them except to keep on. It's gone so far that there's nothing left to do but fight. If anybody wants anything left at all . . .

"So they fight," he said. "Without shoes, without food, without powder. They fight. With nothing except the privilege of dying. They fight to keep alive and to salvage whatever they can of what would never even have been jeopardized if we'd used our brains earlier.

"And they die," he said. "Dying for the Confederacy is not a glorious thing, Mrs. Cameron, believe me. When a man dies in battle, he dies hard. Have you

159

ever seen a man killed violently? Have you ever heard one scream or whine or moan, seen one plunge and twist? Did you know that when a man dies his last earthly act is to befoul himself? There's no glory in it, none!"

He chopped the air with his hand. "I don't give a damn about your silver service or your wedding ring! All I give a damn about is getting as many of the men entrusted to me out of this mess alive as I can. All I want is something to eat for them, so that at least if they do die they die with a full belly. It may just be that a full belly, an ounce of strength, will make the difference between living and dying for one man, and if it does that, if it saves one life, I don't care if your whole confounded plantation disappears as mine did. I'm not concerned with property or politics any more. I'm only concerned with life! I don't give a whit for your arguments! The men need the food you have to live, and, by heaven, I'll—"

Suddenly all the fierceness and anger went out of him and there was nothing left but disgust and the feeling that he'd made a fool of himself and the certainty that he didn't care. His voice dropped to a quiet, normal tone.

"I wish," he said, "that I had some easy answers for everybody. I wish I had some tidy way out for all of us. But I don't. All I know is that out there men go hungry and limp on sore bare feet and shiver when the wind is cold and still do what they can. While you sit here and offer your silver service."

There was a long, taut silence in the room. He looked at the faces and saw no comprehension in any of the three. They don't understand, he thought helplessly. Maybe I haven't said it right. Maybe I don't understand either. . . .

He went toward the door to the kitchen runway. The room was silent. He paused there and turned.

"You won't starve," he said quietly. "This is a rich land. You won't have ham every time you want it and bacon for breakfast and all the coffee you can drink.

But don't be so afraid. You won't starve." He turned and went out the door, across to the kitchen, out the back door, and down the steps and, wanting only to get away from them, out into the yard.

12

"There was a mess of critters down there in the woods," the sergeant said. "Six mules, eight cows, two heifer calves, a two-year-old bull, a couple of saddle horses, and another pen full of hawgs. I reckon they figured if they moved all the stock down there, somebody might start lookin for hit, but if they left a good part of it up here, what they had down there wouldn't be missed. They're pretty coony. I got Boomer an' Brazos drivin the critters up."

"Good work, Mac." Wales stood in an attitude of tension, his thumbs hooked in the front of his belt, pulling down at it. He was aware of the sergeant looking at him keenly.

"You look a mite upset, Capn."

Wales spat.

The sergeant shook his head. "It's a nasty business, ain't hit? But the boys'll sho bless you for bringin 'em some meat."

"Yes," Wales said.

"Troubled?" the sergeant asked. A faint breeze riffled leaves of the big oak in the back yard under which they stood.

"No," Wales said. "Not what you could call real trouble. Just these people. They get on my nerves. And Channing . . ."

"Like you said," the sergeant murmured with gentle irony, "he's a good fightin man."

"I'm sick to my belly with him," Wales said.

The sergeant leaned back against the tree trunk, careless, his face thoughtful. Looking at him, Wales wondered: Lord, what would I do without him? He searched the lined and weathered and long-scarred face of the sergeant—a countenance bereft of illusion or the capacity for surprise or even rage, a face that had seen everything. There was no warning expression on the sergeant's face when he made his next matter-of-fact suggestion.

"Well, Capn, accidents happen on picket duty. There ain't a thing in the world you got to do to git rid of him but send the lieutenant to inspect the guard tonight."

Perhaps at one time Wales would have felt shock at such an offer. Now he did not even feel any surprise. He shook his head as matter-of-factly as the sergeant had made the proposition.

"No, Mac. I don't want anything like that to happen. We'll try to live with him till we get back to Regiment. Then I'll see what I can do to get him transferred."

"All right, Capn. Jest tryin to save you some trouble, that's all."

Wales sighed. "Well, I'm used to trouble, Mac."

"Might be you've had too much trouble, Capn," the sergeant said unexpectedly.

Wales looked at him sharply.

"No more than the rest of you boys."

The sergeant shook his head.

"Naw. You've had more. You was brought up to think, Capn. You use your mind, and the things you got to do ride you more than they ride most other men. You worry about what you do too much. You cain't keep that up for very long, Capn. It'll drive you crazy if you do. Think about how hungry you are if you want to, or how tired you are, or how much you hate the Goddamned army. But don't go to thinkin about right and wrong, Capn, because if you do that, it'll drive you clean outn your mind."

162

He moved uneasily.

"We git along purty good together, don't we, Capn?"

"Fine, Mac."

The sergeant bit his lower lip.

"You got confidence in me, ain't you, Capn?"

"Absolutely, Mac."

"All right." The sergeant rubbed one booted ankle with the other booted foot. "How about doin me a favor then?"

"I don't know. I'll try. What is it?"

The sergeant hesitated before he answered. Then he grinned faintly, but his eyes were serious.

"Send Lieutenant Channin out to pick daisies or somethin—anythin to git him outa the way. Then you take the afternoon off and let me handle things while you git some rest."

"Huh?" Wales was startled by this.

"I mean, hell, I can take care of things. I'll git everything lined up for us to move out in the mornin. You been pushin yourself too hard, Capn. Why don't you jest let me do the worryin this afternoon and you jest take time off." He made a self-conscious gesture toward the plantation house. "I mean, this is the first time in quite a spell that you've had a chance to live like you were used to before the war. I thought you might enjoy takin time to get the feel of it again."

Wales was touched and something inside him trembled and threatened to break loose, but he clamped it down. He looked at the sergeant's expressionless face and felt a burning in the corners of his eyes. He swallowed hard and then grinned.

"Thanks, Mac. But there's too much to do. Besides —you need an afternoon off much as I do."

The sergeant spat. "Hell, I don't worry about anything. I let you do that for me. That's why I hate for anything to happen to you. I might hafta go to worryin full time myself, and I ain't used to nothin like that."

"Well, much obliged, Mac. But I'll—"

The sergeant squatted down suddenly with his back against the tree. He reached out and plucked a stem of grass and put it between his teeth and then he looked up at the captain. Wales saw that his eyes had narrowed; it might be because now he was looking into the sun.

"Now, listen," the sergeant said. "I ain't only thinkin about you. I'm thinkin about what these other men are entitled to also."

"I don't follow you," snapped Wales, inexplicably nettled.

"Now don't git your back up," the sergeant said. "You an' I been through a lot together in this outfit, and most of these other men been with us every jump of the way. I'm sayin that if you're going to keep on leadin 'em, you owe it to 'em to get your mind kinda cleared and kind of git some sort of checkrein on yourself." He cleared his throat. "God damn it, Capn, you're frazzled out. You're jest plain damn tired. A man's got his limits—that ain't nothin to be ashamed of. And when he's reached those limits, he's entitled to kind of set down and git hisself back together again. That's all in the world I'm trying to git you to do." He licked his lips. "All of us been together so damn long. Christ knows, if we don't look out for each other, nobody else will."

"I see." Wales's voice was full of cold anger. "You don't think I'm fit even to lead the company any more —that it?"

"No," the sergeant said flatly. "I don't know anybody I'd trust to lead us any better than you do. That's jest the point. It wouldn't be fair to us for you to let anything happen to yourself. God knows"—he laughed shortly—"wouldn't we be in some fix if Lieutenant Channing was to take over the troop!"

Wales stood rigid, unanswering. He did not know whether to be embarrassed, ashamed, or angry. He swallowed hard.

"The men would like to see you do it, Capn," the sergeant said, coming erect. "God knows, I don't want anything to happen to any of 'em that I could keep from happening, and I know you don't either. It would be a favor to everybody, sir."

Still Wales remained motionless, unanswering. There

was anger in him, but he could feel a stir of response to the sergeant's logic as well. Moreover, what the sergeant was suggesting was undeniably an alluring prospect. An afternoon of solitude, a chance to seclude himself, free of responsibility. It would be the first chance in months to collect his wits, to try to reason things out and get a grip on himself. He thought of the dim coolness of the big library in the house, and it beckoned. Wales rubbed his face thoughtfully.

"In other words," he said slowly, "you're suggesting this for your own selfish purposes."

The sergeant grinned. "You're damn right. I know you ain't goan git my ass shot off for me if you can help it, but I can't guarantee a damn thing about anybody else I might wind up takin orders from."

"All right," Wales said at last. "You're a smooth talker, damn you. I'll give it a try."

The grin on MacLeod's scarred face widened. "Sho. Now if you'll jest send Channin out to reconnoiter or somethin."

"I'll do something with him."

"All right. I'll have everything loaded, counted, and worked out by dark. I'll bring you your inventories then. In the meantime, you forgit about it."

"I'll do my best," Wales said.

"That's all a man kin ask." The sergeant grinned and turned to go.

Wales found Channing in the parlor of the plantation house, and the two men stood alone in the exquisitely furnished room. The sun rayed in through half-pulled draperies and struck gleams from rubbed wood and immaculately polished furniture and the dainty, decorated, translucent pieces of china that, carefully arranged on every flat surface, were the feminine grace notes in the effect of the room. Neither of the booted, spurred men was at ease here; they faced each other with a jumpy tension, part of which came from the fear of colliding with a table and bringing down a fractured shower of irreplaceables. Wales realized this and grinned wryly, thinking: Nobody can say that we don't have respect for other people's property.

Then he realized that Channing was answering him. "I don't understand it, Wales. What are you trying to do—buy me off with one piddling afternoon of free time?"

"I'm not trying to buy you off with anything. Hasn't it sunk through to you yet that I don't give a damn about your threats? All I'm telling you is that you have the afternoon to yourself. What you do with it is your own business, so long as you stay out of the sergeant's way and don't cause any trouble."

Channing looked at him with open contempt. "You're a softhearted son of—"

"Watch that," Wales interrupted flatly, tonelessly.

"All right. But you're too soft, Marsh Wales. You'll never amount to anything. You'll never even get out of this war."

Wales looked at him calmly. "A lot of people won't."

"But you for certain," Channing said. "You're your own bad luck." He turned his back on Wales and stalked abruptly from the room. Wales watched him go, lifted a hand helplessly, then let it drop. He stood irresolutely for a moment. Then, idly, he looked about him, walking from table to table, picking up a vase here and examining its decoration, lifting a carefully placed book there, opening it to the place marked by the big red satin bookmark that seemed to be a decorative fixture in each book, and then closing it.

He was aware that perspiration was running down his flanks. Good Lord, he thought, it's hot in here. Maybe it will be cooler in the library.

It was, a little. And it was blessedly dim. Wales found the old sofa again and slumped on it, grateful for the dimness, swathing himself in it as if it were a blanket. He stretched out on the sofa, closing his eyes, feeling his very bones ache with fatigue.

A short nap, he thought vaguely. Before I start to think, I'll take a short nap to clear my mind.

Lying thus, he sank into half-slumber, not alert, not

166

completely unconscious. He was vaguely aware of little creaking, popping sounds in his ears, as if his entire skull, vascular system, and brain were settling the way a house settles in the evening. His body felt light; he felt himself merging with the dimness. Somewhere in the house he faintly heard the sound of a woman talking; it sounded leagues away and it rose and fell in feminine tones, lulling him. He sighed.

He did not know how long he had lain there before it began. It was not even a dream—not exactly a dream, not quite a hallucination. But she emerged out of the darkness. One moment she was not there; then she was, her bright yellow hair loosened and falling about her shoulders as if she were ready for bed, her skin shining white and fair in the murkiness. She came toward him, arms outstretched, lips forming inaudibly a single word that he knew was his name.

Something filled his chest almost to bursting, an emotion that congested everything in him. He tried to rise, to spring up and meet her, but he seemed chained to the sofa. His limbs would not respond to his will. Panic overwhelmed him that she would go before he could seize her, but not a muscle of his would move. His throat worked futilely, trying to bellow a plea for her to wait; no sound came. Then he summoned all his faculties for one intense effort as she stood there beckoning, her flesh as tangible, as real, as solid as his own. He made a terrific effort of will, and then he was coming up off the sofa. In that instant she disappeared, and in another he was completely awake; the library was empty, and he was sitting there drenched with sick, cold sweat.

"Oh, my God," he said aloud.

He sat there in the unbearably vacant dimness for a long time, his body trembling. I have got to find some way to free myself of her, he kept thinking hopelessly. I've got to find some way to get her out of my mind so that I can be whole again. I can't stay this way, completely in her power, so that even a dream of her racks me to pieces. I can't. I can't.

But how? he thought. What can I do? Pray?

167

No, he thought. That wouldn't do any good either. He stood up. I've seen too much to do that, he thought. Death claiming this man, sparing that one, with no rhyme, no reason, no pattern except one of senseless destruction. How can I pray to a bull in a china shop? No, there would be no use in it. If He exists, He finished with men a long time ago; any fool can see He doesn't give a continental what happens to them any more.

But what, then? He rubbed his head with his hands. Destruction. All destruction. Everything I had gone, and no reason to it, none at all. But just as if someone had shaken a bunch of names around in a hat and pulled one out and said, *Him. He's the one.* As senseless as that . . .

Somewhere there is a key to it, a key that would free me. A reason for it. If I just knew a reason for it. Sometimes I think I have almost got it, but it vanishes before I can grasp it, just as she vanished just now. If I could only find that key, that something, whatever it is . . . If I could only be rid of her, if there were just some way I could take a broom and sweep everything out of my mind and get it clean and ready to start new and fresh.

He mopped his forehead with his sleeve. Still trembling, he sat down again. He sat immobile in the dimness for a long time, but his thoughts would not order themselves. They scurried around and around in his skull in weird patterns until he wanted to scream. In desperation, then, he arose and wandered across the room to the tall shelves of books and took down the first one he reached. It was *Guy Mannering* and, lying down again, he opened it. He had read it before, so when it opened in the middle he began there.

But it was hard to see in the dim light. In only a few moments the desired effect was achieved; his eyelids seemed dragged lower and lower by their own weight. At last, when the book slid from his hand to the floor, he did not stir; he was alseep, this time dreamlessly.

13 _____

"I got everything figgered out," Corporal Dalton said, "but what you aim to do about them air pigs."

The sergeant grinned. Most of the work was done now and things had pretty well slacked off; the sun was beginning to heel down the sky and some of the heat was gone. Not much, but any was a blessing.

"Why, hell, Dalt, ain't you never drove hawgs?"

"You damn right I've drove hawgs." Dalton snorted. "That's how come I'm wonderin what you aim to do about 'em. If we was to try to drive them air hawgs back to Regiment, we ain't goan git back afore next Easter."

"Well, that might not be so bad neither," the sergeant said. He and Dalton were lounging against a big oak tree in the side yard; around them the other men sprawled, resting on the lawn.

"You cain't put 'em in the wagon, neither," Dalton said. "First place, they's too many of 'em. Second place, you hawg-tie a pig and put him in a wagon withoutn no water in this here weather an' he'll be daid afore you gone ten mile."

"Sho," the sergeant grunted. "Dalton, the trouble with you is, you got no imagination. What you reckon I had the men hunt up them two extra wagons and all them boards an' nails for? It ain't no trouble to fix a wagon so's we kin pen 'em up in it without hawg-tyin 'em—where the fun's goan come in is gittin those bastards in the wagon."

"You goan try to do that this evenin?"

"I reckon not. If we jest git the wagon fixed this

169

evenin, I expect we can catch up them hawgs in the morning an' git 'em loaded right quick."

"That's a mean job," Dalton said. "I seed a ole sow take a man's arm plumb off one time when he was tryin to load her."

"It ain't easy," the sergeant acknowledged. "But I reckon twixt us an' the niggers we can git it done."

"You do it," Dalton said without enthusiasm. "I'll *soo*pervise."

"You will, my— Whoa up," the sergeant said. "What we got here?"

The boy came through the notch the driveway made in the hedge and stopped and looked about him. He saw the soldiers on the lawn and he stood very still. Probably eleven or twelve, he was small for his age, and he looked smaller still because of the size of the big old smoothbore musket he was lugging with both hands.

The sergeant squinted at him and rubbed the side of his face thoughtfully. He seemed to be trying to remember something. After a moment he slapped his hand against his thigh. "Smithfield," he said under his breath. "That's hit. Smithfield."

"Who?"

"Nemmind," the sergeant said. He straightened up, almost gingerly. His hand pressed Dalton back. "You stay here," he said softly. "There might be some fire in that air thing." He began to move toward the boy slowly and carefully, walking springily on the balls of his feet, as if he were prepared to jump in a hurry.

The boy watched him come. His gaunt child's face, snubnosed and sunburned under a mat of indeterminate-colored hair, went pale; the washed-out blue eyes stood out very clearly in it. The sergeant, MacLeod, saw the boy swallow hard and lick his lips, and then he saw the boy raise the old flintlock and bring it into line, centered fairly on his, the sergeant's, belly.

The sergeant lifted his hands part way to his shoulders. He called softly, "All right, Smithfield. You hole yo fiah. I ain't meanin no harm."

The boy did not answer. The sergeant saw the gun

170

barrel waver, but he knew it was not from indecision; it was because the boy's arms were inadequate to support it steadily. The sergeant stopped where he was.

"You heah me, Smithfield?"

"How you know my name?" There was a quaver in the child's reedy voice.

"I know yo name," the sergent said. He frowned. "I know whut you come for too."

Behind the sergeant Dalton called, "Mac, you bin took prisoner?"

"You hush," the sergeant called back without turning his head. "An' you stay where you are. I doan crave no two-ounce punkin ball drove through my belly."

He looked at the boy. There was defiance on the boy's face, the lower lip thrust out. The sergeant's gaze traveled up and down the youth, from the dusty, neutral-colored hair down to the widespread bare feet, toes digging into the ground fiercely. The sergeant saw the ragged, unpatched homespun shirt, the equally tattered pants, held in place only by a length of frayed rope; and the sergeant swallowed hard against the emotion that all at once filled him, and he knew that he was going to do whatever he could for the boy. He lowered his hands gently. "All right, Smithfield. You among friends. You can put down yo weapon."

"I wanta see yo colonel," the boy said, not lowering the gun.

"Capn. Not colonel."

"Whatever he is. He the man what took our calf. I wanta see 'im."

"You cain't see 'im right now. He's in the house, restin up. He's plum tired."

"I doan care," the boy said doggedly. "I aim to see 'im."

"All right," the sergeant said. "I allow I can send for 'im. But first you gotta put down that gun."

Something glinted deep in the boy's eyes, a sudden comprehension. Instead of lowering the gun, he tugged the muzzle of it upward. The sergeant looked with fascination at the firing mechanism, the raised lock with its clamped flint, the priming pan.

171

"You the man what beat up my momma, ain't you?" the boy asked softly. "She said the man what beat her up had them things on his sleeves."

"Son, I didn't beat up yo momma," the sergeant said, and then he stepped forward quickly and his hand closed around the barrel of the musket just as the boy pulled the trigger. The lock came down with a dry click, and the sergeant jerked the gun free from the boy's grasp.

"You gotta remember to charge your primin pan," he said tightly. "This here now gun won't shoot without you put some powder in the primin pan." Practicedly, while the boy stood there, frozen, his face blank with astonishment and dismay, the sergeant whisked the ramrod from beneath the barrel and fished out a patch and upended the musket so that the lead ball rolled out of it. The sergeant bent and scooped it up. "Heah," he said, handing it to the boy. "Lead's powerful hard to come by nowadays." He laid the musket down. "Now," he said, "you kin have that back, but doan you lemme see you loadin hit!"

The boy remained standing there rigidly. The sergeant saw tears forming in the corners of his eyes; while the sergeant watched, one welled loose and rolled down the youth's cheek. The boy whisked it away with the back of his hand and his lower lip trembled.

"Now," the sergeant said, squatting down in front of the boy. "Now mebbee we kin talk business."

"I—I come atter our calf y'all stole."

"Sho." The sergeant made a motion with his hand. "Son, we didn't steal that calf. We paid yo momma for hit. We bought hit to feed the Confederate soldiers with."

"I brought yo money back!" The boy rammed his hand in his shirt and jerked out a roll of bills. "Momma say she didn't want yo dirty no-good Confedrat money! I brought hit back!" He stuck out his hand. "Heah!"

The sergeant shook his head. "Smithfield, I cain't take that money back. Now, lemme explain somethin, son. Yo daddy's in the army, ain't he? Well, now, we need that calf to feed soldiers jest like yo daddy is.

The soldiers is powerful hungry. You wouldn't want yo daddy to go hungry, now, would you?"

The boy stared at him, unspeaking. After a while he said, "Momma says my daddy's in Nawth Calina."

"It doan make no difference. He's fightin Yanks same as we are, an' we're fightin 'em same as he is. We all in this fight together. Now, son, you—"

"Doan't call me son!" the boy burst out. It was almost a wail. *"I want our calf!"*

The sergeant bit his lip helplessly. He rubbed his palms on his knees. "Dalton!" he bellowed savagely.

The corporal ambled over, his face a mixture of curiosity and enjoyment. "You havin trouble, Mac?"

"Doan you mind about my trouble. You git yo ass up there and knock on the front door an' tell the Capn I need 'im out heah. Dammit, when I said I'd see to things this afternoon, I never looked for nothin like this."

"Sho," Dalton said easily. "You jest plain outnumbered, ain't you, Mac?" He chuckled and sauntered around the house to the veranda.

"All right, boy," the sergeant said. "Now you come with me. Us'll go around in front an' you can confab with the Capn." He grinned without humor. "I spect you'll make a better impression if you let me carry this," he said and picked up the musket. "Come on," he said, and took Smithfield by the hand and half led him, half dragged him around to the front of the house.

Wales, not certain of what had awakened him, rubbed his eyes. When he opened them, he was staring at the dimness under the ceiling in the library. He lay there for a second or two, trying to gather his wits, then he instantly sat up as he became aware of another presence in the room.

The voice of the girl, Duane Hollander, said, from out of the late-afternoon gloom:

"Are you awake now, Captain Wales?"

"Ummm."

"I'm sorry I had to interrupt your nap. But one of

your soldiers came to the door. He said they needed you out in front. Something urgent, I think."

"Umn?" Wales stood up, awake now, a tight knot of foreboding in his belly. "What is it?"

"I don't know." Her voice was cool and disinterested. Wales could see her silhouette; she was sitting very erectly and formally in the chair across the room. "He didn't say."

"All right." Wales's hand instinctively dropped to his hip and reassured itself on the butt of his pistol. He knuckled at his eyes again and ran his hand through his hair. "If you'll excuse me," he said and went out of the library. He was aware that the girl was following him.

Emerging on the veranda, he blinked at the westering sunlight. His eyes swept the drive before the house and came to rest on the sergeant and the boy standing in front of the steps, the sergeant holding a giant old smoothbore musket in one hand, his other wrapped around the boy's wrist.

". . . an' I reckon he'll be reasonable," the sergeant was saying.

"Mac." Wales's voice was peremptory. "What's the trouble?"

The sergeant lifted his head; his grin was embarrassed and not very mirthful. Wales came halfway down the steps. Gently the sergeant pushed the boy forward a pace.

"This chap here needed to see you, Capn. I had a little talk with him fust, but 'pears like I couldn't satisfy 'im. I figgered maybe you'd better talk with 'im. His name's Smithfield."

Smithfield. Wales's mind raced back, orienting itself. He had a quick, vivid memory of a work-ravaged woman clinging frantically to a calf as the sergeant hauled both of them in on the rope. He remembered her scream. All at once he felt sweat start from his palms. He clenched his fists. God damn it, he thought sickly. Won't they ever leave me alone? Are they going to haunt me forever? An unreasoning irritation flared within him.

174

That should have all been over this morning, he thought fiercely. He frowned at the boy.

"Well?"

The boy looked up at him. Not quite emaciated, Wales noted, observing the skin stretched tightly over the cheekbones, the hollows around the pale blue eyes. But not far from it . . . He expected to feel the relentless pity gripping him again, but it did not. There was no fear on the boy's face; it was taut and half-sullen with defiance, and instead of pity, the irritation deepened.

"I come atter my calf," the boy said.

"I tried to tell 'im, Capn," the sergeant put in. "I done tried to explain to 'im how bad the army needs that calf—how bad they got to have everything they can git."

Wales was suddenly aware of the faint odor of lilacs. He turned his head and saw that the girl had come out on the veranda, too, and was standing on the step behind him. His lips tightened angrily. This was none of her business. This was none of anybody's business. Damn it, they were all trying to hem him in again. He'd been through all this before; he'd explained it all to everybody as best he could. Now he was sick of it. He was sick to his gut with it. He said harshly:

"I'm sorry, boy. We paid your mother for that calf and that's the best we can do. We've got to take it, and I paid her a good price."

The boy thrust a roll of bills forward. "I brung yo money back!" he yelled fiercely.

"I can't take it back," Wales said. "Sergeant," he said, "send this boy on back where he came from. You can have one of the men ride him home on the back of his horse." He tried to soften his tone a little. "How'd you like a ride on a cavalry horse, boy?"

The boy suddenly jerked his arm free of the sergeant's grasp. "I ain't goin home!" he hollered. "I come atter our calf an' you better give it to me, damn yo ole time! You done made my momma cry an' you done beat her up, an' if I git my gun back I'll kill you, damn you!

175

Now you gimme my calf, you hear! You gimme my calf!"

Wales took a step forward in a flare of anger. "I'll give you a rawhiding, you pup, if you don't hush your mouth!" He had the feeling that someone else was in his body now, someone bereft of good nature or forbearance, somebody drained of patience.

The girl's voice was taut and outraged in his ear. "You're a good one at whipping the helpless, aren't you, Captain?" The lilac perfume was strong in his nostrils, then faded, as she moved past him down the steps. She came to the boy and put her hands on his shoulders. Wales saw that her face was very white.

The boy stood rigidly. The girl looked down at him. "Aren't you Smithfield Strikeleather?" she asked. The boy nodded mutely.

"What is all this about?" Her voice was gentle, sympathetic. "What's the trouble, Smithfield?"

The boy looked up at her for a moment, then his defiant lip began to tremble. Wales saw twin streaks of water coursing down his cheeks, but there were no sobs. The child's voice quavered.

"These heah soldiers done stole our calf, ma'am. They come to our house whilest I was out plowin this morning an' they beat up my momma an' went off with our bull calf . . . an' . . . an' he was all the meat we-unses had. That ole gun of mine ain't no good for huntin rabbits an' my momma's been cryin all afternoon an' sayin she didn't know how we was going to git along. I couldn't stand that cryin. I jist cain't stand to hear my momma cry. I come to git my calf an' I want it back. We been savin that calf for winter. We been livin offa poke sallit an' hoecake for a long time now jist so we'd have meat for winter. My little brother, he cries most every night in his sleep, he's so hongry, but we didn't dast eat that calf 'for winter. I want that calf, ma'am. Hit belongs to us an' *I got to git hit back!*"

The girl raised her hands from his shoulders. She stood there with them poised for a moment and then she turned toward Wales a face white as bone. "You're

176

going to give him his calf back, aren't you?" she asked softly.

"No," said Wales flatly.

The girl swallowed. She compressed her lips in a tight line. "If you're worried about us," she said carefully, her voice taut and controlled, "you needn't be. You can give him his calf back and we won't use that to plead our own cause."

"No," said Wales.

Still her voice was under precise control. "You are not fighting children, are you, Captain Wales?"

He swallowed the anger burning his throat. "I'm fighting Federals," he said heavily. "So are my men. They've got to eat to do that, and I wouldn't have taken the calf if we hadn't needed it."

The girl's voice lost some of its control. It was tinged with shrillness.

"But you heard what he said, didn't you? *His little brother cries at night!* Don't you——"

Wales shook his head and turned to go. The anger was beginning to die a little. At any moment it might cease to be enough protection for him. At any moment all of this might start getting through the anger and reaching him. If it did, he knew that he would not have stamina enough to cope with it.

"Cap'n." The sergeant's voice brought him around.

"Yes." Wales's voice was ugly.

The sergeant moved past the boy and ascended two steps of the veranda. He turned his beardy face up toward the captain. His voice was low and earnest.

"Cap'n." He raised his hands helplessly and let them fall. "Sir, thet calf ain't nothing but a rack of bones nohow." His tongue ran over his lips. "There ain't a man here that'd complain did you let the boy have hit back."

Wales looked down at the sergeant. The sergeant's eyes met his, not demanding, only clear and respectful and reasonable. Wales and the sergeant looked at each other for a moment, and then Wales abruptly swung his eyes away.

"I can't set a precedent," he muttered. "I'm not going

177

to have these people after me too. They would be, no matter what they say. For Christ's sake, can't you understand that?" Even the sergeant too . . . he thought. The anger blazed up again. "I said no!" he yelled.

The sergeant's beard stood out, dark and matted, against the white of his face. He did not take his eyes from the captain for a moment, and then he rubbed his hand along his chin. Without further speech he backed down the steps to the drive.

"Oh," the girl began, "I wish—"

Still in the grip of that burst of savagery, Wales swung on her. "You wish . . ." he grated. "You wish . . ." He flung out an arm. "Whose land do these people live on, anyway? These Strikeleathers—who owns their land?"

"We do," the girl said quickly. "It's our land. They squatted there five years ago and we let them stay."

"And his little brother cries at night," Wales said bitingly. His lips curled in a sneer as he faced her. "And that upsets you." His voice dropped to a lower register of profound contempt. "Until we got here," he said remorselessly, "you were pretty well fixed. Did you ever think to find out whether or not his little brother was crying at night? Did you ever offer to do anything about it? Or did you just assume that everybody was as lavishly supplied as you?"

He saw the face of the girl go very white. Her hands laced together, fingers working nervously.

"How many hams have you sent over to them?" Wales asked inexorably. "Or chickens? Or even eggs?"

The girl's throat worked, but she did not answer.

Wales nodded. He made no other comment.

The sergeant moved over to Dalton. "I reckon you better git yore horse," he began.

"Wait!" The girl looked at Wales for an instant with her green eyes blazing incandescently. Then she swung toward the sergeant.

"Those chickens you've got in the coops on the wagon—you send one of your men and tell him to get two—no, four of them—and tie their feet together and bring them to this boy!"

The sergeant stared at her for a moment and then turned his head toward Wales.

There was silence for a full minute. Then, deliberately, Wales nodded. "Two of them," he said. "No more, Sergeant. Be sure to strike them off your inventory."

The sergeant whirled toward the men, lined up at the edge of the drive like an audience at a theatrical. "Boomer!" he thundered. "Git up heah!"

The boy looked back and forth at the girl and the sergeant in confusion. "What about my calf?" he asked again, his voice a quavering mixture of belligerency and fright.

Duane Hollander knelt in front of him, her hands on his shoulders. She looked into his face. "The captain won't give you back your calf, Smithfield," she said. "Now, don't. It won't do any good to carry on. But don't you worry, Smithfield. There's a soldier coming with some chickens for you. Now there. Stop that and listen to me. There's something I want you to tell your mother, and it's very important. Are you listening? Good. Tell your mother not to worry. Tell her that Miss Duane will see to it that your mother and you and your baby brother won't go hungry. Tell her Miss Duane said she'd see to it somehow. Do you understand?"

He nodded blankly, confused.

"That's a good boy." She patted his shoulders and stood up. There was a shrill squawking from behind the house; in a moment Boomer appeared carrying two chickens, their feet lashed together. He handed the chickens to the sergeant, and the sergeant handed them to the boy, who took them gingerly, batting his eyes, still bewildered.

"Now," Duane Hollander said gently. "Now, Smithfield, one of these soldiers will carry you home."

"No!" the boy jerked away from beneath her hand. "No, I ain't goan ride with no damn soldier. I'll walk!" He turned fiercely to the sergeant. "Gimme my gun!" he yelled. He grabbed the big musket from the sergeant's hand. He clamped the stock of it between his

179

knees and looped the cord that bound the two squawking chickens together around the barrel. Then he raised the gun and put it over his shoulder, like an infantryman on parade, with the two chickens hanging head down from the muzzle, screaming and beating their wings.

"You remember what I told you to tell your mother!" Duane Hollander called after him as he whirled around. He made no answer but strode off down the driveway, his thin back defiantly erect, the chickens fluttering wildly. They watched him as he moved off, having a hard time balancing the heavy gun. Then the girl turned her eyes on Wales, and they were twin green cold flames.

Wales said nothing.

The girl made a sound deep in her throat. Then she suddenly ran blindly up the steps. Wales heard the rustle of her garments, caught again that lilac fragrance as she went past him. Behind him he heard the front door slam.

Mopping sweat from his forehead, Wales looked down at the sergeant without any expression on his face, hoping that he would not have to meet the sergeant's eyes.

"You need me for anything else?" Wales asked the sergeant coldly.

Mutely the sergeant shook his head. He did not look at Wales.

"All right," Wales said. "Carry on." He turned then and went the rest of the way up the steps, across the veranda, and into the house.

14

Corporal Dalton and the sergeant fell into step together on the track leading to the barn. The sergeant was walking slowly, almost wearily, and there was no spring in the awkward, plow hand's walk of the corporal either. They moved along thus, silently, for several moments before Dalton grunted a few words.

"That kinda made me feel funny," he said.

The sergeant did not answer.

Dalton's fingers played idly with his mustache. Then he went about the business of pulling a twist of tobacco from his pocket and dusting the lint and grime off it and biting off a chunk. He held the tobacco toward the sergeant in an offering gesture, and the sergeant shook his head. "Unh-unh," he muttered.

Dalton nodded and put the twist back and spat a long greenish-brown, satisfactory stream. "All right," he said around the chew.

"I reckon hit's all in the business," he said after a while.

"Uh-huh."

Dalton looked at the sergeant. His eyes narrowed down to thin, shrewd slits. "You're thinkin powerful hard about somethin."

"Naw," the sergeant said.

"Horse apples," Dalton grunted. "I know you, Mac. You got somethin on yo mind. I been around you too long. You jest like a ole woman about this outfit, an I reckon I know when they's somethin upset you."

The sergeant slowly raised his head and turned to look at Dalton.

"How would you like to mind yo own Goddamned business?" he asked quietly and fiercely.

Dalton's mustaches fluttered. His lips clamped shut.

After a while the sergeant said, "Why, the pore sonofabitch couldn't even look me in the eyes."

Dalton paid him no attention.

They walked the rest of the way to the barn in silence.

Wales went back to the library, but he did not want to stay there any longer. He did not want to sit down and be alone and have time to think; he did not want to do any more thinking at all. He paced restlessly back and forth across the room, feeling a remorseless nervous energy, a massive tension, building up within him. He had the weird impression that his entrails had fused into one gigantic coiled clock spring: click by click events were winding that spring tighter and tighter and tighter. He wondered how much more slack remained; how many more clicks could the spring sustain before it exploded, fracturing the vessel that held it and sending parts flying wildly. He shook his head in an attempt to clear it of all the ominous ragtags of incoherent thoughts and forebodings jamming his brain, and then, driven by that unbearable tension, he stalked out of the library, down the hall, through the dining room, and out through the dogtrot into the back yard.

He noticed then that he must have slept nearly two hours before the girl had awakened him. The afternoon was drawing on; there was a subtle change in the light. The heat was still oppressive, but it was the airlessness that made it so, the lack of breeze, rather than the hard, direct pounding of the sun that had made the earlier part of the day so miserable. Wales paused at the edge of the back lawn and squinted at the sky. In the southwest clouds had begun to join to form the first heaped structure of a building thunderhead. Wales nodded. Likely rain before night, he thought. Crops could use it . . .

That ordinary thought made him feel better; he could

feel the spring unwind a click or two. He began to walk, very rapidly.

It felt good to stretch his legs. It felt good to do something swiftly and violently, even walking. He cut across a field of peas, the crop of these almost finished. If this was mine, he thought, I would turn the hogs in here after one more picking . . . Only, he thought then, they won't have any hogs left. He walked on as fast as he could.

Sodden with sweat, he reached the end of the field and entered a grove of pines. His breath was coming harder now, but his pace did not slow as he passed among the trees. The pines were second-growth, not very large, and the ground in here was littered with slashings. It was hard going. The limbs of the live trees whipped about his face and body as he shoved his way through the woods; the dry stubs of the slashings caught at his boots and trousers like claws. Artillery would set this on fire in a hurry, he thought automatically, remembering the wounded men burning in the woods fires at Chancellorsville. The sweat on his forehead felt cold. He looked for a way out of the pines and saw daylight to one side and emerged on a slope. To his right he could see the hog pens of the plantation and above them the slave quarters and other outbuildings. He went down the slope and into the swale, past the pens, and up the lane toward the slave quarters.

By the time he had reached the quarters he was almost completely breathless. His shirt and trousers were saturated with perspiration; his face was sticky with spider webs from the woods. He rubbed his face with his sleeve and leaned against the back of one of the little brick buildings to rest.

In a moment or two he became aware of voices within the slave hut, and he tensed as he thought he recognized one.

"Here, Tansy. I think this will fit her."

"Yas'm, Miz Duane. Dat a mighty fine dress. She sho be laid out purty in dat dress."

"I hope it will be all right. Mayrene was a good girl."

183

"Yas'm, she a good girl. Po sweet lil thing. She sho will lay out purty in dat dress, dough."

Wales heard Duane Hollander's voice drop until it was barely audible. "How's Yance?"

"He takin it powerful hard, Miz Duane. Powerful hard."

Wales heard the girl say, "Yance?"

There was an inaudible murmur. It went on for some time. The girl said finally, "I'm sure he will. I'll see to it."

The murmur went on a little longer. The girl said, "Yes. I wouldn't wait any longer than that. It's terribly hot."

"Nome," Tansy's voice said. "She woan keep atall in dis kinda weather."

If the girl made any answer to that, Wales did not hear it. He straightened up, mopping his brow with his sleeve again. He walked around the building, wanting to get away from here before he encountered the girl again, and, stepping out onto the street between the cabins, he almost collided with her.

She drew back abruptly. "Oh! It's you! You—startled me."

"I'm sorry," Wales said briefly.

The girl looked at him questioningly. "I was taking a walk," he said.

"Oh," she said. Silence hung awkwardly between them for a moment and then she said, "Were you going back to the house?"

Wales nodded. Without any further conversation they fell in step together then. She did not take his arm this time.

They passed a cluster of slaves gathered in the street. Wales looked at them curiously. They were all men, grouped around two sawhorses across which fresh, raw pine boards, sap oozing from the grain, gleamed in the slanting light. Wales heard one of them say to another, "Heah. You saw awhile. I'se tiahed."

Wales bit his lip. "Funeral this afternoon?"

"Yes. This evening, just about sundown. Whenever they get the coffin ready. They had to rive the boards."

184

The smell of the resin was pungent in the heat. The men bowed and nodded to them as they went by. Then the girl added, "You have been asked to attend."

"Eh?"

"Big Yance—Mayrene's father—he asked me to tell you that he would be honored if you could possibly attend."

"Oh?" Yance, Wales thought. "That would be the big buck my men were roughing up this morning?"

"Yes." Her voice was taut. "He hasn't fared very well at the hands of your men today, has he? Nevertheless, he seems to . . . to admire you a great deal. I suppose it was the . . . ah . . . prompt action you took this afternoon."

"Yes," Wales said. "I'm very good at whipping the helpless, you know."

He saw the girl stiffen. They walked in silence for a moment longer. Wales thought: I didn't need to say that . . . But he felt no regret.

"Mother and I will ride to the burying ground in our carriage," the girl said. "Would you care to join us?" She hesitated. "Of course, you're really under no obligation to attend if you don't care to."

"No," Wales said, his voice quiet and serious. "I'm very touched, very pleased to have been asked. I'm glad I've been able to win the approval of someone around here. But I suppose you and your mother would really prefer that I go on horseback."

"Not at all," the girl said promptly. "We'll be delighted to have you go with us."

"Very well," Wales said. "I will impose myself on you to that extent then. I'll need to go over the accounting of the property which we've requisitioned with you and your mother later this evening. I hope you will be available?"

"Of course," the girl said coolly.

After a moment she said, "I didn't think you were interested in winning anyone's approval."

"I'm not," Wales said promptly.

"No," the girl said, "I didn't think you were." She suddenly moved a pace ahead of Wales and then turned

185

to face him. Wales halted. Now, he thought wearily. Now it begins all over again. The pleading, the recriminations, the attempts to shame me ... He took a deep breath, bracing himself.

A lock of red hair had slipped loose and fallen down over her eye. With a quick motion of her hand and a toss of her head she replaced it.

"I've got to talk to you privately, Captain Wales."

Wales felt the skin on his face tighten as if it were drying into a mask. He looked about him. They had reached the back lawn of the house. Soldiers were moving about, lugging oddments of gear to pile in the wagon. Wales noticed that Houston had paused nearby, a trailing string of harness in one hand, and was staring at them curiously, his eyes traveling up and down the girl with open admiration.

"Of course," Wales said tiredly.

"Let's go in the house," she said quickly. "Into the library. There's some brandy in my father's desk. Would you like a drink of brandy, Captain Wales?"

"Yes," said Wales heavily. "Yes, I'd like that ..."

In the library she opened a drawer of the desk. "Apple brandy," she said. "We make our own. There's always a decanter here—Father used to say the sunlight would spoil it. Ah, yes . . . and glasses." She brought out a decanter and some glasses and followed these with a metal humidor. "There should be some cigars in here too. Father always kept—yes. Well, I don't suppose they're too fresh, but if you'd like to smoke, please go ahead." She extended the humidor and he took a cigar. It was not as dry as he had expected, and its mild scent was totally different from the improvised cheroots of raw leaf tobacco he had been smoking. While she poured a measure of brandy, he, with some of the heedlessness of a starving man assaulting food, bit the end of the cigar and lit it and sucked in the harsh, dry, but satisfying, smoke. At the first draught he sighed and settled back a little on the sofa.

She handed him the brandy glass. He took a sip and ran his tongue around inside his mouth. It was a rich, mellow brandy, with an authority he could feel gratefully as soon as the first swallow reached his stomach.

Duane Hollander restoppered the decanter and sat down in the chair behind the desk, her hands folded in her lap. Looking at her over the glass, he thought that she seemed smaller, lonely, and perhaps a little afraid. For one fleeting moment only he felt a twinge of pity for her. Then he thought with disgust: Now. Now, with me softened by the brandy and the cigar, she will begin the new gambit, whatever it is . . . He waited for her to speak, feeling an unutterable weariness despite the burning of the drink.

There was silence as she seemed to be trying to find words. Then she almost blurted, "I'm not going to oppose you any more."

Wales blinked.

"I beg your pardon?"

Her hands were tightly together, fingers lacing and unlacing quickly; it was a nervous gesture he had noticed was characteristic of her. She said, "I'm not going to oppose you any longer. Do what you will. Take what you want. I'll cooperate as well as I can."

Wales lowered the brandy glass, his mind probing for the trick in all this. "Why," he heard himself saying unctuously, drawing her out, "I knew that I had no cause to doubt your patrio—"

"It's not patriotism," she said quickly. She arose abruptly and walked across the room to a window and parted the draperies and looked out. After a moment her voice came to him, small and low and tired.

"It's just that I believe in God," she said.

Wales got to his feet. "I beg your pardon?"

She turned from the window; the draperies closed; she was only a silhouette against the faint light trickling through them.

"I said I believe in God." Her voice was a little shrill. "What's the matter, Captain Wales? Don't you believe in God?"

"I don't know," Wales said. After a moment he added, "I don't understand what you're driving at."

"Neither do I," she said. "But I believe in God and

187

I believe each of us gets what he deserves. I've thought about it ever since . . . ever since that boy came here." She walked across the room, back to the desk; her face was a white blur in the dimness of the room. "If I had been able to tell you," she said, "if when you had asked me, I had been able to say, we have sent thus and so many hams to them, we have been furnishing them with milk, we have seen that they did not want for food. If I had been able to say that we had shared with them . . . But we knew they were there. I guess we would even have known that . . . that the little child would be crying in the night with hunger if we had troubled ourselves to think about it. But we didn't. We didn't trouble ourselves at all . . ." He heard her take a deep breath.

"I said that I believe in God and I believe He sends to us what we deserve," she said. "I believe we deserve you, Captain Wales."

Wales stood there unansweringly.

"I wouldn't know," he said finally.

"Whatever the reason," she said, "I'm not going to try to stand in your way any more. Take whatever you want to take and then please leave us. I have only one thing to ask of you. That is that you send their calf back."

"No," Wales said.

She came over and stood before him. The dim air was full of the lilac fragrance. "Surely," she said, "what you're getting from us ought to satisfy you. Surely you could—"

"No," Wales said again sharply. He drank the rest of the brandy in his glass and turned away from her. He walked over to one of the bookshelves and stood there looking at the backs of the volumes for a moment. After a while he said, without turning around, "Only civilians have the luxury of making decisions based on moral issues as you have just done, Mrs. Hollander. I don't make decisions based on moral issues any more. I make them in accordance with the orders I have been given."

"I see." There was no intonation in her voice. "I suppose it's easier that way."

"Yes," Wales said. "It is." He heard his own voice thicken with a sneer which might have been directed either at her or himself; he could not tell. "Call it the coward's way out if you like."

At first he thought she was not going to answer him. Then she said, "All right. I didn't expect you to anyway. But it would have made it easier for us to look after them. Because you've not only taken everything we have; you've given us a new obligation at the same time. All right. Well, I'll contrive to look after them somehow. If I can contrive to look after my mother and six dozen slaves, I reckon I can work them in somewhere." Her voice became sharp, though it did not rise. "May I ask an alternate favor of you, then, Captain Wales?"

"I'll not deny you anything not contrary to my orders."

"Thank you. Will you, then, please be gentle with my mother?"

Wales turned. "Ma'am?"

"My mother."

"I don't understand. If I've done anything rude or discourteous, I apologize."

"Oh, of course not." Her laugh was a short, husky, sardonic bark. "You have been a perfect gentleman, Captain." Her tone became intense, deadly serious; Wales could sense the worry in it.

"This afternoon," she told him, "is the first time I've ever seen my mother afraid. She's . . . she's becoming panic-stricken, Captain Wales. It's finally sinking into her that when you leave there'll be nothing left for us to manage with. She's old and she's tired and she's worried about Father and Webb, and now you've added these additional worries and they're more than she can cope with. She's terrified at the thought of the fix we'll be in when you go. I'm not afraid," she said. "Not really. I'll find some way for us to survive. But my mother has finally given out. Consequently her attitude during the rest of the time you're here may be—un-

189

seemly I suppose is the word I want. If it is, Captain Wales, will you forgive her? Will you excuse her and overlook it?"

"Mrs. Hollander," he said, "nothing that's happened here today has distressed me more than the fact that you felt it was even necessary to make that request. You can be certain that I—well, I only hope . . ."

"All right, Captain," she said quietly. "Now if you will excuse me, I must go attend to the evening meal." She paused.

"Lieutenant Channing," she added suddenly, "finished his story this afternoon. You were right. It was in very poor taste."

"I assumed it would be."

"If you want more brandy, Captain Wales," she said, "please feel free to help yourself." He could not tell if there was mockery in her voice or not. "I know," she said just before she went out, "that it's been a very trying day for you."

15

The food was excellent, but that did not help supper any. When they had come to the table, Mrs. Cameron was missing. Duane Hollander had announced, "With your permission, gentlemen, Mother has asked to be excused from eating at the table with us tonight. She has a headache from the strain and will have a light meal in her room before going to the funeral." Now, throughout the meal, Mrs. Cameron's empty chair some-how, to Wales, seemed to fill the dining room with an outraged clamor; it made him nervous and uncomfortable, as if she were actually sitting in it, those fierce old blue eyes fastened on him. Even Channing was subdued. He ate rapidly and without looking at Wales, his lips, between bites, unconsciously held in a slight pout not unlike the sign of sullen resentfulness in a child. The girl, after a few halting tries at conversation, had given it up, and there was no sound in the dining room but the clink of silver and china.

When the cake was brought in for dessert, Duane Hollander broke the hush. "Would you care to go along to the funeral, Lieutenant?"

Channing shook his head. "I'm not much of a hand for funerals. Especially nigger funerals."

"I see." It was the last word spoken until the girl said, "I'll leave you gentlemen with your coffee and cigars, if you will excuse me. I must go get ready. Tansy came up to tell me the coffin is finished, but they won't start until we get there."

After she had left, Channing scraped back his chair.

"If you want me," he muttered, "I'll be around somewhere."

"All right," Wales said. He was glad to be left to finish his coffee alone. When the cup was empty, he arose and wandered through the house out onto the veranda.

Outdoors the light had lost its luster; the sun was half down now behind a tall, gaunt black clump of pines far to the west. But there would be daylight and afterglow for perhaps another hour yet. Wales lit a cigar and inhaled the dry smoke of the old tobacco. He coughed and leaned against one of the columns of the porch, looking out across the lawn.

He could hear the sound from the slave quarters clearly out here. It was not that high-pitched, grief-shivering shriek now; it was a low noise, soft, steady, insistent—gently swelling and falling like a wind blowing through treetops. Wales could distinguish no words, but he knew that it was a chant, and he recognized a primal rhythm in it and had a fleeting picture of naked forms sitting around a fire in a jungle, making a savage obeisance to death.

191

Then, as it was punctuated by a new sound, the mourning abruptly rose in pitch and intensity, full of a quality of excitement It swelled up suddenly through the quiet air of sundown, while a hammer banged again and again and again with businesslike regularity. Wales felt the short hairs rising on the back of his neck. I have never heard such a sound of loss, he thought.

Loss.

He stopped perspiring as his pores closed with the chill it sent over him.

Loss.

Out over the lawn lightning bugs were already beginning their flickering dances, their dim flashing barely visible in the remaining light. A cool breeze had sprung up and was carrying the smell of dew and a thousand sun-distilled essences of weeds and grasses and flowers across the lawn. There was honeysuckle, its sweetness funereal tonight, like the cloying aura of banks of flowers placed around a casket in a hushed room.

The hammer stopped. The wailing from the quarters died away, subsiding again to that low, wavelike chant.

Loss.

Wales's hand, resting on the column, tightened; his fingers dug suddenly, convulsively, against the wood.

It's all I need, he thought. That requiem—it's enough to tear a man apart. Gone, that's what they keep singing. Gone. And, oh, God, it's not just the nigger wench . . . It's Vivian and Ashbrook and—and everything I ever had, everything that ever meant anything. All gone.

He dropped his head, blinking rapidly. Before Christ, he thought, I wish I knew how to cry. Like a woman. Like a child. If I could just get all this burnt, helpless misery out of me . . .

"Captain Wales."

He heard the front door opening, and he turned. The two women came out onto the shadowed porch, their black dresses rustling stiffly. "We are ready," Mrs. Hollander said.

"Yes," Wales said. "Yes. Good. Shall we go?"

He offered Mrs. Cameron his arm as they went down

the steps, but she did not seem to see it, and he let it drop to his side. Together he and the women followed the flagstone walk across the grass to the drive, where a landau with its top down had just pulled up, a Negro youth holding the reins of the two chestnut horses. The boy was off the carriage seat in an instant, offering clumsy help as the women climbed carefully in, maneuvering their skirts precisely. All this was wordless; the only sound in the evening was the beginning shrill and chirp of the night insects and that wavelike chant of grief from the quarters.

The boy remounted, said, "Hyup, hawses," and the carriage wheels crunched on gravel. He turned the horses carefully, sawing the reins, and the horses' jaws champed and slavered, tongues rolling, as the bit pulled them backward and around. Then the horses were trotting slowly and without enthusiasm toward the quarters. Once the off hind wheel hit a rock and the landau lurched. Mrs. Cameron grabbed the side and said testily, "Watch out, Jubal!"

"Yazm," the boy said. "I sorry. Hyup-heah!"

"I suppose you'll take the horses too." Mrs. Cameron turned her taut, chiseled face to Wales.

"We need them," Wales said.

"Yes, of course," the old woman said. "We need them too."

"Cavalrymen must furnish their own horses in our army," Wales said patiently. "If a man loses his horse, he goes to the infantry. There are men in my company I can't afford to lose. I must see that they get mounts."

Mrs. Cameron said nothing.

"I'll leave you a couple of draft animals," Wales told her. "You couldn't plow with these two hacks, but they'll make excellent cavalry mounts once they're used to the sound of guns."

"Robbery," the old woman said tightly.

"Mother, please," the girl said. "We're going to a *funeral.*"

Wales looked at her. I was wrong, he thought. Her mouth isn't too large. She's very beautiful.

Her dress was of black silk, and its high black neck-
193

line set off the ivory paleness of her skin, the cameo perfection of her features. The only adornment she wore was a massive solid-gold brooch at the base of her throat; it was just enough. I hope, Wales thought, I hope she meant what she said about not opposing me any longer. I would like— He canceled the thought before it was completed. It is too bad— He canceled that one, too, and leaned back on the seat of the landau, feeling a curious unease and a vague, formless sense of regret that heightened every time he looked at her.

"It's only a slave," Mrs. Cameron snapped.

"It's a human," Duane Hollander said quietly. "One of our people. Yance's daughter."

"Murdered." There was venom in the single word.

"Yes," the girl said. "But at least Captain Wales has seen to it that justice has been done."

"We have not yet been paid," the old woman said.

Wales bit his lip and gripped the side of the carriage. "You shall be paid when my sergeant has brought me the inventories," he said slowly and precisely. "I'll attend to it directly after the funeral."

"Whoa-up, hawses," the boy on the driver's seat said.

They were at the head of the street that ran between the cabins of the quarters. It was darkening now. "Jubal," the girl said, "go see if they're ready."

The boy jumped off the seat. The street between the houses was filled with slaves. As Wales watched, pine-knot torches abruptly flared into greasy yellow flame, bringing the dusk alive with dancing shadows. The chant which had affected Wales so had died away now, resolving itself into a low, minor-keyed, seemingly sourceless hum, lacking distinguishable words, only a grief-laden moaning.

Then the crowd parted slightly. A mule backed a wagon up to where the fresh pine box sat on the saw-horses in the middle of the street. The raw new wood gleamed yellow in the torchlight. Two men seized the box and hoisted it into the back of the wagon, and when they did this, the humming suddenly rose to crescendo. Cleaving up through the formless music like a knife of melody came the first discernible words in a sweet, piercing soprano, part shout, part song: *"Oh, she gwine home! Good Lawd, she gwine home!"*

Jubal climbed back to the seat of the landau. "Yazm, dey ready."

"Drive us to the burying ground then."

As the carriage rolled away from the quarters, Wales heard the chant surge entirely into words, a shouted chorus: *"She gwine home, good Lawd, she gwine home . . . She gwine home, sweet Jeezus, she gwine home . . ."*

The carriage rolled down the lane past the pigpen, its way illuminated by two slaves marching ahead with torches. As they passed the pens, Mrs. Cameron delicately put a square of white lace to her nose. Then the carriage started uphill, toward a ridge crested with pines. The twilight was deeper now, and it had become graciously cool; the air was full of the clean smell of dew.

Behind them Wales could see the brightness of the torches strung out like a procession of glowworms as the mule-led cortege left the quarters and started into the lane. Faintly the sound of the singing and chanting came to them. The girl said something almost inaudibly, and Wales bent forward. "I beg your pardon?"

"I said, I think it's the saddest sound in the whole world, the way they sing when somebody's died. It's beautiful, but—somehow it just breaks your heart to listen to them."

He nodded. "They don't bottle up their feelings inside themselves the way we do."

The girl said something he didn't catch all of. ". . . wonderful to be like that . . ." was as much as he heard.

It would be, Wales thought. It really would be. Instead of having it inside you, always clawing to get out. Why, if I could yell and carry on like that, maybe I would be all right.

The landau had reached the top of the ridge and started into the pine woods, murky in the evening light.

"It won't take long," the girl said. "They've just barely got time to get it over with and be out of the woods by black-dark."

"Superstitious children," Mrs. Cameron said crisply.

"Mother," the girl said, no reproof in her voice, but a tinge of exasperation.

"Well, they are," the old woman burst out. "They're like children. Little children. You can't get along without them, but they're a curse and an abomination when it comes to looking after them! They'll worry you plumb to death over trifles that don't mean a thing and drive you crazy with their superstitions and their miseries!"

"I don't know what we'd have done without Yance," the girl said. "We couldn't have kept this place going without him."

"Sometimes I think," her mother said bitterly, "that when this stupid war is over I'll sell them all South."

"Mother, you wouldn't do that."

The old woman shook her head. "Say what you will—they're a curse. If it weren't for them, there'd be no war."

"Hush, Mother," the girl said intensely, gesturing toward the driver.

"A black curse," the old woman said stubbornly. "A black curse that's now robbing us of everything we've got except the responsibility to feed all their hungry mouths." She turned on Wales. "If you're going to take all the stock with you, take the slaves too. What am I going to do about them? Don't you know they're all going to be coming to me with"—her voice rose in unpleasant mockery—" 'Miz Alice, wese hongry. Wese got to have somethin to eat,' and standing there looking at me like oxen waiting to be fed. What am I to do? I can't perform the miracle of the loaves and fishes. What am I to do? I say, take them along with you, Captain Wales, and leave my daughter and myself to starve in peace."

The road through the pines was just a white sand-clay wagon trace, bumpy with tree roots. As always, it was hotter inside the pines, breezeless, and Wales began to sweat.

"I don't know," he heard himself saying. "I don't

pretend to know. I guess there's not a person in the South who hasn't thought himself nearly crazy about it. All I know is that if you've got the right to buy and sell them, breed them and kill them, then there is no way you can dodge the responsibility to feed them, so long as they remain loyal. You know why I whipped that man of mine today? If you take away their right to protect themselves, why, then you are responsible for protecting them . . ." He spread his hands.

"We own them," he said, "so of course they also own us. Maybe we're even fighting their war. I don't know. The thing about it is, you can't chain somebody to you without you being equally chained to him. It mixes things up. You can't tell who's chained to who. Maybe if the abolitionists had only announced their purpose as the unenslavement of the slaveowner, we'd have welcomed them with open arms . . . I don't know. All I know is that we're so entangled in the whole business now that we may never get loose. But I believe you will find that you can lean on them as well as having them lean on you, Mrs. Cameron. That Yance—if you have many like him, you'll make out all right . . ."

"Hmf." It was just a sound Mrs. Cameron made through her nostrils.

The driver, Jubal, pulled up the horses. "Heah de buryin groun," he said.

It was a clearing in the pines where the ridge leveled out into a plateau.

In the last ebb of light Wales saw that the clearing was separated from the woods by an old field-stone wall, built so long ago that only the vines and the creepers swarming over it in a solid mass held it together and kept it from crumbling. The same vines ran in a creeping tangle across the burying ground, covering the ground with a springy mat, dipping into the hollows that were the old graves, sunken from the collapse of crude wood coffins long since rotted.

They have been burying slaves here for a long time, Wales thought. There were many graves, and each had its own marker. Here there was a rotting pine headboard, there a makeshift slab laboriously quarried from ordinary field stone and perhaps chiseled with crude and childlike ornamentation. For some graves there were only plain granite boulders, unworked, the rough edges not even smoothed, but at least enough marker to say *He lies here*. Nor was any grave without some pathetic token or decoration contrived from the pitifully thin resources of the mourners. The outlines of some were carefully bordered with jagged bits of broken glass of all colors; on others sat whitewashed bottles, tilted awry by burdens of withered flowers. Wales saw a plowshare painted white and stuck point down on one. Among these old, vine-smoothed depressions of past burial there was something raw and shocking about the pile of fresh red dirt and the new black hole gaping beside it, squarely in the center of the graveyard.

Two slaves sat on the rock wall, a mattock and shovel between them. They arose as the carriage pulled up and parked where the road made a turnaround, then they sat down again. It was very dim in here. The wind lifted, and the whispering of the pines became a solemn, awed sound, mingling with the singing and chanting coming nearer up the slope. Far in the distance a hound bayed; the two slaves on the wall looked at each other with eyes gleaming whitely in the twilight.

The hush of the pines seemed to be contagious: even Mrs. Cameron was silent now. The horses stamped and chomped and wiped sweat from their heads against their forelegs with a slap and jingle of harness.

Wales looked at the girl. Her hands were lacing and unlacing nervously. The breeze dropped; Wales sensed a faintness of lilacs.

There is something I would like to tell her, he thought. Regardless of whatever shabby tactics she may have tried to use on me or Channing earlier, she has strength. She has strength enough to have held this plantation together and run it right. I wish I could tell her that I admire her for that, despite the rest . . . If Vivian had only—

He knew immediately that thinking the name had been a mistake. The picture came at him suddenly, clear, complete, and vivid, imaged on his brain behind his eyes. Vivian. The Englishman. In bed. Locked, straining, writhing. Real in every sickening detail. Wales groaned.

"Captain Wales?" The girl's voice was alarmed; it cut through the scene, obliterated it. "Is something the matter? You look ill."

He could feel the blood climbing into his face while his brain searched for a suitable lie. "Eh? No, Mrs. Hollander. I'm all right. I was . . ." The clopping of hoofs, the jolt and bang and squeal of the wagon, the slow swelling of the chant and the flare of torches on the narrow road: these saved him from further invention as the cortege arrived. The torches fanned out in the clearing, spreading pools of yellow light. The wagon and then the double file of slaves, marching with a ragged, shuffling co-ordination and filling the pines with their song, moved past the carriage in dark, sad procession.

The driver halted the wagon outside the wall, and the files of slaves flowed into a group circled around it. "Oh, swee-utt Jee-suss La-a-am' . . ." The chant rose and fell over and over again. "Oh, swee-utt little Jee-suss La-a-am' . . ."

Wales saw a gaunt figure raise itself erect on the wagon, thin, and spectral against the glow of torches. The figure stood there for a moment, waiting, then suddenly spread its arms over the crowd as if in benediction. Wales heard a resonant voice gong out in the clearing above the chant: "Dat's right, chilluns, praise He name!" Somebody moved around with a torch, forelighting the figure, and Wales saw it was a thin, ancient slave wearing a castoff swallow-tailed coat far too big for his scrawny torso. The old man's white chin whiskers wagged as he sang out: "Praise He name, chillun! You, Shad, You, Brutus. Take de po' sweet dove outn de waggin an' carry huh to 'uh las' restin place, while de chilluns praise He name!"

Two bull-shouldered men wrestled the pine box out of the wagon and heaved it to their shoulders; a lane opened through the crowd. Then the old man laboriously got down out of the wagon and followed the coffin, and the rest of the mourners moved after him, following the pallbearers into the burying ground.

There they ringed around the yawning hole, more than four dozen of them, rising and falling and swaying on the balls of their feet in unison to the chanted rhythm of the singing. Wales saw that some of the women clutched dried gourds, holding them high, shaking them in time to the chanting, their harsh rattle dry and eerie above the wave-like rise and fall of voices.

Then the pallbearers bent and slipped their burden to the ground beside the yawning grave-hole, and immediately the singing stopped.

Now the burying ground was silent. The old man in the swallow-tailed coat moved slowly and deliberately around to the head of the grave, facing the others. He raised his hand. The torchlight glimmered on his lined old face, and in it his eyeballs flickered yellow and his long white chin whiskers were golden.

He confronted the mourners thus for perhaps a minute without speaking, his silence pregnant and impressive and even a little regal. Wales found himself leaning out of the carriage, holding his breath, waiting for the words to come.

"Oh, chilluns . . ." It came at last, in a voice like the surge of an organ's bass notes.

"Yes, aaymen!" The woods seemed to ring and tremble with the answering shout.

"Oh, my chilluns, we done come heah fo' a buryin . . ."

"Yes, bless Gawd!"

"One ob his lambs done gone to jine de sweet Jesus!"

"Yes! Gone! Ayymen!"

"Flewed off an gone, like a bird takin wing! Ain' it de trufe I tells unto you?"

"Lawd, lissen to de trufe!" At each response the gourds rattled frantically.

"Well, He got a right han' an' a left han'! He left han' full of fearful venjunce! He right han' soft wid mercy an' love. Now tell me, chilluns—which han' she sit at? Tell me, chilluns, tell me!"

The answer was a roar, not a shout:

"She sit on He RIGHT han'!"

The old man smiled, his face radiating satisfaction and benevolence. The organ voice dropped; the crowd hushed; its swaying ceased.

"Dat's right, chillun, you done tole hit right. She sit on He *right* hand!"

He leaned forward. "An' you know whut she find dere?"

"Whut she find?"

Startlingly he bellowed the answer.

"She find PEACE!"

His voice dropped again, low, but still sonorous as an organ tone. It reached the people in the carriage clearly.

"Whut is dere down heah below? She gone, but we earthboun'. Whut is dere for us earthboun' chilluns? Why, dey ain't nothin fo' us but de curb and de spur. Dey ain't nothin fo' us but a long road wiffout end— nothing but daytime heat an' nighttime chill, winter widout fire an' summer widout coolness. Dere's thirst— we go to de spring, an' de spring dried up . . . an' de debbil's cloven hoofprint, hit dere in de dry mud. We hungers—we go to de fields, but de fields laid waste— an' de debbil's cloven hoofprint show clear in de ground. De wind blow, an' we seek shelter—but dere is no shelter! De sun beat down an' we seeks shade— but de shade all gone! Hit's a weariness, ain't it? A weariness ebrywhere we turn—a weary land, a desert— an' de debbil's cloven hoofprint dere before us no mat- ter whur we go!"

He gestured upward.

"But not fo' Mayrene! She done gone to He right hand! She done find de spring dat nebber run dry! She find de field dat nebber lay barrun! She find de shelter de coldest wind cain blow troo. She find de shade whose leaves nebber fall. She usin a star fo' a pillow an' a cloud fo' a blanket! She leanin agin de moon an' wawmin huh han's at de sun! De daybreak hawn doan blow. De curfew time doan come. An' de

201

cloven hoof doan't leave no track!" He jerked his hand demandingly. "Ain't hit so?"

"Hit's so, Good Lawd!" The shout swelled out massively, ringing in the pines. Dark figures rose and swayed, the gourds rattled wildly: *clackety-clackety* . . .

Again the preacher's voice dropped low:

"Who kin fly as fast as de kildee? Who kin ketch de kildee bird? You all done seed 'im! You all done heah de kildee gib his cry an' stretch his wings an' rise up outn de pasture low ground like a angel goin home! Kin you fly lak dat? No! Kin I fly lak dat? No! But Mayrene—*she fly* lak dat! She stretch *her* wings an' she done fly home!"

Now his voice rose, became shriller, did not pause for the litany, went on through it and over it: "Lak a kildee, I done said it—wingin up to de sky. Leavin de worl' behine, leavin trouble behine, flying up to peace. Pooshin up troo de air wid wings dat beat so fast de eye cain't behold 'um! Gwine home! Home, I say! Home, whur hit's allweez Sunday, wheah de winds blow gentle—wheah de streets are *golden,* wheah love covers *ebrything!* Dat's wheah she done gone—aflyin up lak a kildee—little old Mayrene!"

At the name a woman's shriek rose up. The old man pointed a finger.

"Whuffo you grieve? Whuffo you cry? Ain' she loose from de troubles, de toil an' de worry? Ain' she walkin golden streets, eatin from golden dishes, drinkin from golden cups? Ain' she enfolded in de buhzum ob de Gret Gawd Almighty?"

His voice sank to almost a whisper; he leaned forward, out over the grave, finger still pointing, eyes shining in the torchlight.

"She lef us behine, but we see her again. Ole Death, he come for all. He come for us, same as he come for her. But we ain' feard, is we? Ole Death, he come an' we meets 'im at de doah. Come in, Grandsir Death, dat whut we say. Come in, Grandsir Death, come in an' take yo chile—'cause we tiahed plumb out an' we ready to go. Den old Grandsir Death, he take he cloak. An' he say—an' he voice be gentle—Come heah to me, chile; you done played too hard an' you done played too long. Hit time to rest, he say, he voice fulla kindness. Den ole Grandsir Death, he wrop you in he cloak an' he hole you close, an' he say: Come long, chile, doan be afraid. We be home in a little bit. *An' you ain't afraid!* You ain't afraid atall, caze old Grandsir Death, he hole you close an' he carry you home, lak a chile go home to hits mammy!

"An' day ain' nobody evah lost! Dey ain' nobody whut believe in de Sweet Lamb Jesus evah lost! So when you gits dere, all wropped in ole Death's cloak, dey's all dere to greet you. De ones you tought wuz lost—day ain't losted! Yo daddy an' yo mammy an' yo loved sons an' daughters—dey all dere an' dey all awaitin! An' dey say: Welcome—lak dey sayin hit now to Mayrene—an 'all you feel den is de splosion of happiness. Oh, chilluns, I tell you—dere ain' no happiness lak de happiness Mayrene done gone to—dere ain' no comfort lak de comfort she done got! Dry up yo' teahs an' wipe yo' eyes an' let de woods an' fiel's ring wid yo' gladness—caze she up deah wheah we all wants to be—up dere enfolded in peace an' love—an' verly I sez unta you, Jesus Hisself done got her in He arms!"

The big Negro, Yance, was on his knees now, with his hands over his eyes, his great shoulders shaking beneath his rough huck shirt.

A many-voiced shriek of affirmation exploded high and clear and triumphant through the pines, trembling with ecstasy: "Good Lawd, goan see um *all* again some day!"

"You right, sisters, you right! Goan see um all again some day, in white robe an' soft white wings. Oh, hit'll be a gret day when we meets again! Oh, hit'll be a gret day when we meets again. Hit'll be a gret mawnin when de trumpet blows, I tell you, when de trumpet blows. You goan rise when de trumpet blows, evvabody goan rise, de quick an' de daid goan rise—hit'll be a gret day when de hawn blows cleah in dat mawnin!"

Then the old man gestured; the two bull-shouldered men lifted the coffin by rope handles, moved over to the grave, began to lower the box into the remorseless hole. The torches shed pools of eerie yellow light; a woman shrieked. The man on his knees cried with great dry husking sobs. The preacher waved his hand aloft: "To de uth she returnith! Dirt we all is and dirt we goes to, but we lives everlastin! Verly, I say unta you, we lives everlastin!"

A single voice, high, clear, piercing, soared into the night in faultless soprano: *"Oh, de ribber is wide an' de ribber is deep . . ."* The answering chorus seemed to rock the night: *"Yes, mah Lawd . . ."*

There was joy in the requiem, joy and excitement; the singers rocked back and forth; the big man on his knees was still crying. Wales saw that the preacher at the end of the grave was jumping up and down excitedly, flapping his arms, as that lone high, pure voice carried the melody and the rest joined in:

> An' death ain' nothin but a long quiet sleep . . .
> Yes, mah Lawd!"

> . . . We'se all gotta journey across some day . . .
> Yes, mah Lawd!"

> . . . An' de soun' ob de trumpet will lead de way . . .
> Yes, mah Lawd . . . !

Wales could feel some of the excitement communicating itself to him; his heart was pounding; his hands were sweaty against the side of the carriage as the singing went on:

> . . . Oh, de worl' is full of trouble an' hate . . .
> Yes, mah Lawd!

> . . . But dere's peace on de udder side ob de Gate . . .
> Yes, mah Lawd!

Then, abruptly, the song broke off. For a moment the torchlighted clearing hung starkly empty of sound.

Then it commenced, starting down low, moaning,

swelling with a rush, coming like a slow, strong wind moving through big pines:

> I know de moonlight,
> I know de starlight,
> I lay dis body down . . .

Something about that chorded tidal wave of sound pierced Marshall Wales. He felt the hair rising and prickling on the back of his neck; his spine went chill. And then, without warning and in a rush, his defenses were stripped away, all the careful checks and balances of reasoning and self-control fading and crumbling before that unutterably sad human music, that distilled lament of man's plight. His throat constricted painfully; there was a burning in his eyes, a sudden involuntary trembling of his muscles. Oh, Christ, he thought, I can't stand that . . .

He gripped the side of the carriage desperately, thankful that it was so dark now that no one could see the working of his face.

> I walks through de graveyard
> I walks to de grave.
> I lay dis body down . . .

If they don't stop it . . . he thought helplessly.

But, inexorably, it went on, simply, slowly—naked grief and loss and resignation throbbing through the dark, lonesome woods. Vivian, Wales thought, shaking all over. All of time, all of living, thick and bitter in his mouth.

> I lay in de grave,
> I stretch out mah arms,
> I lay dis body down . . .

He jumped.

Startled by the sudden sickly flickering illumination of heat lightning in the distance, dancing dryly on the horizon.

I know de starlight . . .
I know de moonlight,

"It's going to rain," Mrs. Cameron said harshly and matter-of-factly.

I lay dis body down . . .

Wales shivered. A slow, cold shiver that racked his body. A slow, cold certainty that hollowed out his belly and filled it with ice.

I lay dis body down . . .

I've never had it like this before, he thought, suddenly terrified. They say you get it sometimes. I've never had it. Fear, yes. But not just this simple, clear—knowing . . . But they say you get it like this.

Then he sucked in a deep breath. He sat up straight, squaring his shoulders.

Fool, he sneered at himself. Self-pitying, superstitious fool. You've heard niggers sing before . . .

"Jubal," Mrs. Cameron said. "Go tell 'Badiah to come light our way with a torch. We'll go now. It's going to rain."

The torch made dancing goblin shadows in the woods as the carriage lurched and bumped down the hill.

In the distance there was the slow, sullen, gathering rumble of thunder.

"A good rain will cool things off," Mrs. Cameron said, looking up toward the sky.

After that the three of them sat in silence all the rest of the way down the hill.

16

Lieutenant Channing had found both the brandy and the cheroots in the desk in the library; he had helped himself liberally to each. Now he strode angrily across the dew-wet lawn to a bench under an oak, licking a cigar to lessen the dryness of it. He halted before the bench, and his teeth clicked together savagely as he bit the end of the cigar. He spat the tiny chunk of tobacco into the grass with a sound of disgust that came from deep within his chest and then, shifting his pistol scabbard, sat down on the cool, damp marble of the bench. He found a match and lit the cigar, but the smoke did nothing to quell the rage and frustration boiling inside of him.

He said, softly and viciously, "God damn her," and he scoured a dent in the yielding turf with the heel of his boot. Smething had gone wrong—completely wrong. Everything had slipped from within his grasp.

He's done something to her, Channing thought bitterly. I don't know what, but it's something . . .

Because, he thought, she was just asking for it this morning. Just inviting me. That business about the rose . . . the way she leaned on me . . . God damn it, he thought, I reckon I know when a woman wants it. I can tell the minute I see one whether she wants it or not. And she wants it. I know she does.

But Wales—

Gone off together now, he thought. Him and all his high-and-mighty mouthing. Leave her alone, he said. And now they've gone off together—and not a damn thing I can do about it.

He stood up suddenly and slammed his fist against his thigh in anger.

Because he's got all the cards, Channing thought ferociously. He's in command, and he's got something to bargain with. But I've got nothing. This morning she didn't know that. Now she's found out that nobody runs things but Wales. That's why she's buttering up to him now. That's why she asked him off with her in that carriage. That's why he's made a point of slapping my ears down every time he gets a chance . . . because he wants her for himself. Like as not she'll be in his bed tonight. Like as not . . .

He began to walk swiftly, aimlessly, seeking expression of his anger in action.

Because nobody else but him can say what to leave and what to take, he thought—and now she knows where to peddle what she's got to peddle. So I'm dirt under her feet now. And that's why I couldn't get anywhere this afternoon.

Indeed, Lieutenant Channing? he thought savagely. *Really, Lieutenant Channing? How very interesting, Lieutenant Channing.* Nothing all afternoon but that crap! Like I was somebody she'd just met at a church sociable . . . Well, by God, if I just had the command of this detail, I'd show her this was no church sociable!

His mind painted lascivious pictures as he walked; he could feel his entire body throbbing with bottled-up desire. She's not fooling me, he thought. I've flipped the skirts on too many of her kind. All they want is to be sure nobody will know about it . . . I'll bet she's already made her deal, he thought. And tonight I'll bet she—The bitch, he thought, the damn scheming bitch—

Near at hand the bawl of a calf jerked him out of churning thoughts; he raised his head to see that his blind pacing had brought him to the cattle pen in the barn lot. Within it he could see the black shapes of resting animals, blots against the lesser darkness of the ground. Only the scrubby calf was awake, roaming around the pen and blatting lonesomely.

Then Channing saw and recognized the figures of the

two men leaning on the fence in front of him and he barked:

"Sergeant!"

The taller of the two figures detached itself from the fence, turning unhurriedly.

"Evenin, Lieutenant."

The courteous, affable words for some reason tripped open a spillway in Channing's mind through which his pent-up rage could pour.

"Sergeant! God damn it, stand up when I'm talking to you!"

Very slowly the sergeant's lounging figure came erect.

Channing stood there for a moment, searching his brain for something—anything—to serve as a carrier for his anger.

"Where's your guard on this cattle pen?"

"Suh, Lieutenant?"

"I said, where's your guard on this cattle pen. You got one, ain't you?"

The sergeant shook his head. "No, sir. I got outposts out yonder and yonder and yonder. With Davis laid up, that gives me jest enough men to man them outposts an' still let the boys git a little sleep."

"I want a guard on this cattle pen!" Channing experienced a pleasurable pride at so easily having found an issue. "Suppose one of them niggers tries some monkey business tonight. Suppose one was to let these animals out—"

"But, Lieutenant"—the sergeant's voice was as patient and gentle as if he were reasoning with a child—"I done tole you, I ain't got enough men for a extra guard post."

"Put Davis on, then. He's had all afternoon for his back to well up. He's still in this Goddamned army! You can stretch out the time ons and shorten the time offs and get your extra men that way. Hell, the men haven't had anything to do today but sit around on their butts and feed their faces anyway!"

"Davis' back is mighty sore, Lieutenant."

"I don't give a crap about Davis' back! I'm going to check this guard at midnight sharp tonight and I

209

want to find Davis on here. Davis. Nobody else. You understand?"

"Yes, suh. I understand perfectly. You expectin trouble, Lieutenant?"

"I don't know. I do know that we've pussyfooted with these people long enough. From here on out it's business. You tell your men not to take any Goddamned nonsense tonight. Anybody comes messin around, tell 'em to shoot to kill. I've got a bellyful of prissing around here. You hear that? I got a bellyful!"

"Yes, sir," the sergeant said tonelessly.

Channing stood there a moment longer, silent, still tapping on his thigh with his doubled fist.

"Has the captain come back yet?"

"Ain't seen 'im. Reckon the funeral's still going on. Never heerd such moanin an' carryin on in all my life."

"Niggers always like that, carry on like animals. They stirred up, no telling what they might try tonight. I want your guard here to shoot to kill. We'll use a password tonight. The challenge will be Stuart and the password Beauty. See that the men have got it. I don't want one of them shooting at me."

"Yes, sir."

"You've got your orders, Sergeant."

"Yes, sir." The sergeant turned away.

"Sergeant."

"Sir?" The sergeant turned questioningly.

"Goddamn it, don't you know how to salute an officer?"

For a moment the sergeant just stood there, a long, astonished silhouette against the moonless sky. "Yes, sir," he said at last in an odd voice, and his hand whipped up.

Channing returned the salute, wheeled, and stalked off. His explosion at the sergeant had calmed him a little, but not much. He walked back toward the house with long, fierce strides.

In his bed . . . he thought savagely.

Then he halted. He raised his head with an attitude of alertness, like a bird dog sniffing the air. "Now," he said aloud. "Well, now."

210

He stood rigid like that for a moment. Then he rubbed his hands along his trouser seams. His face broke into a slow, pleased grin.

"Well, by God," he said aloud softly, "it'll be at his own risk." His right hand stroked idly the flap of his pistol holster. "If she's entitled to protection against me," he said, "she's entitled to protection against him too."

He was beginning to feel better now. He raised the stub of the cigar to his mouth. It had gone out, and he relit it without moving from where he stood. He dragged in a lungful of smoke. This time it seemed to take effect, and he could feel some of the frenzy going out of him. He savored the smoke; he exhaled it in a long, sensuous puff. He was surprised to see that the smoke was visible in the darkness, twisting and writhing in gray skeins that faded, first imperceptibly, then completely. He drew in another breath of it.

"Why, hell," he said, "there ain't anything to it. All I got to do is keep my eyes open." He grinned at the darkness. "That business can work two ways," he said to the vacant lawn. He went over to a bench and sat down, stretching his feet out in front of him, crossing his ankles, turning the damp cigar round and round in his fingers. "There's always Slater," he said, "and I reckon I better talk to Davis. But the other way would be better. The other way would be the nicest of all."

The cigar had gone out again. He did not bother to relight it this time but pulled a fresh one from his pocket. With a snap of his wrist he threw the old one away, sending the burnt stub whirling over and over into darkness.

The sergeant grunted deep in his chest. Standing next to him, Dalton remembered the sound a bull would make when it had been maddened just enough to charge.

"What'd you say?" Dalton asked.

"I said," the sergeant rasped, "shit."

"My, how you talk."

"You go to hell." The sergeant raised his hand and slammed it down on the top rail of the fence. His voice

211

rose in bitter, inaccurate mimicry of Channing's voice. "'Doan you even know how to salute a officer?'" He spat out another obscene word. "For cripes' sake! Why, I ought to take the little pimple-head an'—"

"Ease off," Dalton said. "Calm down." He was a little worried. Usually the sergeant's anger vented itself more in sarcasm than in fierceness. Dalton laid his hand on the sergeant's forearm.

"He kin go screw hisself," the sergeant snapped, jerking his arm away. Then, abruptly, Dalton heard the sergeant let out a long hoarse breath. "Now," the sergeant muttered, "now what in the hell am I gonna do?"

"Huh?"

The sergeant whirled on him. Dalton involuntarily jumped back a pace. "I said, what in the hell am I gonna do?" the sergeant yelled.

"Do about whut?"

The sergeant raised his hand; Dalton tensed to dodge. Then the sergeant dropped his arm, and his shoulders, limned in silhouette against the night, seemed to sag. "Nothin," he muttered. "Fergit it. Fergit the hell all about it."

"Mac, you feel all right?"

The sergeant turned on him again. "I feel fine," he yelled. "There ain't nothin wrong with me. The only wrong with me is all you helpless ole granny-women I got to think for an' look after an' nurse along all the time. Some damn times I git so Goddamned disgusted I—"

"Now, lookahere, Mac—"

"Oh, shoot." The sergeant's voice dropped to a more normal register. "I didn't go for to git you all riled up, Dalt. I jest got somethin on my mind, that's all."

"I allowed you had. You doan hafta be so damn shut-mouthed an' touchy about it though."

"No. It's jest—well, hell, you wouldn't understand. You got folks at home an' everything. But . . . I doan know," the sergeant said wearily. "I kind of figured for a spell that Channin might do all right. I musta been crazy. Hit's jest that now I doan know what to do.

212

They got me all boxed in." He spat. "Well, the hell with it," he said. "Come on, let's go see how Davis is an' give him the bad news. That oughta go over big," he grunted, and now Dalton could hear a grin in his voice. "That'll make Davis reel happy. Him an' Channin oughta be partners for life. Come on, Dalt," the sergeant said, and he began to walk toward the barn.

17

The flickering antic shadows cast by the greasy yellow flame of the pine-knot torch made grotesques of the commonplace things of the night, as the slave trudged ahead of the carriage up the lane toward the house. Wales blinked his eyes against the light. On either side of him, the crossed posts of rail fences jutted against the sky like the muzzles of stacked arms; under him the carriage jolted and bumped with a deplorable slam of running gear; behind them, far back in the darkness, the side of the pine-clad plateau was winking with the lights of more torches as the slaves started from the burying ground.

". . . and insist upon immediate settlement," Mrs. Cameron was saying. "I shall demand payment in gold." Wales listened to her with only a fraction of his mind; that throbbing, mournful requiem around the grave kept ringing through his head, drowning out everything else. He had the disembodied, unreal sense of being caught up in a dream. The two women might as well have been shadows; he felt as if he himself had no more reality than a shadow. The woman had been talking for five minutes now, rapidly and angrily; he had paid no more attention to the swarm of words buzzing around his head than he would have to so many flies.

". . . and shall certainly see that my husband takes this up with—"

"Mother," the girl said.

"Well, I shall. And payment in gold is—"

Wales forced himself to turn his attention to her. "You must realize, of course, Mrs. Cameron," he said heavily, "that what you're asking is impossible. I'll have to pay you in treasury notes."

"I shall insist—"

"Mother!"

"In treasury notes, Mrs. Cameron. Redeemable after cessation of hostilities."

"Worthless," she said bitterly. "Worthless and you know it."

Wales grimaced; the thought of haggling with her made him sick—he was too empty and strengthless. That damned singing, he thought. I can't talk about things now. It stirred me up too much. Don't have enough control . . .

The carriage hit a terrific bump.

"Jubal! Can't you watch where you're going?" Mrs. Cameron pulled herself back squarely on the seat, straightening her hat. "Blamed nigger," Wales heard her mutter under her breath.

"Mother, please," the girl said desperately. "Everybody is tired tonight. Worn out. Must you—"

"Yes," the old woman snapped. "I must. I have no intention of turning one iota of your father's property over to the army or anyone else without being properly paid . . ."

Damn her, Wales thought. She knows. She knows I'm worn out. And she knows it won't do her any good, either, but that now she can irritate me the most with her whining and snapping. She knows that, and by God, she's aiming to have herself a time with me before we leave with any of her belongings.

The hell with her, he thought. I'm just too tired to worry about her tonight.

Now they were on level ground, moving past the square dark hulks of the slave cabins.

"And furthermore," she went on, as if the buildings had reminded her of it, "the fact that girl was only fourteen years old makes no difference. She'd have been ready to breed in two years. That has to be taken into account in establishing a price. She was excellent Coramantee stock."

"Mother!"

No, Wales thought grimly, clutching the side of the carriage tightly. No, I can't hit her. But, Lord, what a satisfaction it would be. . . .

The carriage wheels crunched on the gravel of the drive. They rolled up before the house. Inside, lamps had been lit; brightness spilled out of the tall, fan-lighted windows onto the porch, making puddles of black and yellow around the columns. Wales released a thankful breath. Now, he thought. He had suddenly realized that he had been trembling all the way up the hill. Now, if I can just get this trembling stopped before I have to get out.

Jubal said, "Whoa-up yah, hawses."

Now, Wales thought desperately. Stop it, he commanded the trembling; stop it. I can't let them see it. But it would not stop. It was like the trembling of the thigh muscles when one had ridden too long and too hard, only it was general. *Stop it,* he commanded again, mustering all his will.

It ceased, and carefully he arose, descended, and lifted his hand for the women to take. First the girl, then when Mrs. Cameron was clear of the carriage, Duane Hollander said, "All right, Jubal." Still following its fat-pine star, the carriage crunched away into the night, and Wales and the women started up the flagstone walk.

A piece of shadow detached itself from the darkness of the veranda and moved toward them slowly and gracefully, becoming Channing, thumbs hooked in his belt. His white teeth caught the lamplight, shone mutedly in the darkness. "Ladies? Marsh? Have a nice ride?"

Just the sound of his voice made Wales stiffen. And

him, too, he thought savagely. I've had all of him I can—

"As nice a ride as a journey to a funeral can be, I suppose," Duane Hollander said. Channing missed the rebuke; he nodded sympathetically and helped her up the steps to the porch. At the top step the girl freed her arm. "Mother, don't you think some brandy would be good for everybody?"

Mrs. Cameron did not answer.

"Well, I think it would. We're all worn out. I am and I know you are, and I'm sure Lieutenant Channing and Captain Wales are simply exhausted. I don't suppose any of the house people are back yet. Why don't you make the gentlemen comfortable in the drawing room while I see about the brandy?"

"I'll be delighted to help you, Mrs. Hollander," said Channing quickly.

"Thank you ever so much, Lieutenant. I feel sure I can manage."

"Cap'n Wales."

Wales turned. The sergeant had come around the corner of the house and stood now in a pool of lamplight. He extended some folded sheets of paper.

"Sir, here's the inventories. We got all the stock in the pens down at the barns, 'cepn pigs an' chickens. I done fixed some wagons to haul the pigs in an' we'll ketch 'em up in the mawnin. Chickens are shut up in the roosts. We kin grab 'em whenever we ready to move out. Ever'thin else's already loaded in the wagons."

Wales took the inventories. He said a single, disgusted, obscene word inaudibly. He had been hoping that the sergeant would not have had them ready until morning. Aloud he said slowly, "Thank you, Sergeant."

The sergeant stood there, waiting. Wales could feel the sergeant's gaze on him. He racked his mind trying to imagine what the sergeant was waiting for. Then, vaguely, he realized that the sergeant was waiting for him to ask the necessary questions. He tried hard to think of what it was the sergeant expected to hear, but he could not seem to focus his thoughts. He was genuinely startled to hear his own voice speaking involuntarily and instinctively: "Pickets out?"

He thought that the sergeant relaxed, almost imperceptibly. "Yes, sir. Tight guard. Lieutenant Channin give us a password. The challenge is Stuart. The password is Beauty. In case he forgot to tell you, Capn. I wouldn't want nobody gittin hurt by accident tonight . . ."

"All right," Wales heard himself say. "Stuart. Beauty. Anything else, Sergeant?"

"Yes, sir. I had yo horse an' the lieutenant's horse brung up here to the house an' hitched out in back. They're already saddled an' bridled an' so are all other mounts, in case sumpin happens . . ."

"That's good." Wales turned to go.

"Capn."

Wales swung back.

"Lieutenant Channin had me put Davis on guard at the stock pens. I— Well, suh, the way his back is, I jest wanted to—"

Beside Wales, Channing stepped forward angrily. "Well, confound you! When I can't give an order without a sergeant presuming to—"

Wales rubbed his eyes. "All right," he said. He knew he should think about that a little. Davis' back . . . But he did not feel up to listening to Channing wrangle. "Let Davis pull his hitch, Sergeant," he said harshly.

There was a second's pause before the sergeant answered. "Yes, sir," he said then.

Wales stood looking at the rigid form just beyond the edge of light. Finally he remembered to say, "All right. Thank you, Sergeant. Good night."

"Good night, Capn. Good night, ladies." The sergeant put on his cap and then, soundlessly, melted into darkness.

Wales remained where he was, tapping the papers against the palm of his hand, not quite sure what he wanted to do with them.

Mrs. Cameron's sharp voice brought his head around. "Well, Captain, I presume at last you're ready to talk business?"

Wales looked at her bright, antagonistic eyes. Shit, he thought.

He let out a long, weary breath. "Really, Mrs. Cameron, don't you think it'd be mighty exhausting for you tonight? Why not in the morning . . .?"

Under her stare in the yellow lamplight his voice trailed off.

"Not at all, Captain. I propose to have my due."

"Very well." He tried hard to keep the disgust out of his voice. "Well, I shall see that you get it." He opened the door for her.

She went in, and then the girl brushed past him—scent of lilacs, scent of woman . . .

"Thank you, Captain Wales."

"Not at all, Mrs. Hollander." He stood in the doorway for a moment, dreading to enter. In the distance the horizon was shimmering with cloud-veiled lightning. There was a far, faint throb of thunder. The breeze rose slightly, fingering the leaves of the trees over and around the house. The thunder growled again, closer. Wales and Channing went in the house and shut the door. It was hot in the house.

"Coming up a storm," Channing said.

"Yes," said Wales. He shook his head, hoping that would order his thoughts. Nothing, he thought. Nothing seems real any more.

Now it had got to the point that when he heard her voice he didn't even hear the words. All he was conscious of was the excruciating irritation to his nerves, as if, instead of talking, she were rasping two pieces of slate together, incessantly and willfully.

". . . I don't propose to argue about it with you, Captain. You asked me to set a fair value on each of these items and I have done so."

The old woman sat primly, defiantly, on the sofa, her hands folded in her lap, her face a thin-lipped, stamped-iron mask.

Wales looked up from the secretary, where he had been adding the figures.

"It's an impossible sum."

"More than you have with you?"

He hesitated a moment. "No."

She moved her hands with an exasperated gesture. "Why is it an impossible sum when the money in which you will pay for it is worthless? You have refused my demand for gold. So this is all a charade anyway, the robber giving the victim a promissory note. I have discounted the money to its true value in arriving at my prices in the hope that perhaps I may realize a little something tangible. Now, I am very tired, Captain. Do you propose to agree to a settlement so that I can retire, or must we prolong this argument further?"

"Mother," the girl said.

"Duane, I am handling this."

"I only wanted to ask if anyone would like another brandy."

"No, thank you. Captain Wales?"

Wales stood up heavily and rubbed his hand over his face. Oh Lord, I am tired, he thought. I shouldn't. But anything to end this damned haggling. If I don't she'll go on all night.

"Very well, Mrs. Cameron," he heard himself say. "I agree to your terms." He started to reach for his pocket, but Mrs. Cameron raised her hand.

"That will not be necessary tonight, Captain. I merely wanted to be sure that we understood each other. You may pay me in the morning."

"No," Wales said. "I'd prefer to pay you now."

"And I would prefer to wait until morning."

"We've agreed on the sum, Mrs. Cameron. I have a receipt right here. It'll only take a moment to enter the total. And it will only take a moment for you to sign."

"No, Captain. I insist. I'll sign in the morning."

Wales felt anger rising in him. He started to blurt: You'll damn well sign it now after all this haggling! Instead he heard himself saying politely, "I can assure you, Mrs. Cameron, that I'll not change my mind during the night about taking anything on this list. Neither will I agree to any other negotiations in the morning. You might as well accept payment now and sign."

She waved her hand almost airily. "Oh, we're both entirely too tired tonight to discuss business any further, Captain. Besides, I shall want to make my own tally of what you have in the morning to verify the correctness of your inventory." Her eyes gleamed spitefully. "It is not an easy thing to strip a plantation and leave two women destitute, is it, Captain Wales? It requires a great deal of clerical work." She turned toward the door. "Good night, gentlemen. Duane, are you coming up?"

"In just a moment, Mother." Wales saw that the girl had poured herself another brandy. Her mother's gaze fixed on the glass unwinkingly. "Please come along now. I should like to talk to you."

The girl sighed.

"Very well, Mother. I'll come up for a moment. Then I'll show these gentlemen to their rooms." She put down the brandy glass and the two women went out the door.

From where he sat sprawled in a chair in one corner Vance Channing chuckled softly. He arose and walked over to the tea table and picked up the girl's brandy. He turned to Wales, lifting the glass.

"Here's to Mrs. Cameron. You've met your match at last, Marsh."

Rage exploded behind Marshall Wales's eyes in a blossoming red flash then, set off by that mocking tone. It flared and faded in the same instant; he was left empty, white-lipped, standing there looking at Channing with contempt.

Channing sipped the brandy, his eyes still bold and jeering behind the poised rim of the glass. "You're pale, Marsh. And—why, you're trembling. What's the matter, Marsh? Dealing with an old lady too much for your nerves? Or—is it that filly?"

He took another sip, while Wales remained frozen in place, rigid.

"You know, Marsh, you haven't been looking at all well lately. You've been working too hard, that's it. I always did say you take your duty too seriously. Hell, no point in having a war if you don't get some fun out of it." His eyes narrowed in exaggerated judicial appraisal. "Yes, sir, Marsh, you sure look bad. No two ways about it—you look bad."

Wales did not move.

"Now, what you need—" Channing had finished the brandy. He smacked his lips. "You know, this isn't bad for homemade stuff." He turned to the decanter and poured still another glass and then turned back to Wales. "What you need is something relaxing. Like, say—" He paused, eyes rolled upward as though in thoughtful consideration. "Well—like, say, a roll in the hay with a redheaded woman. That would be relaxing, wouldn't it, Marsh?"

He tossed off the brandy and set down the glass in a smart motion. There was no mockery left in his voice now or in his eyes—only hate, naked, cold and ugly.

"Come off it, Wales. You're not fooling me. I know why you told me to stay away from her. Have you made a deal with her yet? Or does that come later tonight?"

"Channing—" Wales heard himself bite the single word off clean. He felt a tremor going through his body; he had risen until his weight was all on the balls of his feet.

Channing did not even appear to notice. "Well, if you don't get her, you're crazy. You've got plenty to trade with—all the stock and supplies of a whole plantation." His lip curled. "And she'll trade with you, too—don't think she won't. Only, there's one thing, Marsh. You remember what you threatened to do if I bothered her? Well, that works two ways . . ."

Wales's hand curled around the back of a chair. The knuckles stood out like round white knobs.

Channing grinned. "You don't like that, do you, Marsh?"

Wales opened and shut his mouth. Then his words came hoarsely. "Will you meet me out on the lawn?"

"Rough and tumble?" Channing pretended to be shocked. "That's no way for *gentlemen* to settle differences."

Wales shook his head mutely, impatiently. His hand motioned toward his hip.

"Uh-uh." Channing smiled happily and his voice was silky now. "No siree. I'd like nothing better, Marsh. The sergeant could be the referee. But I'm afraid not. If I did it right now, there might be trouble. I might wind up under a cloud for shooting my own captain. You see, Marsh, you wouldn't have a chance. You're coming to pieces. Hell, it sticks out all over you—you stink of it. You're through—finished, worn out. It wouldn't be any trouble at all to put a ball through your head. But not now, Marsh. I prefer to wait until I can do it as a hero, protecting the honor of our fair womanhood left behind, rather than merely as a disgruntled junior officer." He shrugged. "It really don't matter much one way or the other, Marsh. I'd as soon kill you as keep you alive, but I'd as soon keep you alive as kill you." His smile widened. "Soon as I can see General Slater, you'll probably wish you was dead anyhow." The smile went away. "But if you mess with that redhead, I just reckon I'd have to—"

He broke off and shook his head.

"I really feel kind of sorry for you, Wales. No matter what you do from now on, I'll have your ass. You're damn near pathetic."

Then, slowly and deliberately, he turned his back on Wales and sauntered unhurriedly from the room.

Wales watched him go. Gambler, he thought bitterly, wondering why his anger was not greater than it was. Trash . . . But there was no intensity within him. I feel dead inside, he thought. Channing's not real. Nothing's real. Nothing . . .

Moving blindly, he left the house and walked out into the cool night.

The wind was definitely rising. Wales could hear it making the leaves all around the house murmur and whisper excitedly. It felt good against him, and he loosened the collar of his shirt.

The world was asleep. The mourning was no longer coming from the quarters, and there were no lights down there. He walked across the lawn, his boots making a faint, sloshing rustle in the already dew-wet grass. All around him was the high, thin, reedy hysteria of night bugs in the foliage. Everything dark, he thought. That's fine. Dark is what I want.

He halted at a magnificent old oak and leaned against it, feeling the cool rough bark through his shirt. He shut his eyes. He could hear blood making a noise in his temples.

He stayed like that for a long time, doing his best to keep his mind blank. At last he straightened up, biting his lip. I guess Channing's right, he thought. I guess I am finished. Even the sergeant's lost his confidence in me. He said as much. But even if he hadn't, I could tell. And—he shook his head wearily—and I don't blame him, he thought.

He looked out into the darkness. It's all because of this place, he thought. I had just about trained myself not to think, not even to remember, until I came here. Then, everyone pushing at me about right or wrong, forcing me to make decisions, how could I help thinking? And these fields . . . and a house like that . . . and a woman like that—how could I help remembering? And . . . He ran his fingers up and down the rough bark of the tree. I've lost so much, he thought. Everything I've lost has taken something away from inside of me. Now I am hollow. Now I don't have anything left. If Vivian— Oh, God damn her, he thought, God damn her for what she did!

When will it happen? he wondered, watching clouds scud and gather to cut off the moonlight. When will the shell collapse? Will it happen on the way back to Regiment? At the next skirmish? Or maybe just when a superior officer speaks harshly to me next time? Anything could trigger it, and when it happens, then I will be finished. I might have lasted longer if it hadn't been for this place and these people; I might have postponed it for quite a while. But not any more. I have used up too much strength today. It will come soon, and I don't know anything I can do about it. Except watch myself as carefully as I can and hold on to all my faculties with whatever strength I can muster and hope that when it does happen, it won't happen under fire and get somebody killed.

But her, he thought. It all comes back to her. She's the one to blame, damn her. . . .

The horizon was cloud-banked now; the shielded light of the moon did not illuminate, only emphasized, the darkness. He watched a branched artery of lightning flicker downward miles away and disappear. The thunder was a long time coming.

I remember once, he thought, there was a terrific electrical storm, the way we have them down home. Lightning flashing and glaring all around the house, thunder like cannon fire—only I'd never heard any cannon fire then. Flash, explode, boom, all over us, all around us, like hell itself let loose. But it wasn't the lightning that awakened me; it was her shoving into my arms. "Hold me, Marsh, hold me. I'm afraid. This kind of thing scares me." And how I held her all night long, held her tight, close, the way you should hold a child, while the lightning flared all around us. And I remember how, finally, we even made love, with the glare and the noise coming in the window. And how the next morning I found the maple tree near the back porch split right down the middle by a bolt. You would have thought we'd have heard it when it happened, but we didn't. It was a close thing. . . .

"Captain Wales."

The soft voice in the darkness made him turn. Against the few windows still lighted in the house he saw the figure of the girl coming toward him. Then she was at his elbow; his nostrils were full of her. Scent of lilacs, scent of woman, mingling with the cloying sweetness of honeysuckle and the cleanness of coming rain on the wind.

"I'm sorry if I startled you, Captain."

"Oh no. You didn't startle me. I just—needed a breath of fresh air."

"I'm sure you did, after all that sordid haggling. I'm sorry, Captain."

"There's nothing to be sorry for." He found a cigar,

snapped a match on his thumbnail. In the quick bright flare of light he thought her face seemed startled, as if she'd had to change expressions instantaneously. Her eyes were very wide, looking directly at him.

He swallowed a tightness out of his throat and bent down, shielding the match from the wind. When the cigar was lit, he dropped the match and stepped on it and leaned back against the tree.

"You haven't done anything to be sorry for," he said again. "You've done nothing but follow your conscience. That," he said bitterly, "is a luxury I am not privileged to enjoy."

She turned away from him, looking off across the lawn. "Please," she said wearily, "let's not start debating again. Let's not talk about consciences. I don't think I can stand any more of it."

"I'm sorry," Wales said. "I was only feeling sorry for myself."

"I think that must be the trouble with all of us," she said almost tartly. Then he saw her shoulders unstiffen as if she were relaxing. "I hope it rains," she said.

"Perhaps it will."

"You know," she said, "it would feel so good to stand out here in the rain and just let it pour all over me. I am so hot and so tired and confused." He realized that she was talking to herself, not to him. "Rain feels so cold and clean."

She turned on him suddenly. "It's been an uneasy truce, hasn't it?"

"Ma'am?"

Her voice softened. "I told you I wouldn't oppose you, Captain, and I haven't. But I haven't said that I understand your position, have I? I haven't offered any sympathy at all for your difficult position, have I?"

He wondered if she were being sarcastic, and he wished that he could see her face in the darkness. He felt the tingling of wariness within himself, and automatically he came on guard.

"I don't expect any sympathy," he said in a hard voice.

"I wasn't being smart, Captain," she said quietly. "I

meant it." The wind changed direction; he caught again the faint perfume of the lilacs. "I know enough about you now to know that what you have done today hasn't been easy for you."

"No," he said, "it hasn't." Then, unbidden, his ears were full of the sound of a woman crying, a child crying, a calf blatting. He was afraid the trembling was going to start again. "The things I have had to do," he said thickly, "the things I have had to do—"

She laughed suddenly, a curiously high, thin laugh. "We can't seem to stop talking about it, can we?"

Lighting came and went on the horizon in a quick flare; in the instant fleeting blue-whiteness he saw that she was looking up at him with strained tautness. She looks haggard, he thought. But even so . . . He turned away from her.

"I don't know what to do," he heard himself saying. "I don't know what's right any more." The crying seemed to be louder in his ears now. "I guess the war is right—" He whirled on her. "It would be quite a joke on me if it weren't right, wouldn't it?"

"I don't know." Her voice had gone as weary now as her face had looked. "Would it?"

"Yes," he said, not liking the shrill pitch of his own voice. "Yes, it would be a fine joke, wouldn't it?" He tried to stop himself, realizing that somehow he had come to the thin edge of hysteria with no warning. But the chaos within him poured out in words he could not restrain. "On me," he said. "On everybody." His fist slashed the air in an agonized gesture. "Think of it," he said. "Think of all the men alive five years ago and dead now! Think of all the children who'll never even be fathered. Think of all the seed dead on Marye's Heights at Fredericksburg, in those woods at Chancellor's place, on that ridge in Pennsylvania . . . Generations obliterated before they were even born—"

"Captain," she said. He felt her hand on his elbow. He threw it off.

"And the ruined plantations," he said thickly, through his teeth, "and the ruined farms and the ruined cities—Christ," he snarled at her. "Think of it! Think of all

226

the unbelievable waste of it!" He turned on her almost viciously. "And don't you see, that's where the joke comes in. That's the great joke of it . . ."

Some of the excitement went out of him. He leaned back against the tree. "That's why we've got to win," he said hoarsely but quietly. "To keep it from being the greatest, foulest joke in history. We've poured everything we had into it. I've poured a wife into it and a plantation and all my wealth, and it's swallowed them up without a trace. So much gone . . . Don't you see? The only way we can justify all that waste is to win. If winning isn't the most important thing in the world, important enough to justify all that—why, then we're not just fools, we're madmen. Do you think I can't still see that woman? Do you think I can't still hear the crying of that dirty-faced brat? Hell, I'll always hear him!" He straightened up, trying to get his voice under control; it had risen again. "But winning takes precedence over everything—we've got to win or be the perpetrators of the rottenest, maddest jest that ever was. That's why I've had to—I've tried to figure it out and I can't, and if after all we've done, we don't win, we're insane and always have been."

"Of course," she said. Her voice was cool as frost. "By all means. We've got to win."

He was sick and empty and trembling with reaction. "I'm sorry," she said. "I didn't mean to— But I had to tell you . . . I can't help what I have to do."

"None of us can," she said calmly. "That's the awful part."

"But I—"

"You!" she said. Her voice rose suddenly. "You! Do you think you're the only one who feels—" She broke off abruptly. "Ah," she said, "I wish—"

The crash of thunder startled them both. Wales felt her hand suddenly touch his wrist.

He blinked. "That was close," he said thickly.

"Yes," she said. The lightning flared again; her face was upturned. Wales bent forward.

Her lips were soft and only slightly parted; her fragrance was all around him. Under his hand her body

227

tensed, strained toward him, and then eased and moved back.

He raised his head.

"I am very sorry, Mrs. Hollander. I should not have done that."

"No," she said. A few spattering drops of rain began to fall. Wales heard them striking the oak leaves overhead. They were cool on his face. "I shouldn't have let you," she said.

He could not see her face in the darkness.

Damn it, he thought, stop it. Stop this trembling.

"My apologies," he said. "My sincerest—"

"We'll dismiss the incident," she said. There was a reedy note of strain in her voice. "We'll dismiss it. Completely, Captain Wales. We shall dismiss it and not let it happen again, isn't that what we shall do?"

"Yes," he said, "I think that's what we'd better do."

The thunder slammed close at hand. The breeze lifted. More lightning. In the flash Wales could see that she had turned away from him. "It's raining harder," she said in a voice that sounded oddly off key. "I think we'd better go in the house."

18

In the darkness of the barn loft Jeff Davis awakened, sweating. He opened his eyes and saw only blackness around him. He drew in breath, and his lungs were drenched with the sweet fresh tang of hay. He stirred a little, and arcs of fire seemed to flash across his back. The pain brought with it remembrance of where he was, and he let out a hoarse gasp of relief. There was agony in wakefulness, but it was better than the terror of the dream.

He licked his lips and tried to burrow further down in the hay, clenching his teeth against the protesting soreness of his stiffened back. God damn, he thought. God damn. He was not cursing because of the pain; he was cursing the dream.

I wush it would go away, he thought. I wush I wouldn' never dream hit again. But he knew he would. Because, although he never thought of it awake any more, he never knew when he lay down to sleep whether he was going to relive that day on the Trace or not; and sure as fate, just when he was most upset, that dream would come and then, despite the fact that he could consciously remember feeling nothing toward the Old Man but fear and hate, he would be flooded with that vague, helpless sadness and upset even more.

Because after the dream it all came clear in his mind—as clear as if it had happened this morning instead of when he was only six years old.

First he would see again the cabin, see it as vividly as if it were in front of him. See the worm-eaten logs of the little square two-room structure in the wilderness, the bench and hitch rack in front, the pole pen in back where the wayfarers on the Trace put their horses. And, oddly, see himself, too, scrawny and dirty and ragged, playing in the dropping-littered dirt around the hitch rack. He would be playing with the only toys he had—blocks he'd made from mud.

And he would see—or remember—the time he had built a house of mud blocks in front of the doorway of the cabin. It was the biggest block house he had ever built. It had two rooms, just like the cabin. He had spent a long time balancing the blocks, so that the house would have windows and a door, too, just like the cabin. He had just been getting up to call his mother to look at it when his father had come out of the door and knocked the house over with the toe of his boot. Jeff Davis could remember how he had cried, and he could remember his father's face with its rim of black beard looking down at him and grinning, the

229

rotted teeth broken to points like an animal's fangs. He could remember the horrified fascination as his father lifted his foot and said, "I'll learn ye to play whur people gotta walk," and how the big leather boot had come grinding down on the blocks and powdered them back into dust. He could remember, too, how he had screamed and flung himself at his daddy then, and how the Old Man had backhanded him across the yard.

He would recollect, too, the nights when there were no travelers at the ordinary and he, lying up in the loft, could hear the Old Man flailing the Old Woman. She would beg and holler and plead for mercy, and Jeff Davis would bite his lip because he knew that somehow the Old Man was hurting his mother, but he was afraid to see it and didn't know what to do about it. After a while he had made a game out of it: when the Old Man would beat the Old Woman, he would lie up there in the loft and silently mock the yells and the pleading, because it made him feel bad inside just to lie there without doing anything and listen to it.

And then, helplessly, there would be the memory of the day the men came. A bunch of them, riding up in a group with guns across their saddles, instead of coming singly or in pairs the way the travelers did. He could still see the hard, cold blue eyes of the man on the front horse, a man with a square face and an iron-gray beard that hung all the way down to his belt buckle. And he could see his father standing before the men, gesturing wildly. He could see the man with the long beard shake his head and swing the gun barrel around to point at his father. Then the men had got down and tied his father up, roped him to a tree, and Jeff Davis had thought that this was a funny game to play and wondered if they would rope him too. He remembered that while all that was going on his mother had sat huddled and silent on the bench in front of the cabin; he had run to her once and she had pushed him away distractedly. Then he had run after the men, who had gone into the cabin, to see what they were going to do. They wandered around the cabin as if they were looking for something, but whatever it was, they seemed not to find it. Then they went out in back. One of them picked up the ax from the chopping block and looked at it thoughtfully. The rest of them went on to the horse pen, with a shovel they had found, and Samuel Alexander Davis followed them. They paid no attention to him as they dug in the hard-packed earth of the horse pen.

They dug for a long time, trying a lot of different places, before they turned up some funny white things. After they had turned up enough to seem to satisfy them, they went back around to the front of the cabin, and Samuel Alexander Davis scooted into the pen to see what the white things were. They were bones.

He had run back around to the front yard. The men were standing there, talking among themselves. His mother still sat huddled and silent on the bench. He remembered that the men had gone over to the tree and untied the Old Man. They kept their guns pointed at him while they talked there in the shade for a while, gesturing up and down the Trace, the wilderness path that ran in front of the cabin. Then one of the men had walked up leading a horse, and another one had thrown a rope over a limb. Samuel Alexander Davis had wondered what sort of a game they were fixing to play now.

One of the men pointed to the horse. His father shook his head wildly, yelling something. Samuel Alexander Davis began to feel scared inside. He had never heard that sound in the Old Man's voice before. It was scary-feeling to hear his father sound afraid. He went back over to where his mother sat, and this time, absently, she put her arm around him.

Then the men lifted the Old Man onto the horse. He saw that there was a rope around the Old Man's neck. A man stood at the horse's head, holding the cheek strap of the bridle so that the horse could not move. The Old Man turned in the saddle, his eyes big, and yelled something at Samuel Alexander Davis' mother, crouched there on the bench. Then all at once she had sprung up, waving her fist at the man on the horse. "Swing, damn ye!" he remembered his mother shouting at his father. "You done laid fist on me fer the last time! Swing, damn yo mean soul!"

He remembered thinking it was a funny way to swing as the man at the horse's head turned and led the horse forward. When he swung on grapevines in the woods, he always held on with his hands.

It was not until he saw the way his father's legs acted that he actually realized that they were hurting the Old Man. The legs kicked crazily, jerking and twisting as if they were cutting a buck and wing. Samuel Alexander Davis, six years old, stood absolutely still, not breathing. Then the legs quit kicking and dangled limply, and the Old Man began to turn gently, revolve in the breeze. There had been satisfaction in the voice of the man with the long beard: "Now I reckon a wayfarer can travel the Trace without fear of gittin his haid knocked in with a ax an' his pockets emptied."

Then the men had mounted up and left. After a while his mother went around in back and hitched a mule to a wagon. Before long they drove out of the clearing, away from the cabin. His mother had not cut down the Old Man. Samuel Alexander Davis could remember turning around on the seat of the wagon and looking back. At the end of the rope the Old Man was still swaying and turning gently, pushed by the breeze that made a secret, murmuring sound in the trees overhead.

Jeff Davis gingerly brought up an arm and wiped the sweat off his forehead. That Goddamn capn, he thought. If he hadn't whupped me, I wouldna dreamed that-air dream tonight. . . .

His throat was dry and he wanted a drink of water. He started to fumble in the hay for his canteen, and then he froze, motionless. He shut his eyes and began to snore carefully and regularly. Somebody was coming up the ladder to the loft. In a moment he felt a hand on his shoulder.

"Awright, Davis." It was the voice of Boomer. "I know yo back's sore, but the sergeant said you was to relieve me. Git up."

Davis did not move.

"Goddamn it." Boomer's voice was at once sympathetic and exasperated. "They ain't nothin *I* kin do about it. I cain't stay out there all night. I gotta have some sleep too. Wake up, I said!"

"Boomer." The sergeant's voice came in a whisper out of the darkness of the loft. "Matter?"

"Aw—Davis won't wake up."

"He ain' daid, is he?"

"Naw, jest asleep."

"All right, then." Davis heard the sound of a body slithering through the hay. "I'll wake 'im."

As the hand took his collar, lifted, Davis kept his body limp.

There was the angry smack of flesh on flesh.

The sting of the slap made tears well into his eyes. So they goan be that way about it, he thought. Allatime pickin on me . . . All right . . . He shook his head. "Huh?"

"I figgered that would do it." The sergeant shook him by the collar. "Wake up, afore I backhand you again. Time for you to pull guard."

"Goddamn . . . I cain't pull no guard. My back's pure killin me."

"I done tole you earlier tonight, it's Channin's orders. He's out after somebody's ass tonight, an it ain't goan be mine. Now you git yourself up outn that hay an' go stand yo trick."

"Well, if hit was yo back—"

"Hit ain't my back. Now—up!"

"Aww . . ." Slowly, carefully, Davis sat up, making a great show of knuckling at his eyes. He let out a groan. There was nothing feigned about that; his back was one stiff, gigantic, scabbed-over sore.

"I know hit hurts." There was a certain measure of sympathy in the sergeant's voice now. "But you brung hit on yoself. Besides, hit ain't my idea. Now git on down there."

At first it was agony to move, but in a moment or two, as the stiffness wore away, it was better. Jeff Davis cursed softly under his breath, using every obscenity he

233

knew, as he pawed around in the hay for his gun and his cap.

After he had climbed reluctantly and painfully down the ladder and reached the ground, he groped his way through the absolute darkness of the hallway to the open door, and there he halted, looking out at the night.

He licked his lips. It was mighty black out there tonight. Clouds all piled up in front of the moon. The smell of rain still lingering, though there couldn't have been much. He felt the short hair prickle on the back of his neck. He didn't much like the idea of going out there in that blackness and staying there for three hours. That dream had left him upset and jumpy. It would be mighty lonesome out there. And it was so dark that if someone *did* come sneaking up . . .

The sergeant's voice was like a whiplash coming from the loft. "All right, Davis. Git the hell out there an' take over yo post!"

Still cursing, Jeff Davis moved through the door and on out into the darkness.

19

In the dark upper reaches of the house the girl led the way with a candle. Marshall Wales followed wearily. But too conscious, too acutely conscious, of the perfume of the girl trailing back to him—mixed with the coarse, fatty smell of the candle smoke, but nonetheless discernible and bitterly stirring. The long upstairs hall danced with shadows. The girl paused before a door.

"I hope you will find this room satisfactory, Captain," she said tonelessly. "I had it aired this afternoon." She handed him the candle.

Cameo face in flickering yellow light. Green eyes—unreadable—and red hair struck bold by the little flame. Long mouth and firm chin . . . Marsh Wales stood looking down at her.

"Thank you," he said.

"You are welcome," she said. "Good night."

"Good night," he said. "Wait. Won't you need this candle? You can't see in the dark."

"Just stand there a moment and hold it if you will," she said. She moved down the hall to its extreme end and opened a door. "Good night," she said again.

Wales watched her enter. He watched the door close behind her. He remained standing there a moment, still holding the candle high, for the first time in a long while not liking it that he was alone.

Finally he entered his own room. Another candle sat in a small silver holder on a bureau. He went to it and lit it with the one he carried. Then, in the illumination of the twin greasy flames, he looked about the room.

Like all the rooms of the house, it was large and so high-ceilinged that the candlelight could not reach that far; the entire upper part was in shadow. For furniture there was a tester bed, a rocker, and the bureau. The room smelled faintly musty still, with the half-repugnant, half-disturbing odor of a space long closed and secret. Wales felt a certain amount of tension eke out of him. A hideaway, he felt rather than thought. She's given me a sanctuary. Dark, remote, quiet . . .

I'm not sure I like it, he thought. Because it is too perfectly designed to think in. And I don't feel like thinking tonight. I'm too damned tired to think any more. I am so tired . . .

He put the other candle on the bureau, and then he grinned. The brandy bottle and a glass were sitting on the bureau, the brandy gleaming amber in the candle-light.

And that, he told himself, takes care of the thinking

235

problem. I must remember to thank her. It was considerate.

He began to undress. It was good to pull off the heavy boots and stockings and free his feet. But there was more of a sense of liberation when he had unfastened the heavy leather belt that held the two Colts and had loosened the waistband of his trousers so the air could circulate around belly and hips where the monstrous iron weight of the guns had molded the cloth to his skin. When he had done that, he stripped off his shirt.

There was a washstand next to the bureau and a pitcher of clean water. He laved his face and torso and scrubbed with the rough towel. It awakened him somewhat, refreshed him. He hung up the towel and went to his blouse on the bed and withdrew a cigar from the pocket. He moved to the bureau and lit the cigar from the candle flame. He picked up the glass and held it high while he poured it half full of brandy. Then he sat down in the rocking chair with his legs stretched out in front of him, leaned back, removed the cigar, and lifted the brandy to his lips, sipping it.

All at once none of it was any good. The brandy was sour on his tongue, the cigar dry and harsh and stale.

A lightning flash outside the window limned everything in the room in its white, bright flame, but the roll of thunder came far behind and distant: the storm had moved over and the abortive little shower of rain had quit.

Wales turned the cigar around and around in his fingers.

How did it happen? he wondered. I wasn't even thinking about it when I did it. The first thing I knew, I had— And she let me. That is the incredible part of it. She let me . . . He shook his head. No, he thought, she shouldn't have let me do that. She should have screamed or slapped hell out of me or dodged.

But she didn't.

Damn her! he thought. She had no business letting me do that to her.

His palms were sweaty. He rubbed them on his

pants. He kept holding her in his mind. He kept feeling the softness of her lips; the places on his chest where her breasts had pushed against him still seemed to retain a certain special aliveness, as if more blood ran through the skin there.

Why, I'm getting as bad as Channing, he thought contemptuously.

But she let me . . .

He reached down for the brandy glass. The brandy tasted better this time.

He stood up, restless, bone-tired and unable to yield to it. I've got to quit thinking about that, he told himself. I've got to get to bed and get to sleep. There's too much to do tomorrow. I have got to build up some strength. If I keep thinking about this . . . But she— How long has it been since I touched a woman anyway?

Then, without warning, his throat tightened and welled with nausea, as his mind betrayed him. Unbidden, treacherously, it flung up before his eyes, bright, clear, and vivid, the one crystallized, unbearable picture— Vivian's face, framed by the whiteness of a pillow, contorted and twisted in the blind, heedless, agonized grimace of orgasm.

Wales began to tremble.

No! he thought wildly. Nobody but me! Nobody but me should ever see that! It's not right for anybody else to see—she is my wife! That moment when it quits being even love, becomes raw animality—when woman becomes beast—only her husband should—

But he has seen it! he thought savagely. *How could she let him see her like that?* How could— Lying before *him*, lying under *him* like that, striving up to him, biting, whimpering, all reason gone, no shame, no modesty—It's wrong! his mind screamed. Without love it's wrong!

Rage and shame and hate and grief boiled through him, shaking him viciously. He flailed the air with a hand, wanting to cry out. The picture unbearable—the uncaring sacrilege before his eyes . . . Stop it! he shrieked voicelessly. Stop it!

Her face, eyes closed, teeth bared, hair tangled—

desperate, savage, animal lusting . . . I taught her! he thought. I taught her so well! I loved her and I changed her from a woman to an animal and back again, and it was all right because I loved her and treasured her and— Stolen, worthless, he thought, his neck tight and swollen. Him and now how many others? Not love! She was like that all the time underneath. I taught her nothing! It wasn't love . . . But he has her and he has no right— The picture too vivid now, Wales raised his arm. *God damn you, take your eyes off her. Get your body away!* And then suddenly he had slammed his fist into the hard plaster wall with an impact that thudded all through the vibrant silence of the big old house and the wonderful cleansing shock of pain was tearing through him.

He dropped his hand, his mind suddenly empty.

He stood there, panting.

I might as well face it, he thought exhaustedly. There isn't any way I can get rid of her.

He turned away from the wall. He could feel cold sweat standing beaded over every pore of his naked flanks, feel it trickling down to the waistband of his trousers.

The rest of the glass of brandy was sitting on the arm of the chair. Wales reached for it with a hand beginning to bleed at the knuckles. He was shivering. He drained the glass at a gulp and then went to the bureau and poured another glass and drank half of that and let out a long, rasping sigh. Gradually the shivering ended. He stood there by the bureau with the glass in his hands, rubbing his aching knuckles.

I can't control it any more, he thought wearily. There's no way I can bury it, forget it . . . I can't make my mind stop doing that to me.

He drank the rest of the brandy. And *she,* he thought, with her red hair and her green eyes and her long mouth and the way she was looking up at me, would she have—?

He walked to the window and looked out. The moon was veiled by a murk of clouds. The thunder still rolled but muted and far away.

We shall dismiss it, he thought, her words echoing in his mind.

But how can I dismiss it? he wondered. It's torn me apart. Not out of lust for her. But because it ripped away my defenses, left me vulnerable to memories like that.

The brandy was helping him get his control back, he felt; his mind was at least thinking now in coherent sentences.

Now, he thought, if I am ever to be free of Vivian, I have first got to be free of her too.

The only thing is, he told himself, she is so different from Vivian. She has strength that Vivian never had. So that kiss was an accident. Neither one of us knows how it happened. Neither one of us even meant for it to happen. It had no significance, and I must forget it. Because she's not Vivian, a weak, lusting little creature running to the first man she meets when her husband's away. *We shall dismiss it.* She was strong enough to say that. She is strong enough to hold this place together, to face what I am doing to her without fear. She is strong enough to be faithful to her husband. *We shall dismiss it* . . . Her husband is lucky, Wales thought. He's lucky to have a wife with strength enough to say that . . . I wonder if he knows, Wales thought bitterly, how damned much I envy him?

He went back to the bureau and poured another brandy and then slumped down in the chair, rocking gently, staring at the two candle flames on the bureau, trying not to think any more at all. The air had grown hot and still again, and the candle flames burned fat and tall and bright without even flickering.

I'm afraid, Wales thought after a while. I'm afraid that there isn't any way at all that I can keep from thinking. . . .

20 _____

Somewhere away off, from the blackness of a pine-clad ridge, an owl hooted—eight strung-out notes, rising in idiotic laughter. Jeff Davis opened his eyes and shivered. His hand closed more tightly around the gun. He looked up at the sky and wished the clouds would hurry and move away from the moon.

He had been trying to sleep, but he'd had no luck at it. There was no fear in his mind that anybody would be around to inspect the guard. Them officers, he had thought, an' that-air big-mouthed sergeant—they ain't goin to be losin no sleep that they can help. So he had found himself a wooden bucket which, overturned, made a good seat, and he had settled himself at one corner of the cattle pen, gingerly leaning back against the rails and at last finding a position which didn't make his back hurt.

But for a long time sleep would not come. Perhaps he had slept too much already, or maybe it was the dream that had stirred him up beyond relaxing. Whatever it was, he had had nothing to do but sit out here thinking and remembering, going back over all the things that had happened to him since that day the wagon had bumped away from the cabin on the Trace.

Things were pretty blurred for a long time after that. He had a vague recollection of the shack on the waterfront in Mobile, the drunken laughs of sailors mingling with the high-pitched giggling of his mother; he could remember the midnight panting and grunting and thumping from the corner of the shack in which his

240

mother had her bed; he could remember how she would disappear for one or two days at a time and how hungry he would get then, and how cold, if it was in winter. . . .

And he remembered, too, how she had gone off like that one time when he was about nine years old and had never come back. He had never seen her again since then and he had no idea what had happened to her and hardly ever even thought about her any more. Except on nights like this, after he'd had the dream.

Somehow he had wandered onto a steamboat, and the next thing he remembered was being helper to a big black free-nigger cook in the galley. That cook had been meaner'n gar broth seasoned with tadpoles. Davis could still feel the impact of the cook's great hard-soled bare foot on his behind every time he thought about it; his skin still ached with the cook's savage pinches; his cheeks burned with the cook's sudden slaps. Just thinking about that cook, Davis could feel hot, dry, helpless anger burning in him.

He'd stayed on the steamboat for a few years, though, and then one day, while they were tied up at Vicksburg, the cook had hit him without warning and the eleven-year-old boy had seized a kettle of boiling water and thrown it at the cook. Davis grinned, remembering the big black man's screaming. But he had never known what damage he had done—blindly he'd turned and run ashore.

He helped in a grocery store for a while; it gave him a place to sleep. He did chores around a tan yard; sometimes he caught fish and sold them. Then he had worked on a farm for a while. But he hadn't liked the farm work; he'd missed the excitement that was always afoot on the river front, and before long he was back prowling around the docks.

By that time he'd reached puberty; his voice had deepened as much as it was ever going to, and there was something about his face that made people think he was older than he really was. Nobody took him in because of pity any more. And there were no jobs for a white

241

man. The niggers did everything. Anybody who had more work to do than he could do himself had a nigger to do it; nobody wanted to pay wages to a white man. It was a hungry, lonesome, dislocated time.

Until he'd met old Whit Winecoff.

Winecoff was a fat old man who'd been first mate on a blackbirder until he'd got too old to go to sea any more. Then he'd started dry-land slave trading. He'd needed somebody to help him move a bunch of slaves from Mobile to Decatur, and Samuel Alexander Davis had hired out to him for ten cents a day and his meals. Now you talk about a man that knowed handling niggers, Jeff Davis thought, shifting his rifle in his lap, that was old Whit Winecoff . . .

Yes, sir, he owed ole Whit a lot. He'd worked with Whit for five years, and Whit had taught him everything he'd needed to know. It was funny, Jeff Davis thought, how he'd known right from the start that he'd found what he wanted to do. On the first day Whit had shown him how to use a flat leather strap to beat the niggers along when they moved too slowly. "Doan never hit a nigger with a ox whip," Whit had told him. "It leaves a scar, an' nobody wants to buy a nigger with whip scars. It's a sure sign he's a troublemaker." And he remembered that second night, too, sitting around a campfire with the slaves all securely chained in the darkness beyond the firelight, and Whit saying in an offhand way, as he poked the fire, "Now, iffin you feel like a leetle fun, bucko, why don't you try out that fat black Gaboon gal over yonder? She ain't much to look at, but she sho do know how to wiggle an' she ain't clapped up." Jeff Davis' throat tightened as he remembered then how he'd moved into the darkness with his heart pounding terrifically in his chest, to take the first woman he'd ever had. . . .

Jeff Davis stood up. He yawned and stretched and looked all about him. No lights showed anywhere about the slave quarters and outbuildings. Only at the big house were yellow squares of illumination visible through the tree foliage that screened the second story. Davis spat on the ground.

242

Takin hit all an' all, he thought, you cain't beat the nigger business. I-God, I'll sho be glad when I kin git back home an' git a little stock together an' git started again. Then, when I want me a black gal, I doan need to worry about no—

Whut was that?

He swung, raising the gun, ramming it forward at the blackness from which he was sure a sound had come. Sudden fear rose thick in his throat. Whut if they doan lock them slave houses? he thought in terror. Whut if that big black buck that was the daddy of that gal—Do you reckon—?

He saw blackness moving within the blackness. He eared back the hammer of the gun.

"S-Stuart," he husked, and the gun barrel jerked uncontrollably.

"Beauty," Channing's voice said from the night, and Davis let out a great gush of air, almost sick with the relief that surged through him. He lowered the gun.

"Lord Gawd Amighty, Lieutenant, you scairt me. I thought at fust you was—"

"You watch your trigger finger, Davis."

"Yes, suh." Davis put aside the gun and leaned weakly against the fence.

"How're things? All quiet?"

Davis licked his lips. "Yes, suh. I reckon so . . ."

"Good," Channing said crisply, and then his voice changed its tone. "How's your back?"

Jeff Davis blinked in surprise at the unexpected solicitude. His mind searched quickly for any possible trick before he whined, "Hit hurts like pure dee hell, Lieutenant."

"Yes, I reckon it would. That was a hell of a thing to have done to you, being hauled up and whipped like a nigger right out there in front of everybody."

It must be some kinda trap, Davis thought blankly. He held his tongue.

Then he could see the faint gleam of Channing's teeth, smiling in the darkness. "Hell, Davis, you ain't got to be afraid of me. I come out here especially to

243

talk to you. I said, I think that was a rotten thing Wales did to you."

"Sho," Davis whined. "God damn hit, hit hurts, Lieutenant. I think somethin's busted in it."

"I wouldn't be surprised. Wales sure hit you hard enough to bust something in it." The lieutenant leaned against the fence. "You're goin to make a complaint, ain't you?"

"Complaint—whut you mean complaint?"

A match flared in the darkness as the lieutenant lit a cigar. Davis heard him exhale smoke. "Have one?" Channing asked.

Startled, Davis groped and found the cigar the officer was thrusting toward him. He did not look at the lieutenant as he bent to light the cheroot off Channing's match.

"I mean," Channing said after he'd blown out the match, "you're going to let me take you on up to Brigade Headquarters, so you can tell the story to General Slater, ain't you?"

I knowed it was a trap, Davis thought quickly. "I ain't messin around no general," he blurted.

"Oh hell." Channing's voice was disgusted. "God damn it, Davis, you got Wales by the short hair and you ain't even got sense enough to see it. Look," he said. "General Slater that commands this brigade is a friend of mine. We come over here together from Tennessee. He hates niggers worse than poison. Now, you let me take you up to Brigade and you tell General Slater just what Wales did to you—and then Marsh Wales will be in one hell of a mess of trouble."

"Whut kind of trouble?" Davis asked the question in spite of himself.

"Hell, I doan know. I ain't a lawyer. But plenty of it. A court-martial of some kind. They'd bust him down to private. Maybe even give him a prison term." His tone thickened with disgust. "If this was where I came from," he said, "old Slater'd probably have Wales whipped, too, just like he whipped you. I've seen Slater use the lash on many a deserter. But with this damn prissy little tin god Lee they got over here, I don't know. Just the same, there'd be trouble—plenty of it. Enough to teach Wales a lesson, you can bet your spurs on that. If I know Slater, he'll make sure Wales winds up somewhere where he'll get his hand shot off soon as possible."

"All on account of what he done to me?" Davis asked incredulously.

"All on account of what he did to you."

Davis ran his hand along the top rail of the fence. Suddenly he felt a rough, warm wetness against it and jumped, then he realized that a calf was licking the salt off his skin. He struck out with a balled fist in the darkness, felt his knuckles slam into the softness of the animal's nose. He heard a startled grunt, then the blatting of the calf as it lurched away into the darkness. Davis wiped his hand on his pants.

"All on account of me," he said. He stood a little straighter. It made his back hurt. He spat.

"How come you want me to do this?" he asked Channing bluntly.

"Why, I just hate to see a white man whipped like he was a nigger. That's all. It just ain't right. It just naturally gripes me. Ain't that reason enough?"

Davis hesitated. "I reckon. But—

"How do I know hit won't make no trouble for me?" he asked after a pause. "If I go up there talkin to that general. I mean, when they find out about that nigger gal?"

Channing's chuckle was short and harsh. "Hell, what kind of trouble? She was a slave, wasn't she? The old lady's going to be paid in full for her, ain't she? She was—resistin while you were searchin her cabin, wasn't she? Pulled a knife on you—made an attack on your life. I believe that's what you said?"

Davis was silent.

"Oh hell, Davis," Channing said. "Get some sense into you. She wasn't nothin but a nigger. Nobody gives a good Goddam what the details were. That's something that don't amount to a hill of beans."

245

Davis let out a breath. It made sense. The thought of getting even with Wales put a glow in his belly, not unlike that of the corn whisky he'd had that morning.

"All right," he said. "When we git back, if you'll take me to that-air general, I'll go along with you."

"Good." Channing clapped his hand down on Davis' shoulder. Davis flinched, grunting with pain.

"Oh. Sorry. I forgot."

"Lieutenant, my back hurts mighty much right this minute. I reckon you wouldn't let me go off duty right now, would you?"

Channing shook his head. "Don't call your relief yet. I don't want nobody knowing I talked to you. But, hell, there isn't going to be anybody else around. Just find yourself a place and get comfortable. Only—don't spill a word of this, you hear? Now have another seegar to help you pass your trick."

"Yes, suh." As the realization came to him that Channing was about to leave, Davis licked his lips. He looked about him at the darkness.

"Lieutenant, uh . . . you doan happen to know if they locked up them slave quarters tonight, do you?"

"No. Why?"

"Well, I jest—I got to thinkin about that big buck that was that gal's daddy. I was jest wonderin if anybody had sense enough to chain 'im in. When a nigger gits to grievin, there ain't no tellin whut he's liable to do an'—"

"Oh, crap. If he comes fooling around, just blow a hole in 'im. Your orders are to shoot to kill, and I'll see you don't get no more whipping. Now I'll see you tomorrow, Davis. I'm going up and go to bed. But you remember. It might be that I won't have to call on you to go to the general. But if I do, between you and me, we'll take Captain Wales down a peg or two yet!"

"Yes, suh," Davis said. He stood there, watching the gray uniform fade into the night. By God, he thought, feeling something warm stir within him, there's one officer got a little consideration for a private soljer. He stuck the cigar in his shirt pocket.

Yes, by jingo, he thought, I'd love to see 'em whup that bastard jest exactly like he whupped me!

After Channing had gone the night seemed even darker, more vast and empty. Still the clouds would not leave the moon. Davis paced up and down along the fence, unable to settle down and rest. Jumpy, he thought. A man's been whupped like I been got a right to be jumpy. . . .

He told himself that he would be glad when his hitch was over, when he could crawl back into the loft, burrow down into the hay, listen to the comforting sound of others breathing around him. It was, he thought, a queer kind of night. If a man believed in hants, this was the kind of night on which they'd walk. That owl kept hooting over and over; sometimes there was a whippoorwill down in the lane; miles away there was the faintest threadlike sound of a hound baying. Most anything's likely to be prowlin on a night like this, he thought.

But the main thing that worries me, he thought, is that big nigger. I doan want that big sonbitch sneakin up on me in the darkness. He's strong as a ox. Did he lay a hand on a man, I bet he'd . . .

But they shet him in, he thought. They're bound to have. Sholy they know enough about niggers to have locked him up tonight.

Nevertheless, at the faintest stir of sleeping cattle, he jumped. That calf still would not settle down; it kept walking around and around the pen, nuzzling the other cows and disturbing them, making a soft lowing sound to itself. It began to get on Jeff Davis' nerves. I-God, he thought, a whole damn bunch of calvary could run right over a man and he couldn't hear hit on accounta that blasted calf.

Once he stopped and looked down toward the quarters. The black shapes of the buildings were only dimly discernible in the night. I oughta go down there an' check, Davis thought. But hit's so damn dark—

Then his thumb, running idly over the mechanism of his carbine, suddenly discovered that the cap had dropped off the nipple. A sudden fear thickened his throat. Hastily he fumbled in his cartridge pouch. Until the percussion cap had been replaced his gun was useless.

But he ain't got no call to come after me anyhow, Davis thought, his hand shaking as he pressed a new cap in place. I didn't go for to hurt her. I didn't mean to hurt her. If she'd jest laid still . . .

Finally the cap was on; the charge in the gun was alive again. Davis let out a long breath and straightened up. Now, he thought. Now let 'im come.

He squinted up at the sky. Behind the clouds the blob of useless light that was the moon was heeling down toward the horizon. Hit's about over, he thought, feeling better. In jest a minnit I'll go wake Houston.

He walked along the fence, running his hand along the top rail, seeking in the darkness the bars that served as gate. His back was too sore for climbing. I-God, he thought, it'll feel good to git down in that hay. . . .

He still had not found the gate when he halted. There was absolutely no sound in the night. Everything was perfectly still. But for no reason at all the short hairs on the back of his neck had just stood up and a chill had gone down his spine.

He swallowed.

His eyes were large as he looked about him. He opened them as wide as he could, trying to pierce the darkness. But he could see nothing. He stared until little red patterns danced across his vision, and he could see nothing at all.

Hmmf, he muttered inaudibly. He took a step more, certain that he must be almost at the gate. Once he was inside the fence, he would be all right. Nothing could come over the fence without revealing its presence.

Then he smelled it.

Nigger smell! he thought instantly, and his heart dropped and his throat closed up and his knees began to shake.

He sucked in another breath of air.

There was no mistaking it. Smell of sweat, smell of greese, smell of wood smoke. Slave smell. It came to him strong and pungent on the moist night air.

He stood there paralyzed for a moment, then he

managed to force his limbs into action. He swung the gun up. He stared into the darkness.

"All right, nigger." His voice was high and reedy. "I know yo're out thur. Now you git! Git, or I'll blow yo ass off!"

Nothing answered him.

But that rankness was still pungent in his nostrils. There was no mistaking it. He had lived with it too long. It had always meant money in his pocket. He knew what that smell was. He had chained up too many nigger men. He had laid too many nigger women.

His mind raced. I cain't crawl through the fence, he thought. I cain't go over. My back'll slow me up. He kin git me befo I'd make it!

He's got to make a sound, he thought desperately. Iffn he comes at me, he's got to make some kinda sound.

Only he's got the advantage, Jeff Davis thought sickly. He's so all-fired black. He kin see me an' I cain't see him.

And they kin move like cats, he thought.

"Nigger?" It should have been a roar; it came out a fear-squeezed tremolo.

And still there was no answer.

"Now, lissen to me." It was taking all his strength to squeeze the desperate words through his throat. "I didn't go for to kill 'er! It was a accident! Now, you lissen, nigger! You go on back whur you belong! If you doan't, I'll hafta kill you too!"

But only silence from the darkness.

Am I imaginin it? he wondered.

But that smell was rank in his nostrils. He thought it was getting stronger. Smell of a man who worked all day in the hot sun and had no place to bathe. Smell of a man who lived on greasy side meat. Smell of a man who spent his nights shut in a tiny, smoke-filled cabin . . .

"Now go on!" Jeff Davis shrilled. *"Go on!"*

The red patterns danced before his straining eyes. He thought he saw blackness move, a bulk blacker than the

249

blackness all around it. He let out a yelp and swung the gun up and pulled the trigger.

The lock came down with a dry snap and his mind went blank for an instant in astonishment and dismay. *It done dropped off again,* he thought. Then he was sure the blackness towered over him; he choked on the odor of slave—

He squealed and threw the gun as hard as he could and heard it clatter on the hard ground somewhere in the night, and then he tried to yell. He tried with every muscle and nerve in him, but his throat betrayed him. There was a reedy squeak that might have been the squeal of a rat, and then he was running. Wildly, blindly running.

He ran away from the fence. He ran across the plantation yard. He ran toward the lane that led to the fields.

Black shapes kept springing up in front of him, jumping out at him. Somehow he dodged them—the smokehouse, a corncrib, a parked wagon; somehow he knew that what he feared was still behind him. But it was coming after him. He could tell it by something in his back—a nakedness, a vulnerability, a waiting for something to strike.

His lungs became blobs of fire. His breath was a rasping choke. His thighs were stiff as fire logs, and his calves and feet weighed tons. But he had to run on. Because it was still behind him, loping, intent, murderous, and there was no salvation except in running.

Then he slammed into the rail fence of the lane. He hit it blindly, full force, with an impact that jarred each bone and snapped him into the air. He landed on his back in the tall grass of the lane, stunned, sucking in great draughts of breath.

Then all at once his lungs were rank with it again.

He shrilled a chittering cry and rolled between the poles of the fence. He dragged erect again and began to run across a field.

His back was a sheet of fire. Ain't you got no mercy? he wanted to cry out. Oh, damn you, ain't you got no mercy?

Suddenly he crashed into a fibrous wall that yielded and then sprang back. A thousand voices rustled in his ears. A cornfield! he thought. He cain't find me in here! And he plunged into the corn.

Stalks caught at him, crunched beneath him, tripped him. Long rough leaves whipped sharply at his face. He held up his arms to shield himself, the noise of his progress tremendous as he smashed his way along. Finally, deep in the corn, he could go no further. He sank to the ground, sobbing for breath, straining his ears to listen.

First there was the thump-thump-thump of his heart. Then, above that and the rush of blood in his ears, he heard something creeping toward him. *From over there,* he thought. *Or is it over there? Or yonder?* He trembled. The breeze had risen. The whole field was alive with the scrape and play of leaf and stalk against leaf and stalk. There was no way to tell which sound was the one that threatened him, to tell which sibilance was wind and which the intent, implacable blackness seeking him in the corn.

He cowered close to the ground in the dark. Surely it could not find him. Surely it must—

Then it enveloped him like a fog. He gagged on smoky rankness. Then he screamed. He screamed and whirled and plunged on through the corn.

He was screaming all the way across the cornfield. He was actually making no sound, but he did not know it. The breath was wheezing gaspingly up through his paralyzed throat, but he was certain that he was screaming. There was a red fog before his eyes; the night was red. He no longer knew from what he ran; he no longer knew whether he ran from man or blackness or slave smell, from one presence or from hundreds. He plowed and blundered through the corn and he thought there was an army behind him—whip-marked, shackled, black, relentless . . . He ran from all of them, screaming as he went.

Then he had cleared the field. He broke out of the corn and onto a rise of ground. Dimly he was aware

251

that a hill rose before him. He gasped for breath, sagged, then struggled to his feet.

Briars and honeysuckle yanked and clawed and threw him. Pine boughs slashed his face. Oh God, he begged soundlessly, as he tried to make wooden legs push him up the slope. Oh God, oh God, oh God.

Then he had gained the top of the plateau. Red lights exploded in his head. He sank to his knees, wheezing. Make it stop, he begged. Please make it stop. But it was still coming. He could not hear it but he could feel it. Behind him. He could feel it in his back.

He scrabbled to his feet and lurched through the woods, blundering from tree to tree, hanging on to each a moment for breath, but never daring to stop, driven by a fear that seemed now the only reality he'd ever known. He whimpered with the wild, uncontainable, inchoate horror of the blackness behind him. Then a low stone wall hit him right beneath the knees and, helplessly, he went toppling over it to sprawl on the vine-massed ground.

He went clawing on his belly across the burying ground. He could not even get to his feet any more. Sobbing, knowing that he was helpless and alone and finished, he crawled. He rolled into sunken graves and fought his way back out somehow. He cut his hands on the bits of broken glass around them. He came to a mound of fresh wet earth and hitched himself across it.

Hide, the pounding of the blood drummed in his brain. Hide, hide, hide.

He slithered down the other side of the pile of clay. He rolled across some more vines. Covered with wet earth, he came to a clump of honeysuckle, where it had formed a mass against the wall.

And that was all he had strength for. To burrow down in the vines like a helpless, frightened animal. Like a rabbit cowering before a hawk.

He forced himself into them as far as he could. He did not know whether they covered him or not. It did not matter. Nothing mattered any longer. Because it was coming for him. He could smell it again, and he knew it was inside the wall with him, and there was nothing that he could do.

He closed his eyes and held himself rigid, waiting for it to take him.

He thought he could hear it padding up to him on giant bare feet that touched the ground as lightly as a panther's.

Then he knew that it was there.

Slave smell. Sweat and grease and wood smoke. It filled his lungs. It seeped into his pores. It became a part of him. He felt the vast black shadow covering him.

No part of him moved. His body waited for death.

The shadow stayed over him interminably. The smell was rank around him. His fingers dug into the ground.

He waited.

And then the shadow lifted.

He felt it lift. Without looking, unable to look, he felt the pressure off his fear-blind spirit.

But still he did not move.

Gradually the sureness of death flowed out of him. Gradually, through his exhausted and pain-racked body, there came the knowledge that he was not to be extinguished.

He could hear nothing but the blood in his ears, but somehow he knew that the blackness had moved away.

The owl that had been hooting all night laughed again, this time near at hand.

Jeff Davis opened his eyes.

The clouds had passed away from the moon. Light flooded the woods, casting silvered harlequin patterns beneath the pine trees.

Still he did not move.

He was safe now. He knew that. The air he sucked in was pure and sweet, full of the smell of pine and dew and fresh-turned dirt. Nothing else. He was safe.

Exhausted and sick, he lay there for a long time, wondering if he had been, inexplicably, deliberately spared or if he had only been missed in the darkness.

It did not matter now. He would not rise from here till daylight, though whatever had pursued him through the night was gone now. It was not chasing him any more.

But even that did not matter either, he knew. Because he was not ever going to feel safe again. That rankness—sweat and grease and wood-smoke—slave smell—he had sucked in too much of it. He had sucked in so much of it that it would never come out. He would never be free of the smell of it again. And always before it had smelled like money to him. But he knew that when he arose from where he was it would never smell like money to him again.

From now on, he knew, it would always be, instead, the smell of fear.

21

The candles had burned down half their length now, and the little silver dishes were full of wax.

Marshall Wales, slumped deep in the rocker, stared at them dully. Their fat little yellow flames winked back at him sociably.

I have got to get up from here, Wales thought. I've got to get up from here and go to bed. It's past midnight now. If I don't, I'll never make it through tomorrow.

He rubbed his hand over his face. The skin of his face was taut and greasy-dirty, rough with the stubble of sprouting beard; his eyes felt burnt and gritty.

I don't think I have ever been this tired, he thought. Worn out like this. Never that I can remember. Not even after any engagement I have been in. Not after

Gettysburg even. Today has worn me out. Emptied me. I feel as if I'd been turned upside down and drained.

It's a most peculiar sensation, he thought. You say, "I'm at the end of my rope," and it's a figure of speech; it doesn't mean anything. Until you really are. Then you find that it is the most peculiar sensation you have ever felt. To know that you have nowhere to go from here. To realize that whatever it is inside a man that keeps him going, tells him what to do, makes him plan and hope and pushes him along from one minute to another one—to realize that this has entirely quit functioning inside yourself. It feels strange.

He shook his head and looked down at the empty glass in his hand. You'd think the brandy would at least help, he thought. But damned if it hasn't made it worse. The more I drink, the soberer I get and the more clearly I see how empty I am. With everything gone from inside me. Finished. Used up. No hope, no courage, no particular desire to die and no particular desire to go on living. Only a void. The only desire, to stop thinking . . .

He stood up, rubbing his palms down his trouser legs. The candles threw the shadow of his shirtless torso long and gaunt and mocking on the far wall behind him, ripping and flickering in a kind of manic dance.

If only I had never come here, he thought. I was managing all right until I came here. I was keeping going somehow. I had it all pushed down inside, and the lid was fastened tight. Then— Christ, this has been a terrible day. That woman and her calf. That damned Jeff Davis. Channing . . . Mrs. Cameron . . . everybody and everything tearing at me all day. Using up everything I had in me. Everybody but the girl. And she—without meaning to, she's been the worst of all. He ran his hand through his hair. Now everything's roiled up inside of me, he thought. Vivian, Ashbrook, everything I had tied down has broken loose today and is banging around inside of me, and I can't stand it.

He looked at the brandy decanter sitting on the bureau. It was still three quarters full. He shook his head. No, he thought. I don't want any more drinks

255

out of you. You're too dangerous. One more drink and there's no telling—

All around him he was aware of the sentient quietness of the vast, sleeping house. There was continual small sound throughout it—the scurrying of something small in the attic; the occasional creak or snap of a settling timber. He thought, I must be the only one still awake. The last human sound he had heard had been the clump of Channing's boots ascending the stairs an hour before, as Channing had returned from inspecting the guard.

Maybe I ought to quit fighting him, Wales thought. Maybe everybody would be better off if I turned over command to him.

But something in him revolted at that thought. Channing was a killer. Moreover, he was a stupid killer. It would be a death warrant for the men.

But it may be one for them, too, if I try to lead them any more, he thought bitterly. How many of them will *I* manage to get killed?

He went to the window and spread back the curtains and looked out at the earth, lying black and obscure in the moonless night.

What have I done wrong? he thought baf8edly. Grant that there is such a thing as sin, and grant that people are punished for it, what have I done wrong? Why was I picked out to be the one to be destroyed?

I only tried to do my best, he thought. I have done the best I could, the best way I knew how. My home was threatened. Perhaps I could have stayed there, but I chose to fight to defend it. I took a wife and loved her and tried to earn her love in return. What have I done wrong? What sin have I committed in that?

There had to be one, he thought. How else explain it? I've fought as well as I know how. I've carried out my orders as best I could, and still . . . It's senseless, he thought. My God, it's senseless. If there were just a pattern to it, just a reason for it . . . If I could only put my finger on a single cause . . . but it's just a jumble, things happening for no reason, no way that I can understand any of it. I don't have the strength left to puzzle over it any more, he thought wearily.

So now, he thought, here I am. Alone in a room in a big house. Tomorrow I have to begin again. And I can't begin again. I can't quit and I can't begin again. Because I can't think, I can't fight. I can't command. And if I try—disaster, he thought. Channing saw it and he told me. The sergeant saw it and he told me too. It must stick out on me like a mold, a fungus. And there's nothing I can do about it. Courage and hope are like water in a shallow well. You can't keep on pulling out more than will seep back in. I've had to use up too much —and today even the seepage stopped. The well, he thought, is dry now.

He stared out the window.

What am I supposed to do now? he asked the darkness.

The silent black earth yielded him no answer. He turned away from the window and faced the room again, rubbing his sweaty hands on his pants once more.

There are two alternatives, he thought.

I can go to bed. And in the morning I can get up. And see how far I go before I come apart, see how long it takes for me to cave in completely. And pray that when I do, I don't drag anybody else with me. I can go on living without being alive. Because maybe, after a while, this damned misery and hate will stop again. Maybe after a while I'll be dead inside again and never think of Vivian again and nothing will hurt me. But, he thought fearfully, suppose I can't make that happen? Suppose I'm never able to shut it up, to get the lid back on? Suppose I stay aware? What if this just keeps on eating at me? For as long as my body is alive? For as long as my brain is capable of thinking?

A chill ran over him and he shivered. The fat little candle flames winked as if they would like to help him if they could. He looked around the room, still rubbing his hands on his trousers. The room was a jumble of ragged shadows, black and orange, and one cold, dull, winking gleam from the blue steel of one of the pair of Colts hanging in their scabbards on the bedpost.

257

He stared at the guns. The chill grew deeper.

Or, he thought . . .

The rounded cylinders of the gun shone coldly. The little brass caps on the nipples of the cylinders were little red stars in the candlelight.

Wales blinked at them. He shook his head as if he had water in his ear.

Cowardice, he thought. That's what they call it. A contemptible thing to do . . . Self-pity . . .

But this isn't self-pity, something within him wailed. This is agony. Agony real as a gut wound, agony real as a surgeon's saw on bone—only a thousand times worse. Because a gut wound is over, sometime, somehow. The saw cuts through and stops biting. But this just goes on and on and on. Why, it wouldn't be self-pity. I've seen horses shot to put them out of their misery for things that hurt less than this. . . .

But he turned away from the cold, winking gleam of the cylinders.

There ought to be something besides that, he thought. Isn't there any way I can fasten my mind into the future? Hang my sanity on that? The war's end—rebuilding Ashbrook—why, there could even be another woman . . .

He tried hard. He made a desperate effort to visualize a future. But he did not seem to be able to imagine anything. It was as if all the mechanism for hope, for looking forward to anything, had been smashed or disconnected; it would not function. All I can imagine, he thought, is a void. The past keeps getting in the way. I'm not even sure the war will end. It may never end—it might just go on forever and ever, a seven years' war, a hundred years' war, an eternal war . . . And how could I go back to that heap of charcoal? How could I go back there, where every piece of rubble, every tree, even the flowers she planted that still may be coming up in all those choking weeds—how could I go back there where everything I saw or touched would stir it up all over again? And a woman? Another woman? To be that much fool again? After Vivian . . . to hold her, to kiss her, to love her and put myself at her mercy? To always wonder within me—when? When

258

will she choose to destroy me? Christ, no! he thought. Time is dead. I can't go back in time by going forward.

His fists clenched and unclenched at his sides.

Mixed with the thrum of the blood in his temples, he could clearly hear the mocking voice of Channing ringing suddenly within his head:

You're your own bad luck, Wales—you're through, finished, worn out.

Yes, he thought at last. Yes, I guess I am. I guess this is what it is like when you are really finished.

When it is not only easier but more logical just to quit living.

He stood in the middle of the room for a little while. Then, very slowly, as if stalking something or as if seeking his way through fog, he moved over to the bed. He reached out gingerly and drew one of the Colts from the scabbard. He looked down at it curiously, as if he had never really seen what a Colt revolver looked like before.

It was a beautiful weapon. Its long, clean octagonal barrel with the hammer underneath was blue and cold; the cylinders were rounded at the ends like a woman's breasts; there was an almost female curve to the downsweep of the ivory stock. It was a very beautiful weapon, and the cylinder made a dry clicking noise as he turned it round and round and the little brass caps winked up at him.

He stood there looking down at the pistol for a long time.

Then a shudder ran over his body. His lips curled downward bitterly. He cradled the pistol in his palm, while the candle gleam danced up and down the long blue length of it. His chest heaved as he sucked in a deep, whistling breath. Then slowly, very carefully, so as not to disturb the loads, he shifted the gun in his hand and then eased it back into the scabbard on the bedpost and turned away.

He walked over to the bureau and poured a glass of brandy and turned, sipping at the brandy and looking at the two guns across the room.

Not yet, he told them silently. I don't seem to be put

together in such a fashion that I can do that. But maybe the Federals will—

But it was a long while before he could take his eyes off the guns.

Finally he finished the rest of his brandy in one gulp and set down the glass. No, he said. No. I'll make this one decision. I'll resolve this much of the dilemma. I shall still be alive in the morning. He started across the room toward the bed and then whirled as very gently behind him the door opened and shut with only the faintest whisper of wood against wood and the click of the latch, a tiny sound in the night.

Somehow he was not even surprised to see that it was the girl standing there with her back against the door, a dark-blue robe belted around her and the candlelight striking golden sparks from the loosened fell of coppery hair that cascaded about her shoulders and halfway down her back.

They stood looking at each other across the flickering half-lit space for perhaps half a minute.

Her eyes were large in the candlelight. Wales could see no emotion whatsoever in them. They did not shift under his gaze. Her voice was toneless, flat.

"I drank up all the brandy I had in my room," she said. She gestured toward the bureau. "May I?"

Without speaking, without even allowing himself to think just yet, Wales inclined his head.

"Thank you," she said, and she went to the bureau and opened the top drawer and took out another glass. Her movements were not so much unsteady as they were just a fraction out of rhythm. "I hope you'll join me, Captain," she said, and poured both glasses so full that only surface tension kept the liquid in the one she passed to Wales. The room was full of the sharp smell of the brandy; mingled with it was a faint sweetness of lilacs.

The girl faced Wales and leaned her back against the bureau. "Your health, Captain Wales," she said and raised the glass and drank half of it at a swallow.

Wales stood there looking at her without answering.

She raised one hand and let it fall in a little aimless gesture.

"Ladies shouldn't drink," she said. "Except just a little spot of brandy or wine at dinner, or maybe a toddy for the chill." She finished the glass at another gulp, lowered it, and turned to pour another. The brandy shone amber-red in the candlelight. Almost, Wales found himself thinking, exactly the color of her hair.

"Ladies shouldn't be left all alone to run a thousand-acre plantation either," she said. "In the middle of a war, with a crowd of slaves depending on them. Well, I'm sure Webb will be shocked when he comes home to find how much I drink. But—your health again, Captain." She drank once more.

This time she set the half-empty glass down on the bureau and looked at him directly. "You're not drinking, Captain Wales," she said. She moved across the room toward him. "You haven't any shirt on either."

"No," Wales said.

"That's no way to receive a lady," she said. She put out one hand and her finger tips ran down the side of Wales's upper arm, slowly, lightly. "Most ladies would be shocked." Her green eyes looked upward into his. The cameo face was not quite smiling and not quite grave. The scent of the lilacs was very strong. "I," she said, "rather like it."

"Yes?" said Wales. He stepped around her and went to the bureau and put down his still full glass. Then he turned to face her once more.

Probably intentionally the robe had come open at the top. Wales could see the white rounded flesh of the beginning of her breasts. Desire came to him then in a sudden flame that roared up through him. Desire—the first positive emotion in months. A little tremor of shock went through him. Why, he thought in surprise, I feel real.

She did not move toward him. Her face looked sad. "Poor Captain Wales," she said softly. "You are so thin."

I feel real again, he thought. And all I have to do is take her. Because it is what she wants . . .

He moved across the room toward her without speaking. She threw back her head with a motion that sent the hair to shimmering in the candlelight and held her face up and was waiting for him, with the robe dropping completely away from her shoulders in one fluid motion. Her breasts were soft and warm and silken against his chest, and his nose was full of the scent of lilacs and of her; and her lips were parted ferociously beneath his, and her body strained against him . . .

Then in the middle of the kiss he saw them again—Vivian and the Englishman locked together, writhing and twisting obscenely; but somehow Vivian's swirling hair was red, the Englishman was bone thin from four years of war—and a vast sickness and revulsion boiled up in him, killing all desire as it rose, making her flesh a rotten thing to his touch. Then the hate and anger were there, complete, absolute, transferred to her in totality, and Channing's mocking voice rang inside his head: *She'll trade with you—don't think she won't!* And in the blur of fury and disgust he had wrenched loose and heard his own voice, harsh and snarling, "You bitch! If you think you can bribe me to—"

Her eyes went wide and startled and her face went white with shock, and the slamming impact of her immediate slap whirled his head halfway around. Then she was fighting desperately to get the robe back over her shoulders, her breasts rising and falling furiously, her mouth opening and shutting wordlessly.

At last, as she backed against the bureau and pulled the robe around her, the words found shape. "Oh," she forced the whisper between clenched teeth, "oh, you stupid, stupid man!"

"You had it all planned, didn't you?" Wales said in quiet blind fury. "Carefully planned, even to the spare glass in the bureau. Channing was right. He said you'd come. You bitch," he said. "You Goddamned adulterous bitch." He could feel himself trembling all over.

"Oh," she said. Her voice was thick and vibrant with rage. "Oh . . . I feel so sorry for you. You're so pitiful. I feel so sorry for you . . ."

262

Her hands knotted the robe more tightly, savagely. "You think I came here to—to trade with you," she said slowly and distinctly. Biting off each word. Honing the edges of each word and sending it flying at Wales. "You think that. You stupid, stupid man. No wonder your wife fled from you . . ."

He took a step forward, complete, perfect, blinding rage in possession of him. She did not flinch; she even leaned toward him, still throwing the words at him as weapons, each one quiet, edged, deadly:

"Listen to me, Captain Wales. Listen to me. Listen to me and I'll tell you why I came here tonight. Listen to me and understand." Before he could touch her, she had slipped quickly sideways and had reached the bed, and her hand closed over the butt of one of the Colts. "I'll kill you if you don't stop and listen and understand!"

He had never heard such scorn and contempt concentrated in a human voice.

He halted where he was in the middle of the room, his hands knotted at his sides.

"War," she snarled at him. "You men start it with your loose talk and your bragging and your stupidity and then you go off to fight it and expect everybody to crow about how brave and self-sacrificing you are." She said a word he had never heard a woman use before. She said it with more complete disgust than he had ever heard put in it before.

"Yes," she said, "you go scampering off to win your medals and your honors and have your fun and get yourself killed. And want your women to tell you how strong and wonderful you are. But"—for the first time her voice trembled—"but we're the ones who have to face the music . . ."

And now her voice was trembling more, rising, edging toward hysteria. "We're the ones left with the little things too minor for you brave male soldiers to concern yourself with. Like having to run a plantation with no more training for it than you have for crocheting . . . like having to figure out how to feed dozens of mouths

263

depending on us for food after you brave soldiers have taken all our food . . . like learning how to be planter and overseer and doctor and nurse and Jesus Christ performing the miracle of the loaves and fishes all at once, when we've never had to be anything before but women. The weaker we were, the better you liked us—and then you suddenly told us to be strong and went off and left us. We're the ones who have to face all the problems that don't have any answers, with the fear and the loneliness and the waiting, the Goddamned waiting! At least *you* can do something! At least you can fight! And then you only have one problem—you either kill somebody else or you get killed yourself. And you can solve that problem—with your trigger finger—because that," she shrieked, "is how you fool men have *always* solved your problems. But ours don't have any answers! They just come one right after another and there isn't any solution for them, and always we're at the mercy of whatever you crazy, senseless, wasteful men take a notion is your duty at the moment!"

Her voice dropped back to its low, scathing tone, and she clutched the robe around her as if she were suddenly very cold.

"You get scared in battle sometimes, don't you?" she said huskily, tremulously. "You want to run and hide sometimes, don't you? Well, what makes you think we're any braver than you are? Sometimes we get scared, too, and have to run and hide. But where are we going to run to? Where are we going to hide?"

Her green eyes gleamed savagely in the candlelight.

"Sometimes we have got to hide somewhere," she said, and then all at once tears were rolling down her cheeks.

"All I wanted," she whispered, trying to fight them back, her voice strained and thick, "was some place to hide. Because I was so scared. And you seemed so strong and confident that I thought maybe you could hide me and protect me for a little while and I could get some strength from you so I could go on for a little while longer, because I have had just about all I can stand. All I wanted, all I needed, was to be held for a little bit by somebody stronger than me so I could be safe and forget about everything but just being protected for a while."

She dropped her head for a moment and then she raised it and looked at him defiantly.

"It has nothing to do with loving my husband," she whispered. "I love him terribly. But, don't you understand, I just had to hide somewhere for a little while . . ."

Wales opened and shut his mouth, but he did not really have any words formed.

The girl moved away from the guns on the bedpost. Her face seemed completely without blood. She was like a wraith as she went to the door.

"War," she said bitterly, halting there. "Fighting. Patriotism. Country. Duty. All sacred. Yes. Everything's sacred to you men but people. People you can slaughter or starve or leave to die of loneliness if any of those other things require it. Because people don't matter— it's all those other fine things that are . . . sacred. If there is a God in heaven," she said with her teeth clenched, "I hope he damns you all to hell. Because people are more sacred than anything."

She put her hand on the knob. "I'm terribly sorry to have bothered and upset you, Captain Wales. I shall stay in my room tomorrow and I shan't be seeing you again. Good night."

Then she was gone. Wales stood rigidly in the middle of the room, looking at the door she had closed behind her.

A faint breeze stirred the leaves of the red oaks outside. The curtains billowed and flapped listlessly, with small popping noises. The candle flames winked and sputtered. Still Wales did not move. He was breathing deeply.

After a while he turned and walked over to the window and looked out. The wind was cool against his naked chest, but he did not notice it. The clouds had left the moon and the plantation lay limned in shadow and silver beneath him, but he did not see it.

He was possessed of no thought and no emotion. His entire body and his brain, too, felt insentient as clay. Something in the encounter had purged him of every feeling.

He did not know how long he stood at the window before he turned back into the room. The room smelled of brandy and candle fat and lilacs. He frowned.

There was something deep in the recesses of his mind clamoring for recognition. He did not know what it was. It was an unformed thought or an emotion which could not find expression.

He stared at the candles.

There was an urgency to whatever it was that glimmered in the blackness of his consciousness. It had vitality; it wanted to grow.

He paced around the room, as if to walk away from it. But he was beginning to feel a tremor of excitement. Whatever it was, it was important. But he did not dare reach for it. It was still too delicate for that. The only thing he could do was to let it grow as it would.

The excitement became a little stronger. He kept his mind blank. He could feel a tumescence of thought and emotion which must not be interfered with. It was going to be of utmost significance. It was going to be something he had lost and would find again.

Without conscious volition he turned and moved across the room to the bureau and picked up his brandy glass, still untouched. He knew now what it was going to be.

Truth.

Without looking at the glass, he raised it slowly to his lips, that peculiar lassitude giving away now to eagerness, to the certainty that in a minute there would be revealed—

Then the glass dropped from his fingers, hit the floor, and shattered with a disastrous smash, and the room was rank with brandy. Wales trembled all over, face to face with a monstrous reality that he had never imagined.

I am the one, he thought.

His lips moved soundlessly; his body was cold all over.

I destroyed everything, he thought.

The enormity of his guilt sickened every entrail, every nerve, each muscle.

All she wanted, he thought, was a place to hide. *And I refused it to her.*

He trembled more violently.

She tried to tell me, he thought. On the furlough. She tried to tell me that she was finished, used up, exhausted. She cried and begged me—

And I, he forced the words silently between clenched teeth, said *nonsense!*

It was the plantation, he thought in agony. I sold her out for the plantation. Protecting our home, I told her. But she knew. *She knew.*

I thought I loved her, he told himself. I thought I loved her more than anything in the world, and I even had myself fooled into believing it. But she wasn't fooled. She knew that I loved Ashbrook more. The land, the buildings, the ownership. She knew that it was part of me and that I loved that part of myself more than I ever loved her. She knew I was prepared to sacrifice her for it. And she begged for mercy and I told her nonsense, and after that she was too proud to plead any more, too brave to beg. She knew then; she had her answer. She knew I wouldn't let her hide if it meant hurting Ashbrook . . .

"Oh, Christ," he said aloud.

And then, he thought, later she had to write that letter . . .

Christ, he thought, What it must have cost her to write a letter . . .

Because she hadn't meant to . . . He whirled toward the candle flames. God damn it, he yelled soundlessly at them, she hadn't meant to! She was just used up! She needed shelter! And I hadn't given it to her!

But *he* did. And then she found out what it had cost her. And she knew that there was no way she could

make me understand. Because I had said *nonsense!*
She knew she'd get no help from me, no sympathy—
she knew I didn't love her enough to understand—*and
where else was there to turn but to him?*

The trembling ceased.

She needed me, he thought with crucial gravity. She
needed me and she wrote that letter. Because she already knew that I would never understand the simple
fact of weakness.

He looked across the room at the two Colt revolvers.

I understand it now, he thought. I understand everything now. He sank heavily into the rocker.

Then, without any more warning, the break came.
After ten months there was nothing left strong enough
to stop it. Everything that had been pent up for so long
flowed out of him in paroxysms that racked his skinny
frame as if he were retching; all the black bile of hate
and guilt in which he had drowned for so long came
vomiting invisibly out as his body shook and the room
echoed with the awkward sounds of his grief as he
buried his face in a circlet made by his arms. The
candle flames on the bureau flickered; the wind rose
and the curtains flapped like pale, beseeching arms.
One of the candles went out, but he did not know it
for a long time.

Eventually he raised his head. He sat inert for
several moments. There was nothing left within him
that could be called emotion. After a while he realized
that he was cold. He arose stiffly from the chair and
moved slowly and painfully, as if he were very old,
across the room and picked up his shirt from the bed.

It was while he was fastening the buttons that the
second truth came to him.

"Why," he said aloud as he looked at the single
candle flame, "suppose she still needs me?"

He began to tremble again, but this time it was with
excitement.

"Suppose she still needs me?" he said to the flame.
"Suppose something's happened? Suppose he's deserted
her? What if she's alone? She's so weak. What if she's
alone, with a baby, in a strange country?"

The excitement flamed higher.

"Is there a chance?" he asked. "Is there a chance that I could regain something? Is there a chance that I could make it up to her?"

The flame danced and winked; a thin black wisp of greasy smoke boiled upward from it. The little dancing fatness mocked. Derided.

Then a gust of wind blew it out.

Wales turned to the window. He stared out at the darkness. Below he saw the two saddled horses, heads down, cropping the dew-wet lawn in the moonlight.

He dragged his hands across his eyes; he rubbed his face.

It would be desertion, he thought. I couldn't do that. I have my responsibilities to the men.

He turned and began to pace the floor.

Anyway, he thought, I would have to leave now. Tonight. Otherwise, when we get back to Regiment, Channing will have me tangled up in that Jeff Davis thing. I might never have a chance again. But I took these men out. I have the responsibility to— They depend on me . . .

She did too, he thought.

How can I tell? he thought desperately. How can I tell what I should do? This is war. You can't just pull up stakes without . . .

But the horse is down there waiting, he thought. He halted his pacing, stopped breathing, and listened intently. The silence of the house was absolute. And everybody is asleep, he thought.

But it's fantastic, he thought. That I could get away, that I could get to England . . .

His hands clenched and unclenched with excitement. Then the one decisive phrase clanged in his mind: *She may need me!*

He knew then that there was no other decision to make, and in that one instant he could feel the well refill itself. As soon as he had thought the phrase he was full of strength again.

"The hell with the war," he said aloud, flatly and harshly, and he went to the bed and began to dress.

269

There was no more fog in his mind, no more compression within his skull. His thoughts came clearly and with as much precision as if his brain had been a clockwork mechanism. Cotton buyer, he thought. That means Manchester likely. Or maybe Liverpool. A place to start, anyway. Armstrong. Even if it's London, I can find him. A cotton buyer named Armstrong. I can find him and I can find her.

Now, blockade runners—they still make it out of Wilmington. If I can just get to Wilmington—if I can just get on a ship. From there to Nassau and from Nassau to England. I still have credits in England from before the war.

He buckled the heavy guns about his waist.

Then all at once he froze in a quick moment of terror. But what if I'm wrong? he thought. Suppose she went with him because she loves him? Suppose she won't come with me?

His lips tautened into a thin line.

Well, that, he thought, is a chance I am obligated to take.

Then all doubt, all worry, all indecision sloughed away from him. Something within him lifted, soared. There was only eagerness left. He could see now where his duty lay. He could see where it had lain all along.

"With my wife," he said aloud, and ducked out the window onto the roof of the veranda.

Crouching, Wales stood there on the roof for a moment before moving. Then, oriented, he padded softly across the moon-flooded shingles toward the back of the house.

The sergeant will get 'em back all right, he thought. They're grown men, and I'm useless anyway. They told me so. He reached the edge of the roof and halted. And someday, somehow, he thought, I have got to find a way to tell that girl how sorry I am and how grateful I am. I don't know how, but if she lives and I live, I will find a way to thank her.

He looked down into the yard. The horses were still

tearing at the moon-silvered lawn. He felt a tremor of excitement throb along his nerves.

Now, he thought happily. Now it's time to leave. He pushed himself feet first off the roof, edging over until he hung in space, hanging by his fingers in the gutter. Then he swung inward. He groped with his legs, found the column. He let go of the gutter, dropped, grabbed the column, and slid the rest of the way down.

His horse snorted as he came up to it and gathered up the reins. Wales whispered, "Easy, boy," and struggled with excited fingers at the knot which tethered it. For some reason it would not come loose, and the horse snorted and sidled away from him. "Easy—" Wales began again, and then, behind him, Channing's voice came, low and amused.

"Going somewhere, Marsh?"

Wales stiffened and then, very slowly, he turned around. Channing stood there almost negligently, not ten feet away, and somehow Wales was not surprised to see that in his hand Channing held a pistol which was trained on Wales's chest.

Wales did not even feel any fear. Only a sort of wild, raucous joy because he was challenged and he was alive and had the strength to answer the challenge. His eyes narrowed as he looked at Channing.

"Put down that gun, Vance," he said slowly and quietly, restraining the joy within him. "That's an order."

Channing's teeth shone white in a grin. "An order? An order from who? From a hound who has another man's wife in his room in the middle of the night? From a deserter, obviously trying to slope out ahead of a court-martial with God knows how much of the regiment's money still in his pockets? Why, good Lord, Wales, do you expect me to honor an order from a man like that?"

Then all the good humor went off his face; the grin remained, but it was pure savagery.

"Do you think I didn't watch you?" he snapped. "Do

you think I didn't see that girl come out of your room? Do you think I didn't see you when you prowled the roof past my window? Hell, Wales, I've made it my business tonight to keep up with what you were up to. And now——" His voice was thick with satisfaction.

"Shot while trying to desert," he said. "That is going to save us a lot of trouble back at Regiment."

"How do you know I'm deserting?" Wales asked calmly. His mind was ticking off the possibilities. There were none. Channing was too far away for a lunge, too close to miss with the pistol. Suddenly a vast rage, a frustration, replaced the joy of being challenged. It's not fair, he thought bitterly. Not when I just found out what I had to do. Not when——All at once he was afraid—not for himself, but for Vivian.

He knew of nothing to do but to keep Channing talking. Perhaps in a moment or two——it was a gamble, nothing else. But not entirely because of the gamble. Because now he had something he wanted to tell Channing. Wanted to make clear to him. Before it was too late.

"How do I know you were——" Channing pretended to be astounded. "Why, what else? Were you going to make a little moonlight reconnaissance? Is that it? Were you going to check the guard? Do you always start out on missions like that by sneaking out the window and along the roof? How do I know? Hell, Wales, I told you a long time ago, you're finished. Now it's finally soaked in and you're turning tail and running like a scared cur. Of course you're deserting. Aren't you?"

"Yes," said Wales, "I am."

Channing shook his head. "So it's my duty to shoot you. Because I'm patriotic, Wales. That's one of my strong points. I'm patriotic, and if there's one thing I can't stand, it's a man who deserts the Cause." He eased back the hammer on the Colt; the click sounded thunderous in the silence of the moonlit night.

"You had your fun tonight," he said viciously. "Tomorrow I'll have the bargaining power and I'll have *my* fun."

He spat.

"Won't she be disgusted," he said, "when she finds out she wasted it tonight?"

Wales looked at him with contempt.

"You're a fool, Vance," he said quietly.

Channing raised the gun barrel. Wales knew it was coming shortly now; every muscle in his body tensed for whatever blind instinct would tell him to do at the last minute.

"You're a fool," he heard himself saying again. "She won't trade with you."

"The hell she won't," Channing said viciously.

"No," Wales said. "No, she won't." He licked his lips. "There are some things you can't buy, Vance. Not even with a plantation. I know. I traded my wife for a plantation, and now she's lost and I've got to find her. I've got to find her and go to her." I am going to have to kill him, Wales thought wearily. I can see it now. I am going to have to kill him, or I will have her on my conscience, too, for the rest of my life. Because she might. No matter what I say, she might.

But he did not see how he was going to be able to kill Channing, even though it was necessary. He did not want to kill anybody at all, not even Channing, but there was no help for it. He could not leave without doing it. And yet Channing had the drop on him; the muzzle of Channing's pistol looked like a tunnel. The only thing I can do, Wales thought, is keep talking, wait for a break.

"Vance," he said, "you could probably go to bed with her if you were a person. But you're not a person. You're what the sergeant called you. You're just a God-damned mink in a hen house that likes to slit throats to see the blood run.

"You mink men," he went on, his voice thickening with hate and anger, "you Goddamned mink men with no minds, just teeth and the liking of blood. There's so many of you—generals, senators, publishers, ministers, all of you wanting that warm taste in your mouths. You don't care whose throat is slit, as long as you taste that taste." He took a deep, shuddering breath. Still Chan-

273

ning's gun had not wavered; still there was absolutely no chance.

"Bastards like me," he whispered, "are told that they've got to be minks too. They're told that it's fine and noble to be a mink, that the minks will inherit the earth. But they won't, Vance. Because there are people left. And that warm taste gags people, Vance. It gags them and makes them sick and they get to hate it . . .

"Like I hate it now," he said. "Like that girl in there hates it. No," he said, "you'll never get in bed with her, Vance, because she knows the difference between minks and people. She knows all about people, Vance. She knows that people are the only thing you can sin against. Not words, not land, but people. Do you know what she said, Vance? She said people are more sacred—"

"Shut up," Channing said. "And turn around, you talky bastard."

Wales braced himself. I have got to, he thought.

Channing jabbed forward with the gun. "I said, turn—"

Then he stood erect, stretching himself, coming up on his tiptoes and standing there, poised tautly, like a ballet dancer before a leap. The gun dropped from his hand and the words ended in a weird, thick gurgle. He relaxed abruptly, started to collapse groundward, and he landed on his knees, one hand groping at his back.

He twisted his face around to look at the sergeant behind him, and Wales could see that Channing's face was chalk-white in the moonlight and devoid now of all hate—of everything but an injured, childlike astonishment.

"Why?" he gasped uncomprehendingly at the sergeant. "Why did you want to hurt me?"

The sergeant closed his eyes and struck downward with the knife again.

After the body was still, not looking at Wales, the sergeant knelt and thrust the blade of the knife into the ground again and again. Even though it was soon clean, he wiped it on the grass before he stood up.

When he got to his feet, he was panting.

"I was lookin for Jeff Davis," he husked. "He didn'
wake up his relief. I went down to the quarters and
made sure that big nigger was still whur I locked 'im
in. Then I seen you two up here an I come up an' I
heard you talkin and—everything was so still yo words
carried a long way. I come up behind the hawses . . ."

He faced Wales, panting.

"It's too bad, Capn," he said looking down at Channing's body.

"No," Wales said hoarsely. "No, he had it coming to
him."

"I know that." The sergeant raised his head and
looked at Wales with an odd expression on his face.
"I mean," he said, "that you had to kill 'im when he
caught you tryin to desert."

Wales stared at him blankly. "Huh?"

"I said," the sergeant repeated almost coldly, "that
it's too bad he caught you tryin to desert an' you had
to kill 'im."

Wales stared at him with growing comprehension.

"When the outfit gits back to Regiment," the sergeant
went on, "I got to say that somebody knifed 'im. I sho
as hell ain't goan say it was me, Capn. An' you'll be
gone . . ." He made a gesture of reasonableness with
his hands. "It won't make no difference," he said. "If
they ketch you, they'll shoot you anyway."

All at once the tension went out of Wales and he
felt all his muscles sag. "That's right," he said wearily.
"It wouldn't make any difference."

"None at all," the sergeant said. He looked at Wales
steadily. "I'm glad hit worked out this way," he said.
"Hit saves me havin to shoot you. I'd done made up
my mind to do it, first chance I got when it'd look like
an accident. And God knows I'da hated that."

"You—would—have—shot—me?" Wales whispered
in astonishment. His body felt cold all over. *"Why?"*

"Because there wasn't no other way to save the men."
The sergeant's voice was intense, earnest; he was
genuinely trying to make Wales see. "Because you
woulda got 'em all killed. And because—because I been

275

with these men a long time. They're . . . they're all the fambly I got."

He rubbed his jaw. "I'm sorry, Capn. I heard whut you said about yo wife. I knowed hit musta been somethin like that. But I didn' know of nothin else to do about it. I . . . I got to look after these men."

"Sergeant—" Wales shook his head hopelessly— "you—" He sought for words to make the sergeant see and could find none. "They'll all get killed," he said after a moment.

The faintest look of pain crossed the sergeant's face. "I got to do what I can to help it," he said. He took a deep breath. "Jest like you got to go wherever it is you got to go."

"England," Wales said. "It's where my wife is."

The sergeant jerked his head up. "England? You got to make it from heah to England? Why, Capn, you must be crazy. You ain't got a chance in hell!"

Wales looked at him steadily.

"Neither have you," he said.

The two men looked at each other for a long minute with pity.

Then Wales said softly, "All right." He fumbled in his pocket and found the roll of money and handed it to the sergeant. "You are in command. Make your own decisions and use this to pay for whatever you decide to take." And then, without conscious volition, he heard himself say, "I want to take that calf back."

"I'll take hit in the mornin," the sergeant said. "I already planned to."

"No, I'll take it back with me tonight. I want to be the one . . . it's on my way," he said haltingly. "It's— it's important to me."

"I doan't understand."

"Neither do I," Wales said. "But it is. And it's on my way."

The sergeant ran his hand through his hair. He stuck the knife, which he had been holding all along, back in his boot. "All right," he said. "If you're so set on it. I'll help you git hit. But we got to be quiet. God knows where Davis is asleep at, but we doan want to stir 'im

up and git him to askin questions." He looked down at
the body of Channing, and for a moment Wales thought
he saw the sergeant's face work behind his beard. Then
the sergeant raised his head. "Come awn," he said.
"Mornin won't be long."